Elvi Rhodes was born and educated in Yorkshire, and now lives in Sussex. Her bestselling novels include: *Opal*, *Doctor Rose*, *Ruth Appleby*, *The Golden Girls*, *Madeleine*, *The House of Bonneau*, *Cara's Land*, *The Rainbow Through the Rain*, *The Bright One*, *The Mountain*, *Portrait of Chloe*, *Spring Music*, *Midsummer Meeting* and *The Birthday Party*. A collection of stories, *Summer Promise and Other Stories*, is also published by Corgi Books.

www.**booksattransworld**.co.uk

Also by Elvi Rhodes

and published by Corgi Books

MULBERRY LANE

Elvi Rhodes

CORGI BOOKS

MULBERRY LANE
A CORGI BOOK : 0 552 14905 5

Originally published in Great Britain by Bantam Press,
a division of Transworld Publishers

PRINTING HISTORY
Bantam Press edition published 2001
Corgi edition published 2002

3 5 7 9 10 8 6 4 2

Set in 10½/12pt New Baskerville by
Kestrel Data, Exeter, Devon.

Corgi Books are published by Transworld Publishers,
61–63 Uxbridge Road, London W5 5SA,
a division of The Random House Group Ltd,
in Australia by Random House Australia (Pty) Ltd,
20 Alfred Street, Milsons Point, Sydney, NSW 2061, Australia,
in New Zealand by Random House New Zealand Ltd,
18 Poland Road, Glenfield, Auckland 10, New Zealand
and in South Africa by Random House (Pty) Ltd,
Endulini, 5a Jubilee Road, Parktown 2193, South Africa.

Printed and bound in Great Britain by
Cox & Wyman Ltd, Reading, Berkshire.

Another for Stephen

Acknowledgements

To my son, Stephen, who took part with endless patience in many transatlantic phone calls about this book.

To Elizabeth Morgan, for her usual intelligent and immaculate research.

To Shirley, my secretary, who is never cross, no matter how often I change and rewrite things.

To Mary Irvine, agent and friend, for her wise advice and encouragement.

To Chief Inspector Graham Davies, who answered my many questions about police and court procedures. If any errors have cropped up they are mine, not his.

To Steve Pratt, who did likewise.

THE RESIDENTS OF
MULBERRY LANE

NORTH HILL

TO TOWN CENTRE

THE GREEN MAN
Jim & Betty Pullman,
Maisie the Labrador

Harry Ford **1**

2 Winston & Bella Grange

Robert & Anne Nelson **3**

4 A. Jeremy Fielder &
Dulcie James
B. Keith Barnes

Eric Spurling &
James Mercer **5**

6 Karen Jackson,
Fiona (6),
Neil (2½)

Michael & Dawn Blake,
Daren & William
(twins, 9) **7**

8 Nigel & Mary Simpson,
Titus the Yorkshire terrier

Peter & Meg Fenton,
Samson the cat **9**

10 Dermot & Laura O'Brien

Esther Dean **11**

12 Students:
Jennifer, Grace, Imogen,
Caroline Philip, Stuart

Ralph &
Michelle Streeter **13**

14 CORNERWAYS
Gary & Lisa Anderson,
Nathan (6),
Amber (4),
Bruno the Great Dane

Brian Carson, Colin Myers,
David Jessop, Mark Leyton,
Fergus O'Connor **15**

&

16

MULBERRY LANE

BELL LANE

TO TOWN CENTRE

UPPER
MULBERRY

1

The car drew up and stopped outside Number Fifteen. A woman of smart, even elegant appearance – dark suit, silk blouse, well-cut shoulder-length blond hair – got out of the driving seat, went around and opened the boot and took out a signpost and a mallet. She had already put on a pair of work gloves before she left the car. No way was she going to risk chipping the silver-blue enamel on her newly manicured nails. This was not her job anyway. She was a senior executive in the firm, wasn't she? She was not employed to drive 'For Sale' notices into the ground. There were lesser beings to do that but unfortunately, for various reasons, not one of them was available this morning and since, in any case, it was necessary for her to view the house the boss had decided that she might as well kill two birds with one stone. 'From time to time we all have to do things we don't want to do,' he'd reminded her tersely. 'Anyway, you are quite capable!'

Of course she was capable! That wasn't the point, was it? Manual labour was not in her job description but now she was stuck with it. She picked up the sale board, marched, as well as her slender four-inch heels would allow her to march, into the small front garden, selected the place where the board would make the maximum impact on passers-by whether in cars or on foot, and set to work. Driving the post into the ground was no sweat. Thanks to five sessions a week at the gym she was a fit and strong lady. Also the very act of hammering relieved her ruffled feelings.

When the sign was fixed to her satisfaction she surveyed it. FOR SALE, it announced, APPLY PROCTOR & SONS, 16 BELL STREET, SHIPFIELD. She next turned her attention to the house. It had been seen briefly by Trevor, another member of Proctor's staff, who had suggested a possible price to put on it and reported that it was awful, but the agency rules were that anyone who might be involved in the selling of a property should be familiar with it, and not just on paper. They had to be able to talk knowledgeably to any client. This went for all properties, large or small, good or awful. So here she was unlocking the front door (badly in need of repainting) and walking in.

Someone would have to do something about the smell, she thought, wrinkling her nose the minute she stepped into the hall. It was damp, dank and fusty, as if the house had very little acquaintance with fresh air. It also smelled of mice. She took a notebook out of her handbag and made an entry. 'Air freshener!' After that she went from room to room. All this awful furniture would have to be cleared out, though furniture hid a multitude of sins. Threadbare carpets or dingy lino still covered the floors and shabby curtains hung at the windows. She moved from room to room making entries – mostly adverse – in her notebook. Trevor was right.

It *was* awful. It was diabolical. Chipped sink, ancient bathroom with broken tiles and a brown-stained lavatory, peeling paint everywhere, crumbling window sill in the kitchen, no central heating, almost certainly needed rewiring. Looking out of the bedroom windows she saw neglected gardens front and back, with a dilapidated shed, its door flapping in the wind, at the bottom of the latter. Name the dozen worst drawbacks of any property and this house had them all.

That was not surprising. They knew it had belonged to an old lady who had lived there most of her life and had never done a thing to it. In the end, too frail to look after herself, she had been carted off to a nursing home and her daughter had put the house on the market, firmly stating that she wanted the best price they could get in order to meet her mother's nursing home fees, and a quick sale. Didn't they all, Rita thought.

So how in the world would she describe it in order to get this good price and quick sale? Impossible! But then every client expected the impossible. They came into the agency with inflated ideas of what their property was worth, gained from rumours of what houses were fetching all over the town, and the farther the rumour travelled the higher the price soared. How would she word the advertisement for the *Shipfield Courier*? And how would she write the blurb which would accompany the photograph in the agency window, and what sort of a photograph could it possibly be? In fact the photograph would be easier. Although the camera could not lie, it could certainly distort or enhance simply by taking whatever point of view it chose. The written description was, however, another matter. The description had to be true. But mercifully, she reminded herself as she descended the stairs where in parts the carpet was so worn into holes that it was potentially lethal, not necessarily the whole truth, not nothing but the truth.

Phrases listed themselves in her mind. 'Scope for modernization.' 'Offers potential for those wishing to refurbish.' 'A chance to make changes!' And of the garden: 'Back garden – opportunity to redesign.' 'Front garden – walled, hedged, laid to lawn.' Never mind that the only wall was a low one, badly in need of repair, which simply separated the front garden from the street, that the hedge was three yards of dusty privet between this house and the next and the patchy lawn was no more than five feet by six feet. Never mind all that, the facts as stated were true. Also, of course, 'Early possession available.' 'No chain.'

There were a number of minuses which need not be stated. For instance, there were no garages to these houses. Cars were parked right now on both sides of the street, but since the street was wide there was still ample room for two lines of traffic to pass.

And what could one say about the neighbour-hood? Rita sighed. She had little personal knowledge of Mulberry Lane. All she knew about it was what she had been told. In the eighteen months she had been with Proctor's she recalled only one house there being on the market and she had not dealt with it. It seemed to be a place where people lived until they died or, like the owner of this run-down place she was looking at, were carried off regardless.

The houses were spacious semis, with room for

large families. They had originally been built, she had learned, in the second half of the nineteenth century as suitable residences for the managers of the factories which had sprung up on the level land down by the river when the railways had brought light industry to Shipfield. The workers had lived in streets of small houses huddled close to the factories but it had been thought more suitable for the managers to put a little distance between themselves and their employees.

The speculator of the time had seen Mulberry Lane as just the place to build, and his foresight had brought him a nice sum of money. Also, Victorian houses were now back in fashion, but it was the state of this one which would tell against it.

There was nothing wrong with the position of Mulberry Lane. It turned off to the right halfway up North Hill and less than a mile from the town. North Hill itself climbed steeply, as did everything to the north of Shipfield. Where the semis finished – there were not many of them, it was quite a short street because an untimely death had claimed the builder – Mulberry Lane forked. To the right Bell Lane went back into the town and to the left, where, as some of the local inhabitants remembered, there had once been no more than a footpath to the fields where one could gather wild flowers – cowslips, coltsfoot, primroses – the former footpath had become Upper Mulberry Lane. Well named. It was undoubtedly superior. To begin with the houses in Upper Mulberry had names rather than numbers. Fairdene, Hill House, Mulberry Lodge, The Beeches (though no beech tree grew or had ever grown there). The gardens were bigger, the lawns greener, the trimmed hedges higher and thicker.

Rita gave a last glance around, then left the house, locked the door, shook herself slightly as if to shake off the smells, looked around her and sighed again.

Now if only this *were* Upper Mulberry! It was so near and yet so far. If it had only been on the other side of the street and just a few yards further along it would have qualified. What faced her across the way as she stood on the steps of Number Fifteen was what had been the last of the semis but in this case the two had recently been knocked together to make one house. That it was recent was obvious from the fact that the stone had been cleaned – a mistake in her view. She slipped on her glasses in order to read the name on the gatepost: Corner-ways.

Really, she thought, the house looked quite imposing. Two front doors had been made into one and furnished with a rather splendid oak-panelled double door, with wide steps leading down to the drive. A circular drive had been constructed with wrought-iron gates at each end, though these were an expensive and unnecessary luxury because they were almost always open in order to allow the occupants of the house to drive in on the right, sweep around to the front door and later exit on the left. Right now a Toyota Amazon Landcruiser in a rich green was parked by the front door.

The house, because it was built where the road began to curve around, was actually half in Mulberry proper and half just about in Upper Mulberry. Could any use be made of that fact, Rita asked herself? 'Adjacent to Upper Mulberry

Lane'? 'Facing Upper Mulberry Lane'? She would consider it. She wondered what the owner of the Landcruiser gave as his address. Upper Mulberry, she guessed.

Laura O'Brien, who lived at Number Ten which was on the opposite side of the road to Number Fifteen and two doors along from Cornerways in the direction of North Hill, was sitting in her bay window engaged in a telephone conversation with her mother when she looked up and saw a smart young woman hammering a signpost into the ground. At this distance she couldn't read what the sign said but she didn't need to. She had been closely involved with the whole episode of old Mrs Harper falling down the front steps while picking up a bottle of milk, breaking a leg, being taken into hospital and then finally whizzed off to Bristol (where her daughter lived) to spend the rest of her days in a nursing home. That last day in Shipfield General Hospital had been a sad one for the old lady. Laura, dropping in to wish her bon voyage, had found her in floods of tears and indeed had shed a few sympathetic tears with her.

'I've lived most of my life in Mulberry Lane,' Mrs Harper had sobbed quietly. 'You never know where you're going to end up, do you?'

'I expect you'll settle in quite quickly,' Laura had said. 'You'll make friends. You won't be lonely. And you'll be looked after.' She had tried to comfort Mrs Harper but the old lady was not to be comforted.

She wondered how she was getting on now. It had all happened so quickly; the daughter had put the house up for sale and now, as she watched, the estate agent was going inside, presumably to inspect it.

'Hello!' her mother shouted. 'Are you still there, Laura, or have I been cut off?'

Laura held the telephone several inches away from her ear. When Beryl Moffat was on form her voice was probably audible all the miles from Bath, where she lived, without the aid of a phone. When she wasn't on form her voice would sink to a whining whisper. At the moment she sounded hale and hearty but annoyed.

'I'm sorry, Mother,' Laura said. 'I'm still here. Something in the street caught my attention for a minute.'

'There's always something happening in your road,' her mother said. 'Have you finished then?'

'I was going to ask about Dad,' Laura said.

'I don't mean have you finished talking. I mean have you finished decorating the sitting room?'

'All except for the frieze,' Laura told her. 'I'm stencilling a frieze around the top of the walls.'

'I didn't know stencilling was fashionable,' Mrs Moffat said.

'I don't know that it is,' Laura admitted. 'I just happen to like it. A Greek key pattern in a terracotta shade. It looks quite good on the pale blue walls. So how is Dad? You sound well enough.'

'I keep going,' Mrs Moffat said. 'You have to.' Her voice weakened by several decibels. 'Your father is out playing bowls. Where else would he be?'

Almost anywhere, Laura thought. In his shed at the far end of the garden, where he'd installed a comfortable chair, a radio, an electric fire, a shelf of books and a solitaire board, and put a Yale lock

18

on the door. Or when the weather was inclement, wandering around the inside of Bath Abbey re-reading the memorials. Anything to keep him away from the four walls of his home.

'So what was going on in the road that took your attention?' Mrs Moffat asked.

'Only that the estate agent was putting up a For Sale board outside Mrs Harper's house,' Laura said. 'I told you last week she'd left.'

'I wonder who you'll get?' Mrs Moffat said.

'It's what we all wonder,' Laura told her. 'It's a while since there was anyone new in the road.'

'I hope it's someone decent,' her mother said. 'You never can tell these days. There's a lot of riff-raff about.'

'The students are due back today,' Laura said, changing the subject. 'In fact one of them has already arrived.'

She had seen Jennifer drive her small blue Fiat onto the concreted forecourt next door, which accommodated two cars if they were small enough and took the place of the small lawns in front of the other houses. She had tapped at the window to attract Jennifer's attention as she was unloading the car and they had smiled and waved at each other.

'It will be nice to have them back,' she said to her mother. 'I'll probably pop in later and say hello.'

'You know what I think about young people living on their own away from home,' Beryl said. 'I've said it before and I'll say it again.'

'I'm sure you will,' Laura said. Her mother, though she had only recently touched seventy, had the outlook of someone living before World War One.

'And what about that girl – what's-her-name –

having a baby at university! I can't think what she—'

'She didn't have it in the university,' Laura interrupted. 'She had it in the hospital in Brighton. And you know perfectly well that Ruth got pregnant by her boyfriend when she went home for a weekend.'

And had returned and spent the spring term throwing up and the summer term swelling like a balloon while she got on with her studies. And had permission to come back next year and finish her course.

'She had a lovely little girl,' Laura said, rubbing it in.

'Disgraceful!' Mrs Moffat said. 'They'll be having nurseries in universities next.'

'They have had for years,' Laura informed her.

'Anyway,' Mrs Moffat said briskly, 'I can't stand here gossiping. When your father comes in, weary from playing with balls, he'll expect his meal on the table. And mind what you're doing up and down ladders. You could break a leg as easy as not! One thing I will say for your father . . .'

'Really?' Laura asked. 'What's that?'

'He didn't leave it to womenfolk to do the painting and decorating. Remember what I said about breaking a leg!'

'I will,' Laura promised. 'Goodbye.'

It was strange how a ten-minute conversation with her mother was more exhausting than a couple of hours of climbing up and down stepladders painting walls. Was my mother always like this, she asked herself? When you were a kid you didn't analyse your mother. You loved her, or occasionally when you couldn't get your own way you hated her.

You didn't ask what made her tick. She was just there and she looked after you. Her mother had done all that. Always food on the table. Clean knickers every day, warm baths, pocket money. She had been like any other mother, which was what one wanted. One didn't want a mother who would stand out in a crowd. She had loved her mother because one did love one's mother and of course she still did love her but so often now through a cloud of irritation.

Is that how Therese and Frances love me now that they're no longer dependent on me, she wondered? She hoped not. She loved her children to bits; she would die for them. She had lavished love on them physically and in every way from the moment they were born, partly because her own mother had never been demonstrative. A formal good-night kiss, even a kiss-it-better if she'd fallen and hurt herself, but no quick spontaneous hug for no reason at all except that she happened to be there. And I happen to be stencilling a wall, she reminded herself. And if she didn't get on with it the paint would thicken and the colour would deepen so that the next bit of the frieze would be a rich burnt orange instead of a delicate terracotta and every time she looked at it she'd be reminded about where she'd gone off into a reverie about parental love.

She moved the ladder along the wall and climbed up it. The walls were high, with nicely curved mouldings. It was one of the things they had liked about the house when they'd seen it for the first time but it was a devil when it came to decorating. She smiled at the thought of her mother's dig about men doing the painting and decorating. Dermot

21

had done it once and it had been a disaster. After that they had agreed that decorating should be her job and Dermot should do the re-upholstering of the furniture they bought cheap in salerooms. He was a dab hand at that, and at rugs and cushions. She was a dab hand with a paintbrush.

Her mother had never approved of this arrangement. She considered it unnatural. In any case Dermot didn't spend all that much time on rugs and cushions. He earned his modest living teaching English at Shipfield Comprehensive. It was a job Laura knew he didn't always enjoy. He was passionate about the subject but he worried that he was not cut out to be a teacher, certainly not of children. Adults, perhaps; he would have been happier as an academic, working in a university.

She climbed down the ladder again and moved it around the corner of the room and was pleased that doing the next bit she could also look out of the window from time to time. As her mother had said, there was always something happening in Mulberry Lane, though it was seldom of world-shaking importance. At the moment the estate agent was standing on the opposite side of the road on the pavement outside Mrs Harper's house, gazing around. Then while Laura continued to watch she got into her car and drove off, turning right down Bell Lane.

Laura was fond of Mulberry Lane, as indeed she was fond of Shipfield. It was a pleasant town which had not grown so big that it had lost its character. From the old buildings in the centre – the Norman church, the butter cross, the marketplace – it had spread out onto the hills which surrounded it on three sides. On the fourth side the land sloped south to the English Channel. The railway connected Shipfield with Bristol to the west and Bath to the east. When the people of Shipfield wanted bright lights and serious shopping they went to Bristol and when they fancied a bit of culture they visited Bath.

In the busy town centre there was a Marks & Spencer's, a Sainsbury's, Dean & Docker's department store in Bell Street, WH Smith's and all the major banks, as well as several restaurants serving anything from dainty teas at the Spinning Wheel to Italian at Umberto's and a robust roast at the Carvery. Fish-and-chip shops, of course, and a couple of pizza takeaways. There were also pubs to suit every taste, from the upholstered comfort of the old Shipfield Arms to the flashing lights and sounds of the American Bar on Deangate. There were churches and chapels, schools and hospitals, and for the last few years and certainly now the jewel in the crown, the University of Shipfield on its campus at the very top of North Hill. Among the older factories which had survived there was Venables' toffee factory – 'Venables' Cream Toffee travels the world!' – Fairfield & Hartley's biscuit factory and Benson's Box Company which supplied tins and boxes for the biscuits and toffee, and over the years these had been joined by light manufacturing, retail warehouses, an insurance company and more recently several high-tech firms.

She and Dermot had arrived with their two daughters on an August afternoon fifteen years ago, he to take up the job he had been offered at Shipfield Comprehensive and she hoping, since the girls would be at school, to find a part-time job. That she had done quite quickly as one of the team of receptionists at Shipfield's private hospital, where she now worked full time. At first both she and Dermot had found Shipfield dull, but they told themselves that it was better for the children than living in London and long ago now they had become used to a different pace of life.

Shipfield, however, was no Nirvana. It had one cinema complex, no football team, no longer any live theatre or concert hall, and it was undeniably damp.

She had almost reached the end of the wall, only two metres to go now, thank God! Her back was killing her. For a minute she broke off painting and, insofar as she could while balanced on a stepladder and guarding a tin of paint, she stretched her body. She had vaguely thought that she might do something around the door frame, but now she had had enough. Anyway, less was more, wasn't it?

Five minutes later she heard Dermot's key in the lock. Once she would have climbed down the ladder and rushed to meet him but now she continued with the painting. Last year they had celebrated their twenty-fifth anniversary – they had married the moment Dermot was out of university and had their children quickly – so rushing to greet each other was not really on the agenda. Not that they didn't get on, but mad passion died, or had in their case except on odd occasions.

'I'm in here!' she called out.

Dermot came into the room carrying his canvas holdall which was spilling over with exercise books.

'Is there any tea going?' he asked.

'As you can see,' Laura answered, 'I'm up a ladder which is where I've been most of the day.

But if you'd like to make some I might come down and have a cup with you.'

'You didn't *have* to paint the sitting room,' Dermot said mildly. 'There was nothing wrong with it.'

'There was to me,' Laura said. 'It was looking decidedly dingy. You never notice these things. So how do you think it looks now?'

Dermot looked around, nodded his head.

'Well? Is that it? A nod of the head?'

'It looks great,' he said. 'You've done a good job. How about picking out the ceiling rose in the terra-cotta shade? Just bits here and there, the edges of the petals, the centres of the flowers?'

Laura regarded the centre rose. They had found it in a second-hand shop and their thought was that it had come from a much finer house than theirs. She loved it.

'You're right!' she said. He was always right about colour and design.

'It can wait until tomorrow, can't it?' Dermot queried. 'You don't have to finish today.'

'I want to,' Laura said. 'I thought we might attack the front garden this weekend; tidy it up and plant a few bulbs before it's too late. Have you brought stacks of work home?'

'The usual,' he said. 'A few hours. I'll tackle it on Sunday when we get back from Mass. We can still do the garden.'

'Right,' Laura said. 'Are you going to make that tea?'

He went into the kitchen and came back shortly afterwards with two mugs.

'I'm going to turn the fire on,' he said. 'It's a bit chilly in here.'

'You don't notice it when you're up near the ceiling,' Laura said. 'What sort of a day did *you* have?'

Dermot shrugged. 'So-so! Anyway, it's the weekend. Let's forget it. I'm whacked!'

'You're not the only one,' Laura said. 'I don't feel the least bit like cooking a meal. Can we eat out?'

'We could have a takeaway,' Dermot suggested.

'I don't *want* a takeaway,' Laura protested. 'I want to go out. I've been stuck in the house all week.'

'Whose fault is that?' Dermot said mildly. 'No-one made you spend your week's holiday decorating. It was your choice.'

'I know, I know.' He could be so irritatingly logical. 'So do we eat out or don't we?'

'Of course we do,' Dermot said. 'Where do you want to go? Italian? Chinese? You choose.'

'Right,' Laura said. 'Umberto's!'

'Did you ring Therese?' Dermot enquired.

'I did. The doctor said she should really take another week off work, stay at home and rest. It was a nasty bout of flu and her chest isn't clear. But she wants to get back to work. You know Therese. She blows everything light.'

'She's not going to get her way, I hope?' Though his elder daughter often did, Dermot thought.

'No. Duggie has put his foot down.'

'Good for Duggie!' Dermot drank the last of his tea.

There was the sound of a car stopping, sharp toots on the hooter, doors slamming.

'That can only be Imogen,' Laura said. 'No-one else could make that much noise. You wouldn't think it, would you, I mean being a dainty five feet tall and such a refined little thing?' She moved quickly to the window and looked out.

Imogen was unloading the contents of her car. A large suitcase, untidy bundles of nothing recognizable, boots, a duvet, a radio, a hockey stick. Anyone less like a hockey player than Imogen could scarcely be imagined but, according to the other students, she played left wing and ran down the field like a greyhound. She closed the boot, looked up, caught sight of Laura and waved. Laura opened the window and called out.

'Welcome back! Did you have a good summer?'

'Wonderful!' However enthusiastic she felt, Imogen's voice was never loud but her diction was so clear, so perfect, that she could probably be heard half a mile away. 'Tell you all about it later,' she added.

Laura closed the window. 'Only Grace to come now,' she said to Dermot. 'I mean of last year's. I wonder what the three new ones will be like?'

'I can trust you to find out, dear,' Dermot said. His wife was inordinately – that was *his* word – interested in the students, he felt, but he was wrong, Laura always told him. They were young people away from home, she said. She had a natural interest in them.

'I shall miss Ruth,' she said. 'I do already. She was such a bright spark. Do you think she'll come back and bring the baby to see us?'

'Who knows?' Dermot said. 'It depends on whether she's willing to travel from Brighton with a young baby.'

'I had an earful from my mother today,' Laura told him. 'She thinks all houses shared by students

27

are dens of iniquity. I wouldn't think that about next door, would you?'

'I'm sure you'd know if it were,' Dermot said. 'If we're going to Umberto's hadn't you better pack up and get ready? You know how busy he is on Fridays. And we'll walk down. No point in taking the car if we're drinking a bottle of wine. Anyway we need the exercise.'

'Speak for yourself,' Laura said. 'I've spent the day climbing. OK, I'll do the centre rose tomorrow.' She put the lid on the paint tin and took the brush into the kitchen to wash it.

2

Leaving the house that evening, they walked along Mulberry Lane and turned left down North Hill, crossing the railway bridge close to the bottom and then the bridge over the River Fern. The river meandered from east to west through the town, popping up in unexpected places before making a leisurely turn south and disappearing from view just at the point where Umberto's came into sight.

'I like Umberto's,' Laura said when they were seated at a table on the ground floor. 'I always feel at ease here.'

'Sure,' Dermot said. He was studying the menu. 'And I like the food and I'm starving. I had school dinner today. You don't have to suffer that.'

'When I'm at work I suffer hospital lunches,' Laura said. 'Don't think because it's a private hospital the staff get the same gourmet meals as the patients.'

Umberto came over himself to take their order.

'*Buona sera*, Signora O'Brien,' he said. 'Signor O'Brien! How are you both?'

'Well but hungry,' Dermot answered. He gave the order. 'And a bottle of Barolo,' he added.

'At once!' Umberto said.

They were not kept waiting though already the place was busy and by the time they had reached the main course there was a queue outside the door waiting for tables.

'Do not rush,' Umberto said as he passed them.

'Isn't that nice,' Laura said. 'I always feel guilty when I see people standing in line.'

'I don't,' Dermot said. 'They should arrive earlier. Anyway, I want a pudding.'

He chose Tiramisu, Laura ice-cream. When they had finished she put down her spoon and sighed happily. 'That was lovely! Thank you very much.'

As they were leaving the restaurant the rain came down, sudden and heavy.

'Damn!' Dermot said testily. 'We should have brought the car.' He hated rain. 'Come on, quick! We'll catch the bus.'

They reached the stop in time to see the rear lights of the bus disappear into the distance.

'Blast!' Dermot said.

He set off at a fast pace, Laura trying to keep up with him. When they turned the corner into Mulberry Lane he took Laura by the elbow and pulled her into a run. The rain was sheeting down now, the lights of passing cars reflected in the wetness of the pavement. Dermot broke into a run.

'Stop it!' Laura gasped. 'I can't keep up with you.'

'Yes you can,' he said. 'We're nearly home.'

Between Number Ten and Number Twelve a small, bright purple car was parked up against their Volvo. It was new to Laura, who reckoned she knew the ownership of every car in the street since they mostly belonged to residents. Only during the day when the North Hill shops were open did anyone look for space in Mulberry Lane. It must belong to one of the new students.

Number Twelve was ablaze with light – no curtains were ever drawn there except in the sharpest winter frosts. The sound of loud music poured out into the street. Figures could be seen standing in the bay window, more bodies Laura reckoned than could ever be living there.

'Oh look!' she cried. 'They're having a party.'

'For God's sake, who the hell cares?' Dermot snapped. 'Find your bloody key and open the door. I'm soaking!'

'So am I,' Laura said, fishing in her handbag, 'only I don't make such a fuss about it.'

They went in. Dermot hurried through the hall and up the stairs, reappearing a few minutes later wrapped in his dressing gown.

'You should change,' he said. 'You'll catch your death.'

'No I won't,' Laura told him. 'I'll go up in a minute. Did you see the little purple car? It must belong to one of the new students. And he must be quite well off. It's new.'

'Who cares?' Dermot said.

'You will in the morning,' Laura said. 'It's jammed right up against yours. You won't be able to get out. Shall I pop next door and ask him to move it?'

'Certainly not!' Dermot was adamant. 'It's not a good enough excuse for gate-crashing a party.' He walked over to the window and looked out. 'I'll manage.'

The last thing he wanted right now was to get involved with the students, not that he had anything against them, but he was tired and wet.

Laura's involvement with them was no doubt her maternal instincts coming to the fore again, especially now that they didn't see their own family as often. He missed the family too, especially Frances. He knew he shouldn't have a favourite between his two daughters but he had, and since her marriage Therese had grown away just a little, not from her mother but from him. Duggie was now the first man in Therese's life.

It was as it should be and he was pleased she was happily married. Duggie was just the man for her. He was clever, he was successful. Though not yet thirty he was well up the ladder in Barclays Bank and set to climb several rungs higher. Therese's life suited her: she had an interesting job and she was also a good corporate wife, a charming hostess, and one day, he hoped, she would be an exemplary mother.

Frances was quite different. It surprised him that his two daughters could be so unalike, even in appearance. Frances was like her mother, small, slender and dark; Therese took after him, tall and fairish. Frances was the brainbox of the family – he didn't quite know where she got that from – with a first-class law degree. She was now in her first year with a practice in Bath. It was not far and she could have made the daily journey but she preferred to live away from the parental home.

'I'll pop around in the morning, when we get back from shopping,' Laura said.

The noise was still coming good and loud from Number Twelve. Laura looked across the road and saw the light go on at Number Eleven and Esther Dean in her nightdress standing at her lighted window.

'Oh dear,' Laura said, 'they've wakened Esther! There'll be trouble – but hopefully not until to-morrow. And it's no use her rapping on the window – which she is doing – because they won't hear her.'

'That won't stop her,' Dermot said.

'Why doesn't she sleep in the back bedroom?' Laura said.

'Because she's lived in that house most of her life and always slept in the front bedroom,' Dermot said. 'And she's not been used to students. We've only had them in Mulberry Lane for the last three years. It used to be a rather quiet road before then.'

'They do bring a bit of life,' Laura protested. 'Do you think I should go across and see to her? Get her back to bed?'

'For goodness' sake, *no*!' Dermot said. 'Come away from the window! And draw the curtains and shut out the racket.'

'It isn't a racket,' Laura informed him. 'It's just that you never take the trouble to listen properly.'

On the other side of the students, at what had been built as Numbers Fourteen and Sixteen and was now Cornerways, all one large house as viewed from across the road by Rita the estate agent that morning, Gary and Lisa Anderson were not so troubled by the noise coming from their neigh-bours. For a start, unlike the O'Briens' house which was divided from the students only by a party wall, Cornerways and Number Twelve each had a strip of garden to the side of them. In any case they were used to loud music of their own. It was not quite as up-to-the-minute as that of the students (though they tried hard) but when required it was relayed from the most expensive equipment and poured out in every room in the house, including the four lavatories.

At the moment it was turned off because the two of them were sitting on their cream-coloured leather sofa in their deep-pile carpeted lounge, watching a horror movie on their state-of-the-art television with its Dolby Prologic sound surround system and mega-screen, and the noise level from that was more than enough to drown out the repetitive drumbeats issuing from Number Twelve. Gary, round-faced, shrewd of eye, slightly too plump for his thirty-five years, sipped his sixteen-year-old malt from a heavily cut crystal tumbler. Lisa, though a glass of white wine stood on the low marble table in front of them, preferred to dip into the box of Belgian chocolates on her lap. She was ever so slightly bored by the film. She would have liked to have talked, since most of her day's conversation had been with Nathan and Amber, aged six and four respectively and now fast asleep upstairs in their nursery. Gary, however, preferred to watch his movies in silence. It helped him to unwind, he said.

What he needed to unwind from was his week spent working hard and making lots of money in his computer business. What exactly he did Lisa was not sure. Software, and networking for businesses, but she didn't quite know what that involved. She was not into computers. Gary had once tried to explain to her but she had never really understood and he had told her not to worry her pretty head about it. She had been a photographic model for a mail order catalogue before meeting Gary. Sometimes she missed that a little. However, though she didn't understand the ins and outs of what Gary did, she was grateful for the results. How else would they afford this lovely home, their top-of-the-range cars, Nathan's fees at a private prep school and his name down for a public school.

So now, good wife that she was, she sat quietly through screams and stabbings and gunshots and blood. She would have liked to skim through *Hello!* and *Tatler* but Gary would have been irritated by the turning of the pages.

In the end her patience was rewarded. The film ended. Gary stood up and stretched himself.

'Right!' he said. 'I'll take Bruno up the road and then we'll call it a day.'

Bruno, a Great Dane of impeccable pedigree, hearing his name and knowing more or less what the time was, picked up his lead from the shelf by the front door and ambled into the lounge. He had been lying in the hall all evening. He did not like horror films. Musicals he could put up with, but not horror.

'Good boy,' Gary said. 'Off we go!'

He always turned left into Upper Mulberry. You met a better class of dog there. Afghans, Dobermanns, basset-hounds, mastiffs. They were mostly large, as befitted their homes. The exception was Frizzie, an exquisitely beautiful Bichon Frisé bitch whose sex appeal made up for what she lacked in size – at least to Bruno, who adored her. Her dog walker habitually disclaimed ownership of the small dog. She was actually his wife's, he explained, but his wife did not like to be out, even in Upper Mulberry, late at night.

To Bruno's disappointment they didn't meet Frizzie on this occasion. It was rather later than usual – it had been a long film – so it was a short, sharp walk to the top of the hill and back again. When they went into the house Lisa was in the kitchen, making a hot drink.

'I forgot to tell you,' she said, 'there was an estate agent at Number Fifteen this morning. She put up a sale board.'

'Oh,' Gary said. 'Well, we did expect it, didn't we?' He was actually quite pleased. The shabbiness of Number Fifteen had displeased him for some time now. They had been delighted with Corner-ways from the moment they'd been shown around it by Bill Marston, who had bought the two houses and made such a good job of knocking them into one (in order to sell at a profit, he had no thought of living there). In addition, he had been fortunate enough to buy an extra piece of land at the back so that there was now a fair-sized garden, and that had caught Lisa's eye. Neither Gary nor Lisa had taken enough notice of the house opposite. It was not like Gary. He usually had a good business head on his shoulders, but Bill Marston was a very good salesman. And as Bill had said, Cornerways was practically in Upper Mulberry. Gary never thought of it as being otherwise. Indeed you could say the back garden was.

'Well,' he said to Lisa, 'let's hope we get someone decent there – and the sooner the better!'

When Laura and Dermot left the house at mid-morning on Saturday there was neither sight nor sound from Number Twelve. The small purple car was exactly where it had been the previous night.

'I said you should have let me ask whoever the owner is to move it,' Laura said. 'It's obviously one of the students. Now we shan't be able to get out.'

Dermot eyed the space between the purple car in front of his Volvo and the Ford parked behind it.

'Yes we will,' he said. 'Not easily, but we will.'

'Do you want me to see you out?' Laura offered.

'No thank you. It only confuses me.'

'I don't see why . . .' Laura began.

'Don't argue, darling! Just get in.'

He was already in the driving seat, the engine switched on. He'll never do it, Laura thought. Either she'd have to raise the students or they'd have to take the bus, which would be a nuisance because they had to shop both for food and garden things.

He did it, inch by inch, and in the end he was free and drove away.

'You did that well,' Laura acknowledged.

'Thank you,' Dermot said. 'I don't know why you sound surprised. I've been doing it for years, we're always getting jammed in. Perhaps we should have the front garden made into a parking space, like next door. Reverse in, drive straight out.'

'I wouldn't like to lose the front garden, small though it is,' Laura said. 'I like to see a bit of green when I look out of the window.'

There wasn't much to see in the garden at the moment: orange-berried pyracantha along the wall parallel to the road; two largish clumps of deep pink sedum which needed to be divided; Michaelmas daisies in the side bed and a small late-flowering fuchsia. It looked tired and tatty. I must do something with it, Laura thought, give it some sort of design.

Which was why, an hour later in the market, she spent more than she could afford on large quantities of bulbs – tulips, crocuses, early irises, muscari, even daffodils though it was late to be planting those. Also from the nursery in North Hill she bought two clematis for the back garden. She envisaged them rampaging up the wall which bordered their rectangle of land at the bottom, a riot of mauve and purple flowers. Unless of course they died of root wilt, which was likely. She did not have green fingers.

'Don't you think that's enough?' Dermot said, coming up behind her. 'It's going to take us all weekend to plant this lot.'

Dermot was not enamoured of gardening. In addition to cementing over the front garden he would have turned the back garden into one large patio with chairs and a swinging sofa. Perhaps a barbecue, possibly a container or two with trouble-free small bay trees. The maddening thing was, to Laura, that on the rare occasions when he did plant something it flourished and grew, flowered and fruited, all without an ounce of the painstaking care she lavished on her charges.

'It's strange,' she said as they carried their purchases back to the car park, 'that you care so little for nature, coming from your background.'

Dermot had been born in Kilbally, a fishing village in County Clare. He was the youngest of seven and by the time he was eighteen and about to go to university in Dublin all his siblings had left home because there was no work for them locally. Mostly they had gone over the water to England or America, though he had a married sister in Belfast. In his second year in university he had to return home for his mother's funeral. She, who had never had time to be ill, had died of a swift cancer, though Dermot had told Laura he suspected that all her children having flown and her husband being involved with a woman in Ennis, she had found herself with nothing to do, no purpose in life, and had given up on it.

On the day after the funeral he had returned to the university and once he had his degree he had crossed the water to England. He had always known he would. Kilbally stifled him. The only two excitements, though that was too strong a word, were meeting with his friends after Sunday Mass, and the Saturday night dance in Ennis. It was all the more strange then that he had insisted on taking Laura to County Clare for their honeymoon. They'd driven all over the place, walked for hours along the beaches and over the cliffs of Moher, so high that standing on the edge they'd looked down on the birds flying below them. Laura had been enchanted. She'd wanted to go back, still did, but not so Dermot. Kilbally was now in the past and would remain so.

When they came out of Sainsbury's Laura said, 'Let's look in Proctor's window, see if they've put in anything about Number Fifteen.'

There it was, and though it was not as prominently displayed as some other properties, the estate agent had certainly done her best on the description.

'I hardly recognize it!' Laura said to Dermot. Phrases like 'scope for', 'chance to' and 'potential' leapt out at them, but it was the price which caused Dermot to whistle.

'They'll never get that much,' he said. 'I've not been inside but I suspect it's in a dreadful state. You only have to look at the outside to guess that.'

'Well I have been inside as you know,' Laura said.

She had visited Mrs Harper a few times when the old lady needed help. 'You're quite right, it *is* terrible. I expect it's the daughter who wouldn't let them put it on the market at any less.'

It was noon when they arrived back from the town. The purple car had gone.

'Perhaps it was a visitor,' Laura said as they started to unpack the Volvo. 'I'll pop round and see them when we've dealt with this lot. Just to say welcome back.'

'You mean you can't contain your curiosity,' Dermot said.

'I'm simply being friendly,' Laura defended herself – though it was true she particularly wanted to meet the newcomers.

As she walked up the path, carrying the clematis, she saw someone moving across the room next door. The front bay windows were obligingly large in these old houses. It was someone reasonably tall and wearing a rose-coloured dressing gown, though the wearer moved out of sight too quickly for her to take in any other details. She was sure it wasn't Jennifer, it was too tall for Imogen and even a swift sighting ruled out Grace who dressed all the time in black, grey or mud-brown. It must therefore be a new girl, unless there was a new man who draped himself in a rose-pink robe. Not impossible.

'I'm starving,' Dermot said, walking behind her with several carrier bags. 'Can we eat before you go next door?'

'At once!' Laura said.

She heated the Cornish pasties they'd bought in Marks & Spencer's and made coffee.

'I'll give you a hand with the garden things later,'

Dermot said. 'But I warn you I'm not going to spend all afternoon on it.'

The second she had finished eating Laura jumped to her feet.

'I'll just pop round,' she said. 'I won't be long. Or do you feel like coming with me?'

'I do not.' Dermot was still eating. 'I know nothing I say is going to hold you back but I think they're better left to themselves for a few days.'

He was right, she did not hold back. When she rang the bell at Number Twelve Jennifer answered the door. Jennifer's dark hair was loosely piled on top of her head, with several strands escaping and falling over her face. Her bright blue eyes peered through them. She wore the shortest of skirts which made her elegant legs seem longer than ever.

'Laura! Do come in,' she said, smiling.

'Just for a minute,' Laura said. 'Are you all back?'

'Yes. And we have three new ones so we're a full house again.'

Laura followed her through the hall, with its dingy lino-covered floor and paint-peeling walls, into the sitting room. The layout of the house was exactly like hers, though in reverse, but there all resemblance ended. No freshly painted walls with terracotta stencilling. No well-upholstered furniture with toning cushions, no elegant floor-length curtains. Nothing of even reasonable quality. Nothing new, nothing polished, nothing shining. There were two sagging sofas, two mock-leather armchairs, a set of DIY bookshelves and two small tables. The porridge-coloured walls were, mercifully, covered in parts by large, bright posters.

The scene was not new to Laura. Apart from the

posters it was much the same as when Mr Lambert, the elderly owner, had left it three years ago to live with his only daughter Eileen. Eileen had pointed out that, with the university being close and having accommodation only for first-year students, letting the house could be a nice little earner. And when the time came (she meant when he was dead) it would fetch a much higher price than now. Property increased in value over the years.

She conceded that it would have to be done up a bit before putting it up for sale but there was no need to do anything fancy for students. They wouldn't appreciate it. All that was needed was to divide the two larger bedrooms into four small ones, buy a few single beds, second-hand, and then the house could easily accommodate six. Put in meters for gas and electricity, install a pay phone, buy a few cups and saucers and there you were! Forty-five pounds per student per week, a month's deposit to be retained against damage or misuse, students to be responsible for finding tenants and liable to share the rent for any unoccupied room. What could go wrong, Eileen asked?

And the few good pieces of furniture her father had she would bring to her own home where they would be well looked after.

Now the only things in the room which were not old and shabby were the television, the video, the CD player and the radio, all of which the students themselves had provided. Jennifer had told Laura that Mr Lambert paid the TV licence but added it to the rent. But now she noticed two large floor cushions, bright and clean. One was occupied by a girl with waist-length white-blond hair – who was wearing the aforeseen pink dressing gown – and the other by a young man whose pale red hair was cropped so closely as to seem no more than an orange glow over his scalp.

The blond girl smiled a welcome, revealing a wide stretch of totally perfect teeth, as Jennifer made the introductions.

'This is Caroline Mason, second year chemistry. And Philip Robson, also second year, computer studies. They both lived on campus last year.'

Anyone less like an aspiring chemistry graduate Laura thought she had never seen. Surely Caroline should be gracing some catwalk, or appearing on television advertising hair products or toothpaste, or both? About Philip she couldn't make a snap judgement because she didn't know what computer students should look like. He greeted her in a pleasant and undoubtedly upper-class voice.

'Nice to meet you,' Laura said. 'And what lovely cushions you're sitting on. Did you bring them with you?'

'Oh no,' Caroline said. 'They were here when we arrived. They are lovely, aren't they?'

'Oh dear!' Philip said. 'I didn't realize they were personal property. You should have said.'

'Imogen brought them with her,' Jennifer explained.

Imogen waved a hand. 'Please! They're for anyone – especially since you're new here. They will soften the blow – literally.'

'We have permanent marks on our bottoms from the springs in the sofa,' Grace said.

'Did you have a good vacation?' Laura asked her.

'Bliss!' Grace said. 'Mostly at home. We were harvesting of course.'

'And were you all having a party here last night?' Laura enquired.

'Not a party,' Jennifer said. 'Just a gathering. A few friends who'd arrived back.'

'How nice. Now tell me,' Laura said, looking at Caroline and Philip, 'who owns the little purple car which was here earlier?'

'Neither of us,' Caroline said. 'It belongs to the other newcomer.'

'Stuart Young,' Imogen informed her. 'Final year English. At the moment he's up at the place where he lived last year, collecting some of his gear. Rumour has it, a larger TV than ours and a great collection of CDs and videos. That and his car were the reasons we let him come.'

'How did he find you?' Laura asked.

'Oh, you know,' Jennifer said. 'Word gets around. Apparently he was with a group that split up last term.'

'Quarrelled,' Imogen said. 'Has anything happened here while we've been away?'

'Actually, yes,' Laura answered. 'Old Mrs Harper collapsed and had to go into hospital and after that she had to go into a home. Near to Bristol, where her daughter lives. I don't suppose you knew Mrs Harper?'

'Not really,' Imogen admitted. 'Poor old thing!'

'And now of course her house is on the market. So we'll be having new neighbours at Number Fifteen,' Laura added.

'Really?' Jennifer said, but she and the others were only interested as far as politeness demanded. They were birds of passage. Two years from now they would all have left Shipfield for good. Only one year for three of them. Who came to live

44

in Number Fifteen would have no effect on them at all.

Hearing a car stop, Grace moved to the window.

'Hey,' she said, 'he's here! You're about to meet him, Laura.'

Stuart entered the room. He was a person who would always make an entrance rather than just come in. He was tall, with dark wavy hair and skin which looked as though he'd spent the whole of the long vacation on some tropical beach. In spite of the October chill in the air he wore a sleeveless vest. His strong shapely arms and upper chest were covered in fine black hair. He was altogether madly attractive.

'That fucking Volvo's here again!' he said. 'Fucking nuisance. Who the hell does it belong to?'

'Me,' Laura said sweetly. 'Or I should say my husband.'

He turned his head in her direction, looked straight at her. 'And who might you be?' he asked, switching on a warm, slow smile.

'I might be the Queen of Sheba,' Laura said. 'Or Claudia Schiffer. But I'm not. I'm Laura O'Brien and I live next door. I came to say hello to my friends and now I'm just leaving. I'm sure my husband would like to meet you some time.' She smiled at everyone and left.

'Did you have to be so rude?' Jennifer asked Stuart.

'Me, rude?' he said. 'I'm a pussy cat. So is she always popping in and out? Keeping a motherly eye or something?'

'She's all right,' Jennifer said. 'We could have a worse neighbour.'

'Who knows, Stuart?' Grace said. 'One day you

might be quite pleased to see her walk through the door.'

Stuart shook his head. 'Not my type, darling. Now which of you is going to help me unload my car?'

3

Laura went to the telephone and tapped out Esther's number. She was not too worried that Esther's curtains were still drawn across but the old lady was usually an early riser, especially on a Sunday, so a call was in order.

After a delay it was answered – well, not actually *answered* but clearly the receiver had been lifted. She could hear the slight clicking noise Esther made with her tongue against the roof of her false teeth. In her presence it was rather irritating but on the telephone at least one knew she was there. Esther was never quick to speak when she picked up the phone. No 'Miss Dean here'. Her way was to listen in silence until the caller, who had so far heard only Esther's clicking, had identified herself. It was usually 'herself'. According to Esther not many men called these days, which was a pity. It had been different once.

One of these days, Laura thought, I will not speak until she has done so – but there was never time to wait for that.

'It's Laura,' she said.

'I thought it probably was.'

'Then why didn't you say something?' Laura asked.

'*You* called *me*,' Esther said with sweet reason. 'Thought you must have something to say. I didn't call you.'

Laura sighed. Telephoning Esther was never simple; she came from a different direction.

'It's Sunday,' Laura informed her. 'It's half-past eight. Don't you want to go to the ten o'clock Mass?'

'Of course I do. Don't I always?' Esther sounded surprised.

'Your curtains are drawn across. I thought perhaps you'd decided to have a lie-in.'

'Are they?' Esther queried. She paused. 'Why yes, you're right! No wonder I thought it was a dark morning.'

'Do you want a hand getting ready?' Laura offered. 'Shall I come across?'

'Of course I don't want a hand. What a strange idea!' Esther was clearly offended.

It was going to be one of those mornings with Esther. She'd probably had a bad night and was confused. But she'd have been furious if I hadn't reminded her, if she'd missed Mass, Laura thought. Missing Mass on Sunday was, for Esther, some-where near the top of the list of serious sins, up there with adultery or armed robbery, which was why she and Dermot had been taking her to St Patrick's for the last three years, ever since she'd made a not very satisfactory recovery from a broken hip.

'Right,' she said. 'Either Dermot or I will knock on your door at twenty to ten.'

'Send Dermot,' Esther ordered. 'I like a man's arm to lean on. Why are we going so early?'

'It's not early,' Laura said. 'If we leave any later

you'll not get your usual seat and you'll not be able to hear.'

It was not a case of not hearing, it was a case of Esther having occupied that seat at the ten o'clock Mass for countless years. Also, at the time of the Queen's coronation Esther had embroidered a hassock on which she'd knelt ever since. She was never totally happy about someone else kneeling on her hassock at other services. Sometimes she wondered if she should carry it to and from church in a shopping bag.

'I don't need to hear,' she said. 'There isn't a homily I haven't heard a thousand times and I know the Mass by heart. I could prompt the priest if need be. I once did, you know! Not this one, not Father Kennedy, it was in Father O'Halloran's time. He wasn't wearing his glasses and he'd lost his place in the book, so I spoke up. "Heaven and earth," I reminded him, "are full of your glory." Did I tell you?'

'You did indeed,' Laura said. 'I'm going to ring off now so that you can get ready. Don't forget to have some breakfast. We don't want you fainting, do we?'

'Did I tell you I once fainted?' Esther asked brightly. 'Right there at the altar! Of course it was the time of the month. I suffered a lot with my periods . . .'

Laura quietly replaced the receiver.

In fact, Esther *had* had a bad night, one of several recently, and all for the same reason. She had lain awake thinking about Mrs Harper, as she had done repeatedly since she had watched the ambulance which had taken her away, never to be seen in Mulberry Lane again. Is that what will happen to me, she repeatedly asked herself. And where would I go and what would become of me and, worst of all, who would care? These were the thoughts which frightened her, and when something really frightened her she could never bring herself to speak about it, not even to Laura. And now they were selling the house. Oh yes, she knew that, she had seen the woman put up the sale board. She wondered why Laura hadn't mentioned it – though to be fair she hadn't seen her in the last two days. It didn't much matter who would buy it. The only way it would affect her would be that when someone did so, Mrs Harper would be finally out of the picture and very soon no-one at all would remember her. It was a bleak thought; no wonder it kept her awake at night.

'What was all that about?' Dermot asked when Laura returned. He was sitting at the table eating Shreddies.

'The usual,' Laura said. ' "The day I prompted Father O'Halloran, the day I fainted at the altar." '

'Poor old duck!' Dermot said.

'Shall we ask her to lunch?' Laura suggested.

Dermot frowned. 'I've school stuff to get through and I thought you wanted to make a full-scale attack on the garden.'

'I do,' Laura admitted. 'It's just that I worry whether she ever eats a square meal except when she comes here.'

'She has meals-on-wheels,' Dermot reminded her.

'She has them delivered,' Laura agreed, 'but does she eat them? Anyway you're right, we do have a lot to get through. I'll take her a tray across.'

At twenty to ten, with difficulty, they manoeuvred Esther into the Volvo. After Mass they took her for coffee in the parish hall. She was found a seat, fussed over by several nice, caring people whose lives were so genuinely busy that they would forget her existence until she turned up again the following Sunday. At about a quarter to twelve Laura and Dermot delivered her home again.

'I'll come in with you,' Laura said. 'I want to make sure you've got some heating on.'

She turned on the gas fire in the living room and fixed the fireguard firmly around it. There was no central heating, not because Esther couldn't afford it but because neither she nor her parents before her had ever had it and she didn't consider it necessary. 'I was taught that when I was cold,' she said when it was suggested to her, 'I should put on another cardigan. Or go for a brisk walk. That was when I *could* go for a brisk walk. Anyway,' she said now, 'what about that lot across the road? Number Twelve. Did you have a word with them about that party on Friday night? You should have!'

'It wasn't a party,' Laura said. 'It was a gathering. Just meeting up after the vacation.'

'I saw the new ones,' Esther said. 'I saw that one with the purple car. He arrived just after I'd seen you and Dermot gallivanting off somewhere.'

'I suppose you just happened to be at the window?' Laura prompted. Esther was always just by the window. She was a one-woman Neighbourhood Watch.

'That's right! I saw him park his car right up to Dermot's. There'll be trouble there, I thought, so I knocked on the window but of course he took no notice. It's a funny colour for a car, purple. But he's a handsome young man.' Her thin face creased in a smile, her eyes brightened at the memory of him.

'Would you like me to bring you some lunch over?' Laura asked.

'It depends,' Esther said. 'What are you having?'

'Beef. Does that suit you?'

'Fine!' Esther said. 'Don't overcook it, will you? It should be nicely pink. When you carve it the blood should follow the knife.'

'I'll bear that in mind,' Laura promised.

Back at home Dermot already had his work spread out on the desk.

'I do wish Esther had some family to keep an eye on her,' Laura said.

'You're not likely to have family if you're eighty-four and you never married,' Dermot pointed out.

'Or friends,' Laura said. 'She doesn't seem to have any friends.'

'Perhaps that's because she's not the easiest woman in the world to get on with,' Dermot said. 'And I suspect she never was. You have to work at friends unless you're stinking rich or famous. I don't suppose that ever applied to Esther.'

'Probably not,' Laura agreed. 'Though one hears occasional whispers that she was . . . well, not so much famous as notorious. But you are cynical, Dermot.'

'I'm realistic,' Dermot said. 'Old people aren't nice just because they're old. If they weren't all that pleasant when they were young they probably grow a damned sight worse.'

Laura sighed.

'Anyway, there's not much we can do about it,' she said.

'Except take her to Mass, do her shopping, pick

up her prescriptions, check she's warm, take her Sunday dinner on a tray,' Dermot said. 'Perhaps you should call a halt there? Has it never occurred to you that she might like to preserve a bit of independence?'

Laura looked surprised.

'Oh, but I *never* interfere!' she said.

'All right,' Dermot said. 'What I'm suggesting is that you don't take away all her initiative. Leave her to work out some things for herself. She's intelligent enough. That won't prevent you taking the odd tray across.'

'Speaking of which,' Laura said, 'Esther likes her beef a mite underdone.'

'Then I'm sure that's how we'll have it,' Dermot said.

He went back to marking his books. They were Year Eleven's and they were doing reasonably well, most of them. He'd known several of them on their way up through the school but now, while they were doing their GCSEs, he would have them for all their English lessons. Since teaching was his job he supposed they were the age he liked best, though they were certainly not all easy. Individuals among them could be hell, especially those whose only goal was to leave school and never mind the qualifications. Possibly, just possibly, one or two of them might take away a love of literature which would last long enough to make his working on a fine Sunday worth while.

At Number Twelve Jennifer was the first down on Sunday morning, though it was eleven thirty when she staggered into the kitchen. She'd been late to bed and then, tired though she was, she'd lain awake missing Liam, wishing he was lying there beside her.

It was almost a year ago that she'd first met Liam, when she'd stayed with Ruth in Brighton for a weekend. He was studying physics at Sussex. Since his home was in Croydon and hers was in Reigate it wasn't difficult for them to meet in the vacations, or even for weekends in term time. There was never much chance for them to be together in her home but Liam's parents were easier. They had a large family, which meant less concentration on their eldest son.

In the summer vacation she and Liam had gone to France. They had travelled in her car, taking a tent and sleeping wherever it was convenient; on a campsite, in a field and, when the rain came down in torrents, in the back of the car. They had lived on fresh bread, pâté, cheese and fruit, saving what money they had for evening meals in restaurants. They had basked in the sun, been soaked in thunderstorms, swum in rivers, and at night made love. It had been so recent and her longing for him was fresh and strong in her mind.

What was he doing at this moment, she asked herself as she took the cafetière from the shelf and the tin of coffee from the cupboard. Sunday was the only day everyone in the house shared proper coffee. Usually they drank whatever instant was on offer. But Sunday was different. Lady Winton, who would never knowingly have allowed instant coffee to pass her lips, had given the cafetière to Jennifer in the hope that her daughter, living away from home with all kinds of people from who knew what backgrounds, would not lose all her standards. She also sent coffee, Fortnum & Mason's finest

Arabica. In fact from time to time the lady ordered Fortnum's to send one of their hampers containing preserves, pickles, own-make biscuits, fruit cake, ham, cheese, anchovies, olives – whatever, whatever. In the beginning this had embarrassed Jennifer to death but as time went by and she observed the pleasure of her friends as she shared the goodies with them she ceased to be embarrassed. Now they all looked forward to each new delivery.

It was good to be back in Shipfield. Her parents didn't know it but she doubted if she would ever live at home again; not that she wasn't loved and cherished there, not that anyone was the least bit unkind to her, but she'd known in her heart on the day she'd first left home for the university that she was leaving for good.

She poured the near-boiling water into the cafetière and was waiting for the brew to gather strength when Stuart walked into the kitchen. He was dressed in a short red-and-navy silky dressing gown, and though his hair was tousled, he was badly in need of a shave and his knees and feet, which were not as beautiful as the rest of him, were bare, he still managed to look drop-dead gorgeous.

He sniffed the air appreciatively.

'Ah, coffee!'

He seated himself at the table and waited while Jennifer depressed the plunger, poured, and put a mug in front of him.

'Would you like a slice of toast?' she asked – and regretted it the second the words were out of her mouth. Why was she doing this?

Hadn't they sworn, she, Imogen, Grace and Ruth, right at the beginning that there was to be none of this women do these chores, men do those? Women make the meals, clean the dishes, do the laundry, shop. Men chop the wood, light the fires (what wood? what fires?), unblock sinks, lift furniture and open screw-top jars too difficult for frail female fingers. All the girls had agreed that though it was the way they had been brought up there was to be no more of it. 'Anyway, one can buy a gadget for opening screw-top jars,' Imogen had said helpfully.

So why am I serving this man's coffee and offering to make his toast while he sits there watching me, she asked herself.

'Two slices, please,' Stuart said. 'Quite lightly done.'

What you got from the toaster, Jennifer knew, was a matter of luck. She was quite pleased to see that this time the bread was darkish brown with black edges.

'Ah,' Stuart said. 'Could I suggest you set it at number three next time?'

He picked up a knife and ostentatiously scraped off the burnt bits, scattering black crumbs over the table.

'Do we have marmalade, Cooper's thick cut preferably?' he enquired.

'Sorry!' Jennifer said sweetly. 'We can't rise to that. Of course there's nothing to stop you buying your own and keeping it entirely to yourself.' Actually she was well aware that there was a jar of Fortnum & Mason's Seville orange with luscious strips of tangy peel at the back of the cupboard. If he had not been so uppity she would certainly have offered it to him.

'So what are you doing?' he asked.

'History.'

'Ah.'

In one short syllable he managed to convey doubt, condescension and faint amusement.

'And what will you do with history?' he enquired.

She knew what she would do. It had been growing in her mind for a few months now. An aunt had returned from a holiday in the Near East which had actually been a tour of archaeological sites. Aunt Rachael had been full of wonder and enthusiasm and had brought back photographs, souvenirs and – the prize of her collection – a video she had made while an eminent archaeologist, with a team of students, had dug out artefacts from the ground.

'You just wouldn't believe . . . !' she'd said.

But Jennifer had, and it was probably from that moment that she'd known what she wanted to do with her life.

'What will I do with it?' she said to Stuart. 'Who knows?'

And where would Liam fit in? That was the question which niggled at the back of her mind and to which so far she had not been able to find an answer.

'And you?' she said. 'You're reading English, aren't you? What will you do with that?'

'Oh, I know what I'll do,' Stuart said. 'I shall write bestselling novels.'

'How exciting!' Jennifer said. She had never met an author but Stuart was not her idea of what they were like. They would be studious, quiet, self-effacing types, silently observing people so that they could put them in books. There must be more to Stuart than met the eye. And how did he know he was going to be a bestseller?

'Have you written one?' she asked. 'What's it about?'

'Not yet,' Stuart said. 'I've got one or two good ideas. Sure-fire winners! I'll probably make a start when I've done my finals. I reckon it will take – say – six months to write, another six months before it's in print – unless they rush it through, of course. They can do that if they think it's something special . . .'

The door opened and Imogen entered.

'Quick,' Jennifer said, 'Stuart's telling us his plans for the future. Terribly exciting, Imo! This you must hear.'

She met Imogen's slightly puzzled look with an expressionless face and eyes wide open.

'He's going to be a *bestselling novelist*!'

'How wonderful!' Imogen said. 'Do go on, Stuart. When's publication day? Will we be invited to the launch party? I've never met an author before, not in the flesh. Have you, Jen?'

'Never!' Jennifer said.

Stuart waved a deprecating hand. 'It's not fixed,' he said. 'Not yet.'

'What's it called? What's it about? Is it sexy?' Imogen persisted.

'I've not yet written it.' He sounded a mite impatient. 'It's just a matter of finding the time, settling down to it. Is there more coffee?'

'I've always thought,' Jennifer said dreamily as she poured the coffee, 'that I could write a book – if only I had the time.'

'Oh, me too!' Imogen said. 'Will it be in the top twenty, Stu?'

'Of course,' Stuart said. 'What's the point otherwise?' He hated being called Stu.

'Surely the top ten?' Jennifer corrected her. 'I can just see it! I shall go into WH Smith's and if anyone's standing next to me I shall say, "I know him!" What if it won the Booker Prize?'

Stuart sighed.

'You just don't get the idea,' he said. 'I have no intention of writing a book which the critics will say is marvellous and then it'll sit on the shelves and sell a few hundred copies. I'm not in it for literature – I've chosen not to go down that path – I'm in it for the fucking money! You're right, I've got it all worked out. I intend to write romantic fiction for the women's market. That's where the money is! At least one a year and they'll walk off the shelves.'

'You make it sound so easy,' Imogen said. 'I thought writing a novel was difficult.'

'Not if you go about it the right way,' Stuart assured her. 'Once you've cracked the formula it's as easy as baking a cake. The only thing is . . .'

'Yes?' both girls said eagerly.

'. . . do I write under my own name or would it be better to use a woman's name? Most of this stuff seems to have been written by women.'

'We could choose a name for you!' Jennifer cried. 'Oh Stu, do let us.'

'Dilys Flower,' Imogen suggested.

'Poppy Fanshawe,' Jennifer offered.

'Charmaine Silver?'

'Pearl Coniston!'

'Amethyst Green?'

'Amethyst is OK,' Jennifer said thoughtfully. 'I'm not sure I like it with Green.'

Stuart held up his hand.

'OK! OK! Don't call me, I'll call you.'

'On the other hand,' Jennifer said, 'don't you

think your own name, Stuart Young, with a wonderful photograph of you on the jacket . . . ?'

'You have a point there,' Stuart conceded. 'I'll think of it while I have my bath.'

Seconds later Grace came into the kitchen.

'What's the matter with Milord Stuart?' she asked. 'He passed me on the stairs like a man in a dream, didn't even stop to say something rude.'

They couldn't answer. They were clutching each other, shaking, Imogen wiping her eyes with a tea towel.

'Oh Grace, you're so right!' Jennifer said presently. 'That's what he is. A man in a dream!'

'That was very nice,' Esther said later when Laura went to collect the tray. 'The meat was good. I think you get a better flavour when you cook it on the bone. A forerib of beef is best.'

'Thanks,' Laura said. 'I'll bear that in mind.'

'Anyway, you did well with the Yorkshire pudding,' Esther said. 'Do you by any chance have Yorkshire blood in you?'

'Not a drop,' Laura confessed.

What she would not confess, at least not to Esther, though everyone else she knew did it, was that the Yorkshire puddings had come out of a packet, straight from the freezer. Cook from frozen, pre-heated oven 230 degrees, fifteen minutes. Hey presto!

'Yes, Dermot always compliments me on my Yorkshire puddings,' she said.

'He's quite right,' Esther said, nodding approval. 'And now I'm going to have a nap. I advise you to do the same.'

*　　　*　　　*

As he was getting ready to go to the pub for his usual Sunday lunchtime drink Nigel Simpson, who lived with his wife Mary at Number Eight, looked out of the window and saw Laura. She was crossing the road from Esther Dean's.

'There's Laura!' he said to Mary. 'She'll have been taking the old lady to church, she and Dermot.'

'I know,' Mary said. 'I saw them setting off. That blue coat she's wearing is new – I mean Laura's coat.'

'Trust you to notice,' Nigel said. 'She looks well in it, but then she's a nice-looking woman.'

'I'll give you that,' Mary said. She was doing the *Sunday Express* crossword and not taking much notice of Nigel.

'We couldn't have better neighbours,' Nigel said. They had lived next door to Laura and Dermot for several years now and never a cross word between them. Not that they lived in each other's pockets, they didn't, but they knew they were there for each other should the need arise. If he and Mary wanted to go away for the weekend, for instance, which they did from time to time to visit Mary's sister Freda in Eastbourne, then Laura and Dermot could be relied upon to have Titus, whom they could never take with them because Freda had a bad-tempered bull terrier and the two dogs didn't get on with each other at all.

'I'm not denying they're good neighbours,' Mary said in an absent-minded way.

'Laura is kind to everyone,' Nigel said.

'Yes, dear,' Mary said. 'Perhaps just a little too much into other people's affairs.'

'She likes to be helpful,' Nigel said. 'What's wrong with that?'

'Nothing.' Mary, with great satisfaction, filled in the last word which completed the crossword and wondered if she should send it in. Not that she ever did send it but someone had to win the prize. 'I just think that sometimes it's better to wait until you're asked. For my part, as you know, I'm more for keeping myself to myself. You're the sociable one.'

'I had to be, working in the bank,' Nigel reminded her. 'The customers expected a friendly face, a smile of greeting. Where I was concerned I saw that they got it.'

He missed the bank. He'd worked there from leaving school until he'd retired three years ago. Always Lloyds, but not the same branch of course; not even the same town. They moved you around, it was part of the policy. In his heart he was disappointed that he'd never risen any higher than assistant manager of a not very large branch. He didn't admit his disappointment, he didn't show it, but sometimes he felt it even now. He never knew why he'd been passed over, he thought he'd have made a good manager, but in the end he put it down to bad luck. After all, as he sometimes said to Mary, not every clerk could expect to be a manager any more than every lance-corporal could become colonel of the regiment. There weren't enough of those jobs to go around.

And if he wasn't totally fulfilled, he was happy enough – and particularly happy that his last posting, several years ago now, had brought him to Shipfield. His was a happy nature and he was enjoying his retirement. He had plenty to do. He was treasurer of the Shipfield Horticultural Society, he played bowls, he walked his dog and had more time for his garden. Most evenings he walked along to the Green Man – the pub was very close, fronting on to North Hill but with a side entrance in Mulberry Lane – where he had two halves of bitter which he made last. He was also in the pub quiz team which played against other pubs every other Tuesday.

'I'll be off then,' he said to Mary. He called to the dog. 'Titus! Walkies!'

Titus ran into the room, all five pounds of him. He was a Yorkshire terrier, an aristocrat of the breed – his great-grandfather had been best puppy at Cruft's – with long black hair like silk and flowing moustaches of a rich tan shade. In appearance, though not in lineage for Nigel had no aristocratic pretensions, Titus and his owner were not unalike. Nigel was small, neatly formed, and held himself well. And though he no longer had dark hair there were tinges of colour in his droopy grey moustache.

'Come along, boy!' Nigel said, attaching the lead to Titus's collar. 'Are you sure you won't come with us, Mary?'

'You know I never go on Sundays,' Mary said. 'Who would cook the lunch?' That didn't prevent him asking her every Sunday.

'Very well,' Nigel said. 'I'll be back one thirty sharp.'

As he left the house he saw the little girl next door riding her tricycle around the front garden. The garden at Number Six, like that of the students at Number Twelve, had been concreted over. He couldn't understand why anyone should choose to have grey concrete when they could have had green grass and flower borders. He was pleased she wasn't playing ball. Not many weeks ago her ball had come over onto his side and had knocked the heads off some special dahlias he was nurturing. He prided himself he had hid his annoyance from the child's mother, merely suggesting that to play ball in the front might be dangerous for Fiona. If it went into the road she might run after it and there could be a nasty accident.

It was not that he didn't like children. Quite the reverse. They had had a little boy of their own once. He had died of meningitis when he was five years old, a year younger than Fiona was now, and it had been his great sorrow, and Mary's, that they had never been blessed with another child. Sometimes now when he watched Fiona and her younger brother the thought came to him that they might have had grandchildren of their age, or even older.

He waved to Fiona as he walked down the path and turned into Mulberry Lane. She dismounted from her cycle and rushed to greet Titus. All the children loved Titus and he enjoyed the fuss.

'Where's Neil this morning?' Nigel asked.

'He's in the house,' Fiona informed him. 'He was sick. He was sick all over himself and on the rug. Mummy was very cross. He was sick because he'd been eating the cat food.'

'Oh dear!' Nigel said. 'You wouldn't do that, would you?'

'Not any more,' Fiona said. 'It didn't make me sick but I didn't like the taste.'

The Green Man was busy, as it usually was on a Sunday lunchtime. Mostly men. Along Mulberry Lane, around the corner in North Hill and no doubt all over Shipfield, the women were cooking beef, lamb, pork or chicken (or in Upper Mulberry

64

possibly duck or venison), with all the attendant sauces, vegetables, puddings. The combined aromas escaping through open windows and air extractors could have made the town smell like one large restaurant. In the pub the landlord, Jim Pullman, and his wife Betty were pulling pints as fast as they could go. When Nigel reached the bar Jim pushed his glass across the counter.

'Your usual, Nigel,' he said. 'How's everything?'

'All right,' Nigel said. 'And a packet of crisps for Titus. Cheese and onion.' He hoisted himself up onto a bar stool. He was not comfortable on a bar stool, his legs were too short, nor did Titus like it because, being low to the ground, he was too far away from his owner and the crisps so they would have to be dropped down to him instead of being put into his open mouth. The trouble was that Nigel had spent too many hours in the garden yesterday and as a result his back wouldn't allow him to stand for long.

'I see Number Fifteen is up for sale,' the landlord said.

'That's right,' Nigel agreed. 'There's a board outside.'

'Oh, there's more than that,' Betty Pullman called out. 'It's advertised in Proctor's window. Do you know what they're asking for it?'

'I don't,' Nigel admitted. 'I'd think not a lot. It doesn't look all that good from the outside. Which is a pity because when a house doesn't look good it lets down the neighbourhood, you get the wrong kind of person moving in. I must say we've always tried to keep our property up to the mark.'

When Jim Pullman mentioned the price there was a united gasp from all around.

'I can't believe it!' Nigel said.

'It's true,' Jim assured him. 'It's there in black and white in the window.'

'My goodness, James, I wonder what that makes ours worth?' Eric Spurling asked the question of his partner, and at the same time voiced the thoughts of all the house owners within earshot. Property prices were always a source of interest, even to those who had no thought of selling. They liked to calculate the amount of wealth they were sitting on.

'And ours is in perfect condition,' James said. 'We're very fussy about that sort of thing!'

It was true. Anything which could be done to a house had been done to theirs. It was the last word in exquisite taste as well as being embellished with choice pieces from the antique shop which they ran together in the town.

'It's way over the top! You wouldn't get that, even in Bristol.'

The speaker was Michael Blake, who felt he could speak with some authority since he worked in Bristol, even though his job as a representative for a firm which manufactured laboratory glass didn't take him at all into the realms of real estate. He lived, with his wife Dawn, at Number Seven Mulberry Lane, which was where she was now, looking after their nine-year-old twins. Dawn was a chiropodist who had a nice little business working in her own home.

'You could be wrong, Michael,' Ralph Streeter said. 'We all know how property has increased in price. Personally, since I live next door I'm pleased they're not selling it too cheap. We could get the wrong sort of person!'

George Potter ordered another pint. Although

he was a regular in the Green Man his opinion didn't count for as much as some because he didn't live in Mulberry. On the other hand he had an interest. Whoever bought Number Fifteen would need no end of materials, obtainable at his shop.

'Are you going to have the other half?' the landlord asked Nigel Simpson.

Nigel nodded. 'A quick one!' He didn't make his drinks last on a Sunday. Mary wouldn't like it if he was late for his dinner.

4

'Will you be late this evening?' Laura asked Dermot as they left the house together on Monday morning.

'I shouldn't be,' Dermot said. 'There's nothing special happening. Are you sure you don't want a lift?'

Laura shook her head. 'Quite sure, thank you. It's a nice morning. The exercise will do me good.'

'I'd have thought all the gardening you've done this weekend would have been exercise enough,' Dermot said.

'I know,' Laura agreed. 'Actually, it's the reason I have to walk. I'm stiff all over. I must loosen up.'

He got in the car and drove away. She set off along Mulberry Lane.

From her window Esther watched them. She knew that envy was one of the seven deadly sins, most of which she'd committed in her lifetime, but envious she was, no doubt about it. She was envious simply because they had each other. If I'd married, she thought, I'd have had a family. Perhaps I'd still have had a husband, though that was doubtful because as far as she could see the world was full of widows. But at least I'd have had someone. If I'd had to go into a home someone would know about it, someone would visit me. You couldn't rely just on friends, they didn't have a duty to you, but family did. Even if your children visited you only out of a sense of duty it was better than nothing.

Ought she to have married? If she'd not been orphaned by the time she was twenty-one no doubt she would have, if only to get away from her over-strict parents, but since she had inherited the house there had been no need to. She'd had several chances but she'd turned them down. There'd always been something more exciting to tempt her – and let's face it, she thought, she'd never been the faithful type. Familiarity didn't breed contempt so much as grinding boredom and that she would never have put up with. She'd been adept at stepping out of any affair the minute boredom stepped in. You couldn't do that with marriage. Too messy!

Also she had much enjoyed, from time to time, being a mistress. She'd liked the excitement, the plotting and planning, the secrecy. She'd savoured living on the edge of discovery, even danger, and she had never allowed some of the disagreeable chores which came with marriage to be hers. No laundry, no nursing, no cooking – she encouraged her men to take her out to meals. And what lovely men she had known! How kind they'd been, how generous, and she had repaid them by making them happy while the affair lasted. She had been equally generous, too, in letting them go when they wanted out. As in the end they always did. She had had some wonderful leaving presents.

But if I'd been married, she thought now, I'd have had company in my old age; someone to talk to, someone to argue with. Someone to care what happened to me. Of course even if he hadn't been dead by now – men didn't live as long as women – he might be doddering, dribbling, possibly incontinent, maybe even funny in the head. Who wanted any of that? No, all things considered she was better off as she was. Loneliness, for a selfish old woman, which she knew herself to be, was better than some of the alternatives. It was just that the Mrs Harper business had unsettled her.

If I'd actually had Archie's baby, she told herself, I would now have a son or a daughter and perhaps grandchildren. But would she have wanted to have been married to Archie all these years? No, she certainly wouldn't! Best not to think about it. It was all a long time ago. She must pull herself together. As her mother used to say, 'What can't be cured must be endured!' Her mother had been full of platitudes, none of them jolly.

Laura being now out of sight, Esther turned her attention to Number Twelve. There was movement in the front room. She could see the owner of the purple car – he would break a few hearts before he'd finished! He was standing close to the window. She'd not yet set eyes on the other new ones but she would, and Laura would tell her their names and where they came from and all the rest. She was a mine of information.

In fact, if Esther so decided she could see far more from her house than she was allowing herself to observe at the moment. There was no doubt that if she were to use her binoculars she could see right into Number Twelve's front room. Her binoculars were on the window sill, always close to hand, but she didn't allow herself to use them often, certainly

70

not for looking through windows. She had her standards. Watching the street was different. The street was public and people must expect to be observed – it was the binoculars which had helped her to read the exact wording on the sale board at Number Fifteen – but only if something very exciting was taking place behind anyone's window would she give in to further temptation.

The binoculars had been given to her many years ago by Henry, one of her gentlemen. He had been a birdwatcher and had tried to interest her in his hobby, dragging her out of the house at dark, misty dawns, but she had never found that birds did anything interesting. Dear Henry! He had been a nice man but dull. He too had offered her marriage, which she'd declined, and she had wondered afterwards if she'd been wise to do so for he had died suddenly, aged sixty-two, after no more than an hour or two's illness, and had left quite a lot of money.

Laura walked along without hurrying. Dermot liked to be at school by eight fifteen at the latest but she didn't start work until eight thirty when she and Susan took over from reception's night staff. As she was about to pass Number Six Karen Jackson, pushing Neil in his buggy while Fiona trailed reluctantly behind, walked down her path. Laura waited to walk along the road with them. She met up with them most mornings except when Karen was all behindhand.

'Hi!' Laura said. 'You all right?'

Karen, manoeuvring the buggy through the gateway, hesitated before answering.

'Not at my best,' she admitted.

71

She looked pale and tired, even so early in the day, Laura thought. And surely Neil had outgrown the buggy stage? He was going on three and big for his age, whereas Karen was five foot nothing and reed slender. She looked as though she was the one who could do with the ride.

'It's easier this way,' Karen said, reading Laura's thoughts. 'He hates holding hands and it's unsafe not to. He's wayward. So is Fiona, come to that. I couldn't cross North Hill without hanging on to both of them.'

'You take Neil, I'll take Fiona,' Laura offered. She turned to Fiona. 'Is that OK?'

'I can do it on my own,' Fiona said, glowering.

'Oh, I expect you can,' Laura agreed. 'I was thinking you could help me. Will you?'

Fiona nodded grudgingly. 'But not until we get to the big road,' she insisted.

Laura turned to Karen. 'So,' she asked, 'what is it?'

'I'm pregnant,' Karen said in a quiet, flat voice.

'Pregnant? Are you sure?'

'Of course I'm sure,' Karen said, slightly testy.

'Sorry!' Laura said. It had been a natural question, even if silly. Karen was a single parent – single because her husband, having found a woman he preferred to his wife, had walked out on her a year ago. So who on earth was the father, and whoever he was why had she let him make her pregnant?

'No, *I*'m sorry!' Karen said. 'I shouldn't have snapped at you. And I know that you want to ask me, but now isn't the moment. Little pigs have big ears.'

'What little pigs?' Fiona asked.

'Anyway, I've done the tests,' Karen said.

'Would you like me to come round this evening? I could, after supper.'

'Yes please,' Karen said.

'Is there anything else I could—'

'Not unless you can wave a wand and make it go away,' Karen interrupted.

They had reached the junction of Mulberry Lane and North Hill. Laura and Fiona looked at each other. Warily, Fiona held out her hand and Laura took it.

'Thank you,' Laura said.

'You have to wait until you see the little green man,' Fiona instructed her.

At the other side of the road they parted company, Karen and the children going down the hill towards St John's Primary School, Laura uphill towards North Hill Private Hospital, her mind full of Karen. If Karen said she was pregnant, then she must be. In her own experience you always knew. She'd never needed the tests to convince her. And Karen had had two children. All the same, it was a surprise. Karen wasn't the type, and in fact she'd never seen her with another man since her husband left, never heard her mention one. She was a devoted mother. Perhaps it was someone she'd met at work? She had a part-time job in the office at Venables' toffee factory, but only since she'd been able to put Neil in nursery school. Laura suspected she needed the money, but perhaps she needed the company almost as much.

Still thinking about Karen, she walked through the hospital's well-kept grounds with their immaculate lawns, clipped shrubs and colourful, healthy-looking flowers in neat beds, and went in at the staff entrance. She deposited her coat and shopping bag – there were things she must buy on the way home – tidied her hair and reported for duty.

'Posh' was the word which best described the hospital reception area. Pale beige deep-pile carpet, chintzy country-house-style sofas and armchairs, low mahogany tables holding the day's papers and the current issues of glossy magazines. Thanks to the substantial fees paid by the patients of North Hill Private the aura was not so much that of a hospital waiting room as of a five-star hotel, meant to reassure those who waited here in moods ranging from stoic to near panic that all would be well. Not to worry!

Susan was already in reception, chatting with Moira and Denise who were about to leave.

'I'm not late, am I?' Laura asked.

'Not a bit,' Moira assured her. ''Tis just that we've had a hard day's night and I'm dying on me feet – if you'll pardon the word "dying" for it's what Mr Florian in Number Seventeen has done, God rest his soul!'

'I'm sorry,' Laura said. Not that she knew Mr Florian. You saw patients when they first came in, but hardly ever after that.

'Right! I'm off to me bed then,' Moira said.

'Me too,' said Denise. 'There was an emergency admission at seven a.m., Mr Dayberry operating. He's still in theatre as far as I know.'

They gathered their bits and pieces together and left.

The customers, if such a word could be used, flowed in and out steadily throughout the day. Those coming in had one thing in common; they all looked anxious. Some tried to cover it up and their mouths smiled though their eyes did not. And there was the way they dealt with the magazines, picking up one, flipping through a few pages then exchanging it for another.

'I feel most sorry for those who come on their own,' Laura said to Susan. 'Especially if they're elderly.' Sometimes she wanted to go up to them and say, 'There, there! It won't be as bad as you think.'

'I suppose you can be just as worried or afraid sitting in one of those comfy armchairs reading *Homes and Gardens* as you can queuing on a hard bench in Shipfield Infirmary with the *Sun*,' Susan said. 'Still, nicer to be miserable in comfort!'

On the same Monday morning when Laura was busy in reception and Dermot was at school taking his first class of the day and Karen had shared her secret with Laura, Brian Carson was exploring Shipfield. It was almost by chance that yesterday, on his way to the West Country, he had turned off the main road to seek somewhere which would give him Sunday lunch – a proper lunch, not fast food – and had found himself outside the Shipfield Arms, which did him proud with succulent beef and apple sponge pudding.

After his ample meal, leaving his car parked at the Shipfield Arms, he'd walked around the town and, as he always did in such circumstances, had checked the estate agents' windows. There were three estate agents in the centre of the town but it was in Proctor's window that he found what might be exactly what he was looking for. Number Fifteen Mulberry Lane.

He didn't know Mulberry Lane. He hardly knew

Shipfield though he had been there, briefly, once or twice before. Even then, he had liked the look of the place and the feel of it. It wasn't large, nor was it too small to have the necessary amenities. It felt alive. There were people walking around the streets, people of varying ages, and, though it was Sunday, several shops were open. It didn't give the feeling of being a boring place, which would not have done for his purposes. It also had a prosperous air about it, which probably meant there were jobs to be had. That was essential, something he would have to look into.

He reread the notice in Proctor's window. He was used, by now, to estate agents' language so it was clear to him that the house which had caught his eye was run down and would need time and money spent on it. If so, the asking price was far too high. But never mind that for the moment. Cash was a great incentive to lowering the price, and cash was what he could offer. He would have to bring Malcolm to see it, if he judged for himself that it was suitable, but Malcolm so far had trusted his judgement and they had never made a bad buy. What Malcolm would want to know was would it be right for the project? If he was convinced that it was, then money would be found from the Trust.

He had spoken with Malcolm on the phone last night and they'd agreed that Brian should look into it.

Which was why he now, on Monday morning, having slept at the Shipfield Arms, opened the door and walked into Proctor's.

An attractive teenager sat behind a desk. She was leafing through a magazine, which she closed and pushed to one side as Brian approached her. There was no other sign of life.

'Good morning, sir,' she said pleasantly. 'Can I help you?'

He looked decidedly dishy, Josie thought. A bonus for Monday morning. He was tall, lean, with close-cropped dark hair over a well-shaped head and a brow almost high enough, but not quite, to be called receding. He had nice ears, which lay flat against his skull. All this she had noticed when he was looking at the ads in the window, but now that he was nearer it was his eyes which took over. Not large, and now narrowed a bit in what might develop into a smile if his lips allowed it. She couldn't decide what colour except that they were dark, with fine eyebrows set straight and rather low, which made him seem as though he could tell what she was thinking. All this she took in with a speed born of long practice, though she allowed that she might be wrong about him knowing what she was thinking.

'Possibly you can,' Brian said. 'I'm looking for a property in the area – at least I probably am, I'm not sure. Is there someone I could talk to?'

'Of course!' the girl said. 'I think Mrs Masefield is free. I'll just check. I'm sure she'd be able to help you. I won't keep you a minute.'

She disappeared through one of the three doors which led from the front office.

'This one is gorgeous!' she informed Mrs Masefield.

'That's lucky,' she said, returning to the front office. 'Mrs Masefield can fit you in right now.'

Fit me in, Brian thought, what's that shorthand

for? It was nine fifteen on a Monday morning, not the slightest sign of any other customers, no ringing of telephones.

A woman sat behind a large, tidy desk.

'Rita Masefield,' she said, rising, holding out her hand. 'And you are – I'm sorry, Josie didn't give me your name.' But she'd given the right description.

'Brian Carson,' he said.

'And you're interested in buying a property, Mr Carson? Did you have any particular one in mind – I mean have you looked in the window?'

'Just a glance,' he said. 'Nothing in particular.' If he told her what had interested him she would concentrate on that, excluding everything else. Also if it came to bargaining – which it would if it was what he wanted – it was best not to seem over keen.

'Do you live locally?' Rita enquired. 'Do you have a house to sell?'

'No to both questions,' Brian said. 'I'm simply interested in buying, if I can find what I want, and at the right price of course.'

'Good!' Rita said. 'Then I'll take down a few details. How many bedrooms, any particular area, that sort of thing.'

'Four bedrooms. I don't know the areas well enough to decide that but something decent, and not too far from the town. I wouldn't mind a place which needed a bit of work done on it but of course the cost of renovations would have to be considered in relation to the price.'

'Of course,' Rita agreed smoothly. This man, for all his evident charm, wasn't going to be the dream customer. She rather thought he'd been through it all before. And in that case he and she would be well matched. 'Of course what you're looking for is what a lot of other people are also after and it's not so easy to come by.'

'Well, if you don't have anything to offer me I won't take up your time,' Brian said, half rising to his feet.

'Oh no, Mr Carson,' Rita said quickly, 'I wouldn't say we had nothing to offer you. There are two or three properties which might well fit the bill. Please wait just one moment and I'll ask Josie to bring the details.'

She picked up the phone, quoted numbers and names of roads, among which Brian clearly heard 'Mulberry Lane'.

'Would you like some coffee while you're looking at them?' she asked.

'That would be nice,' Brian said. 'Black, no sugar. What's the employment situation in Shipfield?' he enquired.

'If you mean are there jobs,' Rita said, 'then the answer is definitely yes. Lots of opportunities. What sort of job are you looking for?' He didn't look unemployed, not at all. In addition to being well dressed and good-looking he was also self-assured. And he was about to buy a house without first selling one.

'Not for me,' he said. 'I wondered what the prospects were.'

Perhaps he was hoping to start a business, Rita thought. Anyway, she doubted if he was going to tell her and she didn't much mind. She was here to sell houses and it would be nice to start the week doing just that.

Josie brought in several sheets of paper, and the coffee. Rita browsed through the sheets and handed over three of them to Brian.

'Take a look at these,' she said.

He saw that one was the Mulberry Lane house advertised in the window, he recognized the photograph at once. He read that through, then put it to one side while he carefully perused the others, though he could tell at once that neither of the last two were of any interest to him.

'What do you think?' Rita asked. 'Is there anything more I can tell you about them?'

'I don't think so,' Brian said. 'The Mulberry Lane one just *might* be possible but the price is far too high. It clearly needs a lot doing to it. A few thousand pounds' worth of work there, I think.' He smiled across at her. 'I understand estate agents' language,' he said.

Rita smiled back at him.

'I rather thought you did,' she said. 'Why don't you let me take you to see it?'

'I wouldn't want to waste your time,' Brian said. Not, he thought, that she seemed to have anything else on at the moment.

'I'd be pleased to do it,' Rita said. 'You'd get a much better idea of the property. It really does have potential.' 'Potential' was a useful word. It was nearly always true, provided one had lots of imagination and a well-lined pocket. She had no idea whether he had or not.

'Very well then,' Brian said. 'If you're sure you can spare the time.'

Dermot was not having a good day. The morning had been reasonable but the class he was facing this afternoon was not by any means his favourite group. Some of them, he knew, would rather not have been there and if the truth were told there were those he would rather not have had, but neither they nor he had any escape. English was compulsory, three times a week.

Children they were, but in many ways no longer children. Some of them had reached the height they would be for the rest of their lives until old age began to shrink them. There were boys as tall as he was and girls not much shorter. The boys were broad-shouldered and muscular, and their voices had deepened. A few had begun occasionally to shave and Charlie Farrar, boasting his maturity – though heaven knew it did not extend beyond the physical – already sported a moustache, which sat oddly on his round babyish features.

The girls were a different matter, so visibly mature with their pert breasts, their slender waists, their hips and behinds already showing womanly curves. The very sight of them drove the boys mad. Possibly the boys also drove the girls mad. The whole lot of them were a mass of galloping, surging hormones. No wonder it was difficult for them to concentrate on Shakespeare and J. B. Priestley.

'Right!' he said. 'Let's make a start. An extract from any poem of your choice from the syllabus.'

Melanie Clarke sprang to her feet. He might have known she would and he should have found a way to pre-empt it. It was a game she had been playing for a week or two now. She was a bright girl. It was a pity she could find nothing better to do than try to entice her English teacher, though it had not always been her English teacher. She had gone hell-for-leather after Bill Foreman, who taught her French, until he announced that he was about to marry. Presumably she'd realized she couldn't compete with a new bride, which was why she'd turned her eyes to Dermot.

'Yes, Melanie,' he said evenly.

She was, he noticed, looking particularly lovely. The severity of her school uniform with its white shirt and navy skirt enhanced her appearance. She was, however, a man-eater. A beautiful one, as is a tiger. Her figure was ripe and full of curves. When she was older it would probably be overripe but now it was perfect. Her dark hair curled tumultuously to her shoulders. Her eyes, meeting his, were large, limpid, and the colour of bluebells in spring.

'I chose Shakespeare,' she said.

That surprised him. He had not thought of Melanie as being a lover of Shakespeare. He wondered what was coming.

'Very well,' he said. 'Let's say eight lines only.'

'Oh sir,' she said, 'it's such a lovely poem. Can't I read it all? I've been practising it.'

'I'm sorry,' Dermot said. 'There won't be time. I want as many of you as possible to read.'

She pouted deliciously, wriggled her shoulders, then took a deep breath which pushed her chest out to its fullest and looked him in the eye.

'Being your slave, what should I do but tend
Upon the hours and times of your desire?
I have no precious time at all to spend
Nor services to do, till you require.

Nor dare I chide the world-without-end hour
Whilst I, my sovereign, watch the clock for you,
Nor think the bitterness of absence sour
When you have bid your servant once
    adieu . . .'

'Thank you,' Dermot interrupted as she reached the end of the second verse. He knew what was to follow. 'Nicely read. Now who's next?' He looked around the room. 'Chris! What have you chosen?'

Melanie remained standing.

'Oh sir,' she begged, 'let me read the rest!'

'I'm sorry, Melanie,' Dermot said. 'There are others. Chris?'

'I chose the one by Auden,' Chris said.

Melanie, still on her feet, started to recite the rest of her poem out loud.

'Nor dare I question with my jealous thought . . .'

'Please be quiet, Melanie,' Dermot said, though not raising his voice, 'or you must leave the room. You mean "Funeral Blues", Chris? A good choice! The rest of you listen carefully and later we'll discuss whether Auden is saying something behind the words, something we should hear.'

'Who wants to hear stupid Auden in the first place?' Melanie cried. 'I'm not going to listen to it!'

'Melanie, that's enough!' Dermot said. 'Leave the class and see me in the interview room at break. OK, Chris! Carry on.'

Making for the interview room at break time Dermot wondered whether Melanie would turn up or whether she would defy him by not doing so, but there she was, waiting in the corridor. He opened the door and she followed him in. He sat behind the desk and motioned her to take the chair in front of it. She sat down and crossed her legs, managing in so doing to hitch up her skirt several inches higher.

'Well,' he said, 'what was all that about?'

She opened her bluebell eyes to their widest, her pretty mouth drooping.

'You know what it was about,' she said. 'You know why I chose it to read to you!'

'I don't know,' Dermot lied, 'nor do I wish to know. You're being a very silly girl.'

Melanie flushed crimson. Her eyes darted anger at him.

'Don't patronize me!' she said sharply. 'I'm not a little girl. I'm sixteen. I'm old enough to be married if I wanted to.'

And soon will be, Dermot thought, if you go on like this. And heaven help the man who does marry you.

'You behaved very badly,' he said. 'You disrupted the whole class. The proper punishment for that is detention, as you well know.'

She gave him a slow smile.

'You wouldn't dare!' she said softly.

'Wouldn't dare? Now that's really very silly, Melanie.' He laughed, trying to diffuse the situation.

Melanie's tone changed again.

'Don't you laugh at me!' she said angrily. 'You wouldn't dare, Mr Dermot O'Brien, because if you did I'd say you touched me up! I'd say you invited me into this room – which you did in front of everyone – and when I got here you put your hand down my blouse, or up my skirt. Or both!'

He felt fear, real fear. He tried not to show what he was feeling.

'Oh, come on, Melanie! Who'd believe that?' he said.

'Lots of people would,' she said. 'Everybody knows what men are like with young girls. But even if they didn't believe me they'd have to take me seriously, they'd have to look into it. I daresay I'd be suspended, which would suit me beautifully. I hate school. But so would you be, which might not suit you at all. It would be all over the newspapers! Just think of the spread in the *Shipfield Courier*!'

He felt suddenly sick to the stomach. She was right. How had he been stupid enough to get himself into this situation? He'd been teaching for years now, he knew all the rules, all the pitfalls, and if he hadn't the powers-that-be were constantly issuing warnings. How could he have been such a fool? He had let a moment's irritation get the better of him.

The fact that he was innocent wouldn't stop enquiries being made, and he would bear the brunt of them. It wouldn't matter to Melanie, she might well enjoy it. The notoriety would give her a status, it would add to her sex appeal for some, but what would it do for him? And what about Laura and his family? Of course they'd believe him, but why should they have to go through it all because of his crass stupidity? All this went through his head with the speed of light while Melanie watched him from the other side of the desk and he tried to think of his next move.

In the end, after a pause, he decided what to do. Please God it would work, though it might as easily not.

'I don't like threats, Melanie,' he said. Though his insides were churning he kept his voice as calm and reasonable as he could. 'And you don't know me very well or you'd know that I would never give in to them, but what you haven't done is listen to what I actually said to you.'

She looked at him suspiciously.

'What do you mean?' she asked.

'I said, didn't I, that the proper punishment for your behaviour was detention. That was true and remains true. You behaved badly. What I did not say was that I would actually give you detention, and I had no intention of doing so. I don't like it. I don't like taking away anyone's freedom. You might have noticed that it's a line I seldom follow and I don't propose to do so now.'

Was it his imagination that she looked relieved? Had she, in the heat of the moment, been ready to set in motion something which she realized she couldn't cope with? How could he know?

'All the same,' Dermot said, 'it's not behaviour I'll tolerate. If it happens again I'll take action which might be far worse than detention.'

'Oh!' Melanie said, her boldness returning. 'Do you mean I might get expelled? Well, I wouldn't mind that in the least. I've had enough of this place, thank you.'

'You'd better go back to your class,' he said. 'We'll both make a fresh start in the morning.'

He watched her go, swinging her hips as she moved. There was one thing he knew he had to do before the end of the school day and that was to report this to the headmaster. It was the rule anyway, but even if it weren't he would still do it. He didn't totally trust Melanie. She was too volatile.

When his last class was over he went along to Jean Naughton's office. Jean was the headmaster's secretary.

'Could I have a word with him?' he asked.

'Sorry, too late!' Jean said. 'He left half an hour ago. Something special on this evening. Can I help?'

'Not really,' Dermot said. 'Can I make an appointment for first thing in the morning?'

She consulted the diary.

'Nine o'clock suit you?'

'Fine!' Dermot said. 'It won't take long.'

'I hope not,' Jean said. 'He has another appointment at nine thirty and he likes a break between.'

'Ten minutes at most,' Dermot promised. It would be five minutes if he had his way but Spencer could be long-winded.

'Reason?' Jean asked, her hand hovering over the diary. 'You know he always asks that. It's not that I want to know.'

All the same, she wondered. Dermot O'Brien didn't spend much of his school life asking to see the headmaster. She would have hazarded a guess that they didn't like each other.

'Personal,' Dermot said. 'Not important, but personal.'

5

Dermot turned his key in the lock and let himself in. He dumped his bag on the chair and went through to the kitchen – he could hear the radio. Laura was standing at the sink peeling potatoes.

'Hi!' she said. 'You're early. What sort of a day did you have?'

'OK in parts, not so good in others,' Dermot admitted.

'Oh really? Well, since you're here we can eat early,' Laura said. 'I thought we might open a bottle of wine. What do you think? You can open it while I finish the potatoes.'

'OK,' Dermot said. 'What are we eating?'

'Lamb chops with rosemary. So a red, don't you think?'

'Is there some celebration I don't know about?' Dermot asked. They didn't often have wine on a Monday. 'Oh God! It's not our anniversary or something, is it?'

'Nothing at all,' Laura assured him. 'I'll drop hints when that's coming up. I just felt like it, that's all.'

Dermot examined the contents of the wine rack.

'There's a Rioja or a Bergerac,' he said. 'Which do you fancy?'

'Let's have the Bergerac,' Laura said.

They had once spent a holiday in the south of the Dordogne with Bergerac as their centre. It was good to be reminded of happy times. Dermot took two glasses from the cupboard and poured the wine.

'Lovely!' Laura said, taking a sip. 'Bergerac always tastes so earthy, which seems a strange way to praise a wine, but it's true, at any rate for me. So which bits of the day weren't as good as the rest?'

Dermot hesitated.

'Oh, I daresay it's something and nothing,' he said. 'I'm not sure it's worth talking about. I daresay I'm making too much of it.'

There was something about the way he said that. He wasn't usually averse to talking about his job any more than she was. There was something not quite right, she could hear it in his voice.

'What does that mean?' she asked. 'If you don't want to talk about it, that's OK. If you do, I'm listening.'

He told her – everything from beginning to end. It was a relief to do so. Thank goodness they could always talk to each other. Dermot watched her face as he spoke. She looked amused when he told her about the poem, irritated when he went on to Melanie's behaviour in class, dismayed and finally angry as he described the scene in the interview room. When he came to the end there was a short silence which Laura was the first to break.

'The bitch! The little bitch! If she were my daughter—'

'If she were your daughter,' Dermot broke in,

'and she came to you and told you the English teacher had made a pass at her, wouldn't you believe her? If it was Therese or Frances you wouldn't think twice about believing them, would you? You'd believe their story before anyone else's.'

'It doesn't arise,' Laura said impatiently. 'Our daughters wouldn't do anything like that.'

'I suppose that's what most parents like to believe,' Dermot said. 'But whatever they came home and told you, wouldn't you believe them, your own daughters, before some teacher you didn't even know?'

'Is that what's worrying you?' Laura asked. 'That she'll tell her parents?'

'She doesn't have a father,' Dermot said. 'Or at least she does but he's not around. I don't think she has an easy time at home.'

'Look here, let's not start feeling sorry for Melanie. Let's not be making excuses for her.' There was a sharp edge to Laura's voice. 'She's a little bitch and possibly a dangerous little bitch.'

'One of the things which actually bothers me,' Dermot said, 'is did I let her get away with it? Should I have called her bluff and given her detention? She definitely deserved it.'

'I think she did get away with it,' Laura said. 'She won that round, but possibly you were right to let her do so. It's not a situation I'd find myself in, so I don't know. It's a risk an attractive man runs when he's in daily contact with an amorous teenager who's heady with her own power. But tell me, as a matter of interest, *do* you find her attractive?'

'What red-blooded man wouldn't?' Dermot said. 'But not seriously. I'm old enough to be her father, and then some.'

Laura shrugged. 'That could be part of the attraction. Boys of her own age wouldn't fill the bill. She's looking for something more exciting, more dangerous. And if she misses her own father . . .'

'But did I let her get away with it to save my own skin?' Dermot persisted.

'In the end does it matter if you did?' Laura asked. 'You saved a lot of people a lot of anguish – me included. Anyway you did the right thing in going to Mr Spencer. It's a pity you can't see him until the morning. You'd have felt better to get it off your chest.'

'I still wonder if I should just have let it go,' Dermot said unhappily.

'You couldn't possibly have done that,' Laura protested. 'You'd be wide open to another attempt. And if not you then someone else – some other unsuspecting teacher, or a priest or doctor – any male who might have a perfectly good reason for seeing her alone. She has to be stopped.'

'You make her sound dreadful,' Dermot said.

'She is, at least right now she is,' Laura said. 'She might not always be, almost certainly she won't, but for now she is a sex-mad and, according to you, extremely attractive teenager and therefore dangerous to anyone who's vulnerable.'

'So you don't think I'm making too much of it?' Dermot asked.

'I do not!' Laura said decisively. 'You must guard your back. She might well tell her mother. Or just supposing out of peevishness or spite she were to spread her version around the school?'

'She wouldn't do that . . .' Dermot began.

'Oh Dermot, grow up!' Laura said. 'Of course she might! You turned her down, didn't you? You didn't fall for her charm. She won't like that one little bit. It's more than likely she'll want to get her own back. She'll tell whatever story she likes to make up, but since you'll have reported it to the head first, without being required to do so, you'll be in the clear. Don't worry!' She reached for his hand and covered it with hers.

'Thanks, love,' Dermot said.

Laura leaned across the table and planted a quick kiss on Dermot's cheek, then went to put the chops under the grill.

Dermot sighed deeply. 'I don't look forward to tomorrow morning,' he said.

'You'll be all right,' Laura assured him.

'If you say so.' He wasn't convinced. Nor were Laura's thoughts as cheerful as her words.

'Good!' Laura said. 'So shall we stop thinking about it while we eat? Will you lay the table while I see to the rest? The chops won't take long. And you can pour me another glass of wine.'

They ate in near silence for a while, both occupied with their own thoughts, then Laura said, 'I saw Jennifer earlier.'

Damn Jennifer! Dermot managed not to say it out loud, but did the students have to come into everything? And then on second thoughts he was glad; he'd had enough talk about school, he'd like to forget it.

'How come?' he asked.

'I was walking along the road, coming home from work. She caught up with me,' Laura said. 'I offered to lend them a video. *Pretty Woman*. Some of them saw it ages ago but some of them haven't. She thought they'd all like it so I took it round.'

That didn't surprise Dermot in the least.

'None of the others was at home. She said the new people were quite nice – except Stuart. They don't seem to like him much.'

'Right,' Dermot said. He was only half listening, it didn't require more, but he didn't mind it when she prattled on. Right now it was soothing, like the sound of a running stream.

'But fortunately, Jennifer says, he's out a lot. They reckon he might be researching for his novel.'

'What novel?' Dermot enquired. Had he missed something on the way?

'It seems he's got his career all mapped out. He's going to write a string of bestselling novels. We shall all be seeing his name in the charts – once he's decided what his name's to be!'

'I shall watch out for it,' Dermot promised.

'Jennifer was telling me about her holiday in France. She misses Liam dreadfully, especially in bed.'

'The things you girls talk about!' Dermot said.

'It's not we girls,' Laura informed him. 'They see me as a middle-aged woman, all passion spent.'

'You get so involved with them,' Dermot said.

As you do with school, Laura thought, but school was not something she intended to talk about. She put the fruit bowl on the table and took a banana. Dermot chose an orange.

'I have about an hour's work to do,' he said.

'Then when I've stacked the dishwasher you wouldn't mind if I nipped across to see Esther, would you?'

'I don't mind,' Dermot said, 'though I sometimes wish you'd allow yourself just to sit and read a book. Why do you want to see Esther? You saw her twice yesterday.'

'I'm not sure,' Laura confessed. 'There was just something about her yesterday. She seemed to be not quite herself.'

'She's never quite herself! Who knows with Esther what herself is?' Dermot said. 'She seemed all right to me.'

'I could be wrong,' Laura admitted. 'Anyway, since you're going to be busy I'll go across.'

The fact was, there had been a woman waiting in reception today who had somehow reminded her of Esther. She'd been about the same age and there'd been a look in her eyes, a mild confusion, a slight fear, but more than anything a lack of confidence in what was happening. It had made Laura wonder what it felt like to be really old. Was it an altogether different country of which one had no notion until one came to inhabit it?

'I won't be long with Esther,' she said to Dermot. 'Oh, and by the way, I promised to nip along to Karen some time this evening.'

'Karen? What for?'

Laura gave a shrug of her shoulders, a vague shake of her head.

'Not sure, actually. Something to do with the children, I think. She wanted it to be after they'd gone to bed.' She didn't feel it was quite right at the moment to discuss Karen's possible pregnancy with Dermot. Well, not so much possible as certain, according to Karen. There were too many questions attached to it, and who knew what Karen's story was, and how much of it she wanted told, even to Dermot, discreet though he was.

'I suppose you'll be back in time to sleep in your own home?' Dermot asked.

'Oh, don't be put out, darling!' Laura pleaded. 'I

94

really couldn't refuse. I honestly won't be long.'

Considering the kind of day he had had, Dermot thought, it might have been quite nice to have his wife's company for the whole evening.

There was no light showing from Esther's sitting room, which was disturbing, though perhaps she had simply fallen asleep. The radio was on at full volume – Classic FM, to which Esther listened much of the day. Laura crept in as quietly as possible so as not to startle her. The light was out but there was a glow coming from the gas fire and in that glow Esther sat in her chair conducting Beethoven's Emperor Concerto, with all the flourishes of the late Sir Malcolm Sargent, of whom she had been a great admirer. Her arms waved, her head moved from side to side, and so quiet had been Laura's entry that for several moments Esther did not see her. Laura waited in the shadow until the movement had ended and Esther laid down her baton.

'That was lovely!' Laura said, switching on the light. 'You seemed to be enjoying it. What sort of a day have you had?'

Esther was pleased to see her – not that she admitted it, but there was a gleam in her eyes which said as much.

'A bit boring,' Esther replied. 'No-one came – not even the electric man to read the meter. Television was full of stupid quiz shows – they're all stupid except *Countdown*. I reckon I could have been on that if I'd been younger. I can do the numbers, you know!'

'Which is more than I can,' Laura said.

'Oh, and that estate agent woman brought someone to look at the house. Rather nice-looking, he was, and on the right side of forty. You'd have thought he'd have had a wife with him but he didn't. What have you been doing?'

'The usual,' Laura said. 'I saw Karen on the way to work. You remember Karen?'

'Of course I do,' Esther snapped. 'I haven't entirely lost my memory!'

'And I popped in to Number Twelve,' Laura added. 'Took them a video. Have you ever thought of having a video recorder? You could see lots of films.'

She doubted that Esther was short of money, though she didn't throw it around much. Everything in her house was of good quality and she treated herself to single malt whisky and decent wines.

'I'm not sure I'd like today's films,' Esther said.

'Did you go to the cinema a lot when you were younger?' Laura asked.

'Oh yes,' Esther said. 'I've seen hundreds of films. They used to change the programme every Monday and Thursday at the Regent. I often went twice a week.'

'And who were your favourite film stars?'

'Difficult to say,' Esther replied. 'I doted on James Mason but I think it was his voice more than anything else. I always fell for a man who could speak beautifully or who could play the piano, and if he could do both those things then he could have anything he wanted!'

'And was there anyone who could?' Laura asked.

'Two or three,' Esther said vaguely. 'Let me see . . . there was Ronald . . . I think it was Ronald. Yes, definitely! Ronald Unsworth. He had a voice as near to James Mason's as dammit is to swearing, and he played the piano beautifully.' Many were the times, she now remembered, he had played just for her.

'He played a lot of Chopin,' she told Laura. 'And Scriabin. Of course he couldn't have risen to the Emperor. Or Rachmaninov. Rachmaninov's Third is the real test.'

'I suppose so,' Laura said.

'He was consumptive, you know,' Esther said.

'Ronald was consumptive? But how terrible!' Perhaps this was why Esther had never married? Young lovers, united by music, separated by Ronald's early death.

'Chopin, not Ronald,' Esther said tersely. 'He went to Majorca.'

'And you went with him? You never told me you'd been to Majorca!'

Esther clicked her teeth.

'I'm talking about Chopin! He went with that writer woman, Georges Sand. It wasn't a good place for him.'

'Really?' Laura said. 'I would have thought the climate in Majorca would have been good for a consumptive.'

Esther sighed deeply. Why couldn't she make herself understood – or was it Laura who was dense?

'Not the climate,' she said. 'It was no good for his music – at least that's my opinion. It was a backwater. And then that woman taking his attention.'

'I see,' Laura said.

But now Esther, suddenly exhausted, had stopped talking and was deep in her own thoughts. She enjoyed thinking about the past. It was less lonely than the present, filled as it was by so many people who were still real to her. Friends, a few enemies, lovers, parents. Her father had fought on the Somme, been wounded in the leg and gassed twice. Every winter his wound flared up and his chest troubled him, which was perhaps why he died young, in his forties. Her mother seemed not to have the energy to live long after that. Esther had never been as close to her mother as she had been to her father.

Yes, she enjoyed her journeys into the past and Laura was good at prompting her memory. The trouble was, Esther thought, she doesn't always know when to stop and leave me to it.

'What did you work at?' Laura asked, proving the point.

'I was a barmaid,' Esther said.

'A barmaid? In Shipfield?'

'Oh no!' Esther said. 'That would never have done! I worked in a public house near the Bristol docks. I didn't ever tell my parents what my job was. They thought I worked in a shipping office. I lodged in Bristol and came home on a Sunday, my day off. They were strictly teetotal, you see. It was always a bone of contention that I wouldn't join the Band of Hope.'

'Band of Hope?'

'It was connected with the chapel. You had to promise you'd never take alcohol, not even sherry in a trifle. "The lips that touch liquor shall never touch mine." That was the song. I couldn't possibly promise that.'

'Well, Esther, that *is* interesting,' Laura said brightly.

'Yes,' Esther agreed. 'And now I'm quite tired so I think you'd better go.'

'Would you like me to make you a hot drink?' Laura offered.

'Thank you, no,' Esther said firmly. 'A hot drink at this time means I'm up and down to the lavatory all night.'

But a tot of whisky, she thought, will make me sleep.

Karen opened the door almost immediately on Laura's ring, as if she had been waiting for it. Finger to her lips, she led Laura into the living room.

'They've just gone off!' she said. 'I don't expect they'll waken now, but I wouldn't want them to. Would you like some coffee?'

'No thank you,' Laura said. 'I'm sorry I'm a bit late. I nipped across to see Esther. I was a bit worried about her.'

'Oh, is there something wrong?' Karen motioned Laura to an armchair and took a low stool facing her. Like a penitent, Laura thought.

'Not really,' Laura said. 'It was just a feeling I had. She talked a lot about the past. In the end I think she was glad for me to leave. I think she wanted to stay with the past.'

'Poor old thing!' Karen said.

'And what about you?' Laura asked.

'Poor old me!' Karen said.

'Do you want to tell me about it? Don't if you'd rather not.'

'Oh, but I do!' Karen said. 'If only to put you right. In any case, there'll be no disguising it in the end, will there? I was a fool, I know, but I wasn't quite as bad as you might think.'

'I haven't thought anything,' Laura said. It wasn't

quite true, how could it be? The truth was, she somehow couldn't think it of Karen.

'You see, I had this invitation to a party. From one of the parents at school. I was so tempted – I haven't been anywhere for ages – and she knew where I could get a babysitter – so . . . !'

'You accepted.'

'Yes. I had my hair done, dressed up and went. There was a lot of drink around. I had one vodka too many, I suppose. They kept coming, and I drank them. I don't usually drink much, truthfully I don't! I couldn't stay late because of the baby-sitter, and this man said he'd run me home, which he did. He insisted on seeing me into the house, which seemed OK at the time. I thought he was all right. The babysitter was all ready for off, and she went. She could hardly have been farther than the gate when—' She stopped; bit her lip as though she couldn't get the words out.

'And?' Laura prompted.

'That was when he pushed me onto the sofa. I suppose I shouted, but he put his hand over my mouth. He was like a savage. I tried to fight him off. I won't tell you the things he said, the names he called me while he was doing it. I can't . . .' She buried her face in her hands. Laura went down on her knees and took Karen in her arms, stroking her hair as the sobs now tore at her body.

'He raped you?' she said softly.

Karen nodded. 'He said . . .' She struggled to get the words out. 'He said . . . I was asking for it. I wasn't, Laura! Truly I wasn't! I'm not like that!'

'Of course you're not, darling,' Laura said. She felt tight with anger, but anger was no good to

Karen now. Her need was for comfort, compassion, love.

With a visible effort, Karen pulled herself together again and continued.

'Then Neil cried, quite loudly. "You'll have to let me go to him," I said. "You'll have to! If I don't, he'll come downstairs! He always does." I couldn't bear the thought of that. Not Neil! He rolled off me. I jumped to my feet and hurried upstairs.'

She stopped. Laura gave her a minute, then prompted her gently. 'And?'

'I pacified Neil and he went off to sleep. I had to go downstairs again, for fear he'd come up. I was afraid, but I had to. So I did.' There was a long pause. Finally she said, 'He'd gone. I hadn't heard the car start, so I thought he might come back, but I looked through a crack in the curtains and it wasn't there.

'I didn't tell anyone. Who would I tell? A while after I asked the woman who'd given the party who he was, but not as if it mattered. She didn't know. He'd come with a friend of a friend. She thought he probably lived in London. I couldn't ask any more. I never wanted to see him again. I can't help it if he's got away scot free. But oh, Laura, I don't want this baby! I don't want this poor little baby.'

She broke down in tears; tears of relief that she'd told someone, tears of despair that nothing was solved, tears of downright fatigue as if the burden of it all was a physical weight on her shoulders. Laura held her, let her cry, at the same time searching for what she should say. She felt her own burden now, a lifetime of belief that abortion was a sin, a sin akin to murder. How was she fitted to advise Karen? But on the other hand, she told herself, I must not expect Karen to suffer for *my* beliefs. She's her own person. She has her rights.

'Oh, Laura, what am I going to do?' Karen cried.

'Take one step at a time,' Laura said. 'You've done enough for this evening, but make up your mind to see Dr Craven as soon as you can. Make totally certain you are pregnant before you face the next step.'

Karen took Laura's proffered tissue and dried her eyes.

'All right,' she agreed. 'I'll do that. He won't be pleased. He told me I shouldn't have any more babies after Neil. And I'll have to tell him the circumstances, won't I?'

'It would be best. He'd be the one to advise you.' It would buy time, Laura thought, time in which to think straight.

Which was much the same as Karen's own thoughts at this moment. 'All the same,' she said, 'I'm sure I *am* pregnant.'

'How was Esther?' Dermot asked.

'Fine. Would you ever think she'd been a barmaid?'

'Oh I would,' Dermot said. 'I always reckon there's more to Esther than meets the eye.'

'She said someone had been to look at Number Fifteen. A man. Forty-ish.'

'Really? Actually I'm whacked,' Dermot said. 'Shall we go to bed?'

He didn't even bother to ask after Karen, for which Laura was grateful.

Surprisingly, he fell asleep quickly, but when he awoke at four o'clock in the morning thoughts of the coming day rushed into his mind. After that he didn't sleep at all.

Brian knew almost as soon as he stepped into Number Fifteen that it was the kind of place he was looking for, though there was no way he would tell that to Mrs Masefield who stood beside him in the hallway. He looked with distaste at the dingy wallpaper, the peeling paint of the skirting board.

'Yes,' he said. 'I see what you mean. It has been neglected, hasn't it?'

'As I told you,' Rita said, 'it belonged to an old lady. I think in her last few years here she wasn't able to do much to it.' She knew almost nothing about the previous owner but it seemed a reasonable supposition and one which might just move this man to make allowances.

'More than a few years, I would think,' Brian said.

'Shall we take a look at the rest of the house? Shall we start at the top?' Rita suggested.

He followed her up the stairs and in and out of the bedrooms. There were three double rooms, all with fireplaces, and a fourth which, though supposedly a single, was no more than a box-room. The bedrooms were well proportioned and basically sound, he thought, casting an expert eye, aside from the window sills, some of which would need to be repaired or renewed. He could see little else which a thoroughly good clean, several gallons of paint, new floor covering and curtains wouldn't take care of. The larger of the bedrooms at the front would be his, and the single room might be his office-cum-study unless he decided to put in another bathroom, which might be more sensible with four or five of them in the house.

'And I take it there's only the one bathroom?' he said.

'That's right,' Rita agreed, 'though there is a separate lavatory on this floor and another one leading off the back porch.'

'Right,' Brian said. 'Shall we take a look downstairs?'

He followed her down and looked at the rest of the house: sitting room, dining room, kitchen. The last of these, he decided with a single glance, would need totally gutting and refitting – not that that couldn't be done. From the small scullery, with an ancient, once-white sink, a door led down stone steps to a sizeable cellar with a window so grimy that it let little light in. A mouse scuttled across the floor as they entered. All the same, it could be a useful room once it had been cleared of the cartload of rubbish on the shelves and the floor.

Rita shuddered. She hated mice, though she wasn't going to show it.

'Shall we take a look at the garden?' Rita said. 'Of course that *is* neglected, and a garden soon shows, doesn't it?'

The garden was quite good, Brian thought. It was about a hundred feet long by thirty feet wide and surrounded by trees. Something could be made of the garden and it would provide work to be done, should that become necessary. They might even grow food, he thought; vegetables, salads.

'Right,' he said. 'Thank you very much.'

'Is there anything you'd like to take a second look at?' Rita asked.

'I don't think so,' Brian said.

He didn't need to spend a lot of time, he could tell most things at a glance. It wasn't the first time he had done this. In any case, there would have to be a surveyor's report.

'So what do you think?' Rita asked. 'Is this the kind of thing you're looking for?'

'I suppose it could be,' he said doubtfully. 'Would there be any restrictions on what could be done with it?'

'I don't know of any,' Rita said. 'It depends what you mean. I wouldn't imagine there'd be any at the back if you wanted to build on there, though I doubt you could do so at the front. Perhaps you'd like to bring your wife to see it?'

'I don't have a wife,' Brian said, smiling. 'But if I decided to go any further I'd want to bring a friend to look at it.'

'Of course,' Rita said. She wished she had the slightest idea what he was up to. He gave her the impression of a man with a purpose and she couldn't think what that purpose might be.

'There is one thing I know,' she said. 'You couldn't start a business here. It's strictly residential. Well, I suppose you could if you were a doctor or a solicitor. Something like that.'

'I'm not either of those,' Brian said. 'Nor do I want to set up a business.' He could tell she was dying to know what the score was and, as a matter of fact, it might not be a bad idea to tell her, get her reaction.

'What I want premises for,' he said, 'is to house three or four young men who have just come out of prison.'

She looked decidedly taken aback, eyes widened, eyebrows raised.

'You mean *ex-convicts*?' Rita said.

'Strictly speaking, yes,' Brian agreed. 'But don't get me wrong, we're not talking here about hardened criminals, thugs and murderers. Nothing like that. No-one dangerous. We're talking about young men who've probably just served their first sentence and have nowhere to go when they come out of prison. We're offering them a few months' rehabilitation.'

'Why?' she asked. 'Why are you doing this?'

'Because they need it,' Brian said. 'And it's not me doing it, or not me financing it I should say. I'm employed by a man who has a lot of money, no dependants, a large heart and a social conscience.'

'He must have all of those!' Rita said.

'It wouldn't be the first time,' Brian said. 'He's done it once before.'

'And who is this gentleman?' Rita asked.

'That doesn't matter,' Brian said. 'Publicity is the last thing he'd want. The point is, he has the money and this is what he wants to do with it.'

'And did it work?' Rita asked. 'I mean the first time?'

It was obvious to Brian that she could hardly believe it but in that she was no different from most people. Once a convict, always a convict!

'Yes it did!' he said. 'That house now has its second intake and the man supervising it was himself once an ex-prisoner there.'

'And who would supervise this one?'

'I would,' Brian said, 'as it's a new place and I have the experience. I supervised the first one.'

'And you don't mind? You don't mind living with these men?'

'I like it,' Brian said. 'And I'm quite safe. They're

not going to gang up on me, I'm not going to be murdered in my bed.'

'And don't other people object – I mean neighbours?' Rita asked.

'That's the problem,' Brian admitted. 'Some do. Oh, they think it's a splendid thing to do, rather noble, as long as it doesn't happen too close to them. So what do you think the reaction would be in Mulberry Lane?'

'Me? I haven't the faintest idea!' Rita said. 'I don't know anyone in Mulberry Lane.' All the same, she thought, I wouldn't like it next door to me. And who was to say there'd be no danger?

'Unfortunately,' Brian said, 'you can't test the water. You have to make up your mind and jump in. In the end it'll be up to my boss and me.'

Suddenly, Rita felt she was on the edge of a sale. Her mind switched round to the job in hand. And what had it to do with her who lived there? Nothing at all as long as they could arrange the mortgage, or in this case, she reminded herself, produce the cash.

'Well, all that's your affair, isn't it?' she said affably. 'Do you like the house?'

'I suppose it would do,' Brian admitted, 'but of course the price is ridiculous! I certainly wouldn't advise my boss to pay ninety thousand pounds for it. I can't imagine anyone would.'

'Unfortunately,' Rita said, 'that's what the owner is asking.'

'Then she's in for a disappointment, not to mention a long wait,' Brian said.

'Nor does she want a long wait,' Rita said. 'She needs the money. Would you like to make an offer?'

'I'd want my boss to take a look at it first,' Brian

said. 'In the meantime you can suggest seventy thousand.'

Rita shook her head. 'I doubt she'll take that.'

'Cash. On the nail. No waiting. I could get my boss to come tomorrow.'

'OK,' Rita said. 'I'll see what I can do.'

6

It was with a slight misgiving that Dermot, when he came to register his tutor group on Tuesday morning, realized that Melanie Clarke was not present. It was not unusual for Melanie to be late, or even not to turn up at all. She had a record of short absences from school for minor ailments, and it was not unknown for her to truant. All the same, this morning he would have been pleased to see her in her usual place.

'Does anyone know why Melanie Clarke isn't here?' he enquired nonchalantly.

No-one did, though there was a small frisson of excitement as they heard the question. Leaving school yesterday, Melanie had given her own, rather guarded version of what had taken place in the interview room. No exciting details, but a hint of a promise that there might be more to follow. 'Just you wait and see!' had been the tone of it.

As it happened, Year Eleven was Dermot's first class of the day. Knowing he would have to leave them he set them some reading from *Great Expectations*.

'Make sure you do it,' he said. 'I'll question you on it when I get back, and that's a promise!'

Two minutes later he knocked on the headmaster's door.

'Come!' Mr Spencer called.

The headmaster was seated behind his extremely tidy desk, the only items on it a report which he was studying and a black ballpoint pen. He continued to read when Dermot entered, not looking up until he had reached the bottom of the page.

'You wanted to see me, O'Brien?' he said. 'Is it important? I'm rather busy.'

For one brief moment Dermot wanted to say, 'Not really. It can wait,' and make his escape. Was it, in fact, all that important? But Laura had thought it was, and the knowledge that Melanie had not shown up niggled at him.

'Perhaps not madly important,' he said. 'Something I just thought I'd let you know.'

'You'd better sit down,' the headmaster said. 'Keep it as short as you can, will you?' He leaned back in his chair, pressed his hands together as if in prayer, and waited.

Dermot told his story as briefly as possible, showing no emotion whatever, as if it was all too trivial to mention but he was simply doing his duty. The headmaster's only reaction was a very slow nod of the head on one or two occasions and a widening of his eyes as the story progressed.

'And that's about it,' Dermot said in the end.

There was a pause. The headmaster sat up straight, unclasped his hands and placed them palms down on the edge of his desk.

'And you thought this was not important?' he said in a smooth voice.

'That's right,' Dermot said. 'But of course best to let you know.'

'Then you are a *fool*, O'Brien!' the headmaster said with a complete change of tone. 'You have broken every single rule in the book and, I don't doubt, a few which aren't laid down in the book but which one ounce of common sense would have made plain to you!'

'But, sir—' Dermot began.

'Listen to me and don't interrupt!' the head bellowed. 'You might learn something, though God knows a man of your experience should know it all! I'm going to take you through every single bit of the staff rule book. Do you never read it, O'Brien? What do you think it's there for?'

It was a fact, Dermot thought, that though he had skimmed through it once, a long time ago, he'd never felt the need to do so again, and when updates or additions came he gave them a cursory glance and pushed them away. There were better things to do; marking papers, planning lessons. He opened his mouth to say something but the headmaster silenced him with a wave of his hand.

'In the first place,' he said, 'and this is common sense, it doesn't require written rules – this Melanie Clarke – oh, I know Melanie Clarke when I see her! You might not believe it but I know most of the pupils in my school. I make it my business to do so, especially the ones who might one day cause trouble. This Melanie Clarke – did you never see the possibility of some difficulty arising with her?'

'Not really,' Dermot admitted – then immediately knew he had given the wrong answer.

'Then you must be blind!' the headmaster said. 'It's obvious. For a start, the way she dresses . . .'

'She always wears school uniform,' Dermot put in.

'It's the *way* she wears it,' the head said testily. He did not like being interrupted.

It was true, Dermot thought. No-one could make school uniform look as sexy as Melanie could.

'So am I to take it that until yesterday you never had the slightest trouble with her? She was a model pupil, was she?'

'I wouldn't say that,' Dermot admitted. 'But there was nothing I couldn't handle. Her problem is, she likes to be noticed.'

'Quite!' the headmaster said. 'Quite. And how did you deal with that?'

'I didn't give in to it,' Dermot replied.

The headmaster thumped his desk with such force that his ballpoint skittered across the polished surface and dropped to the floor.

'Wrong, wrong! You handled this abysmally! The last thing you should do with a child who craves attention is refuse to deal with it. It leads to even more demands. For heaven's sake, O'Brien, didn't you learn any child psychology?'

Did I? Dermot thought. All that time ago? If he had then it had not been the same as Spencer's. And he had helped to bring up two children, which was more than Spencer had done. The Spencers were childless.

'According to your own story,' the headmaster persisted, 'when she complained you didn't stop to listen, you didn't attempt to sort it out, you invited Chris Benton to read. Am I right?'

'Yes,' Dermot agreed. 'Except that I did ask her to sit down and be quiet.' It was plain that Spencer was going to give his own interpretation of the facts, he would lend no weight to the circumstances let alone to the sheer bloody awkwardness at which Melanie excelled.

'And when she complained, when she was disruptive because she felt – rightly or wrongly – she'd been unfairly treated, your reply was to send her out of the room?'

'She wasn't unfairly treated,' Dermot protested. 'She was allowed to read her verse.'

'But not to discuss it?'

'I thought it wasn't suitable—'

'You didn't think, O'Brien! That's the trouble! If you'd given her just a few minutes more of your time . . . but most important of all you should *not* have sent her out of the classroom. A pupil nursing a grievance, when sent out of the classroom, can get up to anything. There was an instance in my last school where a child who was sent out alone and unsupervised set fire to the cloakroom. The fire brigade had to be called and a great deal of damage was done.'

Well, at least we were spared that, Dermot thought, but forbore to say so.

'All these things are in the book,' Spencer said. 'And while sending her out of the room on her own you told her to see you in the interview room at break?'

'It only wanted ten minutes to break,' Dermot said.

'A lot can happen in ten minutes,' the head said.

Like burning down the whole school, Dermot thought. Reducing it to a smouldering ruin.

'And then you proceeded to see this girl on her own. Did it not occur to you that you should have sought a third person to be present?'

'Not at the time,' Dermot confessed. 'But with

113

hindsight . . .' I was a fool, he thought. I really was a stupid fool!

'Hindsight will not do!' the headmaster barked. 'Did you close the door of the interview room?'

'Of course not,' Dermot assured him.

But had he? Did he go into the room first? Did Melanie follow him? Did she close the door? He simply couldn't remember.

'This is not the first sign of trouble from Melanie Clarke,' the headmaster said. 'As I daresay you know, it seemed there might have been a problem between her and Mr Foreman, but fortunately he managed to avoid that.'

You mean he handled it better than I did, Dermot translated.

'Well, all this is very disturbing,' the headmaster said. 'And the fact that Melanie hasn't turned up for school this morning does not augur well. It probably means she's told the whole story to her mother—'

'Her version of it,' Dermot interrupted.

'The version which her mother will believe.'

Dermot couldn't deny that. Wasn't it exactly what he'd said to Laura last night?

'And if she has, we will hear more. Let me spell out for you, O'Brien, what could happen if her mother lays a complaint. It could be very serious indeed, and not just for you but for the whole school. I value the reputation of this school.'

'And I value my reputation,' Dermot said.

'Naturally! And I wish you'd thought of that sooner. If the mother wishes to take the matter further – which she has every right to do – then you would most certainly be suspended, pending an enquiry. You would have to get in touch with your union, the school governors would be involved, the Department of Education, the Social Services – who will *always* take the part of the child. It could eventually go to court. Even if at the end of that you were judged not guilty you might well have to leave this school and I'm afraid you would find it almost impossible to get another job in the teaching profession. There will always be that element of doubt, which will be fed by publicity. We have no power to stop Mrs Clarke going to the press.'

Dermot felt sick. What an idiot he had been! What a naïve, stupid fool! Listening to Spencer, he realized that everything the headmaster was forecasting could come true. It was the kind of thing one read about in the tabloids, not what happened to oneself.

'Do *you* think I'm guilty?' he asked Spencer. 'I mean of whatever Melanie might accuse me of?'

'Good heavens, no!' the headmaster said. 'Such a thought never entered my head. If it had I wouldn't have had you in the school for a minute.'

'Thank you,' Dermot said. 'So possibly others would think the same way as you?'

The headmaster shook his head.

'I wouldn't count on that, O'Brien. Your word against hers! But in any case you'd still have to go through the hoop. No, you've been incredibly foolish and almost entirely lacking in common sense. And now we must await events – and hope there won't be any.' The tone of his voice said he had no hope of that. 'In the meantime you'd better get back to your class.'

Dermot did not go back at once to his class. He went to the staff cloakroom and doused his face liberally with cold water, as if he was trying to wake himself from a nightmare. He wanted to rush out to his car and drive home. He wanted to find Laura. But he couldn't go home, and if he could Laura wouldn't be there. He felt totally alone and – a feeling unfamiliar to him – afraid. And every single bit of it was his own fault. That was so clear to him now. Was he fit to be a teacher?

He wasn't sure how long he might have stood there if someone hadn't come in. Dermot left quickly. There was nothing else for it. He went back to his classroom.

Heads were raised as he entered. When he sat behind his desk he was aware that twenty-three pairs of eyes were focused on him. The air was thick with unanswered questions.

'Right,' he said briskly. '*Great Expectations*. Let's get on with it.'

He was fifteen minutes into the lesson when the classroom door opened and John Fenwick, who taught English lower down the school, entered.

'The head wants to see you.' He spoke quietly, but not so quietly that the pupils in the front desks didn't hear. 'Pronto! I'm to stay with your class in the meantime.' He looked enquiringly at Dermot, waiting for an explanation which Dermot did not give. He simply nodded and walked out without a word.

What now? The short walk to the headmaster's room seemed like a mile. What was happening? Was anything? Or had Spencer thought of something else with which to upbraid him? Passing through Jean Naughton's room he wanted to ask her what it was about but, head bent over the filing cabinet, she avoided his eye. He knocked and went in.

Seated in front of the headmaster's desk were Melanie Clarke and what was presumably her mother. Dermot felt rooted to the spot, as if his feet were weighted by lead, and his heart and his head were leaden too. In that second his whole future loomed blackly before him. And all because, he thought, bitterly angry with himself, he hadn't kept his cool when confronted by an awkward child.

'Mrs Clarke,' the headmaster said, 'let me introduce you to Mr O'Brien.'

Mrs Clarke acknowledged Dermot with a brief nod. Melanie gave him a look of deep dislike.

'Good morning,' Dermot said.

'Sit!' the headmaster commanded Dermot, who obeyed like a well-trained dog. In the short silence that followed he studied Mrs Clarke. It was clear from whom Melanie inherited her good looks, though she was in every way a bolder edition of her mother. Melanie's figure was fuller, her eyes darker; her mouth was pinker, wider, more sensuous. She could not but exude sex appeal, it shouted out loud, whereas her mother, though cast in the same physical mould, was in every way toned down so that she had an air of refinement totally lacking in her daughter.

How can I be noticing this, Dermot asked himself, when my mind is chock full of what's going to happen to me in the next few minutes?

'Mrs Clarke is here because she has received from Melanie a complaint about your treatment of her daughter yesterday.' The headmaster's voice was flat, monotonous, totally devoid of feeling. 'I have already heard what she has to say but now she wishes to speak for herself.'

Dermot did not look at the headmaster. His eyes

were fixed on Mrs Clarke. She was looking down at her hands which she was twisting in her lap, and then she looked up and her eyes met his and Dermot could tell she was summoning up her courage to speak, as indeed he was to listen to what she had to say. It seemed an age before she said anything, and then when she spoke the words rushed out of her.

'I'm very sorry, Mr O'Brien. I'm very sorry for what happened. In fact I'm ashamed. It's not the way Melanie's been brought up to behave, not at all, but she misses her dad. She's very fond of her dad and she's not found things easy since he went—'

'Please, Mrs Clarke . . .' Dermot interrupted – but she was not to be stopped.

'I do my best, but I won't have her talking back to her teacher and misbehaving in school. I've told her times without number she's got to work hard and pass her exams or how will she ever get a decent job? So she's here to apologize and I'm here to see she does.'

She gave her daughter a sharp prod between her shoulder blades which brought Melanie to her feet.

'Right!' Mrs Clarke said. 'You know what you have to say. Get on with it!'

Melanie, her gaze on the floor somewhere near Dermot's feet, muttered, 'I'm sorry.'

'Sorry, who?' her mother prompted.

'I'm sorry, Mr O'Brien.'

'Thank you, Melanie,' Dermot said. He could hardly believe that this was happening.

'I hope you'll put this behind you, Mr O'Brien,' Mrs Clarke said. 'I hope you'll not hold it against her. I assure you Melanie won't ever do such a thing again.'

'Then we'll consider the matter closed, shall we?' Dermot managed a smile. 'Thank you for coming, Mrs Clarke.' She would never know, this anxious-looking woman, how much he owed her.

'And I add my thanks,' the headmaster said. 'I wish all parents were as co-operative as you are, Mrs Clarke. And now I expect you want to get on. My secretary will see you out and Melanie can go back to her class. I'd like you to wait behind for a minute, Mr O'Brien.'

You bastard! Dermot thought furiously. You knew when you sent for me that everything was going to be all right, but you let me sweat it out. And now you're going to continue the lecture. But then it's the least I deserve, isn't it, he told himself.

'You got off lightly,' the headmaster said when Jean had led the Clarkes away. 'Far too lightly for someone who acted as foolishly as you did. A teacher of your long experience! I can hardly believe it. I suggest you think about the whole episode very, very carefully. I also suggest you take the rule book home, read it thoroughly and digest it.'

Dermot went out through Jean Naughton's office. Looking at him, she raised her eyebrows in a question.

'Pompous bugger!' Dermot said. But Spencer was right.

Lisa drove her Amazon Landcruiser through the entrance to the drive of Cornerways. The width between the gateposts was only just enough to allow her through but she was a skilful driver. She came to a stop at the front door, jumped down and went around to release Bruno who was locked into the back. The children liked to have Bruno in the car when they were taken to and collected from school and nursery and he was always ready for any little trip that came his way. His life was exceedingly comfortable, bordering on the luxurious, but it was a touch boring. Now he made an elegant exit from the vehicle then sauntered to the front door, where he sat on his haunches while waiting for Lisa to collect the shopping.

There wasn't much of it this morning: fresh bread, milk, organic salad things, a bunch of flowers, chicken nuggets for the children and two nice fillet steaks for her supper and Gary's. As she gathered things together she glanced across the road. A man and a woman were emerging from Number Fifteen. The woman she recognized as the estate agent, she had seen her before when she put up the board. The man, she guessed by the way he was peering intently at everything, must be a prospective purchaser. He looked all right, quite nice actually. Casually dressed, but a good haircut. She noticed such things. He was gazing up at the house, after which he turned his attention to the front garden and then looked across the street. He might have seen her watching him but he gave no sign. Looking to the right, she saw Esther at her window. Nosy cow, she thought. She misses nothing. It would not have occurred to Lisa that, given a few more years, she would have been almost on a par with Esther and both of them for the same reason. They had little else with which to occupy large parts of their days.

In Esther's case not much was done in the house,

not only because she was old but because all forms of domesticity bored her. Fortunately she was not the least bit fazed by what was left undone. Layers of dust passed unnoticed, except that when she was in a light-hearted mood she would write 'Dust me!' with her finger on surfaces. In Lisa's case she was not over-occupied because she had Mrs Litton who came every morning except Saturdays and Sundays and saw to the dust, as well as to the washing, ironing, vacuuming, emptying the dishwasher, making the beds and the rest.

But, Lisa reminded herself as she unlocked the front door and was preceded into the house by Bruno, she wouldn't have Mrs Litton for long because the lady had given in her notice and a fortnight from now she would be living closer to her daughter in Reading. Nor was there, so far, anyone else to replace her. Gary was not the sort of man who would lift a finger in the house. He had made that plain from the beginning. His job was to earn the money, and at that he couldn't be faulted. He worked long hours, which was what left Lisa a lot of time to herself.

Who would have thought, she mused, filling Bruno's water bowl before putting the shopping away, that she, who had been born and brought up in a small council house in Leeds, where her parents still lived, would be living in a house like this, furnished with the best that money could buy – and Gary had let her choose everything – the children in private education, her Landcruiser out there on the drive? At the time she'd left Leeds you could have bought a flat, or even a small house, for the money Gary had paid for that vehicle, let alone that he had also bought a BMW coupé for his own use, which occasionally she was allowed to drive.

It wasn't that she thought any the less of Leeds. She had been happy there and from time to time she took the children to visit her parents, but her life had changed so much since the day she had met Gary there at a trade fair. He had not been in the computer world then. He had been a salesman for a company which supplied the essential ingredients – oils, fragrances, chemicals, powders and pastes – to the pharmaceutical companies represented at the fair. They would be used in deodorants, make-up, nail varnishes, shampoos – anything and everything to make the body look beautiful and smell nice. She had been one of the models hired by the pharmaceutical companies, chosen not only for their beautiful faces but because every company was vying with the others to have the most glamorous girls. They were there to show what their company's products could achieve. No-one was tactless enough to say that these girls were near perfect before anything at all was done to them.

Gary had singled her out from the beginning – later he'd said he'd fallen in love with her at first sight – and before the trade fair was over he had made love to her in his hotel room. That was when Nathan had been conceived. He had told her while they were in Leeds that he planned to get out of what he had been doing up to now and go into computer software. He had observed what was needed in the many firms he visited and he was sure he could design the software for it. It was a cert, it was a money spinner.

Having had some money left to him by his parents he was determined to set up on his own.

His outfit would be small to begin with, he'd told Lisa, but it would grow. No doubt about that! He was ambitious, hard-working and sure of his skill; in fact he had bags of confidence. And so far it had all been a wonderful success. It had brought them to where they were now, and who knew where it would take them in the future?

But at least, Lisa sometimes thought, I didn't marry him for his money. She had taken the gamble with him. And for his part he had not hesitated to marry her as soon as he learned she was pregnant. She still loved him, as she knew he did her.

Her head filled with thoughts of the past, she turned around from the fridge where she had deposited the steaks and the salad things, and immediately tripped over Bruno who was sprawled out on the floor.

'Bruno!' she shouted. 'For heaven's sake go into your bed!'

He heaved himself to his feet and, tail between his legs and a hurt expression on his face, he slunk away.

She loved him dearly, she really did, but he was so big. She would really have preferred a small dog, a poodle, or a Yorkie like the one down the road, or a Bichon like Frizzie in Upper Mulberry; a dog which could sit on her lap and be cuddled. It was Gary who had wanted a big dog, the bigger the better, which was strange really because Gary wasn't a big man physically. Putting on weight, but not big. When Bruno stood on his hind legs with his front paws on Gary's shoulders the two of them were eyeball to eyeball. Still, Bruno *was* a nice dog, and so good with the children. Gary said he would be a deterrent to burglars, and of course when they saw his size he would be, but in her opinion such was his nature that if he hadn't frightened them off immediately he would make them welcome and give them whatever help he could.

She arranged the flowers in a glass vase and took them through to the sitting room where she put them on a low table in the window. It was natural that she should look out of the window. She always did. The estate agent and the man who was with her were getting into a car, and while Lisa watched they drove away. She wondered if the man would buy the house. She wondered if he had a wife and, if he had children, what ages they were. It would be nice to have someone with whom she could make friends.

7

As far as Karen was concerned, the evenings were far and away the worst part of her day. That had been the case ever since Ray had left her. It was then, after she'd put the children to bed, that she missed him most, felt the full weight of her loneliness. And now, added to that, she had the weight of the child growing inexorably inside her. Not physical weight, of course. It would be – how big? Possibly not more than an inch or two long? She didn't know. But she did know that it would be, in its almost infinitesimal way, a human baby. It would have arms, legs, minute hands and feet, fingers and toes, a beating heart – each and all of which were reasons – if reason came into it and not just emotion – why she could not bring herself to do anything about it. Kill it, she meant, forcing herself to use the word.

She had been to see Dr Craven, had told him the exact circumstances. He had told her that in her case he could point her in the direction of a termination. (Termination, she thought, was a better-sounding word.) She had not been to blame, she had no redress. But was I to blame, she asked herself? Or was I totally blameless? Sometimes she was not quite sure. She had told Dr Craven that she needed more time to think. He had said, 'Very well, it's your decision, but the time isn't infinite, in fact it's quite short.' He had also told her that if she decided to have the baby she must take great care of herself.

And that was where it stood. She had not made up her mind. Day and night she tussled with it, and got nowhere. And now she was eight weeks pregnant and sick every morning, rushing away from her desk in the office, returning white-faced with some sort of story about dodgy mushrooms or whatever. She didn't think anyone believed her but they were a nice lot and didn't push it. Actually, it had something to do with the fact that the office was in Venables' toffee factory and the all-pervading smell of toffee, which she had once found quite pleasant, now came over to her as nauseating.

Apart from being pregnant, she enjoyed her work there. It was a change to be with other people and also to earn a little money. Ray paid the mortgage and supported the children but there were other expenses to be met. She could only work part-time because of the children, whom she had to deliver – Fiona to school proper, Neil to the nursery – in the morning, and collect when she finished her shift in the afternoon. In the afternoon it was a worse rush than in the morning. Fiona had to be collected from school first, and then she had to retrace her steps to pick up Neil. It would have suited her better to have reversed that, but it was impossible. She needed almost to run to be at the school on time because if she was late there was trouble from the teacher who had to stay until every child had left the premises. Karen was usually the last to arrive. The nursery was a little more flexible. They were used to working mothers picking up their children at different times.

So today, as on every other weekday, she had dragged an unwilling Fiona – unwilling because she wanted to stop to look in the shop window in North Hill and hoped to persuade her mother to buy something – to the nursery, where she bundled Neil into his outdoor clothes, fastened him in the buggy and walked the length of Mulberry Lane again.

Every time I look out of the window, Esther thought, that young woman is walking along the road!

But now at last they were home, and their tea was on the table. Baked beans on toast. It was too often beans on toast – she was guiltily aware of that – or fish fingers. She knew, it niggled at her, that she ought to give the children a more varied diet, but beans were quick, they were also nutritious and, mercifully, the children liked them. She salved her conscience by frequently serving a salad on the side, which neither Fiona nor Neil relished and would not eat at all unless it was drowned in salad cream, and by offering them fruit.

She wished she could enjoy beans herself, it would save trouble, but the sight of Neil spreading them liberally over his face, his clothes and the table was enough to put anyone off for life, especially these days. So now, while the children ate, she sipped a cup of weak, milkless tea and nibbled at a slice of dry toast. She would eat properly later, when the children were in bed, and whether she wanted to or not. She knew she must try to eat well for as long – or short – a time as she carried this baby. Poor little devil, she thought. She wanted neither to nourish him nor to love him, she just wished he would leave her unwelcoming body with the least possible fuss. So why was she so reluctant to help him to do that? Was it because she was in some way scared? She didn't think so. Her God, if she had one – which sometimes she had but he came and went – was not an Old Testament God dealing out retribution. No, it wasn't that. It was that somewhere deep down she had a – perhaps reverence was too strong a word – respect for life. Any life. Which was why, she supposed, though large moths frightened her half to death, she could never actually kill one.

If it had been Ray's baby would she have been happy? He had left so suddenly. She had taken the children to Bedford for an overnight visit to her mother, who wasn't well, and when she returned he was gone. Nothing left of him except a note on the kitchen table. His clothes had gone from the wardrobe, his fishing tackle from the hall, his collection of CDs. Everything gone. Had he done it on the spur of the moment or had he been planning it for weeks?

Perhaps she should have run after him, but she hadn't. His note had been so final, she had read no hope into it. In any case where would she run to? She'd been so numb she'd felt as if she couldn't speak, couldn't think, couldn't even move. Perhaps it would have been better if she'd been consumed by a tremendous anger, an anger which would have made her run off somewhere; confront him, drag him back. But the anger hadn't hit her until later, and by then it was too late. She had lost him.

She had telephoned her mother who, though sorry for her, was short on sympathy.

'I warned you!' she said. 'Didn't I warn you? He wasn't a man who was ever going to settle down. He was always one of the lads. What he cared about was meeting his pals in the pub. That's not what you need in a husband, is it?'

She had never seen him like that. Perhaps she hadn't wanted to? All she knew was that she had wanted him. She'd been head over heels in love with him, as she had thought he was with her. Even now she didn't know what had changed him.

'Nothing changed him,' her mother said. 'He was always like that.'

But he hadn't gone off to seek his mates in the pub. He had found another woman. And after too many evenings spent alone she had fallen for a lightly given invitation to a party.

And what was he really like, this other man who was now part of her, in her, whether she liked it or not? She knew almost nothing of him. His first name was Terry. He was blond, handsome and well spoken. More than that she didn't know. Was he clever or stupid? Was he criminal or straight? Was he healthy or sick? What sort of genes had he handed down to this child she was carrying? With Fiona and Neil she would think 'That's your father coming out!' or 'That's just like your grandma!' There would be nothing she would recognize as his in this child – if she should keep it.

'I want to watch the telly!' Fiona said.

'Telly!' Neil echoed.

'Not until you've finished your tea,' Karen said. 'You don't watch telly while you're having a meal.'

'Everybody else does,' Fiona grumbled. 'Everybody I know in the whole world does. Michael does, and Darren, and Kelly, and Hattie, and Liam . . .'

'If you don't stop talking and eat your tea there'll be no time left for the telly,' Karen warned.

And after that it would be baths – hairwashing night – and a story to read. She'd be glad when Fiona could read them for herself, even perhaps to Neil. Then bedtime, and soon after that she herself would go to bed. There was nothing better to do – well, there was always washing and ironing, but she was dead tired. She would have to try to find time for it tomorrow or the day after.

It was Reading Week in the university, which meant that no-one at Number Twelve had to attend lectures or tutorials. In theory the university library would be crowded with students, heads deep in books, intent on learning more and more about their chosen subjects. In practice it was practically deserted, as were the refectory, the sports centre, the car parks and indeed almost every part of the campus. The students might well have been doing some deep reading in their own digs, though it was more likely that they had had a long lie-in and were now off on pleasure bent for the evening.

Imogen, on the other hand, had driven off early in the day to spend time at home with her family. This suited Jennifer admirably. It was also Reading Week at Sussex, which left Liam free to spend some time with his love in Shipfield. The self-inflicted rules at Number Twelve, which had been finally agreed after prolonged discussion, stated that no-one was allowed to double up their room with a visitor. This was nothing to do with moral reasons but everything to do with finance (who is paying for this accommodation, food, heating, etc.?) and amenities, the prospect of queues for the bathroom and lavatories. As Grace had pointed out, if they all had a friend to stay they would have twelve people sharing facilities designed for six. Therefore it had been decided that a visitor could only be accommodated in the absence of a paying tenant who had agreed to the use of his or her room by the said visitor, financial arrangements to be agreed between the interested parties. So in theory Liam would occupy Imogen's room, though in practice only his belongings would do so.

He was due to arrive any minute now. Jennifer longed to see him, she longed for his arms around her.

Grace was out – who knew where? She had lots of friends. Caroline and Philip had gone off together somewhere or other, into the town perhaps, or to Bristol. The two of them appeared to be getting on very well though to judge by appearances alone that seemed unlikely. Caroline was so gorgeous, while Philip was . . . well . . . He was nice of course, always polite, always considerate. He never hogged the bathroom for ages, never fought for his own way about television programmes. A really nice guy, in fact.

Stuart, unfortunately, was still here but at the moment in his own room. He was a man who gave the appearance of having scores of friends, of being in constant demand, but Jennifer suspected that he had very few friends – and who could wonder at that? Anyway, for the moment Jennifer hoped he would stay in his room.

And then she heard the sound of a car drawing up and stopping, and when she ran to the window to look out, there he was. She ran out of the house and was waiting with outstretched arms the moment Liam got out of the car.

Esther, from her window, watched with interest and not a little envy. She wished she could hear what they were saying.

'Oh, Liam,' Jennifer said, 'it's so good to see you! It seems ages.'

'Six weeks,' Liam said.

'It seems like six months!' Jennifer said.

Liam disentangled himself from her embrace and took his overnight bag from the car.

'Am I OK parking here?' he asked.

'Of course,' Jennifer assured him. 'But better still you could take Imogen's spot. I'd do it now if I were you, before Stuart pips you to the post. That little purple car is his. I can't think why he hasn't moved it already. He always has his eye on Imogen's place.'

'I'd as soon have it off the street,' Liam said. It was his mother's car. She hadn't been easily persuaded to lend it to him even though it was an old banger.

He got back into the car and manoeuvred it into Imogen's parking place and then, arms around each other, they went into the house and closed the door behind them.

Esther sighed. That was the end of that little diversion. It was getting dark and they had only one lamp lit in the front room, which was nice and romantic for them but meant she could hardly see a thing. In fact there was very little happening on the street at the moment. Two men – the one she had seen before and another who was a stranger to her

– had spent quite some time at Number Fifteen during the afternoon, but they'd left. It might be a good time for her to leave her post and think about making some supper.

'I really have missed you!' Jennifer said. 'Let me take a good look at you, make sure you haven't changed.' She stood back and appraised him. 'No you haven't,' she assured him. He was still six feet tall, thin to the point of emaciation. He had the same unkempt look, fair hair in need of cutting falling over his eyes. Almost certainly he was wearing the same frayed jeans and beige sweater. He was not a man who cared about his appearance. But at least it couldn't be said she loved him for his looks. It was her mother's theory that part of his attraction was that he was so unlike most of the young men she was used to, and in this lay Lady Winton's hope that Jennifer would come to her senses before it was too late.

'Coffee?' Jennifer offered.

Liam hesitated. Was there time for what was uppermost in his mind?

'Where's everyone else?' he enquired.

'All out except Stuart,' Jennifer said. 'But having heard you come in I don't doubt he'll be down any minute.'

'In that case, coffee,' Liam said.

He followed her into the kitchen and stood close to her, running his fingers up and down her spine as she dealt with the coffee.

'Ah!' he said. 'The real stuff. So your ma is still sending food parcels to the hungry.'

'She is,' Jennifer confirmed. 'So how about a little Gentleman's Relish on some toast?'

Liam shrugged. 'She'd not see me as the person to have that. Your ma is an out-and-out snob, my love!' He turned Jennifer round, took her in his arms and kissed her long and deeply.

'So you keep telling me,' Jennifer sighed. 'She wasn't quite as bad before Daddy had his title.'

Four years ago her father had, to her mother's great delight, been knighted for services to the textile industry, though her mother's delight had been mitigated by the fact that the honour had not been for something more illustrious than textiles. 'Why couldn't it have been for the arts?' she had complained. 'Think of all those classical concerts, all those exhibitions, and your father contributed generously to all of them. Still,' she had concluded, 'a title is a title and I shall live up to it!'

Her mother would never understand Liam. How could she? For instance, she didn't know what a revelation he was in bed. The juxtaposition of thoughts of her mother and of sex with Liam was incongruous. Sometimes she wondered how she herself had come to be born. When it comes to sex, she thought, I must have my father's genes – though what he had done about it other than devoting himself to textiles she couldn't imagine.

It was rebellion against her mother's values that had made her apply for a place at Shipfield when on her results she would have been offered a place at Oxford. That had been another thorn in her mother's flesh. In Lady Winton's view the newer universities were not quite real. The only thing Jennifer could not manage to do was to lose her educated accent, her posh way of speaking, which stood out against Liam's South London accent.

There were footsteps down the stairs and Stuart

burst into the room, switching on all the lights as he did so.

'A bit dim in here, isn't it?' he said. He held out his hand. 'You must be Liam. I'm Stuart Young!' He had a way of announcing his name as if he already saw it in gold letters on the cover of a book and expected it to be instantly recognizable.

'Right,' Liam said nonchalantly.

Stuart crossed to the window and looked out.

'Ah!' he said. 'I see you've parked. Actually, old boy, that's residents' parking, but not to worry for the moment, we'll sort it out in the morning.' He peered out of the window again, then jumped back suddenly, as if he had seen an apparition.

'Bloody hell!' he exploded. 'That fucking woman is looking out of the window again!'

'That's because you've switched all the lights on,' Jennifer said. 'She thinks she might see something interesting – like a fight, or an orgy.' She turned to Liam. 'It's Esther. She lives opposite. She's very old and doesn't get out much. I think she relies on us for entertainment.'

'Then I'll give her some, the silly bitch!' Stuart said. He stepped into the full light and made a rude sign in Esther's direction.

'Ooh,' Esther said out loud. 'It's that handsome one! The cheeky monkey!' She had a soft spot for cheeky monkeys. She raised her hand in the air and returned his sign. 'And you,' she shouted, 'with knobs on!'

Stuart turned away. 'Do I smell real coffee?' he asked.

'In the pot,' Jennifer said. 'Help yourself.'

He did so, then sat with them at the table to drink it.

'Are you going out?' he asked.

'No!' Liam said.

'Yes,' Jennifer said simultaneously.

'We thought we might just go along to the pub,' she added.

They had thought no such thing. She had planned an evening in, with the earliest possible bedtime, and she was sure Liam was of the same mind, but the thought of an evening in with Stuart there was too much. He and Liam had nothing in common, but nor could she contemplate leaving Stuart while she and Liam went off to bed. Her bred-in-the-bone good manners, which she cursed, forbade that. And if they did go to bed Stuart would hear every sound, every creak of the bed. It wouldn't put Liam off but it certainly would her.

Stuart looked up with interest. 'Now there's an idea,' he said. 'I might go with you.'

He had plans vis-à-vis Jennifer but he would wait for the right time to put them into practice. He prided himself on being a skilled strategist. He had worked out that to be super successful he must sell himself. Those who reached the top were the ones – in addition to writing the books, which was no sweat – who had a high profile. They were in the news – it didn't matter what for – and they were seen everywhere. Being a shrinking violet would do him no good at all. And it would be easier to achieve this, he had calculated, if on his arm he had the right female. She must be presentable, though not a raving beauty; he had his own good looks to put into the equation. She must be intelligent – the people he would mix with would not want a bimbo – and she must have class.

And where did all that lead but to Jennifer Winton?

It was a plus that her parents were titled and well off. That should open a few doors, though it was a pity her father wasn't actually in publishing. He had no qualms about being acceptable to them. After that lout Liam they would welcome him with open arms. It was sickening that for now he had to sit opposite that shit, watching him with his arm around Jennifer, his hand resting lightly on her breast in a proprietary manner. He could have smashed his face in except that physical violence – at any rate violence in which he was personally involved – was abhorrent to him.

Michelle Streeter's last customer of the day, as it happened, was Rita Masefield. It was a last-minute appointment and Rita was not a regular customer. As she explained on the telephone, she usually went to Cut-and-Come-Again, but for some reason – it was to do with extensive renovations being made to their salon – they were closed.

'And just when I need them,' Rita said. 'I'm desperate! My husband has had this important invitation for the two of us for this evening and my hair's an absolute mess. I know it's a cheek to ask you at such short notice . . .'

'Don't worry – did you say the name was Masefield? Don't worry, Mrs Masefield,' Michelle said soothingly. 'If you don't mind coming in as late as six o'clock I'm sure I can fit you in. A blow-dry was it?'

So there Rita was, in the chair, and there was

Michelle standing behind her wielding the styling brush and the hairdryer. And there they both were, finding out about each other by means of small talk.

'So do you live locally?' Michelle asked.

'I live nearer to Bath but I work locally,' Rita said. 'I'm an estate agent.'

'How interesting!' Michelle said, scrutinizing Rita's reflection in the mirror. 'Shall I give you a bit more height on top? I think it might suit you.'

'Please do,' Rita said. 'My hair does tend to go flat on top. So do whatever you think, I leave it to you.'

She settled back in her chair and gave herself up to Michelle's expertise. Thus so quickly had they reached the intimacy which exists between hairdresser and client. From now on this would be not only a salon but a confessional where absolutely anything could be said by the client and heard by the professional. Marital infidelity, money problems, awkward children, bodily ailments. Everything was of interest and up for discussion.

'So is business good?' Michelle asked pleasantly. 'Are you selling lots of houses?'

'Not bad,' Rita said. 'Mustn't grumble.'

'Is it an exciting job?' Michelle enquired. 'I expect it is.'

'Sometimes very interesting,' Rita said. 'I sold a house the other day which was interesting – not so much the house, but the people who were going to move in.'

'Really?' Michelle said, looking critically at Rita's reflection, not critically at Rita herself but at her coiffure. 'I know you didn't ask for a cut,' she said, 'but I think it would be better if I trimmed a few ends. I can do it when it's dry.'

'Feel free!' Rita said.

'So what was it that was especially interesting about these people?' Michelle enquired.

'They were ex-convicts,' Rita said. 'Some rich guy has this thing about helping young men who've just come out of prison. He sets them up in a house where they can be rehabilitated – sort of. It's very public spirited, isn't it?'

'Absolutely,' Michelle agreed. 'Mind you, I wouldn't like them living next door to me, would you?'

'Oh no!' Rita said. 'Do you think you could go over my hair with the tongs? It stays in longer.'

'Sure!' Michelle said. 'I meant to. They're plugged in.' Wielding the tongs, she added the finishing touches to Rita's hair. It really had come up nicely.

'So where is this house?' Michelle asked, making conversation.

It was at that point that Rita, intent on her image in the mirror – she was really pleased with it – forgot all about discretion, professional ethics and the high standards maintained by estate agents. She was, after all, in the hairdresser's chair.

'Mulberry Lane,' she said.

Tongs in hand, Michelle paused fractionally, just long enough to forget the hot tongs, which now touched Rita's scalp, causing her to cry out.

'Sorry!' Michelle said.

8

They were all there in the Green Man. It looked like being a profitable evening, Jim Pullman thought, looking around with satisfaction. He took great pride in his pub and in his running of it. It dated from near the end of the nineteenth century when Shipfield had been growing fast towards the north end of the town, but in its hundred years of life it had benefited (or not, according to one's point of view) from every modern convenience which breweries and owners had added to it. Now there were coloured lights around the bar, also outlining the windows, inside and outside, and framing the large old fireplace which had once burned huge logs but was now fitted with the most ornate artificial coal fire Shipfield's gas showrooms had been able to supply, capable of bursting into flames at the turn of a tap. All it could not provide was the sweet smell of burning wood and the excitement of flying sparks which in former times had threatened to set the rug on fire.

It seemed now to be unusually busy for a week-night, but you never could tell. There never seemed to be a reason for whether he was busy or whether there was hardly a soul in the place.

The O'Briens were there – Dermot not looking all that happy. There was that very pretty Jennifer, one of the students, with a double escort of young men, one messy-looking, the other smartish and well spoken. Jim wasn't surprised she had two in tow, he'd not be surprised if she had a dozen on a string – and he wouldn't have minded being one of them if he'd been twenty years younger. She was a corker. He wished she came in more often.

Peter and Meg were there from Number Nine, which was itself unusual, at least for them to be as early as this. They both commuted to and from Bristol and arrived home late so that when they did come it was more often for the last hour before closing time. Eric and James had just arrived. Dawn and Michael were also present.

'We don't often see you, Dawn,' Jim said.

'My mother's here,' Dawn explained. 'So she's looking after the twins for an hour or two.'

'We can't find Samson,' Peter said as they came up to the bar. 'He's always there when we get home – you'd swear he knew the time – but this evening he wasn't. We wondered if anyone might have seen him?' He looked around but was met with shaking heads.

Samson was a large tabby cat – his name fitted him – and because his owners were away all day he came and went as he pleased, through the cat flap. Most people in Mulberry Lane knew him. He was a friendly animal who paid regular visits to other houses and at several of them – unknown to Peter and Meg – he was fed.

'I've never known him be missing before,' Meg said miserably. 'I've put a dish of pilchards outside

141

the back door – he's mad on pilchards – but there's no sign of him.'

'Oh, he'll come back all right,' the landlord said. 'He knows his way around. He's probably gone courting! Even pilchards wouldn't keep him off that. But he'll be back.'

'I hope you're right,' Meg said. 'I just hope he hasn't strayed into North Hill. There's such a lot of traffic there.'

'I didn't see him around,' George Potter said.

'Well, you wouldn't, would you?' Meg said. 'I mean being in the shop.'

'You'd be surprised what I see without going out,' George told her.

'We'll keep our eyes open, Meg,' Laura promised.

It was not all that usual for Dermot and Laura to be in the pub during the week either. Dermot brought too much work home. But this week was half term so he was on holiday, and if he looked less than happy, which Jim Pullman thought he did, there was a reason for it. Laura had not managed to book herself a week's holiday to coincide with his, so he had been left to his own devices, which he didn't much like. It was to cheer him up, and because there was nothing fit to watch on television, that she'd suggested they went along to the pub after they'd eaten their early supper.

'For God's sake let's not sit with her!' Stuart said when he saw Laura coming in. Hastily he gathered their drinks from the bar and moved them to a table a few feet away, then quickly ordered a second round and brought those across. To Jennifer's surprise it was Stuart who had paid for all the drinks so far, quietly and without fuss. Apparently he was not mean. Arrogant, big-headed, intolerant, rude – all that and more besides but not, it seemed, mean with money.

'She's not all that bad,' Jennifer said.

'She is for me,' Stuart replied.

Jennifer was annoyed that Stuart had tagged on to them and she knew that Liam was furious. In the two minutes when Stuart had gone to the loo he had said so fervently.

'Why did you let him?' he demanded. 'Why didn't you stop him?'

'How could I stop him?' she'd questioned. 'It's a public place.'

'You're too bloody polite,' Liam had grumbled. 'I didn't come to Shipfield to spend time with that sod!'

'Then why didn't *you* stop him?' she'd retorted. 'I can't see *you* letting politeness stand in the way!'

So here they were, an unhappy trio – or, rather, an unhappy duo. Stuart, having dodged Laura, was relaxed and amiable. Let's hope, Jennifer thought, that a couple of drinks will soothe Liam.

Nigel and Mary Simpson sat side by side on an upholstered banquette against the wall. It was always Mary's chosen seat because it supported her back. Titus sat at Nigel's feet, eating crisps. Six feet away Maisie, the landlord's overweight yellow Labrador, lay stretched out on the carpet. She and Titus seldom had anything to say to each other. Titus knew who was top dog – size had nothing to do with it – and Maisie was too laid back to mind.

'This is turning out to be a very pleasant evening,' Betty, behind the bar, said to Jim. She was not a lady who noticed undercurrents.

Five minutes later the pleasant calm and low

murmur of conversation in the bar of the Green Man was shattered by the dramatic entrance of Michelle Streeter, followed two paces behind by her husband, Ralph.

She made straight for the bar – George Potter who was standing directly in her path jumped out of the way as an alternative to being knocked down – then when she reached it she twirled around so that she faced the company.

'You are not going to believe this!' she shouted. 'I tell you, you are *not*!'

'Why not try us?' Jim Pullman said. 'And in the meantime what would you like to drink?' He sensed trouble and he was all for keeping the peace, he didn't like fuss and palaver on his licensed premises. Not that he would ever have suspected Michelle Streeter of breaching the peace.

'I will,' she said. 'Just listen to this!'

She needn't have worried, there was no-one in the pub who wasn't agog.

'Number Fifteen has been sold!' she announced.

A collective sigh of relief went around, not so much at the news as at the fact that it wasn't as bad as they had feared. Or, in a few cases, disappointment for the very same reason.

'Well, that's good,' Laura said. 'We didn't want it standing empty too long, did we?'

There were murmurs of agreement, which Michelle allowed to go on for several seconds – not for nothing was she a leading light in the Shipfield Amateur Dramatic Society. She knew the value of the pause. When she judged it had gone on exactly long enough she held up her hand and, surprisingly, gained immediate silence.

'You have not heard the worst!' she said. 'Oh no,

144

not by any means. You have not heard to whom it's been sold. You have not heard who is going to live there!'

'Well, tell us,' George Potter said. 'Don't keep us in the dark, Michelle.' Not that it mattered much to him.

'It is to be occupied,' Michelle announced in a slow, clear voice, 'by a gang of *ex-convicts*!'

If she had wanted to create a stir she was not disappointed. After a second's silence everyone spoke at once.

'Ex-convicts?'

'How could ex-convicts buy a house? Where would they get the money?'

'Profits of crime, of course!'

'I didn't say the convicts had bought it,' Michelle said. 'It's been bought for them by some do-gooder – who of course lives miles away. Well, he would, wouldn't he?'

'While Michelle and I live right next door!' Ralph said.

'What sort of convicts?' Nigel Simpson enquired.

'Men who've served a prison sentence,' Ralph said impatiently. 'What other sorts of convicts are there? They've been convicted of crimes!'

'I meant what sort of crimes?' Nigel said mildly. 'There are crimes and crimes.'

'How do we know what sort of crimes?' Michelle demanded. 'Burglary, arson, manslaughter, grievous bodily harm. How shall we ever know? They're not going to tell us, are they?'

'Oh dear! We could be murdered in our beds!' Meg said.

'How do you know about this?' Dermot asked Michelle.

'Straight from the horse's mouth,' she told him. 'Don't think it's not true, because it is! The estate agent, the woman who had a hand in the selling, she told me. I don't suppose she meant to. I was doing her hair and people tell you all sorts of things, they get carried away. Thank goodness I agreed to do her hair at the last minute or we'd never have known!'

'Which might have been better,' Dermot ventured.

Ralph Streeter rounded on him at once.

'How can you say that? At least forewarned is forearmed. We shall know what to look for. If we'd known earlier we might have been able to stop the sale but from what this woman said it's gone through, or just about.'

Eric Spurling broke in.

'Do you think possibly we're overreacting? I mean, it sounds to me as if these men have done their time. I presume they'll be here for some sort of rehabilitation. Perhaps they'll be going straight from now on. What makes us think they're going to commit further crimes?'

'Because that's what they do,' Ralph said angrily. 'It's their way of life. Everybody knows that. Once a villain, always a villain. But it's all very well for you, you won't have them living right next door!'

'It won't just be your end of the road,' Meg told him. 'We'll all be vulnerable. There'll be a spate of break-ins or whatever it is they're up to, you mark my words.'

'I would just like to see anyone break into my house!' Nigel Simpson said fiercely. 'Titus would have them in a flash.'

Titus gave a short assenting bark.

'And there's another thing,' James said. 'It's

bound to send the value of *all* our property down, having those sort of people living here.'

Eric Spurling turned on his partner at once.

'How can you say something like that, James? That's pure prejudice! I'd think you'd remember that you and I suffered from prejudice for years. We weren't acceptable. We'd let the area down.'

'That's a long time ago,' James said. 'Before we came to Mulberry Lane.'

'I know,' Eric said. 'We've been accepted here. That's a good reason why we should give these men a chance.'

'Well, I'm not sure I agree with you,' James said huffily. 'We've worked hard for our house. I don't want to see it lose value. Aside from that, I don't trust them.'

'You're making assumptions about them,' Eric said. 'You could be quite wrong.'

'Of course it would be *me* who's wrong. Never you!' James said.

Dermot decided to intervene. When those two quarrelled it could take over.

'I don't see that property values matter if we're not thinking of moving. Our house will be the same to Laura and me as it is now.'

'In the circumstances, some of us might want to move,' Meg said.

'Well, I wouldn't,' Mary Simpson said. 'Not after all we've done to the house and garden.'

'You never know,' Meg said darkly, 'with convicts living in the road we might feel we have to. Samson would be very upset, I can tell you.'

'Bugger Samson!' Ralph Streeter said. 'It's not cats we're discussing, it's the price of property – and worse!'

At this point everyone started to talk at once. Titus joined in, and even Maisie gave a deep, token bark. It was also the moment when Jim Pullman decided that enough was enough. He didn't like anyone swearing at a woman. Tempers were getting frayed. He didn't think they were the kind of people to start a punch-up but he wasn't going to risk it. In any case it was no way to run a bar. People came into the Green Man for a few drinks and a relaxing hour.

He rapped on the counter.

'Sorry, ladies and gentlemen!' he said in a voice firm enough to quell a riot. 'That will do, thank you! Change of subject, please.'

'But we haven't finished!' Ralph Streeter protested. 'There's still a lot to be said – like what steps are we going to take.'

'But not said here!' Jim was adamant.

Laura spoke up.

'Jim's quite right. We'll get nowhere this way, but there are things to be discussed. Also, not everyone from Mulberry Lane is present. There are sure to be other points of view. So why don't we have a meeting and invite everyone in the road who wants to come?'

'Fine,' Jim Pullman said, 'but I suggest not here, unless you'd like to hire a private room.' He would rather they didn't. It threatened to be a noisy affair.

'We could have it in our house,' Laura said. She looked at Dermot for confirmation and he nodded.

'I don't see why not,' he said.

'Then if we can fix an evening while we're here – without going into the subject again – I will undertake to invite everyone else in the road. They can come or not, as they please.'

'That's that then,' Jim said when the date had been agreed. 'And now a few nice cold beers on the house to cool us all down.' He'd been quite fierce with them and it was not in his interests to make enemies of his customers.

When they left the pub Dermot and Laura walked along the road with Ralph and Michelle. Dermot would rather not have done so – it was quite clear that he and the Streeters held opposite views on the future occupants of Number Fifteen – but not to walk with them would not only have looked unfriendly, it would have more or less declared a split. If they were to come to some future consensus a split was not the best starting point. Since the Green Man was on the even-numbered side of the road they walked along together until Number Ten was reached, at which point the Streeters crossed the road to their own house. Dermot breathed more easily when they left. He had thought for a minute that Laura, with her usual hospitality, was going to invite them in for coffee.

'I did wonder,' she said as they went into the house, 'whether I should have asked them in, but then I thought it wouldn't be a good idea. There'd be only one subject of conversation.'

'Quite right,' Dermot said. 'I think we should avoid having little discussions with different people; let it wait until we all meet together.'

'All the same,' she said, 'it's going to cause a lot of trouble. I can see it coming.'

'I'm afraid that's true,' Dermot said.

'And there's something to be said on both sides,' Laura said. 'Don't you think so?'

'What I think is that we could just go round in

149

circles until we all sit down and have a proper discussion,' Dermot replied.

'I suppose you're right,' Laura agreed. 'Anyway, what are you going to do with yourself tomorrow?'

There were loads of things he could do in the house, odd jobs which had been waiting until someone could find time and inclination to do them. New coat hooks to put up – she had bought the hooks weeks ago and they had been on the kitchen dresser ever since – a faulty plug to see to on the vacuum cleaner, new batteries to fit in both smoke alarms. It would be nice to have all these things done.

'I don't know,' Dermot said. 'I suppose I might walk into the town.'

'Well, if you do could you bring me a pot of growing basil?' Laura asked.

In the event, he left home reasonably early next morning, though not too early for Esther to wave at him from her window. He waved back. He's a nice man, Esther thought. If he were mine I'd keep an eye on him. You never knew who was around.

Further along the road Dermot passed Karen Jackson. Presumably, since she was alone, she had dropped her children wherever she took them. They said good morning to each other without stopping.

Laura hadn't told him what Karen's problem was – or had been – and since it was most likely women's stuff, he hadn't asked. She looked a bit pale though. In Waitrose he bought everything on the list Laura had given him: basil in a pot, also coriander; Wensleydale cheese, bananas, stock cubes. After that, duty done, he felt free to browse in the bookshop and have coffee, which they'd recently started to serve there. A very civilized thing to do, he thought as he chose a book which he might or might not buy, collected his cup of coffee and a Bath bun, and sat at a table in the corner. Why hadn't he thought of doing this earlier in the week? He was well into the book – he decided he would buy it – when he heard his name.

'Mr O'Brien! Good morning!'

The voice was vaguely familiar but it wasn't until he looked up that he recognized its owner.

'Why, Mrs Clarke,' he said. 'Good morning!'

'I'm ever so pleased to see you,' she said. 'Would you think it was a cheek if I asked if I could have a word with you?' She was carrying a cup of coffee and a paperback.

'Of course not,' Dermot said. 'Why don't you sit down and join me?'

He stood up and held out a chair for her.

'I haven't seen you in here before,' he said. 'Not that I'm often here myself. It's just that it's half term – well, I don't need to tell you that, do I? – and I promised to do a bit of shopping for my wife.'

'I sometimes drop in when I'm on the afternoon shift. I work in Sainsbury's,' Mrs Clarke explained. 'Now that they keep open all sorts of hours we work shifts. Mine is twelve noon to seven o'clock this week.'

She spoke hesitantly while at the same time, Dermot noticed, stirring her coffee into which she had put neither milk nor sugar. He supposed it was something to occupy her hands and wondered what it was she had to say to him. He wasn't sure that he wanted to hear it but it would be churlish to refuse her, particularly in the light of what she had done for him.

'Is it a good place to work?' he asked, making conversation, giving her time to get over her nervousness.

'Oh yes, very good,' she said. 'The only thing is the hours don't fit in with the times I'd most like to be at home. If I'm on the morning shift I can't be there to see Melanie off to school and if I'm on the afternoon I'm not there when she comes home. I have to miss out on one or the other, though they're both important, aren't they?'

'I'm sure they are,' Dermot agreed. 'Though these days I think quite a number of parents have to miss out on that kind of thing, more's the pity. Which bit worries you most?' He felt sure this wasn't what she wanted to talk to him about.

'Well,' Mrs Clarke said, 'I do like to make sure that she has a good breakfast and see she sets off in time – I mean so as not to be late for school. Left to herself she'll have no more than a cup of tea. These girls starve themselves for fear of getting fat, don't they?'

'I'm afraid it's a stage they go through,' Dermot admitted. 'In fact I think our younger one might still think that way.'

'Oh, I didn't know you had daughters, Mr O'Brien,' Mrs Clarke said.

'Two. Both grown up now. Fled the nest.'

'Ah! But you've gone through this stage. It's not easy, is it? Sometimes I don't know what to do for the best. But I do think it's important to be there when Melanie gets in from school. I mean for my sake as well as hers. I like to know she's actually arrived even if she does go straight up to her room and put the music on. You hear such awful things these days.'

'I'm sure Melanie's a sensible girl,' Dermot said.

He was sure of no such thing. If Melanie were his daughter, which heaven forbid, he'd want to be there to make sure she came straight home from school. Indeed did she do so – or did her mother have some good reason for her anxiety?

'I wish I could be sure,' Mrs Clarke said. 'Sometimes if I get the opportunity I ring her from work when I know she should be home. Sometimes she is, sometimes she isn't. When she is there she doesn't like it, she says I'm spying on her. When she isn't there I worry like anything, especially now with the dark evenings on us. I can't win!'

'Perhaps she goes to friends?' Dermot suggested.

Mrs Clarke shook her head.

'Melanie doesn't have many friends, not girl friends – and the boyfriends she doesn't bring home. I wish she would. I've always made her friends welcome.'

She fell silent, as though she had come to the end of everything she had to say. She had stopped stirring her coffee, though so far she had not taken a single sip of it.

'Is this what you wanted to speak to me about?' Dermot prompted her gently.

She sighed. A long, deep sigh.

'I'm not sure,' she admitted. 'Really I shouldn't have spoken to you at all. It was just seeing you there. I wouldn't have come down to the school to say any of this. I'm sorry, Mr O'Brien. I shouldn't have bothered you with my worries.'

'It's no bother,' Dermot said. 'Please don't apologize. I'm sorry I can't be of more help.'

'It's a help to me just to be able to say it,' Mrs Clarke said. 'And it's not just me not being there when I should be. I worry about how she's doing at school. I want her to work hard and make something of herself. She's a clever girl really. She takes after her father.'

'Oh, she is!' Dermot agreed. 'She's very bright. If she'd work just a bit harder she could do very well.'

There was a silence, which in the end Dermot apprehensively broke.

'I think you said your husband left home? Might that have some bearing? How long ago was it?'

'Six months,' Mrs Clarke said.

'And . . . will he be returning?'

'Who knows? I live in hope,' Mrs Clarke said. 'I never really understood why he left. There was no-one else involved, he wasn't one to go after other women. He said he had to sort himself out, he needed time and space. He'd been made redundant, you see, and he hadn't been able to find another job.'

'So you don't know where he is?' Dermot said. 'That must be difficult for you.'

'Oh yes, I do know,' Mrs Clarke said. 'He's found a place to live. It's off the Walworth Road in South London. He sent me the address straight away, but he said I was only to use it in an emergency, he wanted to be left alone. He was very depressed and that worried me, but I respected his wishes. He transferred half his redundancy money to my building society account. He was always thoughtful in that sort of way.'

'And does Melanie know where he is?' Dermot enquired.

'Only that he's in London,' Mrs Clarke said. 'I've

never given her his address. I don't think it would be wise. If he wants to get in touch with us, he will.'

'It can't be easy for you,' Dermot sympathized. 'And, of course, it isn't always easy for girls in their teens, is it, even when everything seems all right at home.'

'I daresay it isn't,' Mrs Clarke said, 'though some of them seem a lot more difficult than others. Melanie hasn't been the same since her dad left. It's funny, I never thought she was all that close to him. She doesn't say much, but I can tell she misses him. I think that's why she seems to be turning to older men. There was a man down the street . . .' Her voice trailed off.

'I'm sorry,' Dermot said.

'Actually, Mr O'Brien, she's quite a good girl – I mean in *that* way. I would have said not all that long ago she was a bit of a prude. And I don't think there's any real bad in her. In spite of what she might say, I don't think she'd *do* anything wrong.'

'I expect you're right,' Dermot said. 'Who knows your own daughter better than you?'

'Yes. Thank you for listening to me. It's been a help.' She rose suddenly to her feet. 'I won't take up any more of your time.'

'Don't forget,' Dermot said, 'any time you want to you can come along to the school for a chat about Melanie.'

'Would I get to talk to you?' Mrs Clarke asked. 'About Melanie, I mean.'

'I expect so. She's in my tutor group.' But sorry as he was, he was not sure it was a good idea either for him or Mrs Clarke or Melanie. 'Better still,' he amended, 'you could come when we have an open meeting. Talk to the other teachers, meet some of

Melanie's friends. There'll be one before Christmas. I'll remind Melanie to let you know.'

'Thank you,' she said. 'I'll be off then. I mustn't be late for work.'

He watched her as she walked across the room and down the stairs. Poor woman! She was a nice person too. She deserved better.

He returned to his book, read a few more pages, then paid for it at the desk and went off to catch his bus. He had wondered whether he would stay in town for a spot of lunch, but he'd decided against it. He wasn't one for wandering around town centres and it wasn't the most pleasant of days. There was a chill, damp mist coming from the river. He disliked November. As far as he could see it had nothing to recommend it.

So what shall I do with the afternoon, he asked himself as the bus climbed up North Hill. It was definitely not a day for working in the garden. He had dealt with all his school work. He could, if he wished, settle down and read the rest of the book he'd bought. Though that tempted him, when it came to it his conscience probably wouldn't allow it. There were odd jobs Laura had been wanting him to do for ages; he might make a start on those, earn a few Brownie points.

For his lunch he opened a can of pea and ham soup and cut a slice of bread. While he ate he thought about the jobs. A loose tile in the back porch – he'd need to check whether he had any cement in the shed – batteries for the smoke alarms and a new plug for the vacuum cleaner. He would have to pop out to Potter's but that was only a matter of minutes.

The Potter family had been in the hardware

business in North Hill as long as anyone could remember. George was the third generation to own the shop and, looking at the floor-to-ceiling shelves while waiting for his turn to be served, Dermot thought it likely that there was stock there from the time of William Potter who had founded the business all those years ago. There was no doubt in Dermot's mind that George would have exactly what he needed, and indeed he had.

'I'm afraid the batteries come in packets of four,' he apologized. 'That's the way it is these days. When my father had this shop, if you wanted one screw you could buy one screw. Now you'd have to buy a packet of twenty. That was a bit of an argy-bargy in the pub, wasn't it? Much ado about nothing!'

'I don't think that was the general feeling,' Dermot said, 'though I'm inclined to agree with you. Are you coming to the meeting?'

'Oh, no!' George said. 'None of my business.'

Because of the dreariness of the day it seemed almost dusk as Dermot walked home. If he wanted to get these jobs finished before Laura was home he'd really have to move. Surprisingly – he was not the world's best handyman – everything went well. He had finished and cleared away, and put the kettle on to make a pot of tea, before he heard Laura's key in the lock.

'Hi!' Laura said. 'Everything OK?'

'Fine,' Dermot replied. 'The kettle's on. Tea won't be a minute. What sort of a day did you have?'

'Much as usual,' Laura said. 'Quite busy. Did you go into town?'

'I did. I got everything on the list. Then I bought a book. Oh, I had a coffee with Mrs Clarke.'

'Mrs Clarke?'

'Mother of the dreaded Melanie.'

'Oh, that Mrs Clarke. So why was that?'

Dermot poured the tea and sat by Laura at the table.

'She wanted to talk about Melanie.'

Laura frowned slightly. 'Was that wise?' she asked.

'I didn't have any option,' Dermot said. 'She asked if she could join me at the table. I couldn't pretend I was just leaving, I'd hardly started my coffee. Anyway, I didn't see much harm in it.' That wasn't entirely true. He'd felt more than a little apprehensive.

'Perhaps not,' Laura conceded. 'All the same, I'd think it better to steer clear. What was it she wanted to say about Melanie?'

'I'm not entirely sure,' Dermot admitted. 'Nothing I could do anything about anyway. She talked about her husband.' He related Mrs Clarke's conversation. 'It must be difficult for the woman. She reckons Melanie is basically a good girl but I reckon Melanie gives her a bad time.'

'That I can well believe,' Laura said.

'I suggested that she might like to come to school when we have an open meeting, talk to some of the other teachers.'

Laura nodded. 'Probably a good move. But if she does come, keep your distance. The mother might be every bit as nice as you say, and of course it's a sad story, but I don't trust Melanie – at least what I've heard of her – one little bit. Don't get involved!'

'That's fine, coming from you!' Dermot protested. 'You who get involved with everything and everybody. Anyway, do you want to hear what else I've done today?'

'Sure,' Laura said. 'What have you done?'

'All the odd jobs!' He listed them.

'That's marvellous!' Laura cried. 'I can hardly believe it. And does everything work?'

'Thank you for that vote of confidence,' Dermot said. 'Come on, I'll show you.'

'Right,' Laura said. 'I'll take a look at your handiwork and then I'm going to drop a note in on the neighbours who weren't in the pub last night.'

9

Laura had not found it easy to arrange a date for the meeting convenient to everyone in Mulberry Lane. In the Green Man she'd narrowed it down to either Tuesday or Thursday evening of the following week – there was nothing sooner than that – and there were five other houses to be visited.

'All the same,' she said to Dermot, 'it has to be done. Everyone must have a chance to speak.'

'I'm no longer sure that's so,' Dermot said. 'I think perhaps a meeting wasn't the best idea. We could just let things take their course – in fact in the end that's about all we can do. The meeting might just end up with people falling out with one another, people who've lived amicably in the road for years. And we can't stop these people coming. They have to live somewhere, and why shouldn't it be Mulberry Lane?'

'So you're in favour of them, you're for it?' Laura asked.

'It's not a question of being for it or against it.' Dermot sounded irritated. 'I just don't think it's fair to prejudge them. We don't even know if what's been said is true.'

'Oh, I expect it is,' Laura said. 'I don't see why

the estate agent would have told Michelle if it weren't. It wouldn't be to her advantage, would it? I suspect it just slipped out, the way things do when you're having your hair done.'

'I can see why women's hairdos are so expensive,' Dermot said. 'You're being charged for therapy. All the same, I wish I could find out how much truth there is in it. I suppose only the estate agent knows that and I can't go in there and ask outright, can I?'

'You can't,' Laura agreed. 'Anyway, we said we'd have the meeting, so we must.'

In the end she had either seen everyone who was at home or had dropped a note through the door of those who weren't. 'Next Tuesday is the favoured date,' she told Dermot. 'Eight o'clock. Try not to bring too much work home, darling.'

'I'll try,' Dermot promised. 'What was the general reaction?'

'Anti, I'm afraid. Oh, I don't mean to the meeting, I mean to the thought of ex-convicts.'

'I wonder how long you have to be out of prison, going straight, before you cease to be thought of as an ex-convict?' Dermot said. 'Of course it doesn't surprise me they're mostly anti. That was obvious in the pub. Not Eric Spurling, though – which was pleasing. I just hope that the meeting will go the right way and a few of them will decide to give these blokes a chance. So who's coming, apart from the ones I know about?'

Laura read from her list.

'Bella and Winston Grange from Number Two. Harry Ford from Number One. Dulcie James and Jeremy Fielder, Four A – it's interesting that Number Four is the only house that's been divided into two flats. Keith Barnes from the upstairs flat wasn't in. Dulcie said she'd tell him, but he's away a lot. The Nelsons at Number Three weren't in either. I left a note. Eric and James, Michael Blake, and Dawn if they can get a babysitter.'

'What about Cornerways?' Dermot enquired. 'Did you go there?'

'Yes. I saw Lisa. Gary was out. She wasn't at all happy about it, though she's much more civil when Gary's not there. She actually invited me in. She thinks they'll both come if they can get a baby-sitter.'

'She wouldn't be happy,' Dermot said. 'And he'll be worse.'

'Karen also has to get a babysitter,' Laura said. 'And that just leaves Esther. I'll go across in a minute.'

Dermot looked at her in surprise.

'Do we have to ask Esther?'

'Of course we do,' Laura said. 'If anyone at all is vulnerable—'

'—which they're probably not,' Dermot interrupted.

'Agreed! But if anyone is it could be Esther. She's old and alone and lives very close by. She'd have more reason to be afraid than most. That makes twenty or more, plus whichever students decide to come.'

Dermot sighed.

'Let's hope we can knock some sense into the antis,' he said.

'You mean convert them to our point of view,' Laura said.

'Of course I do! Otherwise what's the point of doing it?'

'Well, I hope you're right,' Laura said. 'We've all

lived fairly peaceably in Mulberry Lane up to now. I'd hate it to change.'

Thirty minutes later Laura told herself that she ought to know better than to be surprised at Esther's reaction to anything. It was usually out of kilter with the rest of the world.

'A house full of young men!' the old lady said, beaming. 'Now that *will* be interesting! When are they coming?'

'I don't know. In fact we're not one hundred per cent sure that it's true,' Laura admitted.

'I certainly hope it is!' Esther said. 'We could do with a bit more life in Mulberry Lane. There's never much going on.'

'That's the way most people like it,' Laura said. 'People don't like change.'

'Then they're mad!' Esther said decisively. 'Not to mention extremely dull. People who don't like change are always dull.'

'That's a sweeping statement, Esther,' Laura observed.

'I know,' Esther admitted. 'At my age you're allowed to make sweeping statements. It's one of the few things you are allowed.'

'Anyway,' Laura said, 'if you want to come across either Dermot or I will fetch you.'

'Send Dermot,' Esther said. 'I expect you'll be busy making coffee and putting biscuits on plates. I take it we shall be having coffee and biscuits? It's not a sherry do, is it?'

'Not really,' Laura told her.

There was a pause. Then Laura said, 'So you're not nervous, Esther?'

'Nervous? Why should I be nervous?' Esther sounded genuinely surprised.

'Well, perhaps you shouldn't be. It's just that . . . well, ex-convicts . . .'

'They're not going to hurt *me*,' Esther said. 'They'll think I'm just a harmless, silly old bat! And I shall be if they behave themselves. And if they don't – and I could well be the first to know because I shall keep an eye on them – I can report them to the proper authorities. If I want to, that is.'

'Esther,' Laura said to Dermot when she was back at home, 'is going to do a Neighbourhood Watch on them.'

'In that case we can tell the others they need have no fears,' Dermot said.

'Not quite,' Laura said. 'Esther will be the judge of what's reprehensible and what isn't.'

The fact that there was no-one to speak on behalf of whoever was going to move into Number Fifteen and that so many would be against them preyed on Dermot's mind. No-one *could* speak for them, except in a general way, citing tolerance and a wait-and-see attitude, because no-one knew quite what was afoot. Who was coming, how many, where from and – most important of all – for what reason had they served prison sentences? Not knowing that, the anti-brigade would assume the worst if only to excuse their attitudes. He felt sure that terms such as rape, grievous bodily harm, assault, even murder, would be bandied about, along with burglary, arson and car theft, and they could not, with any authority, be disclaimed because no-one knew.

And then on Saturday morning came a stroke of luck. Looking out of the window for no reason at all, Dermot saw a man unlocking the front door of Number Fifteen and going into the house. He called out to Laura, who was in the kitchen.

'There's a fellow just let himself in at Number Fifteen. I'm going across to have a word with him.'

Laura hurried into the sitting room, still drying her hands.

'Why?' she asked. 'What are you going to say to him?'

'I don't know,' Dermot admitted. 'I'll know better when I know who he is. He's probably only from the estate agent's but even so he might tell me a bit more than we know now.'

'It's been a woman before,' Laura said. 'Perhaps it's Mrs Harper's son-in-law come to collect bits and pieces.'

'If it's a member of the family they'll appreciate someone keeping an eye on the house,' Dermot said. 'But if it's someone who's actually moving in I might get some information. And he might *want* to know something.'

'Shall I come with you?' Laura suggested.

'No,' Dermot said. 'There's no need. On the other hand, I might bring him back for a cup of coffee. I'll see how it goes.'

He crossed the road to Number Fifteen (observed, of course, by Esther) and rang the bell. The man he had seen enter opened the door.

'I'm from Number Ten, across the road. Dermot O'Brien. I saw you going into the house. I thought I'd better check. Just in case. I didn't know whether you were a member of Mrs Harper's family, or what.'

'Very sensible,' the man said. 'I'm Brian Carson. I'm not a member of the family. I'm going to move in here. I came to take some measurements.'

'Ah,' Dermot said, 'I see!'

He was momentarily at a loss for words. The man didn't look in the least like a criminal. He was well dressed in a casual way, and well spoken. But don't be silly, he told himself. How do you know what a criminal looks like and why shouldn't a jailbird speak the Queen's English?

'Are you moving in soon?' he asked.

'Quite soon,' Brian Carson said. 'The sale's gone through. We have to clear the house – I've gone into that with the previous owner's daughter – and then there'll be a lot to do but most of it can be done when we're in.'

'We?' Dermot queried politely. 'Your family?'

Brian Carson gave Dermot a long look.

'No,' he said. 'Not my family. Do you mean you haven't heard? It's my experience that these things get around like wildfire.'

'We have heard a rumour,' Dermot admitted. 'Of course we'd no idea whether it was true or not. As you say, these things get around.'

'Why don't we get straight to the point?' Brian said. 'If you heard that there are going to be some young men in the house who've served prison sentences, that's true. I'm not one of them but I shall be in charge. I shall live here with them.'

'That's what we heard,' Dermot confirmed.

'And you were all up in arms?' Brian suggested.

'Not everyone,' Dermot said. 'Some were, some weren't. What we lacked was anything other than those bare details. Naturally we're all curious to hear more. But don't assume everyone's against the idea.'

'I'm pleased to hear it,' Brian said. 'I can assure

you we're not going to bring trouble. We'll keep a low profile, but don't expect us to be in hiding.'

'I don't. And I'm not expecting trouble,' Dermot said. 'But you'll admit it's a bit unusual. We'd like to know a little more. There might even be something we could do for you. Would you come across the road with me and have a cup of coffee? Meet my wife; she knows everyone around here.'

'Gladly!' Brian said.

They were in the sitting room. Laura had poured the coffee, and joined them.

'Well, to satisfy your curiosity—' Brian began.

'It's not idle curiosity,' Dermot interrupted. 'Some people are genuinely concerned. I don't go along with them, but they are.'

'OK,' Brian said. 'Point taken. The man I work for is called Malcolm Fraser. He's a rich man with a big heart. He wasn't always rich, his fortune is self-made. As a young man he had nothing and, he told me, he wasn't what you'd call an upright sort of character – far from it – but in his twenties, when it seemed as if he was going rapidly down the wrong road, he met a man who gave him a chance to make something of himself. And he took that chance, and made the most of it.'

'What does he do?' Dermot asked.

'Nothing, now,' Brian said. 'He's retired. He sold his business for a large amount of money. He has no family – he never married. He's chosen to spend his money on giving young men second chances. Perhaps you've heard of the Fraser Trust?'

Dermot shook his head.

'OK,' Brian said. 'Well, it works like this. The Trust buys a house, usually one which needs

167

restoring, renovating – and is therefore bought at a reasonable price. And, by the way, whatever you've heard about the inflated price of the house, they didn't get it. The ex-cons, usually four, but it could be more or fewer, move in with a supervisor – that's me – and live there for as long as it takes. That is, as long as it takes for their rehabilitation – going out in the world with confidence, and as long as it takes to put the house into good condition so that it'll sell at a profit, which is usually between three and six months. The profit goes into the Trust to purchase the next house.'

'Sounds a good scheme,' Dermot said.

'Oh, it is,' Brian agreed. 'But it's not all plain sailing. Mr Fraser chooses to help men who have served a prison sentence and he does that partly because there aren't all that many people who want to be bothered with them – there's a lot of prejudice – and partly because they need help if they're to start a new life. It's all too easy when you come out of prison to slide back into the old ways.'

'I imagine it is,' Laura said. 'How does Mr Fraser get in touch with these people?'

'Through the Probation Service, through organizations for ex-prisoners. That sort of thing. They get in touch with him if it's a case where they think he can help. It's quite a small-scale operation, and all the better for that. And if it sounds like a cushy number, it's not. These men have to find jobs, go out into the workplace. In between going out to work, or if they genuinely can't get a job, they have to work in the house and garden. That's a deliberate policy, they have to be doing something constructive – in fact they need to, it's good for them. This will be the second house we've set up.

And we've had some success. Not a hundred per cent, but enough to make it worthwhile.'

'And do you get opposition?' Dermot asked. 'I mean from the area where you set up house?'

'Always!' Brian said. 'You name any kind of opposition you've heard in Mulberry Lane and I'll have heard it all before. It mostly arises out of fear.'

'I suppose it does,' Dermot agreed. 'And are the fears justified?'

Brian shrugged his shoulders.

'Sometimes they are. I'd be lying if I said otherwise. Things happen, but not all that often. By the way, how did you come to hear about us moving in here? People usually do, of course. We don't try to keep it a secret.'

Dermot told him about the scene in the pub.

'I admit it got a bit heated,' he said. 'The landlord didn't like it – I mean the scene, not the reason – so we decided to meet together here and discuss it. We've invited everyone in the road who wants to come. What I did wonder, and it's why I was so pleased to see you earlier on, is whether you'd consider coming to the meeting and putting your side of things? It's next Tuesday evening.'

'Certainly I'll come,' Brian said. 'I'd be glad to, though I feel I'll be stepping into the lions' den.'

'I think you might be,' Dermot agreed. 'But you'll find not everyone's against you. And who knows, you might be able to tame some of the lions. At the very least you can tell it as it is. Right now it's largely guesswork and foreboding.'

'Do you know who'll be coming to live in the house?' Laura asked.

Brian nodded. 'More or less. It's not totally settled. There might be three men, or possibly four.

We're having the large bedroom divided into two. It's important for each man to have a room of his own, some privacy, after having had none at all in prison. The eldest in this group is twenty-six, the youngest twenty. For three of them it's been their first stretch, for the other one, his second.'

'And are we allowed to know what they were in prison for?' Dermot asked.

'It's a pity you feel you need to know that,' Brian said. 'Whatever it was, they've served their sentence – or enough of it to be let out on parole . . .'

'But I'm sure you realize that that's the first thing people will want to know,' Dermot persisted. 'They'll want to know because they're nervous – frightened, some of them. You said yourself that the prejudice arises out of fear.'

'They needn't be afraid,' Brian said. 'None of this lot were murderers or rapists, or convicted of grievous bodily harm or suchlike. They're mostly thieves or burglars, conmen or that sort of thing. No-one's life is going to be in danger.'

'To some people around here,' Dermot said, 'property is as valuable as life.'

'It's the same everywhere,' Brian said.

'Would you like another cup of coffee?' Laura offered.

He rose to his feet. 'No thank you,' he said. 'I'd better be off. I've quite a bit to do.'

'Then we'll see you next Tuesday,' Dermot said. 'It's very good of you.'

Tuesday evening turned out extremely wet, the rain beating down. Everyone who had decided to come – which was most people – arrived between ten to and eight o'clock, damp and uncomfortable. The umbrella stand was jammed full and wet coats were piled in the hall.

Nigel Simpson was the first to arrive, accompanied not by his wife but by Karen Jackson.

'Mary's kindly sitting in with the kids, so as to let me come,' Karen explained. 'I hope they'll not give her any trouble. They're both in bed but Fiona's had toothache ever since she got home from school. Probably a ruse to prevent me coming!'

'Don't worry,' Nigel said. 'They'll be all right with Mary. She's good with children.'

'In any case,' Laura pointed out, 'if you're needed it won't take two minutes to get you home.'

'I brought Titus,' Nigel said. 'You don't mind, Laura? He hates it when we both go out and I thought if he went to Number Six it might get the children too excited.' What he meant was that he didn't trust the children not to come downstairs and play about with Titus, who was yapping his head off as the doorbell rang again.

By ten minutes past eight everyone who had accepted to come had arrived. Dulcie James informed Laura that Keith Barnes sent his apologies, he was in Nottingham overnight. There was no sign of the Nelsons, from Number Three, nor had they replied to Laura's note. Gary and Lisa Anderson from Cornerways were both there, having persuaded Mrs Litton to sit in. Bella and Winston Grange came in at the last minute. The students were represented by Stuart, Jennifer and Imogen, with the promise that Caroline might appear later. Everyone eventually managed to find somewhere to sit, even if on straight-backed dining chairs or on the floor, and while Dermot went across the road to collect Esther, for whom a comfortable armchair had been reserved, Laura served coffee.

Esther, sweeping in on Dermot's arm a few minutes later, to the accompaniment of further yapping from Titus – as from a herald – had dressed for the occasion. She wore an ankle-length floral skirt, a white frilly blouse and her pearls; and in her thick, untidy white hair she had clipped a rather special Flanders poppy, saved from a Remembrance Day some years back. Automatically, those in her path moved aside to let her through to her chair and this she acknowledged by a gracious inclination of her head and a lifting of the corners of her thickly reddened mouth in a slight smile. When she was comfortably seated Titus took his place at her feet. The Queen Mother could not have done it better, Laura thought, bringing her a cup of tea, which she preferred to coffee, and a ginger biscuit, which she dipped into the tea and skilfully transferred to her mouth the instant before it fell apart.

The low buzz of conversation resumed, none of it, as far as Dermot could hear, about the subject they had met to discuss. It ranged from the weather through increases in the price of petrol, the road works in North Hill, the difficulty of getting babysitters, and back to the weather.

'Anyone like more coffee?' Laura enquired, hoping that no-one would, and pleased when her hopes were fulfilled.

'In that case,' Dermot said, 'shall we get on with what we're all here to discuss? But before we start to discuss it I have some progress to report.'

'It was a rumour!' Nigel said. 'I thought all along it might be.'

'No, it wasn't a rumour,' Dermot said. 'What Michelle heard from the estate agent lady was, in essence, true.'

Michelle smiled, not so much because it *was* true as because she had been the bearer of the truth.

'What do you mean, "in essence"?' Gary Anderson demanded. 'Either something is true or it isn't.'

I am not going to like Mr Gary 'Cornerways', Dermot thought. He had so far had little to do with him. Occasionally Gary had come into the Green Man, but he had never stayed long. He had all the trappings of a man whose bank balance was larger than those of others and wished everyone to know it. Still, he had a right to be here, he had a right to have his say.

'Of course,' Dermot said. 'I mean I have a little more information about the people who are moving into Number Fifteen.'

'You mean they're actually moving in? Are you telling me we can't get together and stop it?' Gary said.

'That's about it,' Dermot said. 'The sale has gone through. We can't stop that.'

'Then we should be able to. It's a danger to the rest of us,' Ralph Streeter said. 'Don't forget Michelle and I live right next door!'

'I don't think there is any danger,' Dermot said.

'Everyone should get a dog!' Nigel Simpson interrupted. 'A dog is the greatest protection.' Titus gave a short bark of agreement.

'Why do you say there's no danger?' Gary asked. 'What do you know about it?'

'I'm trying to tell you what I know,' Dermot said steadily. 'And the reason I know more than you do is because I've met the man who will be running the

173

house, supervising everything. His name is Brian Carson. The actual owner is a man named Fraser who has set up a Trust from his own money to do what he's doing. Brian Carson told me all about the project and I invited him to come here this evening so that we could put any questions we wished to him. He was agreeable to that. I think you'll find he'll be very open with us, but I thought we'd like a little time to ourselves first.'

If he had wanted his announcement to make a stir he was not disappointed. Almost everyone had something to say, if not to the meeting at large, then to each other, and it seemed to Dermot that they were divided into two camps, those who were happy to listen to what this man would have to say and those who were bursting to have a go at him. Eric and James were still not in agreement. At a rough guess the camps were equal in number but there was little doubt that those against were likely to be more vocal. It was always the way, Dermot thought, bad things happened because good people kept quiet. Well, as far as he could he would encourage them to speak up.

'That would be the man I saw,' Esther said, speaking for the first time.

'You saw him?' Nigel said.

'Indeed I did,' she said. 'I remember thinking he was quite like a man I used to know. I can't at the moment recall his name but he was very nice, so I expect this one will be.'

A ring at the door interrupted Esther's reminiscences. Everyone stopped talking.

'That will be Brian Carson,' Dermot said – and went to let him in.

10

Dermot ushered Brian into the hall.

'Thanks for coming,' he said.

'Am I in for a rough ride?' Brian asked.

'You might be,' Dermot admitted. 'I'm sure you'll deal with it.'

They went into the sitting room. Dermot raised his voice so that everyone could hear, though he needn't have bothered since the whole room was suddenly quiet.

'This is Brian Carson,' he said. 'He'll be living across the road from us and he's kindly agreed to come and tell us what we're waiting to hear. I'll not introduce anyone now. Let's get things going and you can introduce yourselves a bit later on.'

He looked around the room, noticing the expressions on people's faces. Gary Anderson's was as dark as a thundercloud; Ralph Streeter's, if possible, was even darker. Some were total blanks and two or three – not more – had a slightly milder expression, as if they had come prepared to hear the evidence. The Granges looked as if their minds were elsewhere. Dermot wondered if they had quarrelled. Actually, no-one seemed to know much about the Granges. They were both in the university all day, and in vacation time they were away attending conferences. Esther alone, a welcome committee of one, gave Brian a warm smile and extended her hand.

'So pleased to meet you, Mr Carson,' she said pleasantly. 'We're all looking forward to hearing what you have to tell us. So exciting!'

'Bloody old fool,' Gary Anderson muttered to his wife, but not so quietly that he wasn't heard by those around him, and also by Brian.

'Would you like a cup of coffee first?' Laura offered.

'No thank you,' Brian said. 'Perhaps afterwards.'

Dermot called the meeting to order.

'I've told people very briefly about the Fraser Trust,' he said to Brian. 'You might like to expand on that?'

'Right!' Brian said. 'Good evening, everyone. I'm pleased to be here and I hope I can clear up any misunderstandings you have or which might arise in the future. I'll begin by repeating, possibly, what Dermot's already told you about the Fraser Trust.'

He watched as the man at the very front of the meeting, the man who had made the remark about the old lady, squirmed in his seat. He had already marked him down as a troublemaker. There was always one like that and you could recognize them at once.

'Mr Fraser,' he said, 'is a rich philanthropist who has chosen to use his wealth to help young men, who have, shall we say, taken the wrong path, to make a new start in life. What he does started out as an experiment but so far it seems to work.'

Gary Anderson couldn't contain himself another second.

'When you say "taken the wrong path",' he asked sharply, 'isn't what you actually mean that these men have committed crimes bad enough for them to be sent to prison? They're criminals, in fact. Let's not wrap it up in social-worker speak! They're criminals.'

There was a faint murmur of assent around the room, a nodding of one or two heads. Few people liked the Andersons, they were considered stuck up and he was invariably rude, but on this occasion the general opinion was that he was right.

Brian gave the man a steady look and answered him with cool politeness.

'They *were* criminals, Mr . . . ?'

'Anderson,' Dermot supplied.

'They *were* criminals, Mr Anderson,' Brian repeated. 'Yes, they committed crimes – not the very worst crimes in the book, but still crimes, and they were sent to prison. They served their sentences and, having paid their debt to society, were released. I think technically they're no longer classed as criminals.'

'I don't believe they change,' Gary Anderson said firmly.

'Ah!' Brian said. 'I'm interested you put forward that theory, Mr Anderson, and it comes as no surprise. It's one that's commonly held and it's exactly what the Fraser Trust is working to disprove, and with some success. Modest success, I grant you, and very individual, but true.'

'Perhaps we should let Mr Carson tell us how he expects it to work here before we go on to any more questions or observations,' Dermot suggested. He was determined not to let Gary Anderson hold the floor.

'I'd be glad to,' Brian said. 'Let me put the facts of what it will mean for Mulberry Lane, which is what you're all interested in. Mr O'Brien has already heard them, so he must bear with me.

'Four young men,' he continued, 'will move into Number Fifteen. They're all in their twenties and they've all served prison sentences. They'll be here for rehabilitation. If you think that this will be a soft option after prison life, then let me disabuse you of that idea. These men will be required to work hard and to follow a strict regime. It will be my duty, living with them, to see that it's carried out.

'In the first place three of the four will have to find jobs in the locality. The Fraser Trust provides the house and pays my salary but the men, rather than depending on Social Security, have to go out to work. They have to earn enough between them to run the house – pay for food, gas, electricity and so on.'

'Why only three out of four?' James asked. 'Why doesn't the other one have to earn his keep?'

'I'm coming to that,' Brian replied. 'The fourth man will earn his keep by working full time in the house, restoring, renovating, decorating. It's in a shocking state, I'd say nothing had been done to it for years. He'll certainly have plenty to do and I've already decided who'll fill the bill. The eldest of the men has served two prison sentences and during that time he's done courses in joinery work and plumbing, and a certain amount of electrics—'

'Two sentences!' Gary Anderson broke in furiously. 'So we're dealing with repeat offenders, are we? Clearly the rehabilitation lark didn't work with him!'

178

Brian took a deep breath and summoned his reserves of patience.

'He wasn't offered it the first time round. He was released from prison, went back to where he'd lived before and immediately got in touch with his old associates. I wouldn't label him as a repeat offender. Hopefully, this opportunity will prevent him ever being one. But to continue – the other three men will also have to help with the house and the garden. They'll have to put in time in the evenings and at the weekends. Also, those who earn money will pay their wages into a kitty and the fourth will be credited with a notional amount. Apart from a small personal allowance – pocket money – to each man the money will be used partly to run the house and a certain amount will be paid into an account for each man, which he can take with him when he leaves, goes out into the world again. While we live in this house we are no burden whatever on the state, on the taxpayers.'

'And when will they leave?' Ralph Streeter asked. 'How long do I have to put up with them as neighbours?'

'Difficult to say,' Brian admitted. 'Possibly six months, possibly only three. A lot depends on the individual. If a man gets on well and is offered a permanent job, either here or elsewhere, then he might leave. These men are not still in prison. They're doing this because they choose to.'

'It might be a good scheme for your man Fraser,' James said. 'He must be making a bob or two!'

'Mr Fraser,' Brian said in a steely voice, 'does not make a penny from this. He set it up with his own money and he continues to pay money into it. The house has to be furnished, very basically: beds,

179

chairs, sheets, towels and so on. Money has to be available for emergencies. Anyway, ladies and gentlemen, that's the plan.'

'Do you mean,' Ralph Streeter demanded, 'that if one of these ex-convicts leaves here before you're ready to sell we might get a replacement criminal?'

'If one of the men leaves before the rest,' Brian said, 'another man just might take his place. There's always someone glad of the chance. If on the other hand by some coincidence all four men are ready to leave at the same time *and* the house is in suitable condition, then we could all move out, lock, stock and barrel, sell the house and start again. It's not always as neat as that, of course.'

'I think we understand that,' Nigel Simpson said in a reasonable tone, 'but would it be possible for us to know something about the men who'll be living here? After all, forewarned is forearmed.'

'We have a right to know!' Gary Anderson said.

'Oh no we don't!'

It was Karen, sitting at the back of the room, who spoke up. Every head turned in her direction. Even those who knew Karen best were not used to hearing anything at all forceful from her, added to which she was the first dissenting voice against everyone who had spoken so far.

Seeing every eye on her, she flushed crimson. It seemed to her that most of these people were sitting in judgement, and somehow, perhaps foolishly, she related it to herself. These were the people who would judge *her* when they found out, *if* they found out. They would show her no mercy, make no allowances. They would be the 'she was probably asking for it' brigade. Where once she might have been indifferent to the ex-cons (though she hoped never hostile), now she felt herself firmly on the side of the men who were not here to defend themselves. She'd spoken because she couldn't keep silent another minute and now she wouldn't go back on it.

'We don't!' she said firmly. 'We don't have the right to know anything about our neighbours, whoever they are. People's affairs are their own business.'

You little beauty! Brian thought. I could kiss you! He jumped in quickly.

'The lady is absolutely right,' he said. 'We don't have that right. Nevertheless, because I know the men wouldn't mind – and in an odd way it might help them, they'd be saved the embarrassment of ever having to confess – I'm prepared to give you some brief facts. I'm sorry you feel the need to know them, but I understand. However, I'm not going to identify these men by name. The youngest was sentenced for car damage and theft. The pair who are both two years older served sentences for burglary and arson respectively. The eldest of the four – he's twenty-six – is the man who has served two sentences, both for theft – from stores, small shops, cars, wherever he saw the chance. Each of these men has served something between nine and twenty-four months in prison. More than that I'm not prepared to tell you. They might, but I won't. And I repeat, they've served their sentences.'

Immediately he felt the waves of antagonism sweep around the room. He spoke up quickly, trying to stop it.

'You might like to know,' he said, 'that these men don't know each other, they haven't served their time in the same prison. None of them are married

181

and none of the men are from this area, which is important because it means they won't be meeting old associates. That can be an ex-prisoner's downfall. But what that also means is that they'll be separated from friends and families – those who have families – and they might well be lonely. If there is hostility towards them they're likely to feel it keenly.'

'What else can they expect? We can't pretend we want them here.' It was Ralph Streeter again.

'Speak for yourself,' Eric Spurling said. 'We might not all think the same way.'

'What they can expect is entirely up to all of you,' Brian said. 'I always start out with high hopes that people will be tolerant – even friendly. Sometimes the hopes are realized, sometimes not.' He turned to Dermot. 'Is there anything else, do you think?'

Gary Anderson chipped in again.

'Theft, burglary, arson!' he said. 'And you expect us to welcome them as neighbours.'

'What if we're attacked?' Michelle asked. 'How will we defend ourselves? How do we know we're safe even to walk along the road?'

'I don't think you need worry about that,' Brian assured her. 'Not one of these men has the slightest reputation for violence towards persons. And incidentally, because I'm sure some of you will want to know, none of them are alcoholics or drug users – we don't allow drugs – and they'll all be on a curfew, in by eleven p.m., at least for a time. And bear in mind they'll still be on parole so if they did commit any of these crimes you're worried about they'd be straight back into prison. I assure you that's the last thing they want! If it hadn't been they wouldn't have volunteered to come on this rehabilitation course. They didn't have to. They wanted to. I know I've said that before but it's worth repeating.'

'You make it sound all fine and dandy, all very plausible,' Ralph Streeter said.

'I just tell it like it is,' Brian said.

'Then answer this,' Ralph said. 'This Mr Fraser, does he have any of these people live with him – or even next door to him?'

'No,' Brian said evenly. 'He's a very elderly man and he lives way out in the country.'

'I thought as much!' Ralph said. 'Easy-peasy for him, isn't it? Not like me. In case you hadn't already realized, I live right next door! I'd be the easiest to burgle.'

'You'd also be the last,' Brian said. 'They'd be unlikely to go for so obvious a target.'

'Tell me something else,' Gary Anderson said. 'Don't these guys have to report regularly to the police?'

'No they don't,' Brian said. 'If they were sex offenders they would have to, but they're not. I should have included that in the list of things they're not. Quite a long list when you come to think of it.'

'Well, I can't think why they don't have to report,' Gary persisted.

'Law of the land,' Brian said. 'They are in touch with the Probation Service, which knows all about them. But there is something you'd like to hear, which is that because they served between six and thirty months their convictions aren't finally spent until ten years have gone by.'

'I'm glad to hear that!' Gary said.

'I knew you would be,' Brian said.

'So if there's nothing else,' Dermot said, 'perhaps we'll break up the meeting and continue informally over another cup of coffee. There might be views you'd like to put individually to Brian.' He turned to Brian. 'Would that be all right?'

'Certainly!' Brian said. 'And there's just one more thing I'd like to say before we break. Three men will need jobs in the locality. I think I can safely say they'll be willing to do anything within their capacity. So please, if any of you can offer anything, or can suggest who might—'

Gary Anderson broke in yet again.

'Do you seriously suggest that I, as an employer, should take on a man I knew to be a crook?'

'An ex-crook,' Brian said. 'Yes, it's a serious suggestion and if you took the risk you might be agreeably surprised.'

'Well, I'm sorry to disappoint you,' Gary said. 'There's no way I'd do that!'

'I am disappointed,' Brian admitted. 'But not surprised.'

Laura had gone into the kitchen to make more coffee and Meg Fenton had gone with her to help. Brian, getting away from Gary, started to cross the room towards where Karen was sitting. It would be a pleasure, he thought, to speak to someone who wasn't against everything he said, but it was not to be. He was waylaid by Stuart. Almost everyone else started a conversation with whoever was nearest. Dermot began to move in Brian's direction, determined to get him out of the clutches of that revolting Stuart, who was clearly haranguing him, when Esther called out to him.

'Dermot dear, am I wrong, or did I hear a glass

of wine being offered? I'd like that. Red. Claret if you have it.'

'I'm not sure you did,' Dermot said. 'But I daresay I could find one, since it's you. Would anyone else prefer a glass of wine to coffee?' He hoped no-one else would. The supply was limited.

'Esther would like a glass of red wine,' he said to Laura, in the kitchen. He took down a bottle from the rack and started to open it.

'I reckon Brian is in for a rough ride,' he said, 'not to mention the lads. It's amazing how fearful people are.'

'Fearful or prejudiced,' Laura said. 'Or more likely both. All the same, I reckon Brian can take care of himself. It's different for the young men.'

Dermot poured the wine and took it to Esther. Brian had escaped from Stuart and was making his way towards Karen who, for the moment, was sitting on her own. He took the empty chair beside her.

She was a pretty woman, Brian thought. Curly dark hair, shoulder length, eyes the colour of clear amber, pale skin. She was slender and long-legged under tight-fitting blue jeans and a polo-necked red sweater.

'Thank you for your support, Mrs . . . ?'

'Karen Jackson,' she said. Her voice was softer than when she'd been making her protest a few minutes ago.

'I was glad of it,' he said. 'It came at exactly the right time.'

'I was only saying what I thought,' Karen said. 'No-one has a right to poke into anyone else's life the way they do. It isn't as if they did it to be helpful. They wanted to hear the worst you could tell them. The worse it was, the more interesting

185

gossip it would have made. It would have been in the pub and everywhere before the night was over. It doesn't give your men a chance.'

'I'm used to that,' Brian said. 'But I'm glad not everyone feels the same way. You, for instance.'

Karen looked hesitant. She was suddenly aware that it was herself she'd been defending, against a hypothetical attack.

'Oh, it isn't that I'm all for it,' she admitted. 'I wouldn't go that far. It's just – as I said before – that I think people shouldn't interfere with other people's affairs. They should be given a chance. All the same, I expect I'll still lock my door at night. I have to think of the children.'

'A sensible precaution in any circumstances,' Brian said. 'I do the same. Is your husband here?'

'I don't have a husband. I did, but now we're separated,' Karen said in a voice which said, 'Don't ask!' 'My next-door neighbour's looking after the children so that I could come here. The man with the Yorkie is her husband – Nigel Simpson.' In fact, it wasn't the reason for the meeting which had greatly interested her, it was the thought of an evening away from her own house, something which might stop the thoughts of her own troubles going round and round inside her.

'He seemed a reasonable man, Mr Simpson,' Brian said.

'He's all right,' Karen agreed. 'They're not all as bad as you might think, I mean from what you've heard so far.'

'I'm pleased to hear it,' Brian said. 'Can I get you a cup of coffee?'

'Thank you,' Karen said, 'though I'll have to leave when Nigel does because of relieving his wife.'

'If you stay right where you are I'll be back with it in two minutes,' Brian promised.

He returned quickly. 'I didn't ask whether you'd like black or white,' he said. 'I risked white. Is that OK?'

'It's fine,' Karen said. 'I prefer it.'

A slightly uneasy silence fell. Suddenly, for both of them, there seemed to be nothing more to say. Karen was the first to find her voice.

'I nearly didn't come,' she admitted.

'Why not?' Brian asked.

'It will sound quite rude,' Karen answered. 'Actually I wasn't madly interested in what the meeting was about. I didn't think it would affect me. I still don't see why it should.'

'I think you're right,' Brian said. 'So why *did* you come?'

'To get away from home,' she confessed. 'Does that sound awful?' She thought it probably did. She didn't know why she was telling this man she'd only just met. She was off men, anyway. She didn't trust any one of them. But she'd better take a hold on herself or she'd be telling him she was pregnant.

'No, it doesn't sound awful,' Brian said. 'In a way, I think I understand. I don't have children – I'm no longer married either – but when the men are living in the house I don't have a lot of freedom, or I tell myself I don't, though really I suppose it's up to me, I make my own hours. It's just that I don't always like to leave them, especially at night. Does that sound daft? Am I making them sound like children? Because they're not.'

'Not really,' Karen said. 'It must be a responsibility.'

'Especially at the beginning. I don't know the

187

men well then. It gets easier – or of course it can get worse – as time goes by. I learn to know who I can rely on.'

Esther's voice suddenly rose above the general chatter.

'Young man, come and talk to me! You can bring Karen with you.'

Brian looked at Karen, raising his eyebrows.

'Your next-door-but-one neighbour to be,' Karen said. 'I reckon she'll be on your side.'

'Then I'd better obey,' Brian said. '*Will* you come with me?'

'For a minute or two,' Karen said.

'So you are Brian!' Esther said. 'And you're going to bring four nice young men to live in Mulberry Lane.'

'Ex-cons!' Gary Anderson said. He was standing quite near.

Esther either didn't hear him or chose to ignore him. It was never easy to know which line she was taking, as she well knew. It was one of the advantages of being old and known to be on the deaf side. There are none as deaf as those who will not hear, she reminded herself.

'So I hope you're going to bring them in to see me,' she said. 'I could do with the company of some nice young men! Are they strong and handsome?'

'When they come,' Brian promised, 'I'll introduce you and you can judge for yourself.'

'Good,' Esther said, 'I shall enjoy that!' She turned to Karen. 'Are you all right?' she asked. 'You look a bit peaky to me. Go and get her a glass of wine,' she instructed Brian.

'No! No, really!' Karen interrupted. 'I wouldn't have time to drink it. I have to go in a minute.'

'As you wish,' Esther said.

Nigel Simpson came towards them, Titus at his heels.

'I think we should go, Karen,' he said. 'Mary may be getting anxious.'

'Right!' Karen said. 'I'll just find Laura and say thank you.' She turned to Esther. 'Good night, Esther,' she said. 'It was nice seeing you.'

Brian held out his hand.

'Good night, Karen,' he said. 'And thank you!'

11

Brian watched with relief as the removal van drove away from Number Fifteen. He himself had arrived at ten past nine that morning, having driven from the hotel in Bath where he was staying until Number Fifteen was at least habitable enough for him to move in there, to find the van already parked outside, the driver – smoking a cigarette in short, angry puffs – and his mate both leaning against the front wall, waiting impatiently for his appearance so that he could let them in. He was ten minutes late, for which he apologized.

'There was a traffic hold-up on the road,' he explained.

'What else do you expect?' the driver retorted. 'Me, when I have a job to do, I set off earlier to allow for it.'

'I'm sorry,' Brian said again.

He saw Esther, standing in her bay window next door but one, watching his arrival. He waved to her and she gave him a cheery wave back. There was no sign of the Streeters next door. That pleased him. Ralph Streeter was someone he could do without. He was not going to make life easier. Presumably, since they had a business in the town, they left home early – and hopefully arrived back late.

He collected a bottle of milk from his car, marched up to the front door and unlocked it. 'There you are,' he said to the men. 'It's all yours. I'll be around if you want a hand.'

'No thanks,' the driver said, dropping his cigarette on the doorstep, grinding it with his heel. 'You're not insured. Much as my job's worth to let you loose on it. If something went wrong I'd be the one to cop it.'

'That's fine by me,' Brian said. 'I'll not interfere. I'll leave you to it.'

'A cup of tea wouldn't be interfering,' the driver said.

From what Brian had seen on previous visits of the contents of the house, though it was crammed full with the lifetime's possessions of an old woman who seemed never to have thrown anything away, there was nothing of real value. It was at the daughter's insistence, when he'd spoken to her, that everything was to be removed, and delivered to her in Bristol. It transpired she didn't want the things for herself but she hoped, even allowing for the cost of the removal van to Bristol, she might make a tidy packet selling them. Brian had not bothered to express his disagreement. She wouldn't have believed him. He recognized a greedy woman when he saw one. It was as well, he thought now, she hadn't been present to see the rough way the removal men had cleared the house and jammed everything into the van.

By eleven o'clock the van was packed and the men were ready to leave. They had done well – two cups of tea each had cajoled them into a better mood. He walked to the van with them and saw them off along Mulberry Lane in the direction of North Hill. As he was about to go back into the house Mrs Anderson, from the house opposite, drove past in her Landcruiser and swept into the drive of Cornerways. That was some vehicle! He wouldn't at all mind owning one of those, but at thirty-five grand or so, much more than his year's wages, it was unlikely to happen. She jumped down from the vehicle, unloaded several plastic bags of shopping and released the dog. If they were as security conscious as her nasty husband made out, why didn't she leave the hound at home to guard the house? The size of it alone would deter any would-be intruder.

Before going back into the house he took a critical look at the front garden of Number Fifteen. 'Garden' was a misnomer. It consisted of a rectangle of overgrown, weed-filled grass. There was a narrow gravel path underneath the window, which appeared to be there for no reason at all, since it led nowhere, a dark green, almost blackish holly bush against the wall which divided the house from that of the Streeters, and a sickly looking fuchsia hedge which might in the summer have borne flowers but was now long past that, against the front wall. Something would have to be done there. His general impression of the front gardens along the road were that they were neat and tidy, even though not bordering on the beautiful. It would hopefully be a good mark for the men if they put the front garden to rights as quickly as possible. And painted the shabby front door, he thought as he went up the steps towards it. The whole house would have to be painted but until that was possible a bright new door would help.

He went into the house and walked around, upstairs and downstairs, standing in every room, simply looking. Not a pretty sight! It was dingy and dirty and it smelled stale. He opened every window as wide as it would go, noting as he did so that there was hardly one which didn't need new sash cords. That would be high on the list for attention. He supposed he could stay in the hotel in Bath until the day of the men's arrival – which was scheduled for next Monday – but he'd need to be in the house a good deal of the time between now and then. There was furniture to be bought and delivered – beds, tables and chairs at the very least; also needed were crockery, pots and pans, a washing-up bowl, cleaning tools – a hundred and one things. He had gone through this before, in the previous house, so he was no longer surprised by how many bits and pieces it took to set up a home from scratch. He'd spent time making lists and he'd been around the town in the last few days, checking where he'd get the best deals in furniture. To fit in with his budget some of it at least would have to be second-hand. That didn't matter.

Standing in the large bedroom he wondered how best to divide it into two. Fortunately it had two windows, one quite large, the other smaller but still adequate. There was a fireplace which, though personally he quite liked the look of it, would have to be blocked up. In any case the plan was to put in central heating. That would be totally necessary when the house came to be sold again. At present there were ancient electric fires. He wondered if Colin Myers was up to doing central heating.

He went downstairs, walked along the narrow back hall and through the back door into the garden. The state of that was worse than the front. He couldn't imagine when anything had last been done to it and it had no design at all. It was simply a long, narrow rectangle of tired grass surrounded by an assortment of lilacs, elders and what he thought was forsythia, which would not be worth looking at until next spring. Of all the trees there were, it was his opinion that, once its flowers were past, lilac was the dullest. The only fortunate thing was that the dull trees cut the garden off from its neighbours. He would not have to suffer the Streeters.

In the decrepit cubby-hole against the house, which was actually the outside lavatory, leaning against the wall was a broom, and hanging on a nail was a dustpan. On another nail hung a pair of shears, red with rust, and in the corner an ancient lawnmower was propped against the wall. He hadn't noticed these things before because everything was festooned with cobwebs. A monstrously large spider took fright and scuttled up towards the ceiling. He was relieved to see it go, he had an aversion to spiders. He took the broom and dustpan into the house. He could make immediate use of them, even though they were a long way past their best. They had, in fact, been high on his shopping list.

He looked at his watch. It was half-past eleven. He would start at the top of the house and sweep through, after which he would find somewhere to have lunch, and after that he would shop. He had noted as he had driven past that there was a pub on the corner of Mulberry Lane and North Hill. With any luck they would do lunches, or at least make him a sandwich.

194

He made a start upstairs. By the time he had swept through every room, upstairs and down, tipping the dirt and dust of ages into the dustbin which the removal men had omitted to take, he felt as though he was not only breathing dust but eating it. He could have drunk a pub dry. He washed his hands and face and brushed himself down as well as he could – that was another thing, when he came tomorrow, even though the place wouldn't be ready for him to stay overnight, he must bring soap and towels and a change of clothing, or at least a clean shirt. For now his car coat would have to hide everything.

There were very few people in the pub. A yellow Labrador, lying in front of the bar, raised its head as Brian entered, then lowered it again and went back to sleep. Brian ordered a half of bitter and drank it down in one go.

'You were thirsty!' the landlord said.

'I was,' Brian agreed. 'I'll have the other half. Do you do lunches?'

'Not really,' Jim Pullman said. 'Except on Saturdays. I could do you a hot pie, chips and peas.'

'That would be fine,' Brian said.

He moved to a table close by the bar. Ten minutes later Jim Pullman put his lunch in front of him.

'Thank you,' Brian said. 'That looks good! Can you tell me, is there a good hardware shop around here? Household things, I mean.'

'There certainly is,' Jim Pullman said. 'Potter's, just round the corner in North Hill. You couldn't do better anywhere. Are you new around here, then?'

'Yes,' Brian said. 'I'm moving into Number Fifteen Mulberry Lane.'

There was a moment of total silence. Brian and Jim Pullman looked at each other.

'I take it you've heard?' Brian said.

'Yes,' Jim said. 'In fact there was a bit of an argument in here last week. I put a stop to it. In my position I don't take sides and I won't have trouble, not in my pub. I keep a decent house where people can have a drink in peace.'

'Good!' Brian said. 'So it won't be a problem if these lads come in from time to time for the odd half-pint? It won't be often because there's too much to do in the house, and they don't have much money, but they need to mix in the community.'

'No problem to me!' Jim said. 'They've as much right here as anyone else, as long as they behave themselves.'

'I think you'll find they'll do that,' Brian reassured him. 'They've too much to lose if they didn't. I just don't want them to be banned.'

'Why would I do that?' Jim questioned.

'You'd be surprised what people do!' Brian told him.

'If they made themselves nuisances to other people then I might take action, but I'd do that whoever it was.'

'Well, thank you,' Brian said. 'I suppose it's too much to hope that you might have a job going for one of them? Anything! Cellar work, cleaning, kitchen work?'

Jim shook his head.

'Sorry! Not at the moment. I've got all the staff I can afford. In any case, I'd need to know them a bit better.'

'Fair enough,' Brian said. 'It was worth asking.'

Jim Pullman went back to the bar to serve a

customer. When Brian had finished his meal he
went off to find the hardware shop.

'Are you Mr Potter?' he asked a man who was up
a ladder, checking shelves. 'Mr Pullman, at the
Green Man, recommended you.'

George Potter descended with surprising agility
for a man of his age and weight.

'I am,' he said. 'What can I do for you?'

'I've got quite a long list,' Brian warned him.
'You might not have everything.'

'We'll give it a try,' Potter said. 'I keep a good
stock but if there's anything I don't have I daresay I
could get it for you.'

They went through the list together. It surprised
Brian how many of the items the shop carried.

'You're right,' Potter said. 'It certainly is a list! It
looks like you've a lot of work ahead of you.'

'That's a fact!' Brian agreed. 'We're just about to
set up in an empty house. We need everything.'

'Empty house, is it?' Potter asked. 'Where might
that be?' He wondered what sort of a set-up it could
be where they had nothing at all to bring with
them.

'Number Fifteen Mulberry Lane,' Brian said.

Potter stopped dead in the middle of measur-
ing out sash cord. I've been expecting you, he
thought.

'Oh!' he said. 'Number Fifteen? That's where old
Mrs Harper lived.'

'That's right,' Brian agreed. 'And I take it you've
heard something?' He could tell by the look on
Potter's face.

'Yes, I have,' Potter confirmed. 'I heard it in the
pub. There's not much happens that we don't get to
know about one way or another.'

'And from what I gather it wasn't well received?' Brian said.

'Not by some,' Potter agreed. 'They had a meeting about it. I didn't go, I didn't think it was my business. I don't suppose they invited you?'

'Oh, but they did!' Brian said. 'At least Dermot O'Brien did. I was glad of a chance to have my say, not that I could have convinced some of them in a thousand years. You'd think a foreign army was about to move in. They weren't all like that, of course. One or two were very understanding.' He thought with pleasure about Karen's intervention. She would never know how it had lifted his spirits.

'Well, I daresay you have a hard row to hoe,' Potter said. 'I wish you luck.'

On Friday morning Brian checked out early, though reluctantly, from the hotel in Bath. He had decided that from today, when the men were due to arrive, he must live in the house full-time with them. It had never really been on the cards for him to stay overnight in Bath, even for a few days, while they were in the house. He would miss the modest luxury of the hotel; having a clean, comfortable room to sleep in, the dining room where he had only to choose from the menu for his food to be placed before him, the bar in which he could relax. In that he had purchased the necessities for Number Fifteen – beds and bedding, cooker, pots and pans, chairs and tables – and that they had all been delivered, you could say that the house was habitable. He had also laid in basic food supplies, which could be augmented when he found out what the men liked to eat or, more to the point, what they disliked. It would be reasonable to expect that after prison fare they would welcome most things, but that had not been his experience previously. Sometimes, it seemed, you grew to like what had become familiar.

The road between Bath and Shipfield was still busy though the morning rush hour had passed its peak. As he drove he thought about what lay in front of him at Number Fifteen, asking himself, and not for the first time, whether he had been mad to choose the kind of life he had been leading for the last three years and would probably now continue to lead for another two at least. There had been no need for it, no way had he been forced into it. It had been a tremendous leap, in sharp contrast to his previous way of life where he had been an account director in a busy, highly successful advertising agency in London's West End. He'd been well paid, had shares in the company, was well liked by his clients whom he regularly lunched, wined and dined. Had he stayed the course he would most likely have been on the board by now. In that world you moved up or you moved out, there was always someone talented and younger pushing up behind you. He'd reached thirty-seven, and at forty, unless you were on the board – in which case you'd be largely responsible for keeping senior clients happy, putting out fires and playing golf – you were over the hill, or deemed to be.

He hadn't wanted that largely hand-holding role. He was a mover and shaker. He liked to make things happen. He'd thought of starting his own business. Even so, had it not been for Helen he would most likely have stayed. She had been engaged as his secretary and within weeks they'd been living together. She'd been the sun, the moon and the stars to him. Six months later they had married, at which point it had been thought better that she shouldn't work directly for him. She had remained with the agency, transferring to an account executive whose main account was with a large travel firm. The perks of that had been foreign travel and more and more often she had accompanied her boss, Charles, until one day, returning from Sri Lanka, bronzed and fit and with a satisfied smile, she had informed Brian that she was moving out of the marital bed and into that of Charles. 'I'm sorry, darling,' she'd said, 'but there it is. We married too young, you and I.'

Too young for her, he'd thought, but not for me. He'd loved her deeply, and continued to do so long after their divorce, which shattered him, was over. Did he still love her, he wondered as he pulled into a petrol station to fill up. He didn't think about her as often. What he did know was that he'd lost his trust in women. If Helen could let him down, who wouldn't. He had felt disillusioned, traumatized. There'd been no way he could stand to watch Helen arrive every morning with Charles, tousled, as though she'd found it difficult to get out of bed, and leave with him every evening to go back to it. He'd begun to dread going in to work every day.

It was while he was wondering what to do that he'd lunched with a senior client who'd told him, in what was no more than a topic of lunchtime conversation, about the Fraser Trust, which was soon to be set up by an old friend of his. A week later, he could never quite understand why, he had been offered the job, at less than half the salary he'd been earning in the agency, but that no longer mattered. It was a plus point that he'd be away from

London and in something entirely new; so was the fact that it would be hard work and totally different, something he'd have to create from the ground up. Had he, he wondered, in his new distrust and wariness of women, perhaps looked forward to it because there would be none involved? It was possible.

Surprisingly, Fraser hadn't baulked at his lack of experience. 'It will be a learning curve for all of us, including the men,' he'd said. 'Common sense, care and compassion, and a good business head! I judge you've got those.'

The next morning he had seen the agency chairman and announced that he was leaving. The chairman expressed his regret, which seemed to be real, and reluctantly reminded him that there was no question of working out a period of notice. He would have to leave as quickly as possible. Clients didn't like working with someone who would soon disappear. It was the usual procedure. He'd been compensated handsomely for his swift departure and he'd sold his shares in the agency. No-one would ever know how much it had hurt him to leave Helen, though in fact it was she who had already left him. Would it have been different, he wondered, if they'd had children? It might have been worse – especially for the kids – but in any case they'd never had time for that. All the same, he would have liked to have kids.

Turning off the main road, driving into Ship-field, he passed the estate agents. He'd thought, when it happened, that he'd call in and tell Mrs Masefield exactly what he thought of her gossiping ways, but it was too late, the harm was done. He'd have preferred the neighbours to have learned the position gradually, it would have been easier for the men than having a wave of hostility waiting for them from the word go. (He was not sanguine enough to think that it might never have leaked out. It always did, by whatever means.)

He drove up North Hill and turned into Mulberry Lane. On the other side of the road Laura O'Brien and Karen Jackson were walking towards North Hill with two small children whom he presumed were Karen's. He waved to them and they waved back. He had told the O'Briens that the men would be arriving today and Laura had wished them luck. He was grateful to have the O'Briens for neighbours, he thought as he let himself into Number Fifteen. They were good news. So was Karen.

He walked around the bedrooms again, checking that everything was as in order as it could be. He had placed a heap of new bedlinen on each bed, intending that the men should make up their own beds, but now he thought, since he had two or three hours before he needed to collect the first arrivals from the station, he would make up the beds himself. It would seem more welcoming. He had not entirely sorted out who would sleep where because for the moment, and until they had partitioned it, two men would have to share the largest bedroom. It might be a little while before they got around to doing the partition so it was important that the two men who shared the room should get on as well as possible together. He had met the men, but only in brief interviews, and he knew their histories, but not enough to know who would settle with whom.

Colin Myers, he thought, will definitely have a room of his own. Myers, at twenty-six the oldest of the four, had served two sentences, both for burglary. In his opinion Myers was the wild card, the one about whom he was least sure. He was not totally convinced that Myers was actually motivated to reform. For this reason, he had already decided that he would not take the risk of having him share a room with any of the younger men. He had no wish for Myers to pass on any of his possibly dodgy ways. On the other hand, Myers would be, in practical matters, the most helpful of the four. In his time in prison he had learned to do joinery and plumbing and, so it was reported, had done well at both. He would be the man who would work full-time putting the house to rights while the others found jobs outside.

So, he was left with David Jessop, Mark Leyton and Fergus O'Connor to sort out, all in their early twenties and with, between the three of them, sentences for burglary, theft from small shops and stores, car theft and damage and arson. Jessop, imprisoned for burglary, car theft and damage, had never done well at school and since leaving school at sixteen had a history of casual, unskilled jobs, punctuated by frequent spells of unemployment. In fact he had been out of work more often than in. He had come from a broken home and had spent much of his early life in care. Poor little devil, Brian thought.

Mark Leyton's background could hardly have been more different. He had had a privileged life, at least in the material sense. His father was well up the ladder in a major oil company and spent most of his time stationed abroad. Mrs Leyton, it seemed, always followed her husband, with the result that Mark was sent off to boarding school at the earliest possible age, joining his parents only for the holidays. He had felt rootless, and still did. Since his father was not yet of retiring age his parents were still abroad and now, because of his behaviour, they had even less time for him.

In a way it was easy, Brian thought, to work out why Mark Leyton had turned to crime. It was not from necessity, it was for excitement, probably to alleviate boredom. On leaving school at eighteen he'd started out by selling insurance. His appearance and his cultivated accent were great assets for a salesman, but he couldn't hold that, or any other job, down for long. His last job – he was now twenty-two – had been as a car salesman. It was in that job that he had worked out the elaborate scam against his employer which had landed him in prison. His employer, however, was several degrees cleverer than Mark was, and totally unforgiving.

Fergus O'Connor had been imprisoned for arson. He had set fire to government property. There seemed no obvious reason except that he was an angry young man with a grudge. He had left his home in County Clare for Liverpool at the age of sixteen and had had a variety of jobs but had been unemployed for eighteen months before he set fire to the Job Centre which he was required to attend regularly. He had done it by night, so that there was no danger to life or limb, but records had gone up in smoke, causing no end of chaos. In spite of the fact that O'Connor had been keen on rehabilitation Brian was not totally sure that he regretted setting fire to the Job Centre, though, oddly, he was the most outgoing of the four men and no longer full of anger.

On the whole, Brian thought as he made up the

last of the beds, which was his own, he was inclined to put Jessop and Leyton in the double room. In spite of the differences in their backgrounds they had in common a difficult childhood. Affluence and poverty met there on the same ground. There was no evidence that O'Connor had suffered as a child. He had left Ireland to see the world, starting with Britain.

By the time Brian had done a few more jobs, including setting his own rather Spartan room to rights, unpacking a few books, his small CD player and other personal possessions – though no photographs – he had to leave for the station to meet Myers and O'Connor. The other two would arrive in the late afternoon.

12

It had been an interesting day for Esther. Fridays were often more eventful than other days, though in fact the previous week had not been without interest, with vans arriving almost daily, delivering furniture and large parcels, the contents of which she could only guess at, and Mr Carson up and down in his car all the time. He seemed a very nice man, he nearly always gave her a friendly wave. And now the young men had arrived, two around lunchtime and two more later in the afternoon. Not knowing when something might happen, she had been at her post almost all day, with hardly time to go into the kitchen and make a cup of tea.

They didn't look like ex-convicts, except that they had close-cropped hair, but then that was the fashion at the moment, wasn't it? Even quite small boys had what Laura said was called 'a Number One'. She didn't like it. She liked a man with a fine head of hair, preferably dark and curly. No, the new arrivals looked exactly like any other men. Had she not known, she would never have taken them for criminals. She had particularly liked the look of one of the last pair to arrive. He was tall and handsome, his fair hair a little longer than that of the others. He carried himself well. He had breeding, that one. She could tell breeding when she saw it. She wished she knew their names but she would have to rely on Laura for that. In fact, for once *she* would have something to tell Laura. Laura had not seen the arrival of the men, either this morning or this afternoon. Esther doubted that anyone other than she had seen that, though she had observed Karen hurrying past on the other side of the road, on her way to pick up the children from school. The way that young woman dashed about, always in a rush!

It would be at least an hour before Laura was home, perhaps longer before Dermot was. She could never think why it took Dermot so long when everyone knew school finished at half-past three. There didn't seem to be anything more going on at Number Fifteen. She'd seen Mr Carson lock the car, and now they were all in behind closed doors. Doing what? She wished she could have been there. For one moment she contemplated whether, with the aid of both her sticks, she could manage it. She could ask for the loan of a cup of sugar. But she knew it wasn't possible. Today was one of her bad days, she could hardly drag herself along the passage and into the kitchen, which she must do soon because what with one thing and another she'd hardly eaten a bite all day, and Laura had warned her that it was when she didn't eat properly that she got confused.

At Number Fifteen Brian and the four men had finished a pot of tea and some toasted buns and were now sitting around talking. Or, rather, Brian was doing the talking. The men seemed subdued.

There were certain matters which had to be said from the beginning, though he had no intention of coming down on them heavily. Now was not the time. They were strangers to one another, in a strange place, and also they were no doubt travel-weary. It was best that they got to know one another a bit before he began to lay down too many conditions. They had seemed reasonably satisfied with their rooms. Even David Jessop and Mark Leyton, on being told they would have to share a room for the time being, had taken it reasonably well. David hadn't looked deliriously happy but it was something all the men had had to get used to in prison.

'There will have to be some house rules,' Brian told them now. 'We'll have as few as possible, but what there are must be kept, for the sake of everyone. Household chores – cooking, cleaning, washing up and so on – will have to be shared. I leave it to you to sort out how you'll do that but the place has to be kept clean, and reasonably tidy. If what you decide between you doesn't work I'll make a rota, which will have to work. No smoking, except in your own rooms, and the two of you who are sharing a room for the present will have to come to your own arrangement about that.'

'I don't smoke,' Mark said.

'Nor me,' David Jessop said.

'Then that's solved,' Brian said. It was too much to hope that everything would be so easy, but it was a good start. 'There are two loos,' he continued. 'In fact there's a third, outside, but it'll need attention. Unfortunately there's only one bathroom. Fitting in a separate shower is an early priority but until then it's a question of consideration.

'Not too much in the way of drinks,' he went on. 'I'm not saying we won't have the odd beer, but no spirits . . .'

'Who can be affording spirits?' Fergus O'Connor asked.

'. . . and definitely no drugs of any kind,' Brian said. 'But you knew that before you came. And it's not my intention to treat you like children, you're not in prison any longer, so when the work's done you're free to go out, though for the moment – we'll see how it goes – curfew is eleven p.m. Which leaves the question of women. As I said, you're free. You'll go into the town, you'll meet women, possibly you'll make friends. I make no rule which says you can't invite women friends to the house, though I expect you to use discretion. What won't be allowed is for them to stay. Anyway, that's enough for now. We'll talk about finances and work and so on tomorrow, but for now there's a meal to be prepared for the five of us and I'm leaving that to you to sort out. There's food in the fridge and in the freezer. I prefer that we eat together most evenings. In the meantime I'm going to put my room to rights. I actually only moved in today myself so I've a few things to do. So I'll leave you to it. If there's anything you need, something I've overlooked, let me know.'

Leaving them was deliberate. They'd want to talk things over, especially they'd want to talk him over. The only thing they had in common so far was that they were new to the set-up and to him. Difficulties would arise along the way, he was sure of that, but it was his policy that the more they could sort out for themselves, or between themselves, the better. He was responsible for them – he took that seriously – but there was no way he was going to be a nanny. The only way this project could, in the end, be counted a success was if the four of them emerged as young men in control of themselves and able to take a proper place in society. He might not say that to them, it sounded pompous, but it was his goal.

'So!' Colin Myers said when Brian had left the room. 'So that's how it's going to be.'

'What do you mean?' David Jessop asked.

'I mean he lays down the rules and we obey them. He cracks the whip, we jump. Might as well be inside!'

'I didn't think that,' David said. 'I thought it sounded all right.'

'Keep things tidy, no smokes, no spirits, form an orderly queue for the bathroom, everybody in bed by eleven? Leave it out!'

'He didn't say that,' David argued. 'For a start he said be in the house by eleven. So where would we want to be after that? We don't know anybody.'

'And not likely to if we're not allowed out!' Colin said. 'I'll bet anything you like he was a school-teacher.'

'You've lost your bet, chum,' Mark Leyton said in his calm, cultured voice. 'He was nothing like that.'

'How do you know?' Colin demanded.

'Because he told me. It just happened he told me at the interview. We all had interviews, didn't we?'

'Except that he didn't favour us all with his life story,' Colin said. 'So come on, what was he if he wasn't a schoolteacher? A probation officer? The filth? A fucking sergeant major in Her Majesty's bloody Army?'

'You're miles off,' Mark said. 'He was pretty high up in a London advertising agency. Earning big money, I'd guess.'

'Oh yeah? You're telling us he left dosh like that to look after a bunch like us? Why? What's the catch? Probably got fired.'

'I'm telling you it's what he did,' Mark said. 'I don't know why. It's not something I could ever imagine doing.'

Fergus O'Connor spoke up. He had kept silent until now. The truth was, he was feeling homesick. He had spent a lot of time feeling homesick in the last year, usually for Ireland though it was three years since he'd left and he'd never been back, but now – and it seemed unbelievable even to him – he felt himself homesick for prison, almost as if in the unchanging routine, the sameness, the security, he had begun to put down roots.

'Is it not as well then that he did so?' he suggested. 'As well for the likes of us, I mean?' He wasn't sure that he was ever going to take to Colin Myers, though he'd be careful never to get on the wrong side of him. Praise be they didn't have to share a room!

That was exactly what David was thinking. He hadn't wanted to share with anyone, he'd looked forward to being on his own, but at least he hadn't drawn Myers. He'd met his sort in prison; always against everything. He'd take care not to tangle with him.

'Let's clear this lot away,' he suggested. 'Then check the fridge and see what's for supper. I'm hungry. We can do our rooms later, can't we?'

'*You* check the fridge,' Colin said. 'Me, I don't like cooking and I intend to do as little as possible!'

211

'Don't worry,' Mark drawled, 'we'll find you some-thing else to do. How are you on scrubbing floors? Anyway, I'll give a hand with the cooking. I quite like it. Who knows, it could be good practice. I might end up being a chef on the telly, earning megabucks.'

'Don't bother to practise on me,' Colin said. 'I don't like fancy stuff.'

Karen, hurrying by when Esther had seen her with the children, had noticed Brian Carson go into the house with two men, though she had been on the other side of the road and not near enough to speak or wave. Now she was at home and the children were having their tea. Scrambled egg today, and since she served broccoli with it she didn't feel the least bit guilty. Actually, she thought, it would be nice to make some small gesture of welcome to the newcomers. Almost everyone at the meeting in the O'Briens' house had been at the worst hostile and at the very best no more than neutral. What an awful start for them if the men should somehow be made to recognize this. She hoped that wouldn't be so, but living next to the Streeters and opposite the Andersons it was a forlorn hope. Esther would be all right. She liked Esther.

But what should she do? What *could* she do? All she could think of was that she could bake a cake. She wasn't too bad at cakes and most men had a sweet tooth, didn't they? So yes, she would do it as soon as the children had gone to bed, and she'd take it along tomorrow. A fruit cake.

'Right, children!' she said. 'When you've eaten every scrap on your plates there's bananas and ice-cream to follow.'

'Pink!' Neil demanded.

'I'd rather have chocolate ice-cream!' Fiona said.

'You can each have your choice,' Karen said. 'I've been shopping today. But you have to eat all your eggs and broccoli first.'

Afterwards, while the children watched television, she cleared the table, put the plates in the dishwasher and sorted out the ingredients for the cake she would make later. Actually, she would make two. It was ages since she'd baked a cake for the children and herself. After the TV programme she read two stories to the children, one Fiona's choice and one Neil's – they could never agree on the same one – and then it was baths and bed. She went upstairs with them, both so clean and sweet-smelling, gave them a big hug and several kisses and tucked them in. Oh, how she loved them!

'You're getting much too big for your cot, Neil,' she said. 'You'll have to have a proper bed very soon.'

She dimmed the light almost to its lowest – neither of them liked the full darkness – put on a quiet music tape, and went back downstairs. They would probably fall asleep before the tape ended.

In the kitchen she turned on the oven, beat flour, butter, sugar, eggs, a pinch or two of cinnamon in the mixer, then switched it off and folded in the fruit – currants, raisins, sultanas, finely cut lemon peel – and spooned it into two cake tins. She should do this more often. It was soothing, though nothing really soothed her troubled mind; nothing at all. It was with her every hour of the day, and when she wakened in the night, this new life inside her.

She questioned herself, reproached herself that she couldn't make up her mind to let it go, though

it wasn't, she would then remind herself, so much
letting it go as having it taken. Not a passive
thing on her part, but a deliberate act. She couldn't
understand, in any rational way, why she felt like
this. She had no religious scruples about it, she had
never had the slightest condemnation for anyone
else who chose to have an abortion. She knew
also, forced herself to think about them, all the
difficulties which would be hers if she had the child.
What would it be like? Perhaps it would be like her
or would it be like this man whose appearance she
could hardly remember? How would she afford it?
How would she be able to go out to work and earn
money? And how could she manage if she didn't?
She had almost gone beyond the stage of thinking
about what people would say. In the end, that was
the least of it. The big truth was that to have this
baby would affect her life for ever. And to choose
not to have it, what would that do?

She recognized that she was asking herself
sensible, practical questions and she knew that she
was normally a sensible, practical person, but now
she could find no answers except to continue
to think that, above and beyond everything, she
couldn't bring herself to have an abortion. Every
day which passed, every day in which the baby was
growing, made it more difficult to do that. Sometimes she felt she would go mad.

She had been to see Dr Craven again but only,
she thought, because she had to talk to someone.
She knew he would say exactly the same things to
her as he had before – and of course he did, only
with more emphasis. But he couldn't make up her
mind for her, he said. Only she could do that. And
if she was going to have a termination then he must

214

remind her that time was slipping by. And if she was going to have the baby she must look after herself; eat well, get enough rest. She knew that everything he said was the truth.

It was the sweet, fragrant smell of the cakes beginning to bake that brought her back to the reality of the moment, that she was sitting at the kitchen table she hadn't even started to clear, that she felt worse than ever and all her thinking had brought her nowhere. She must make up her mind, right now, this moment. And, in fact, having made that simple resolve – just that she would do so: she would make up her mind, stop shilly-shallying, going around in circles, she would make up her mind and accept the consequences of whichever side her decision fell – she did it.

'I will keep the baby.' She said the words out loud. It seemed to give them more validity. 'For better or for worse I will keep the baby!' And then she burst into tears, but some of the tears were tears of relief. She went to the telephone and tapped out Laura's number.

'Can you come?' she asked. 'I need you.'

'Of course I'll come,' Laura said. 'What is it?'

'I can't tell you on the phone. I need to see you. I'm sorry!'

'Don't be sorry,' Laura said. 'It's all right. I'll be round in a few minutes.'

Karen was waiting in the hall when Laura rang the bell.

'Do you mind coming into the kitchen?' she asked. 'If I go anywhere else I'm likely to forget the cakes, burn them.'

'They smell wonderful,' Laura said. 'I didn't know you baked cakes.'

'I don't all that much,' Karen said. 'Not these days. I suddenly had this idea that I'd take a cake to the men at Number Fifteen. To welcome them.' Her voice sounded remarkably steady, in her own ears, but inside she was shaking.

'A nice idea,' Laura said, though there was no way Karen wanted to see her about baking cakes. 'So apart from cakes, what is it?'

'I've made up my mind. I mean about the baby. I've decided what I'll do. I think I want you to tell me I'm not crazy.'

'Try me,' Laura said. 'And shall we sit down?'

'I'm sorry! Of course. Would you like some coffee?'

'No thank you,' Laura said. 'Just to sit down and listen to you. That I'll do willingly, but you know I'm not the best person to give you advice.'

'I told you, I've made up my mind. I suppose I want . . . I don't know . . . reassurance.' Karen sat perfectly still, spoke quietly.

'One thing I can say for certain,' Laura told her, 'is that whatever you've decided, I'll support you. I don't have to approve to support. So what's it to be?'

'I've decided I will have the baby.'

There was a pause before Laura spoke. 'Are you sure?' It was not what she had expected to hear.

'Quite sure,' Karen said. 'It isn't a matter of whether I'm right or wrong. I hardly know that myself. The fact is, I couldn't *ever* cope with the alternative. Some people could, but I couldn't. It's not that I'm nobler than the rest, it's not that at all. It's just that I couldn't.'

'I see,' Laura said. 'And I'm sure you've faced

how hard it's going to be – I mean in the circumstances – three small children and so on.'

'Oh I have! I really have!' Karen said. 'I've spent hours thinking about it.'

'If that's what you want,' Laura said, 'then I hardly need to tell you I'll support you all I can. Not just now, but for as long as you want me to. I promise!'

'Thank you,' Karen said. 'I'm going to be glad of that. I truly am.'

'One thing,' Laura said. 'Can I tell Dermot? I haven't so far, but we don't have secrets.'

'Of course you can,' Karen said. 'He's going to know before long anyway. You can tell anyone you like. They'll all have the same question, even if they don't ask it out loud. "Who's the father?" '

'To which we don't have to give an answer,' Laura said. 'My reply will be "I don't know. He doesn't live around here." Or, in fact, whatever you want me to say.'

'Right at this moment,' Karen said, 'and compared to everything else, it doesn't loom large.'

Next day, being Saturday, there was neither school nor work, about which Karen was relieved. She had slept little on Friday night, even though part of her mind was more settled, and on getting up she had been thoroughly sick. The children had both wakened early, bright as buttons, rushing into her bedroom, climbing on the bed after she had crawled back between the sheets hoping for an extra hour in which to recover herself.

'It's Saturday!' Fiona announced. 'I know it's Saturday but Neil doesn't because he doesn't know the days of the week!'

'I do!' Neil protested. 'Tuesday, Sunday, Friday . . .'

'It doesn't go like that, silly!' Fiona was all scorn. 'Tuesday, Sunday, Friday!'

'How do you know it's Saturday?' Karen asked Fiona.

'Because it's pocket money day. I knew when I woke up. I always do. Can we go to the shops?'

'Later,' Karen promised. 'After breakfast we're going along the road to take one of the cakes I baked to some nice young men.'

'Why?' Fiona demanded. 'Why are we giving *them* the cake?'

'To make them happy. I did one for us, to make us happy.' The cakes had turned out well, she was pleased with them.

'If we had both cakes we'd be two times as happy,' Fiona said.

'Twice,' Karen corrected automatically. 'And we're not going to keep both. That's greedy!'

An hour or so later, after a breakfast she couldn't face because she'd been sick again, she said, 'We'll put on our coats and go.'

'To the shops?' Fiona asked.

'After we've taken the cake,' Karen promised. She put Neil in the buggy and they set off.

Esther, at her window with her mid-morning cup of coffee and biscuit to hand, watched Karen and the children as they came up the path to Number Fifteen. Now why would they be calling there? She couldn't imagine what they could possibly want. Karen was looking under the weather – pale-faced, dark rings around her eyes, not at all her usual pretty self.

*   *   *

Brian, who had been in his room when he heard the bell, ran down the stairs and answered the door, and tried not to show his surprise at seeing Karen standing there. She thrust a tin box at him.

'A fruit cake for the men,' she explained. 'Just to say welcome.' She felt foolish. What would they think?

'How very nice of you!' Brian said quickly. 'What a kind thought.'

'It's nothing really,' Karen said. 'I happened to be making one for us. I hope fruit cake's all right.'

'Wonderful,' Brian said. 'Just the job. Why don't you come in and meet everyone?'

'Oh, I couldn't!' Karen said. 'I've got the children with me. I couldn't leave them, you see.'

'I can see you've got the children with you,' Brian said kindly. 'I wasn't thinking of you leaving them on the doorstep. Do come in, all of you. It would be nice for the chaps to meet a neighbour.' It wasn't something which was likely to happen too often, he thought, at least not many neighbours would bring a cake.

'Well, if you're sure,' Karen said. 'I didn't expect . . .'

'Nor did I,' Brian said. 'It's a pleasant surprise.'

He helped her over the top step with the buggy. Fiona, needing no second invitation, marched into the hall. 'Lift me out! Lift me out!' Neil cried.

'May I?' Karen asked. 'He hates his buggy.'

'Of course,' Brian said.

He went with the three of them into the living room.

'A neighbour, Karen Jackson,' he said to the men. 'She brought a cake to welcome us. A home-made fruit cake. Isn't that nice? And this is Fiona, and this is Neil. They live at Number Six, the other side of the road, nearer to North Hill.'

There was a moment's awkward pause and Mark Leyton rose to his feet.

'Oh, please,' Karen said, 'I didn't want to interrupt you. I'm not staying.'

Mark held out his hand.

'Mark Leyton,' he said. 'Nice to meet you.'

He introduced the others. With varying degrees of awkwardness they shook hands. They were out of touch with women, Brian thought, and it showed – except for Leyton, to whom these kind of manners would always come as second nature.

'Please sit down for a minute, Karen,' Brian said. 'Would you like a cup of coffee? It won't take a jiffy.'

'No thank you,' Karen said. 'We're on our way to the shops.' She paused, wondering what to say next, wishing one of the men would speak. 'Did you have a good journey?' she asked in the end. 'Or I should say did you all have good journeys? I suppose you all came from different places.'

As conversation went, she realized, it wasn't brilliant, but it managed to break the ice so that for the next fifteen minutes they talked amicably about nothing or, rather, Mark Leyton and Brian kept the ball in the air while the others contributed an occasional remark, though it was Fergus who found some chocolate in his pocket and shared it between the children. In the end Karen stood up. 'We'll have to be going,' she said. Brian saw them to the door and walked down the path with them. As they reached the gate Gary Anderson came along the road with Bruno on the lead. He gave them a curt nod and continued on his way.

'That's a beautiful dog!' Brian called after him.

'Yes,' Anderson shouted back. 'And a fierce one!'

Karen laughed, feeling for a moment suddenly free. 'Now I wonder why he's walking Bruno in this direction?' she said. 'He usually sticks to Upper Mulberry.'

'I guess it's a threat,' Brian said. 'See what could happen if you came my way!'

'Actually,' Karen said, 'Bruno's a honey. I've met him with Lisa occasionally. You'd be safer with Bruno than with Titus!'

Brian watched Karen and the children as they walked away towards North Hill, and then went in to join the men in the living room.

'A very nice lady,' Mark said.

'A corker!' Fergus said.

'She's very pretty,' David contributed. 'She reminds me a bit of my Sandra, my fiancée. I told you, we got engaged when she came to see me in prison. She brought the ring with her. I would have gone straight back to her when I came out but she was all for me coming here. She made it part of the deal.' He looked at Brian. 'Will she be able to visit me here? She did in prison.'

'I don't see why not,' Brian assured him. 'In a few weeks' time. But as you know it will have to be a day visit, or if she wants to come overnight we'll have to find somewhere else for her to stay. That shouldn't be impossible.'

'She lives in Croydon,' David said. 'It could just be a day visit.'

'All right for some!' Colin said.

'Are you engaged?' Brian queried. 'Do you have a partner or a regular girlfriend?' He knew he hadn't.

'No,' Colin said. 'As you know, I have an ex-wife. She'd be the last person I'd want a visit from.'

'Then the problem doesn't arise,' Brian said.

'It might,' Colin said. 'I suppose we're not barred from speaking to the opposite sex?'

'I've told you you're not,' Brian said dismissively. 'I'm going into the town. If you've decided what we're having for supper today and tomorrow, I'll do the shopping.'

'What's wrong with takeaways?' Colin said. 'We could have takeaways.'

'The cost is wrong,' Brian said. 'We can't afford them, except occasionally. Anyway, when you make the cooking rota you can count me in. I'm not averse to cooking.'

'Will I be putting the cake away?' Fergus asked. 'Or shall we have a bite now?'

'Do you reckon we'll get cakes from anyone else?' David asked.

'Get real!' Colin said. 'Who do you think welcomes four blokes like us?'

'Well, Karen did,' David said defensively.

'I have to agree with Colin,' Brian said. 'Karen is probably a one-off. I don't think the rest of the street is going to hang out the bunting, hire a brass band.'

'Are you saying that the people around here know about us?' Mark asked. 'If so, how come? Who told them?' He looked accusingly at Brian.

'I didn't,' Brian said. 'But I told an estate agent because it seemed necessary, and she blabbed.'

'Stupid cow!' Colin said.

'I agree,' Brian said. 'It wasn't something I expected.'

'So who did she tell?' Mark demanded.

'Her hairdresser, who happens to live in Mulberry Lane – though the estate agent didn't know that – and she announced it in the pub.'

'And there were objections?' Mark persisted.

'From some,' Brian said. 'Dermot O'Brien, who lives across the road, called a meeting to discuss it. He invited me to put my side of it, which was a good thing to be able to do.'

'So we're already branded?' Colin said.

'By some,' Brian admitted. 'Certainly not by everyone, as you've just seen for yourselves. Some people are afraid. It's down to us to prove they needn't be, that their fears are groundless. Actually, it was bound to come out. In my experience it always does.'

'So I suppose we're barred from the pub?' Colin said.

'As a matter of fact, you're not,' Brian said. 'I've got to know the landlord. He's completely neutral. You'll be just as welcome there as anyone else as long as you don't cause trouble, which he doesn't expect and nor do I.'

'So are you going to tell us who the enemies are?' Mark asked.

Brian shook his head.

'No, I'm not! It might all come to nothing, people might change their minds, so no point in anticipating difficulties. On the other hand, when it comes to finding jobs for at least three of you – which I'm in the process of doing – I'm obliged to tell any prospective employer. I can't give a false reference – but that will be confidential to him, or her. Once again, the rest will be up to you. Unfortunately you haven't paid the price once you're out of prison, there's more to be paid. I wish that weren't so, but it is.'

'It's a bugger!' Colin said. 'What's more, it's what lands you back inside.'

'No it's not,' Brian contradicted him. 'It makes it more difficult to keep straight, I'll agree that, but it's up to you in the end. Anyway, let's not assume that there'll be any trouble. It might be no more than hot air.' He couldn't totally believe that. By the looks on the faces of the men he wasn't sure that they believed it either.

Esther moved away from the window. She had to go to the toilet. If she had stayed in her place just five minutes longer she would have observed something which would have been very useful to know. She would have observed someone hurry up the path at Number Fifteen, push something through the letter box, then rush away.

13

Walking into the hall, to go up to his room, David saw an envelope lying on the mat. He picked it up – a squarish white envelope, sealed, no stamp or postmark on it and not addressed to anyone – and took it in to Brian.

'Thanks!' Brian said, opening the envelope, taking out the single, folded sheet of paper.

Cold, fierce anger swept over him as he read the message.

WE DON'T WANT YOU HERE! WE DON'T
WANT CRIMINALS IN MULBERRY LANE!
GET OUT QUICK OR WE'LL DRIVE YOU
OUT!!
DON'T THINK YOU'VE HEARD THE LAST
OF IT,
THIS IS JUST THE BEGINNING!

Naturally, there was no signature. Crayons in red, blue, green and purple had been used to write the words in block capitals, the letters leaning at all angles so as to disguise the hand. With a blank face, Brian calmly refolded the sheet, replaced it in the envelope and put it in his pocket. He would have liked to tear it into shreds and, in the absence of an all-consuming open fire, throw the fragments into the waste bin but he was determined not to show any emotion. From the first phrase he read he'd known that this was something he wouldn't on any account show the men. In any case, though his anger made him want to destroy it, caution told him not to. It was evidence – though again common sense told him that the best thing was not to pursue the matter, but to ignore it. Not easy!

'Party political drivel!' he said dismissively. 'They come at you all the time.'

Even so, he wouldn't dismiss it entirely. He was too angry. He'd try all he could to find the perpetrator and put a stop to it before it got worse and the men became involved. His first thought on that was to go across and have a word with Dermot, see if he could throw any light on it. Dermot was safe enough, he couldn't possibly be the perpetrator.

'I'm just going across to see Dermot O'Brien,' he said casually. 'Shouldn't be more than half an hour at the most.'

'So in the meantime are we allowed out?' Colin demanded.

'Sure!' Brian said easily. 'By the way, I'd thought we could all go along to the pub together this evening.'

He hadn't thought any such thing, but now it suddenly seemed a good thing to do. It was possible – perhaps highly likely – that the writer of the letter would be in the pub. Even without identifying him it would be no bad idea to show him that his threats – he was assuming, for no real reason, that the writer was a 'he' – were not intimidating anyone, in fact were being ignored.

'Great!' Fergus said.

'It would make a change,' David said.

Mark nodded agreement. Colin said nothing, but Brian reckoned he would probably wait and go with them if only out of curiosity. If the man decided to take off on his own, Brian thought, then so be it. He hoped he wouldn't do anything to bring trouble but, as he'd told the men, they were no longer prisoners.

He looked up and down the road as he left the house. There was no-one in sight, though if there had been it wouldn't have meant much. It could have been an hour ago that the letter had been delivered, and it must have been after Karen left or he'd have seen it. Certainly whoever had put it through the door wouldn't have hung around.

Laura and Dermot welcomed him.

'How's everything going?' Laura asked. 'Would you like some coffee?'

'No thank you. I'm not staying long. As to how things are going, I'd have said fine until fifteen minutes ago.' He brought the letter out of his pocket and handed it to Dermot. 'Which was when I received this!'

Dermot read it, then handed it to Laura.

'Not nice!' he said. 'Not nice at all. Have the men seen it?'

'No,' Brian said. 'And I don't intend to let them. But if it happens again, if it happens frequently I can't imagine they won't find out. They're not stupid. By the way, please keep this to yourselves. I don't want it spread around.'

'You don't have a clue who could have written it?' Dermot asked.

'How could I have? The only people I know are

the people I met here last week, plus the landlord at the Green Man and Mr Potter, the iron-monger. Oh, and the estate agent, but she doesn't live locally.'

'You're right,' Dermot agreed. 'How could you know? It was a silly question.'

'In any case,' Laura said to him, 'it doesn't have to be someone Brian's met. It's fairly sure word's got around. The situation could be known to lots of people we wouldn't even think of, or don't even know. Don't you think you should go straight to the police?'

'No,' Brian said. 'The police would want to question the men. I'd like to keep it from them if I possibly can. And I don't quite agree that it could be just anyone, I reckon it must be someone close by. For a start, there's the reference to Mulberry Lane. Who would care about Mulberry Lane if they didn't live here?'

'Oh, anyone in the near neighbourhood,' Dermot said. 'Fear and prejudice – which is what this is all about – spread like a virus.' He studied the note again, looking for a clue.

'I did wonder if it could have been a child's trick,' Brian said. 'Say an older child.'

'Could be,' Dermot acknowledged. 'Not that I know of one.'

In his time he had seen missives like this written by the children in school. A couple of years ago there had been a spate of them, though the guilty person had proved to be not a child but a temporary cleaner with a grudge.

'Somehow,' he added, 'I don't think it is. Anyway, some people stay childish all their lives. They play childish tricks.'

'So what *are* you going to do?' Laura asked.

'I'm not sure,' Brian admitted. 'That's why I thought I'd talk to you. I know I could go to the police, they'd have a better chance of finding out than I have, but I won't yet. I don't want to blow it up into something bigger than it is. I'd dearly like to work out who it was and find a way to stop him – or her.'

'It would be a start to think of who it wasn't,' Dermot suggested. 'We could go through the people who were here at the meeting and eliminate some of them.'

'For a start we can rule out Esther,' Laura said. 'Physically she couldn't do it, nor would she get anyone to do it on her behalf. She was for you, not against. She was looking forward to a bit of excitement. And Karen . . .'

'We can rule out Karen,' Brian said. 'She'd be the last person. She brought us a cake to welcome us. She'd baked it specially.'

'Well, that *was* nice,' Laura said.

'Yes! She came in and met the men. They liked her.'

'Nigel Simpson was at the meeting,' Dermot said. 'Though I can't see Nigel – I mean, he might not approve, he's conventional, but he's too straight – I can't imagine Nigel doing this messy letter. He's too pernickety. Then there's Stuart . . .'

'. . . Stuart?' Brian queried.

'The less-than-pleasant student from next door. He's an unknown quantity, he hasn't been here long, but I don't think he'd make the effort.'

'And the Andersons,' Laura said. 'Well, not Lisa, but he's not a nice man.'

'He was certainly dead against the idea,' Brian

229

said, 'but I somehow feel he'd come straight out with it, not send anonymous letters, though I don't know him, do I?'

'That was my impression,' Dermot agreed. One by one they went through who had been at the meeting, but without reaching any conclusion. 'So what are you going to do in the meantime?' Dermot asked.

Brian shrugged. 'I'm going to brazen it out, show whoever it is he can't touch us, though in fact that's not true. He can make things quite nasty for the men. Anyway, I'm still determined not to hide them away so I'm going to take all of them along to the pub this evening, let everyone who's there take a good look at them. If the men can make a good impression it will help them, and of course they're aware of that even without knowing about the letter.'

'We'll come along,' Dermot said. 'If we keep our eyes and ears open we might learn something. Who knows?'

It being Saturday evening, and by now raining steadily, the Green Man was reasonably busy. There was also a darts match in progress between the Green Man and its rivals from the Haymakers further down North Hill, a competition of local importance. Brian went to the bar with the men – Colin had decided to come – and introduced them to Jim Pullman before he ordered the first drinks.

'So what will you have?' Brian asked them.

With the exception of Fergus they chose bitter, and Brian ordered half-pints. 'I would like a Guinness,' Fergus said. 'Though I know 'twill be nothing like it is in Ireland because you don't have the waters of the Liffey.'

'Sorry about that, son!' Jim Pullman said.

They took their drinks to a table from which they could watch the darts match. It was there that, ten minutes later and not appearing as if it had been prearranged, Dermot and Laura joined them.

'Are you settling in?' Laura asked the men.

'It's early days,' Mark said politely. The others nodded in agreement with Mark, but said nothing. Brian reckoned they were wary of answering any questions, harmless or otherwise. Without uttering a syllable, Colin Myers gave off an air of hostility strong enough to trouble Brian. Given the circumstances, such hostility could easily erupt into trouble for all of them. Perhaps sheer, hard physical work might be the best thing to contain him.

He had been unsure whether he should take on Colin Myers and he wondered now if he had made a mistake in doing so. The men were four very different characters, which was to be expected, but the three of them seemed, so far, to gel, while Myers stood out like a sore thumb. He wondered why he had opted for rehabilitation. Possibly the real reason, though it was not one which Myers had voiced, was that should he offend for burglary again his sentence would be at least three years. Perhaps he recognized in himself the inability to go straight without help. If that was so, then there was hope, but the man's demeanour so far said that he was already regretting his decision.

'As Mark says, it's early days. There's a lot to do in the house,' Brian said to the O'Briens. 'I doubt if anything's been touched for years.'

'Oh, I can confirm that!' Laura said. 'Mrs Harper

was quite old, almost ninety. She couldn't get out, nor could she move around much in the house. She had home helps from time to time but it never seemed to work. She didn't get on with them.'

'I wouldn't have thought any daughter would have wanted her mother to live in such conditions,' Brian said.

'Bettina is a law unto herself,' Laura told him.

'Anyway, the sooner we set it to rights the better,' Brian remarked. 'We've had the weekend to settle in. We shall make a start first thing Monday morning.'

'In the meantime,' Dermot offered, 'what about another drink?'

'Thank you,' Brian said. 'After that we must be off.'

Not even Colin raised any objection to the prospect of leaving early. Prison regime had made them used to early nights and no doubt they were tired, as he was himself. On Monday he had to get in touch again with three potential employers who had said they would at least interview the men. The jobs would be temporary and unskilled but it would be a start. Colin would be occupied in the house and it was as well that he'd been agreeable to that role because Brian doubted his ability, at this stage, to get on with an employer or with work-mates.

As Dermot returned from the bar with a tray of drinks, Nigel Simpson walked in at the door accompanied by Titus who, recognizing Laura as one of his favourite humans, ran towards her. Nigel followed him.

'I'd forgotten the darts match,' he said. 'I should have been here sooner.'

'There's still a way to go,' Laura said. 'So far, we're winning.'

Dermot put down the tray of drinks on the table and introduced Nigel to the four men. Nigel nodded to them but made no attempt to shake hands, not even with Mark, who rose to his feet on being introduced.

'Let me get you a drink, Nigel,' Dermot said. 'Come and join us!'

'Thanks,' Nigel said. 'I won't, actually. You seem a bit crowded.'

'As you wish,' Dermot said.

Nigel walked away and found a seat closer to the dartboard. Dermot and Laura looked at each other but nothing was said for a few seconds until Dermot spoke.

'Do any of you play darts?' he asked the men.

'I do,' David said. 'I like a game.'

'I guess there's somebody playing most nights,' Dermot said. 'You should come along and join them.'

David nodded. 'Maybe I will. They're pretty good players, though.'

And, Brian thought, I'll buy a dartboard for the house. It would probably pass an hour or two quite agreeably.

A little later he suggested they should leave. 'We have one or two things to sort out,' he told them.

'Me too,' Dermot said. 'I still have some papers to mark. We'll walk along with you.' It was deliberate on his part and Brian gratefully recognized it as such. They were unlikely to meet any neighbours on an unpleasantly wet night, but if they did, then all to the good. They would be making a statement. Jim Pullman called out to them as they left. 'Good night!' he said. 'See you!' No, Brian thought, the letter writer couldn't be Jim Pullman.

They did meet up with neighbours, though not the ones Brian would have chosen to encounter. As they walked along Mulberry Lane – David, Mark and Fergus with Laura, close behind Brian and Dermot with Colin – so from the other end approached Ralph and Michelle Streeter. They met head on at the point where the Streeters were about to turn in at their own gate. Dermot halted.

'Hi, Ralph, Michelle!' he said.

Ralph Streeter, with the briefest nod, took Michelle's elbow and in silence steered her firmly up the path to their own front door, looking neither to left nor right. Dermot stared after them.

'Funny chap, Ralph Streeter,' he said easily. 'You never know where you are with him!'

'They've probably had a row,' Laura said.

It was a fair try on the part of the O'Briens, Brian thought. It didn't deceive him, though he hoped it did the men. Was this going to be the pattern, rather than the pleasant evening they'd had in the pub? Oh well, somehow they'd ride it out. And then his mind went back again to the letter.

Back in the house, Fergus said, 'Shall I make some coffee, or a pot of tea?'

'Is there a video we can watch?' Colin asked. 'I fancy watching a video.'

'No,' Brian said. 'There's the TV and we do have a recorder – given – but so far no videos to go with it. Those you'll have to rent out of your allowance, I suppose between you.'

'What allowance?' Colin demanded.

Brian took a deep breath. One day he might just lose his cool with Myers.

'I told you all that when you had your interviews,' Brian reminded him. 'You know you'll all be paid a small amount of money each week which is yours to do with as you like. You yourself won't actually be earning a wage but you'll be doing valuable work in the house – and a great deal of the time I'll be doing that with you. The others will have to take jobs in the town, and whatever they earn will go into the kitty from which we'll run the house – food, fuel and the rest. You'll each be given exactly the same allowance for pocket money and after that whatever's left over each week will be put into separate accounts in your names so that you'll have something to take with you when you leave. But I've explained all this to you before! So what are you questioning?'

'I don't like the idea that I won't be earning a wage and the others will,' Colin protested.

'But you will be,' Brian said, 'though in a different way.'

He knew what it was. Myers didn't like the thought of not getting his hands on a week's wages before handing the money over. And he is the one I wouldn't trust to hand it all over, Brian thought.

'Anyway,' he said, 'this is a fruitless conversation. You knew the rules. There aren't all that many but that's one of them, and it will be kept. Financially you'll all be treated the same and in the end you won't leave here empty-handed.'

'I'd rather earn my own money and do my own saving,' Colin said sullenly.

'That's not possible,' Brian said firmly. 'For the time being we're a small community. We all have to fit in. If you want to save from your weekly allowance that's up to you. If you don't like the way things are you're free to leave. I can get someone to take your place.'

He was calling Colin's bluff though he didn't think for a moment that the man would leave, he had too much to lose.

'I still think . . .' Colin began.

'Oh, put a sock in it!' Mark interrupted. 'You're being exceedingly boring!'

'I would say you're the lucky one,' Fergus said. 'You don't have to go out and get a job – which heaven knows won't be easy!'

'On the subject of jobs,' Brian said, 'I've been around the town in the last week or two trying to sort something out and I've put out some feelers, but nothing so far. We'll need to talk it over, but not tonight.'

On a Tuesday morning, two or three weeks later, it was almost half-past eleven when Esther finally took up her place at the window. She had been delayed on account of having run out of clean knickers and had had to set to and wash her smalls and a few other bits and pieces – a job she hated. She no longer washed the big stuff, sheets and towels. They went to the laundry once a fortnight, though their charges were daylight robbery.

Earlier on, hearing a car start, she had taken a quick look and had glimpsed Mr Carson setting off, two of the men in the car with him, and a little later a third one left. Eventually, Brian had returned alone. She wondered what that was about. But now there was nothing. You couldn't call a couple of delivery vans and a car or two passing each other happenings. She was looking for people.

Glamour Boy's little purple car was back in its

236

usual place and so was Imogen's. That awful-looking boyfriend of Jennifer's was not, at the moment, on the scene – and good riddance to him! He wasn't suitable for a nice girl like Jennifer, the daughter, it seemed, of titled parents. Anyway, since their cars were there Glamour Boy and Imogen must be at home – they never walked anywhere – but she could see no sign of movement in the house. In any case surely they should be in the university? These students came and went as they pleased.

She turned her head a little to the right – and was rewarded. There, on the horizon, was Karen Jackson, approaching. What was she doing in the street at this hour of the day? She should be at work in the toffee factory. It couldn't be anything wrong with the children. If that were so then they'd either be with her or she'd be at home with them, but she was quite alone and moreover walking rather slowly, she who rushed everywhere. Then suddenly she stopped short, right outside Number Twelve. Her face contorted as if with pain and both her hands went around and clutched at her back. Then she staggered another foot or two before leaning on the first object to hand, which was the little purple car.

Immediately, Esther remembered that Karen was pregnant, though not far gone and it didn't show. She would never have known if Laura hadn't told her, which she had done because Esther showed such concern about having seen Karen looking unwell when she had visited Number Fifteen with the children.

It had been on the following day that Esther had spoken, on the Sunday, when Laura had called to see if she was ready for church.

'She looked quite ill! She looked as though she needed looking after, cosseting,' she'd said. 'I felt quite worried for her.'

'We need to worry about her,' Laura had said. 'Karen is pregnant.'

'Pregnant?'

It was strange, Laura told Dermot later in the day, that all Esther had shown was surprise, not shock. Perhaps when you get so old you cease being shocked, Dermot had said.

'She never once said either then or later, "Who was it? Why?"' Laura said. 'She just said, "Poor, poor girl!" and then went quiet. You must have noticed when you came across, and for the rest of the morning, she never said a word, not about anything.' And he had noticed.

When they'd taken Esther back home and Laura had seen her in, Esther said, 'Tell Karen I offered the Mass for her. I'll pray to Our Lady. In some ways she went through the same thing, didn't she? And she needn't worry about me knowing. I know when to speak and when to keep quiet, though you mightn't think it.'

Clearly, Esther thought now, watching keenly, the girl was in trouble. She might just be feeling sick from the toffee, in which case she had better not be sick over the purple car! And then memories came rushing back, memories from all those years ago and now as clear as if it had happened yesterday. She knew what it was. She knew exactly what was happening!

She rapped fiercely on the window, even using her stick, trying to attract someone's attention. Though there was no-one in the street to attract she hoped and prayed that one of the students would hear her. Her efforts were rewarded – or possibly not; it might have been that Imogen had actually not heard a thing but was in any case about to leave home at that very moment. She saw Karen immediately, and while Esther watched anxiously she went to her aid, put her arm around Karen and led her into Number Twelve, closing the door behind them.

Esther's hand stretched out towards the binoculars, always within easy reach. Was this a legitimate moment to use them? After all, it looked like an emergency, and she didn't want to know from curiosity, she was concerned. Then she withdrew her hand. No, definitely not. How could she know what Karen would say to Imogen? She couldn't intrude, it wouldn't be fitting. Nor, damn it to hell, could she do anything useful at all. She was a helpless old woman, and seldom had she felt it as keenly as now.

'Easy does it!' Imogen said in her soothing voice as she guided Karen into the house and towards an easy chair.

Stuart, who had been sitting on the sofa, reading the newspaper, sprang to his feet as they came into the room – not from an excess of good manners but because he was startled.

'What the—' he began.

'This is Karen Jackson,' Imogen said. 'You might remember her. She was at the meeting at the O'Briens'. She lives just along the road and she isn't too well. I thought she should come in and sit down for a minute.' She turned to Karen. 'Did it come on suddenly?' she asked. 'Would you like a hot drink or something? Shall I call the ambulance?'

Karen shook her head. 'No, no! Please don't. The pain's eased off a bit now. It was very sudden, in my back. I felt . . . strange. I still do.' She also felt unaccountably nervous. 'I can't describe it. Perhaps it's because I'm pregnant?' The words were out, not that it mattered at this moment.

'My God!' Stuart said.

Karen gave him a cold look.

'It's quite all right,' she said. 'I'm only twelve weeks gone. I'm not going to have the baby in your front room!'

'Good! I mean . . . of course not! Well, if you'll excuse me, I'd better be going. I have a lecture. I'll leave you in Imogen's capable hands.'

'Oh no you won't!' Imogen said. 'You're not leaving just yet. I'm going to phone Laura and ask her what we should do. It might well involve you!' She knew practically nothing about pregnancy except she did know you could have a miscarriage and that the most likely time was three months. She gave no thought at all as to why Karen was pregnant. She hardly knew her. She'd seen her walking past with the children but had never spoken to her until the meeting, and then only briefly. And now she had to sort out what to do. She hoped that what ailed Karen might be no more than a simple back strain, or perhaps one of those viruses which went around all the time.

'I'm afraid I'd be of no earthly use to you,' Stuart said.

'You can be of use right away,' Imogen told him. 'Look in the book and find the number of the private hospital where Laura works.'

He took the telephone directory from the shelf – one tended to do what Imogen commanded –

240

found the number and called it out to her. As Imogen picked up the telephone Karen gave a sudden sharp gasp of pain and clutched at her abdomen.

Stuart moved swiftly to the door. 'I'll be in my room,' he said. 'Things to do!'

Imogen was already tapping out the number.

'Don't you dare leave this house until I say you can!' she called out.

'I'm ever so sorry!' Karen said. 'It startled me.' She looked grey. 'Perhaps I should try to get home?' She didn't know how she would manage it. She would be so glad to see Laura. Laura would take over everything.

'Don't worry!' Imogen said. 'You stay right where you are for the moment! You'll be all right. Laura will know what to do.' She spoke into the phone. 'May I speak to Mrs Laura O'Brien,' she said. 'I think she works in reception. It's very urgent!'

She was put through quickly.

'Laura, it's Imogen!'

'Imogen?'

Why in the world would Imogen be ringing her? And at work. It must be something to do with the house. In a split second every possible disaster flashed through Laura's mind and out again. There was a fire! Smoke was pouring out of the windows! There was a flood! Taps had been left on and water was flowing out into the street. A car had crashed into the front wall, someone had been injured!

'Tell me what's happened!' she cried.

'It's Karen,' Imogen said. 'Karen Jackson. You know.'

'Of course I know Karen,' Laura said. 'What is it?'

'She's here. She was sent home from work and

then she had a bad turn in the street, just as I was leaving the house. So I brought her in. The thing is . . . she's pregnant.'

'I know,' Laura said.

'Twelve weeks. That's why I'm ringing you. I want to know what to do.'

'Let me speak to her,' Laura said.

Imogen handed the phone to Karen.

'What happened?' Laura asked. 'Tell me exactly, Karen.'

She listened carefully while Karen spoke.

'Are you bleeding?' she asked.

'I'm not sure,' Karen said. 'I don't think so but I'm not sure. I feel frightened! Oh Laura!'

'Try not to worry,' Laura said. 'Let me talk to Imogen again.'

'Oh Laura, do come!' Karen begged. 'Please do come!'

'Yes, of course! But please let me speak to Imogen,' Laura insisted.

Reluctantly, Karen handed over the phone. 'Please persuade her to come!' she said.

'Am I really needed?' Laura asked Imogen. 'It's difficult. We're busy here.'

'How can I tell?' Imogen asked. 'I'm so ignorant.' If only Grace were here, she thought. Grace knew all about cows calving and sheep having lambs. Grace would know exactly what to do. 'What's more . . .' she spoke to Laura in a whisper, turning her back on Karen, 'she knows I'm ignorant. That's why she's panicking, and I don't think that's going to do her any good.'

'It certainly isn't,' Laura agreed. 'Very well, tell her I'll come. I'll be there as soon as I can and in the meantime she's to keep as calm as possible and

242

try to relax. Give her a warm drink and tell her she's to lie on the sofa with her feet up.'

'Is she coming?' Karen said. 'Oh, please say she is!'

'She's coming,' Imogen said. 'She shouldn't be long.'

14

Karen did as she was told and lay on the sofa. What she desperately wanted was to be in her own home, but it was impossible, and in any case Laura would come here. She looked at her watch, starting to count the minutes until Laura would arrive. The hospital wasn't all that far away; say twenty minutes' brisk walk? If she had left at once she might be nearly there.

'Are you reasonably comfortable?' Imogen asked. 'Would you like another cushion? Would you like a hot-water bottle for your back? I don't think I should offer you any aspirins or anything, do you?'

'I don't know,' Karen said. 'A hot-water bottle would be lovely. I'm sorry to be such a nuisance.'

'You're not,' Imogen assured her. 'Just try to relax.' She opened the door and called up the stairs.

'Stuart, please fill my hot-water bottle! It's in the bathroom. The one with the black-and-white doggy cover.'

'Hell!' Stuart said. 'I'm in the middle of—'

'Do it at once, please!' Imogen ordered.

He thundered down the stairs and went into the kitchen, appearing a little later with the hot-water bottle but standing in the doorway, waiting for Imogen to take it from him. No way was he going to venture into Karen's presence.

The bottle was moulded exactly like a small black-and-white terrier, its head hard and solid, with gleaming plastic amber eyes, and was therefore not the most comfortable shape to fit into Karen's back. Whichever way she positioned it the head dug into her flesh, collided with her bones.

'I'm sorry!' Imogen said. 'He's rather sweet, but I suppose he's designed to put one's feet on.' In any case she wasn't sure that a hot-water bottle, even of the conventional shape, was the right remedy. She felt so ignorant, so helpless. If only Laura would come!

If only Laura would come was also Karen's all-pervading thought. She looked at her watch yet again.

'I'm sure she won't be much longer now,' Imogen said, observing her.

Laura arrived within the next ten minutes, earlier than anyone could have hoped for, since a colleague had given her a lift. Before she could ring the bell the door opened to let out a fleeing Stuart.

'Hi, Laura!' he said, rushing past her. He had never thought he would be pleased to see Laura Busybody O'Brien on the doorstep. 'Go right in!' In a flash he was in his car, driving away.

It was at the moment when Laura walked into the room that Karen felt that, just possibly, she was bleeding. She was not certain, but there was this slight feeling in her body that it was so, which made Laura's appearance more than ever like that of an angel from heaven. Laura would know exactly what to do. Tears spilled over and ran down Karen's face at the sight of her.

'Oh Laura!' she cried. 'Oh Laura, I'm so pleased to see you! What am I going to do?'

'First of all,' Laura said, handing her a tissue, 'we're going to get you home. No! First of all, while Imogen's getting her car out I'm going to ring Dr Craven and ask him to go to your house, pronto! When I've done that the two of us will take you home.'

She picked up the phone, tapped out the number, spoke to the receptionist. 'I see,' she said presently. 'Well then, as soon as he can. Tell him it's urgent. Thank you!'

'He's in the middle of a full surgery,' she informed the others. 'He'll come as soon as he can. In the meantime, Karen, when you get home you're to go to bed and stay there.'

Between them Laura and Imogen helped Karen to the car and Imogen drove slowly and carefully along the road to Number Six. The moment they were through the door Karen said, 'I must go to the bathroom.'

It was as she had suspected. She was bleeding slightly, but unmistakably. Her back ached worse than ever. She came out of the bathroom and told Laura.

'Right!' Laura said. 'Straight to bed! And don't worry. It's early days, everything could be all right!' She didn't entirely believe what she was saying.

'I haven't made the bed,' Karen apologized. 'I was in a rush this morning. I'm afraid everything's in a mess.'

'I'll see to all that,' Imogen said. She was pleased to find something to do.

It was two hours before Dr Craven arrived. Imogen and Laura stayed on, making cups of tea, filling a more suitable hot-water bottle, tidying the house, while Karen lay on her bed under a blanket. Laura rang her hospital. 'It's an emergency here. I can't be sure I'll be back today,' she said. 'I'll have to wait and see.'

Dr Craven's visit was short, his words to the point. He gave Karen an injection and told her in no uncertain terms that unless she wanted to lose the baby she must stay in bed until he gave her permission to do otherwise. A few minutes later Laura saw him to the door.

'Will she be all right?' she asked.

'I don't know,' Dr Craven said. 'It's impossible to be certain at this stage.' He would have judged last time he'd seen her that her greatest wish *was* to lose the child, as long as it occurred naturally. Now her attitude was different. She seemed upset at the thought.

'She'll have to stay right where she is. Who's going to look after her, not to mention the children?'

'I don't know,' Laura confessed. 'I don't think she has many friends around here, and most people go out to work anyway. Her mother lives in Bedford so I suppose we'll get in touch with her. In the meantime, we'll do what we can between us.'

'I'm sure you will,' Dr Craven said. 'I'll pop in tomorrow. Let me know if I'm needed in the meantime.'

'I don't know who'll be here tomorrow,' Laura said, 'but someone will be.'

When she had closed the door on the doctor she went upstairs to Karen, and found her agitated again, crying out as soon as Laura walked into the room.

'The children! How could I only just have thought about the children? What am I going to do? They have to be fetched from school, both of them! And even if they don't go to school tomorrow, how can I stay in bed with them to look after?'

'Don't worry!' Laura said. She seemed to be spending her time urging Karen not to worry. 'We'll sort something out.'

She hadn't the slightest idea what. Karen was right. How could she stay in bed with two small, lively children in the house? Who could come in, or even take them elsewhere to look after them? She herself couldn't be off work after today, and just about everyone she knew around here had jobs to go to. Except, she thought, the Simpsons next door. Nigel and Mary might give a hand, though they were elderly and in any case totally unused to children. Clearly the person to contact was Karen's mother.

'First things first,' she said to Karen. 'One of us will see to picking the children up from school this afternoon, though you'll have to phone both schools and explain, probably send a note. They won't just let the children go with anyone who turns up – quite right too. Then I think you should phone your mother, and ask her to come and look after you for a few days.'

'No! Absolutely not!' Karen was adamant. 'Mum doesn't even know I'm pregnant. I didn't tell her. I knew she'd be horrified.'

'She'll find out in the end,' Laura said. 'She's bound to.'

248

'She will if I have the baby, but the longer I avoid telling her the better. And if I miscarry she need never know.'

'Even if you do miscarry,' Laura said, 'which is by no means certain, it's surely not something you'd want to keep from her?'

'Oh yes it is!' Karen said. 'You don't know my mum. She's a strict Catholic. Oh, I'm sorry if that seems I'm being rude to you. I'm not. You're not a bit like my mother. Actually, she cares more about what the priest says, about what the neighbours think, than she does about me. Anything for the sake of respectability. So as for hearing that I'm pregnant by a man I don't even know . . . !' Her voice trailed off. Her eyes filled with tears again. She thought she had never felt as miserable in her whole life. Everything was against her.

'I'm sorry,' Laura said. 'We'll think of something, somehow.' Privately she thought it would almost certainly in the end have to be Karen's mother, but she would perhaps talk Karen round when she was less distraught. 'For now, I think you'd better start by ringing the school. Perhaps Imogen will go for the children?'

Laura waited while Karen called Fiona's school. Karen spoke nervously, then as she listened, Laura watched the corners of her mouth lift in a slight smile.

'Thank you! Thank you very much!' Karen said. 'That's very kind.' She put the phone down.

'Well, that bit's all right,' she said. 'One of the teachers will bring Fiona home, and what's more, she will also collect Neil. The head teacher thought that was a better arrangement than having them picked up by someone she didn't know. Now I have to call Neil's nursery.'

'A much safer arrangement also from the school's point of view,' Laura agreed. 'Now why don't you try to sleep before it's time for the children to come home? I'll stay, and in the meantime I'll try to sort something out. Karen dear, are you quite sure you wouldn't like to phone your mother?'

'Absolutely!' Karen said.

'Very well. But think about it. If you like, if you change your mind, I'll ring her for you. I'll explain.'

Karen shook her head. 'I won't change my mind.'

I would hate it, Laura thought, if Therese or Frances felt that way about me.

It had been an interesting day so far for Esther. She had watched Karen being helped into the house by Imogen – what a nice girl Imogen was, and so well spoken; she couldn't quite remember where she had met her before, it must have been at Laura's – and then Laura arrive, only to be almost knocked down on the doorstep by Glamour Boy, rushing as if the devil himself was after him. Then Karen had been helped to the car and an hour or two after that she'd seen Dr Craven's car go along the road. A red car, she knew it quite well. And not many minutes ago Karen's children had walked along the road with a young woman she'd never seen before. No doubt when she saw Laura – she hoped she'd pop in this evening with all the news – she'd tell her who that was.

She felt fairly certain about what was taking place. A miscarriage, she was sure of it, and she was truly sorry. It might be almost a lifetime ago but she would never, ever forget how it felt, and not only the pain at the time, which was awful, but the dreadful feeling afterwards, which went on much longer than the pain, went on for months, came back years later, inexplicably, and was worse, far worse. She had felt herself to be truly bereaved, emptied, bereft, and with the certainty that she would never have the chance again, which for her had turned out to be only too true. Perhaps it wouldn't be for Karen, though she would have to find another man, and in any case she had two children already. Why did the chance never come to me again, she asked herself? It was not that there had been no other man to give her a child, simply that she had never conceived.

She had watched Brian from Number Fifteen set off late in the morning with the eldest of the young men – she must get to know their names – and return with loads of wood strapped to his car's roof-rack. He had waved to her when they were unloading it. Later, the others had returned, though separately, not together. The little dark-haired one had been the last to arrive. She rather liked the look of him, he had a chirpy air, though he was not as striking as the fair-haired Adonis.

Mark was the first to arrive back, very pleased with himself – a smile on his face and a jauntiness in his walk – because he had landed the job, which was in the restaurant of the Shipfield Arms where Brian had lunched on the Sunday he had found the estate agent's in Shipfield. Since then he had lunched there two or three times during the period when he was waiting to move into the house and had formed an acquaintanceship of sorts with the manager. It was this which had enabled him to mention the Fraser Trust project and in the end to ask if there was a likelihood of a job for one of the men. All along he had had Mark in mind for this. Mark was educated, well spoken, and cared about his appearance. He was a young man, Brian told the manager, who was likely to get on well with the public and he, though of course no more than the rest of the men, deserved a chance.

'Sure!' the manager had agreed. 'And I do employ one or two men and women who clear and lay the tables, fetch and carry, generally make themselves useful in the restaurant. Not waiters, you understand. They don't take orders or serve. But they need to be intelligent and presentable. If your man fills the bill, and doesn't have sticky fingers, he can come along and we'll take it from there.'

'So I was lucky,' Mark said to Brian. 'And I'll make the most of it. I hope David and Fergus are equally lucky.'

David, arriving back shortly afterwards, had been. He had been offered a job in the shipping department of Venables' toffee factory. It would be largely manual to begin with, they told him, but there was a chance that he might be moved on to the clerical side later. It depended how long he'd be with them.

'It's not well paid,' David apologized.

'Nor is mine,' Mark added. 'Still, they're jobs, aren't they? I reckon we've been first time lucky.'

Fergus had not been lucky. He had applied for a job in the 'While-U-Wait' Tyre Mart, fitting new tyres and retreads to cars. The manager had told Brian a day or two ago that there was a vacancy and that, moreover, the job didn't need much, if any, previous experience except that whoever did it must know the basics about cars, enough to be able to move them around and so on. 'And I do,' Fergus had confirmed to Brian. 'I've been interested in cars since I was a kid. Anyway,' Fergus said, 'I was too late. They'd set someone on two days ago. If it didn't work out the manager said he'd be sure to let me know, but I do not have high hopes.'

'Not to worry,' Brian said. 'It's early days. You *will* find something, and until then you're on benefits and there's plenty you can help with in the house.'

''Tis not the same as bringing in the money,' Fergus objected.

'That's what I say,' Colin Myers interrupted.

'You're both wrong,' Brian told them. 'The work in the house is equally important and it's part of the plan. When everything's finished in the house you can all go out to work – if you're still here, that is. Anyway, on the whole it's been a good day. Who's doing the supper?'

'Colin and I,' Mark said. He didn't like Colin Myers and he was fairly certain Colin didn't like him – didn't like anyone, in fact – but it couldn't be helped, they had to learn to work with each other, change and change about, which meant that at least he wouldn't have to share duties with Colin Myers all the time. He had met his type in prison. Kevin Broome, for example. He was a dead ringer for Myers. At first he had been prepared to like Broome, or at least, since that seemed improbable, to get along with him, but Broome definitely hadn't liked him. He'd made that plain at every opportunity. He disliked him for his education, for the fact that he read different books and liked different music, and most of all because of the way he spoke. Broome was, in addition, a bully and for that reason for the rest of his sentence Mark had given him a wide berth. Now, Colin Myers could easily take the place of Kevin Broome except, Mark thought, I will not allow that to happen. He was no longer in prison. He was a free man – or almost as good as.

This evening he had chosen the menu. Aside from the fact that he was more into cooking than Colin, who had confessed that all he could do was to heat ready-made meals in the microwave, it was his turn to do so. He had decided on tagliatelle with bacon, broccoli and a green pesto sauce, which Colin said was not food at all, there was no substance in it. He would have liked sausages and chips. 'Fine!' Mark told him. 'When it's your turn to choose, you can try that. I like my sausages well done.'

The table was laid, the bacon was on the grill, the broccoli and pasta ready to go into their pans of boiling water, when the doorbell rang.

Brian sprang up to answer it. Laura stood on the step.

'Hello!' she said. 'I'm only going to be a minute. I just wanted to know if you were all OK, if there was anything you wanted?'

'Come in!' Brian said. He went with her into the living room. 'Sit down for a minute. I was just saying we've had a good day today. Mark and David have both found jobs.'

'I'm the fly in the ointment,' Fergus said. 'I've not done so. 'Twas not my lucky day!'

'I'm sorry about that,' Laura said. 'What sort of job are you looking for?'

'Anything at all,' Fergus said, 'except that I'm not all that brilliant in the brain department so I'll not be looking for anything in the way of astrophysics! Something hands-on would suit me best.'

'We had a porter leave last week at the hospital where I work,' Laura said. 'I don't know whether he's been replaced – I don't think so – but I could find out if you like.'

'I would indeed like that!' Fergus said. ''Tis very kind of you. Very kind indeed!'

'I'll ask about it tomorrow,' Laura promised. 'Give me the phone number and I'll ring you right away if there's a vacancy. So what did the rest of you get?'

Mark, who had turned the heat off under the pans and the grill and had come into the room to join the others – there was no point in cooking pasta until they were ready to eat it – told her his news. Colin remained in the kitchen.

'And I got a job in the toffee factory,' David said.

'Venables'?' Laura said. 'That's where Karen works. Poor Karen!' Damn! The last two words had slipped out without thinking.

'Poor Karen?' Brian said. 'Why? What's wrong?'

'Oh, just that she's not at all well. She was sent home sick this morning.'

'I'm sorry to hear that,' Brian said. 'Nothing serious, I hope?'

'Oh, I don't think so,' Laura said. 'But she has to stay in bed for a day or two, which is awkward because of the children. Mary Simpson is there at the moment and I'm going along now.'

'Is there anything we can do?' Brian asked. 'Karen was very kind to us, brought us a delicious cake.'

Laura shook her head. 'I don't think so, but I'll let you know. Anyway, I must fly. I want to look in on Esther.' She was sure Esther would have observed the comings and goings. She'd be longing for news.

'Right!' Brian said. 'While you're there, tell the old lady if there's anything any one of us can do for her, at any time, she's only to ask.'

'That's kind of you,' Laura said. 'I'm sure there'll be something, even if it's only a few minutes of your company now and then. She appreciates that as much as anything, though it's probably what she's given least.'

'Poor Karen!' Esther said, when Laura told her, echoing Brian's words. 'I could tell there was something, in fact I guessed what it was. I sort of recognized it.'

'Recognized?' Laura raised her eyebrows. 'You know about miscarriage, then?'

'Oh yes!' Esther said, nodding her head vigorously. 'From the best possible source. The source nearest to home.'

'You don't mean . . .'

'I do,' Esther said. 'It happened to me, you know.'

'I didn't know,' Laura said. Esther was full of surprises. 'It would have been quite a time ago, of course. Long before I knew you.'

'Not so long that I don't recall every detail,' Esther said sharply. 'People think when you're old you forget everything. Some things you never forget. I might forget your name the very next time I see you, but I won't forget what it's like to lose a child. Because you *are* losing a child, you know, even if it isn't ready to be born it's alive to you. The rest of the world doesn't know that, but you do. Poor girl!'

'It might not happen,' Laura pointed out. 'She might well keep the baby.'

'She might,' Esther conceded. 'And if she does she'll be wondering every day until it's safely delivered whether the child's going to be all right, if you know what I mean, having had this little setback.'

'Oh, I don't think she will.'

Esther gave her a cold look.

'Permit me to know what I'm talking about, even if you don't.'

'Sorry, Esther,' Laura said.

'Of course when it does go well you have the joy of a child,' Esther added. 'That was something I was never privileged to experience. At my age you've experienced most things – well, you have if you've got any guts – but that's an experience which was denied me. I don't know why!'

There was a silence between them, Laura thinking, but does Karen want that experience, in the circumstances? 'I must go!' she said. 'I must get back to Karen. So . . . we'll see what tomorrow brings.'

One of the things which the next day brought was a telephone call from Laura to Number Fifteen. Brian answered the phone.

'Good news so far,' Laura said. 'There *is* a vacancy for a porter and Fergus can come here for an interview at two o'clock this afternoon. We're towards the top of North Hill, on the left. Tell him to come to the main desk and ask for Mr Hennessy. I might well see Fergus. I'll be on duty.'

257

'Thanks enormously,' Brian said. 'Fergus is out at the moment. He's gone along to Potter's shop for some brackets. Anyway, a name like Hennessy sounds like a good omen. The Irish tend to stick together.'

'He's OK,' Laura said. 'He'll give Fergus a fair chance. All the same, Fergus will have to come clean about his circumstances. He won't be taken on without references and I haven't gone into any details at all. I didn't think it was my place.'

'You've been very helpful,' Brian said. 'Do you reckon it would be a good idea if I were to phone Mr Hennessy before Fergus goes there?'

'I think it can't do any harm,' Laura said.

'I'll do that right away,' Brian promised. 'How's Karen?'

'All right, I think. I stayed the night—'

'That was kind,' Brian interrupted.

'It was nothing. The children slept like logs so I've not gone short of sleep.'

'And what about today?'

'Imogen took the children to school. She has to go in for a lecture but she'll be through in time to collect them both, and she'll take them back with her to Number Twelve until I get home. Mary Simpson will be in and out of Karen's most of the day, and she'll see that she has food. It's the best we could do. I want to call Karen's mother but she insists we mustn't.'

'Why not?' Brian wanted to know.

Laura shrugged. 'Some bone of contention between them.'

'Well, you seem to be a pretty neighbourly lot,' Brian said.

'Sometimes we are, sometimes we're not, as

you've already discovered for yourself,' Laura said.

'Is there anything at all I can do?' Brian asked. 'Would it help to go in and see her?'

'I don't think so,' Laura said. 'Not at the moment. I must get back to work. In case I don't see Fergus, wish him luck from me.'

Luck, or it might have been not just luck but the fact that Brian had a talk with Mr Hennessy and put him in the picture, or that Mr Hennessy was a fair-minded man and he saw in Fergus a young man who was eager to work and grateful for any new chance that life might give him. Or again, it could have been that Fergus was from the north of County Clare and Mr Hennessy had relatives who lived just across the bay in Galway. Whatever it was, Fergus was told to report at eight o'clock the following morning.

He ran back down North Hill, too excited to walk, and announced that if they could go to the pub this evening he would stand them all a round, including, if they would honour him, Laura and Dermot O'Brien.

'Oh no!' Mark said. 'Three of us have found jobs.'

'Four of you,' Brian corrected him. 'Colin has already started his.'

'Right then,' Mark said. 'The four of us will share the round.'

Colin said nothing. He'd do it this once, but after that no-one was going to tell him how to spend his meagre money.

In the event Laura could not so honour either Fergus or the rest of them, though Dermot did. Laura was busy at Number Six where at ten past ten in the evening Karen finally lost the baby she was carrying.

Gary Anderson drove along Mulberry Lane, saw Laura in his headlights leaving Number Fifteen, turned into his own drive and parked his BMW behind the Landcruiser. When he went into the house the children, pink and shining from their baths, already in their pyjamas, rushed into the hall to meet him, with Lisa not far behind. He swept the children up into his arms and kissed them, then followed Lisa back into the kitchen.

'Supper in half an hour,' she said. 'The children are ready to go up. Shall I pour you a G and T?'

'Please,' said Gary. 'I'll take the children up in a minute.'

'Will you read us a story, Daddy?' Nathan asked.

'Want a story!' Amber demanded.

'I will,' Gary promised. 'In a minute.'

He turned to Lisa.

'I see Laura O'Brien is hobnobbing with the ex-cons,' he said. 'I saw her come out of Number Fifteen. Just what you'd expect, of course.' He had little time for the O'Briens with their woolly liberal views. They saw everything through a rosy, tolerant haze while he himself saw things clearly. He looked facts in the face and considered himself a good judge of people.

'There's been comings and goings all day,' Lisa told him. 'I've seen all the men, some of them twice. Actually, they look all right.'

'Don't be soft!' Gary said sharply. 'They're criminals, plain and simple. Don't you forget it.'

'But perhaps—' Lisa began, handing Gary his G and T.

'No "buts", no "perhaps",' Gary interrupted. 'And another thing – I've heard they've been in the pub! Well, they'll get short shrift from me if I see them there.'

'You can't start trouble in the pub, darling,' Lisa said. 'Jim Pullman wouldn't have it.'

'*I* shan't start trouble,' Gary said. 'But I'll tell you what I *will* do. I'll take Bruno along with me. I'll show the pack of them what they're up against if they try to burgle *my* house!'

'Yes, dear,' Lisa said.

He could have a point there. Although she knew Bruno was as soft as a brush, wouldn't hurt a fly, the men were not to know that, were they?

Lisa had also seen Karen Jackson being taken into next door and helped out again, driven off in the car; and then later on a strange woman bringing the children home from school. What was all that about? Some days she spent nearly as much time looking out of the window as did Esther. The difference was, Laura O'Brien popped into Esther's, no doubt explaining everything. No-one popped into Cornerways.

15

The men were at the table, eating their evening meal. By common consent they had decided that they would normally eat as soon as possible after they had arrived home from work, and do their evening chores afterwards. Fergus had discovered quickly that, in spite of being given his lunch every day in the hospital canteen, he was ready to eat again as soon as the food could be put on the table.

'I'm as hungry as a hunter by the time I get home!' he said. 'It's all that pushing people about, lifting them on and off the trolleys.'

As early as the second day in the job, because another porter had gone sick, he had been promoted temporarily from pushing supplies around to the more important job of ferrying patients to and from treatment rooms, or down in the lifts to X-ray in the basement; even in and out of the operating theatres.

'I like it,' he told the other men. "Tis far better than taking sacks of potatoes and trays of meat to the kitchen. The *craic* is better. You don't get much talk out of a leg of lamb but the patients, now, like a pleasant word or two!'

And they would get it from Fergus, Brian

thought. He had the true Irish gift of the gab and nothing seemed to dampen his cheerfulness. It was interesting, too, that he spoke of 'coming home' from his work. Neither Mark nor David used that word as yet, though of course it was early days. They didn't seem discontented with their jobs though David, the biggest and brawniest of the bunch, complained that his was heavy work, boxes of tins of toffees were no light weight and his back ached like the devil. Still, he didn't make it a serious complaint so, for the three of them, so far, so good.

Not so good with Colin Myers. It wasn't that he didn't work hard, once he had made his reluctant start on a job. He did. And whatever he'd been taught in prison he'd clearly learned well. When he chose to he worked quickly, but his day was a long string of complaints and when he wasn't vocally complaining he was silently sulking. There was nothing in between. Brian found it difficult spending the hours with him. He wished Colin could have been one of those who went out to work.

In the evenings when they were all doing their chores on the restoration of the house, Fergus would whistle, or sing in his pleasant tenor voice. Mark and David might join in, though mostly they chatted amicably. There was nothing of that from Colin. He objected to working in the evening when he'd been at it all day, though as Brian pointed out, so had they all in one way or another. He saw to it that the very most the men did was a couple of hours' work after their early supper, sometimes no more than an hour, and that, whenever possible, Colin had a different task from whatever he'd been doing during the day. But it made no difference. Nothing suited Colin.

Brian had gone along with him to Potter's to buy tools. Colin had very few of his own and it had been agreed that if he was to do a decent job he must have the right equipment. So they had bought hammers, chisels, a drill, a saw, a plane, screwdrivers and a great deal more, everything necessary for the work – to a total of nearly three hundred pounds. Doubtless there would be more needed, as well as materials. The Trust footed the bill and the tools were on loan to Colin, with a few items for the other men.

Fergus and Mark had been on cooking duty this evening, so the meal they were now eating was a good one: Irish stew with dumplings, exactly right for the chilly November day. No matter who was on supper duty Brian, if he had time in the afternoon, would always make some preparation towards it. Today he had peeled and washed the vegetables. Colin avoided all that. He didn't believe in working hard all day and also helping to make the supper.

'Your mother goes out to work, doesn't she?' Brian had asked. He knew she did. 'Does she set to and make the meal when she comes in?'

'She's a woman,' Colin had replied. 'It's a woman's work.'

'You're living in a bygone age,' Brian told him.

Fergus wiped his plate clean with a piece of bread. 'That was very good,' he remarked, 'although I do say it myself!'

'Agreed!' David said. 'You'll get to do it again. What's for afters?'

'Treacle tart,' Mark told him. 'Which we didn't make on account of not having the time, or the skill. I bought it in the town and I'll reclaim the money from the housekeeping.'

'I thought,' Brian said when they had finished eating and Fergus had made a pot of tea, 'I'd take some flowers along to Karen tomorrow. From all of us. She was very good to us, and just when we needed it.'

'So shall we all chip in?' David suggested.

'That would be nice,' Brian said. 'I'll tell you how much when I've bought them.'

Fergus and Mark murmured agreement. Colin kept quiet. There'd be nothing from him, Brian thought. Nevertheless, he'd ask him.

'What about you, Colin?'

'Count me out,' Colin said. 'My allowance doesn't run to buying flowers for women I don't know.'

'Suit yourself,' Brian said.

At Number Six, the next day, Karen sat in the easy chair reading a romantic novel. When, in the last few years – ever since Neil was born, in fact – had she read so much as a line of a book in the daytime? It had been a pleasure reserved for bedtime, and one never to last longer than the time it took to read half a chapter before she fell asleep, exhausted by the day. It was also something she had only really taken up since Ray had left, and as pleasures go it ranked nowhere compared to that of having a man in her bed. Danielle Steel was not nearly as satisfying.

All the same, romantic novels would be her bed-fellows from now on. She was off men. Her experiences with men had not been good ones. She hoped never again to have to live through anything like the last twelve weeks. But paradoxically, now that it was over and the outcome was clearly for the best – what she would have prayed for if she had not given up that sort of thing – she had this incongruous sense of loss. (It was, in fact, exactly what Esther could have told her would happen.) It was inexplicable since she hadn't, at any point, wanted the baby, and had now been relieved of a burden which she would have been almost incapable of carrying. And it was not just a sense of loss in her mind, it was a feeling as physical as toothache. It was as if her body had been emptied, as if the painful departure of that tiny foetus had left a great hole in her inside, a hole big enough to have nurtured a seven-pound baby. A boy? A girl? If they had known, no-one had said.

I *will* get over it, she told herself, not for the first time. Of course she would. And the bright spot was that now her mother need never know. And she would get over it all the sooner, and more efficiently, Dr Craven had said to her, if she did as she was told and rested. She should not go back to work for at the very least another week. Never mind that she needed the money. When he said 'get over', she thought, he meant physically. Her insides would heal. Never mind the rest. He knew nothing of how she felt. How could he?

So here she was, scorching her legs which were propped up on a footstool in front of the 'living flame' gas fire, reading a novel in which the heroine's life was as unlike her own as it was possible to be. Beautiful and desirable the heroine was; her problem only to make the right choice between the rich and attractive men who pursued her. Karen read quickly, but without skipping a single word. She was desperate to finish at least the chapter before one of the students brought the children home from school and her enforced leisure ended. Probably Grace would collect them today. She was especially good with the children because she had younger brothers and sisters of her own.

The students had been so kind to her, as had several other neighbours. Laura, of course. She was always there when she was needed. Mary Simpson, as well as being almost always on call, had taken the children's clothes and washed and ironed them. Even Nigel Simpson had called in once, bringing Titus with him. 'To cheer you up,' he said. Betty Pullman from the Green Man had twice come across with a hot dinner on a tray. Esther, via Laura, had sent her best wishes. Between them all, as well as taking the children to and from school, they had made meals, shopped, kept the house clean, brought books from the library. Anything, everything. She'd never dreamt that neighbours could be so kind. Though any day now, she reminded herself, she'd have to get back to doing it all herself.

The doorbell rang. It was too early for the children, and in any case the students now had a key. She put her book face down on the footstool so as not to lose the place – she was reluctant to leave it – and went to answer the door. Brian Carson stood on the top step clutching a large bunch of bronze chrysanthemums imprisoned in florist's cellophane.

'I'm sorry,' he said. 'I've disturbed you. I should have had the sense to come later when the children were here and there'd have been someone with you to answer the door. I didn't think.'

'You haven't disturbed me,' Karen said untruthfully. 'And I'm quite well enough to answer the door. Please come in!'

'I won't keep you,' Brian said, stepping into the hall, handing her the flowers.

'They're from all of us,' he announced. 'I'm afraid they're not terribly exciting. There isn't a lot of choice in the florist's at this time of the year.'

'How very kind – and please don't apologize,' Karen said. 'They're lovely! I like chrysanthemums, I really do. My father used to grow them, great big things with heads like plates, but I prefer these smaller ones. I love the scent of chrysanths. I used to pick the petals off and put them in a bottle of water, tell myself I was making perfume!'

'I never thought of them as being scented,' Brian said.

'Oh but they are!' Karen assured him. 'They have a very distinctive scent.'

She paused. It was all she could think of to say about chrysanthemums, though her father, had he been there, could have gone on for hours; cultivation, varieties, feeding, pruning – everything.

'It's very kind of you,' she repeated. 'All of you. Say thank you to the boys for me.'

'I will,' Brian promised. 'We just wanted to know you were getting on all right. I'd better be going . . .'

'Oh, please don't go!' Karen found herself saying – she who minutes earlier had been annoyed at being dragged away from her novel, and had in any case sworn off all men. 'Come into the kitchen while I put these in water and then I'll make a cup of tea.'

'I don't think . . .' Brian began.

'Please!' Karen said. 'If you have time, that is . . .'

'Well, if you're sure you're fit enough . . . or I could make it for you.'

'No, really!' Karen assured him. 'I'm quite fit enough. I shall be back at work in a few days.' She knew he had no idea what had ailed her, and she didn't propose to tell him. All the same she had an uncomfortable feeling of dishonesty about it. He was such a nice man.

He followed her into the kitchen and stood around while she filled the kettle, placed the flowers in a jug of water, put teabags in the pot.

'Do sit down,' Karen said. 'When I've made the tea we'll go into the living room. It's more comfortable.'

Brian seated himself at the table.

'I'm happy here,' he said. 'I like kitchens. I'll be pleased when ours is finished. It's top priority and Colin's working at it but there's a lot to do. I don't know how the old lady managed in it. The equipment – what there is – is as old as the hills and mostly doesn't work properly.'

'You get used to what you have,' Karen said. 'Especially if you've had it for ages.'

'I would think it might even have been dangerous,' Brian said.

Karen nodded. 'I daresay she should have sold the house years ago and moved to something smaller and more up to date, but even if she wanted to, she left it too late. You don't want the upheaval of moving house when you're old. Milk and sugar?'

'Milk, no sugar. Have you lived here long?' Brian asked.

'Nearly seven years. We came here when we were first married,' Karen said. She had been pregnant with Fiona. Otherwise, she had since wondered, though only recently – it had never occurred to her at the time – would Ray have married her at all? Anyway, water under the bridge. She had ceased to have any feelings for him and it was better that way, though she felt sorry for the children, especially Fiona. If Neil had any memories of his father, good or bad, he didn't show them. Fiona would sometimes say, 'When is Daddy coming?' though less often than she used to.

She put the mugs of tea on the table, together with the biscuit jar, and sat down opposite Brian.

'Help yourself to biscuits,' she said. 'Though I don't think there's much of a selection.'

Brian took a ginger biscuit from the jar. 'Am I allowed to dunk this?' he asked.

'Sure! It's the only way to eat a ginger biscuit. All the same, I wish I'd never shown the children how to do it. Especially Neil. His mostly end up having to be fished out of the mug with a spoon, or on the table. There's an art to dunking, isn't there?'

'Are you really feeling better?' Brian asked, dipping his biscuit.

'I am truly,' Karen said. In fact, in the last few minutes she had suddenly felt a whole lot better. 'I told you, I'll be back at work next week.'

'And are you looking forward to that?'

'More or less,' Karen said. 'In any case I have to get back. Because I'm part-time I don't get paid when I'm not there. Anyway, how is everything going?'

'Quite well so far,' Brian said, skilfully catching the last of his soaked biscuit in his mouth before it fell apart. 'Excuse me!'

'Have another.' Karen pushed the biscuit jar towards him.

'Thank you,' Brian said. 'It's a long time since I dunked a ginger biscuit. It's one of the small pleasures of life I'd forgotten about.'

'How are the men?' Karen asked.

'I think they're settling in,' Brian answered. 'It's all very different from a prison routine, isn't it? And then they have to get used to living with each other – none of them had ever met before – and get used to the routine in the house, which you have to have however lightly you do it. I try not to be heavy-handed.'

She couldn't see him being heavy-handed. Though he came over as a strong man, there was a gentleness about him, or perhaps quietness would be a better word. His voice was quiet. She didn't imagine he would raise it much. On the other hand, she thought, he would be firm, probably stand no nonsense. He hadn't given way the least bit in the meeting at the O'Briens', he'd calmly stood his ground, though politely. It was an interesting combination and it showed in his face and his manner. He was a man you could probably talk to freely, but you wouldn't get idle flattery in return. He wasn't smooth-tongued. On the other hand, she thought, what am I on about? She hardly knew him and he was a man, wasn't he? That much was against him.

'What about their new jobs?' she asked. 'Are those OK?'

'They seem to be. All three of them, I reckon. The only one who isn't satisfied is Colin Myers, and of course he's working in the house, not doing a job outside. But even allowing for the fact that he'd prefer to be earning cash I've discovered he isn't a man who would fit into most jobs. He wouldn't get on with people. I'd say he's a loner. I'm not sure I should have taken him on. I might have made a mistake there.'

He finished the tea in his mug and rose to his feet.

'I mustn't take up your time,' he said. 'I'm sure you ought to be resting.'

'I've done loads of that, and I can't remember ever having more spare time,' Karen said. 'Anyway, thank you for coming, and please thank the men for the flowers. I do appreciate them. I hope things go well.'

'Oh, I daresay they will,' Brian said. 'I suppose I was having a bit of a moan, but it was good to have someone to talk to!'

She saw him to the door and when he had left she stood in the window and watched him walk away along the road. Not many people would have chosen me to talk to, she thought as she went back to her book.

On the same morning that Brian Carson took the flowers to Karen, and as Jennifer was about to leave the house, the postman, long past his time because they were short staffed, pushed a shower of unsolicited mail through the letter box of Number Twelve. Jennifer picked it up and, skimming through it, found a letter for herself. It was from her aunt; she recognized the rather flamboyant writing. She opened it and read it as she walked along Mulberry Lane, and in her excitement as she took in what it said she failed to see Nigel Simpson with Titus walking towards her, and almost tripped over the dog's lead.

'Steady, steady!' Nigel said, but kindly.

'I'm sorry!' She bent to pat Titus, who licked her hand.

'It must be a love letter!' Nigel observed.

'No,' Jennifer said. 'It's from my aunt.'

She turned back to it as she walked on.

Here is what I'm sure will be a most interesting piece of news for you! You remember Professor Norman Maitland? Well, at least you'll remember his name because he was the lecturer on the holiday I told you about.

Well, I saw him last weekend, he took me out to dinner (which didn't actually surprise me; he had been hinting at it but he's always so busy, and then living in Cambridge, not London). It was a very good dinner, at L'Ecu de France in Jermyn Street, but you don't want to hear all about that, do you?

Why wouldn't I, she thought? I've never been to L'Ecu de France.

Anyway, he told me that for next year he planned a dig in Athens – probably starting in June at the beginning of the long vacation and returning at the end of September – he has to be back in Cambridge then. *So* – I told him about you and how interested you were and how you might make archaeology your thing and so on, and, to cut a long story short, he said he was fairly certain, if you liked the idea, that he could find a place for you. He's taking students from Cambridge. You would be a dogsbody, of course. Probably all very menial, but it would give you a taste of the real thing. Norman is a very eminent man in his field. I've more or less promised to join him there, but only for two or three weeks, and I'd be a mere onlooker. Let me know what you think, darling. It would be fun, wouldn't it?

She had added a postscript: 'I'm afraid you wouldn't be able to bring Liam.'

It was the postscript which made Jennifer wonder. Could this be, in fact, a ploy between her aunt and her mother to entice her away from Liam? Her mother would be quite capable of such a thing but she didn't truly think her aunt was. She was too direct. So she would discount that idea for the moment. Not that her aunt had exactly taken to Liam. No, the point was, what would Liam have to say when she told him – if she told him – that they would be spending the whole of next summer apart? And how, come to think of it, did *she* view that? Could she bear to be away from him for so long, and with such a distance between them?

Oh, but the offer was madly enticing! And what a marvellous kick start if she decided she was going to do archaeology! She had never been to Athens, though she had always wanted to go there. It was the stuff of travel brochures. The Acropolis by moonlight!

That morning's lecture – Wilfred Owen and his place among the war poets – went in at one ear and out of the other without stopping to lodge in her mind, which was full of the letter and all the questions it raised. Of course the project was still more than six months away, but no doubt Professor Maitland would already be thinking of who would be in his team. She couldn't shelve making the decision for too long, still less trust that doing nothing on her part might result in fate working everything out for the best. Indeed, what was the best? The very best, from her point of view, would be to take up the offer and also have Liam go with her to Greece – the best of all possible worlds. She was dizzy with delight, but not too dizzy to ignore what she knew to be true, that Liam couldn't possibly be included, even if he wished to be. And that was by no means certain. He had no truck with archaeology. He was bored when she went on about it. So what part could he play – other, of course, than that of her lover?

If, on the other hand, she was ready to make up her mind quickly and definitely not to take part, to refuse the offer, all she had to do was write to her aunt and say so. She couldn't really envisage doing that, not immediately. To work with Professor Maitland might be the best chance she would ever be given. And if Liam loved her, she told herself, really loved her, he would let her go and wait patiently until she came back. 'Patiently' was not a word to apply to Liam. When was he ever patient? His impatience was part of his attraction. He never liked to wait for anything. And did he love her so much that he would consent to this, just wait for her to return?

She would ring him as soon as she was back home. It wasn't something to be discussed from a campus phone booth. Almost certainly she must arrange to see him, perhaps this coming weekend. Would he come down to Shipfield? She didn't want to go to him. The problem was, they had a full complement in Number Twelve; no-one had any plans to be away. Why had they made this stupid rule that they couldn't have visitors overnight unless there was an empty room? She supposed she had agreed to it at the time but now it seemed ridiculous. She wanted him in her bed.

About the time Jennifer was leaving her lecture, having absorbed next to nothing and made no notes at all – she would have to get them from someone else – Esther watched an orange van draw up outside Number Thirteen. The driver walked up the path to the door. He'll get no answer, she thought. If he waited long enough she would get herself to the door and tell him that he'd have no luck, they both went out to work. 'Who shall I say called?' she would ask him. Then she saw his lips moving and his arm pointing towards the van, so unless he was a raving lunatic someone *had* answered the door and they were having a conversation.

Then she remembered that though she had seen Michelle drive off she had not seen Ralph do so, and indeed there was his car, a few yards along the road. A car each! Such extravagance!

'You're late!' Ralph Streeter said to the driver of the van. 'You're a whole hour late.'

'Sorry, mate,' the driver said. 'Blame the traffic.'

Ralph was not appeased. He did not expect to have to wait in to receive workmen, but Michelle had been totally unyielding, pleading end-to-end appointments for perms, tints, haircuts, blow-drys. 'I can't let my customers down,' she said firmly. 'I've far more appointments than you!' It was true. He ran the salon but it was Michelle who did most of the hairdressing. She was indispensable.

He showed the man the layout of the house and where everything was, then said, 'I shall have to leave. I can't hang about any longer. Mind you lock up when you go.'

It was only when he was driving down North Hill that he thought, in an unusual (for him) flash of reason, 'Why am I having a burglar alarm installed at the same time as leaving a total stranger the run of my house?'

16

It was the sound of the burglar alarm which brought Brian running down the stairs from his bedroom at the front of the house, where he had been putting up a rail in a cupboard so that he could use it as a wardrobe. So far he had made do with hanging his clothes – what there were of them – over the backs of two chairs. There had been more urgent jobs than wardrobes to deal with.

The noise rent the air; deafening, shrill. He had no doubt what it was but its proximity puzzled him. The only house on which he had noticed an alarm was Cornerways across the road, but this racket sounded near enough to be on his own front doorstep. If it was from Cornerways, remembering his one and only meeting with the owner, he was tempted to ignore it, though he knew he wouldn't because Mrs Anderson might be involved and she, when her husband wasn't looking, had smiled quite pleasantly at him.

When he opened the front door the origin of the ear-splitting din was clear. Though not actually on his own doorstep it issued from no more than three yards away and eighteen feet higher up. A man in brown overalls stood on next door's garden path, a satisfied smile on his face as he pointed to the bright yellow box near the top of Number Thirteen's front wall. He saw Brian, gave him the thumbs-up sign and said something which it was impossible to hear.

'Turn it off!' Brian yelled.

Oblivious to all other sounds, the man continued to smile and nod. Brian resorted to sign language, putting his fingers in his ears, pointing at the box and pulling a face. Comprehension dawned on the man's face. Still smiling, he went into the house, turned off the alarm and came out again.

'Good, isn't it!' he shouted. 'A burglar alarm!'

It was possible, Brian thought, that the man was so used to noise that he never spoke in a normal voice.

'I guessed. Very loud!' Brian replied – and found himself shouting in return.

'We do the loudest alarms the law allows,' the man said with pride.

'So can we expect the boys in blue to arrive any second?' Brian asked.

'Oh no!' the man said. 'I phoned and told them I was going to test it. Well, I think I can safely say it passed the test.'

Colin came out of the house. He had been using a powerful drill in the kitchen and had heard no more than the last few seconds of the noise. Now he looked up at the yellow box, stared for a second, then turned on his heel and marched back into the house, slamming the door behind him. Brian was not surprised. That would be more or less the reaction of all the men.

'I notice you're not alarmed,' the man said. 'I

could probably give you a discount as I'm working in the area.'

'No thank you,' Brian said. 'It's probably the last thing I need.'

The man shook his head.

'I wouldn't be too sure! There's a lot of crime about. Still, mustn't grumble too much at that. It's an ill wind, etc. Good for business! In fact I've got orders for two more to be installed in this road. All I did was put a small ad in the *Courier* and lo and behold, four enquiries the very next day!'

'Four enquiries from Mulberry Lane?'

'Three from Mulberry and one from North Hill. Not a bad return for a small ad, is it?'

'Not bad at all,' Brian agreed.

'So have you been having a spate of burglaries around here?' the man asked.

'None that I know of,' Brian answered.

'Just a coincidence, then? Anyway, I got all three jobs in Mulberry. I'm doing one more this after-noon and the other tomorrow. In fact I daresay I could fit you in tomorrow if you're interested. You're sure you wouldn't like to take advantage of a good offer?' the man persisted.

'Thanks, but no!' Brian assured him.

The man fished in his pocket. 'Well, here's my card, should you change your mind. But bear in mind you'll get a better price if I'm working in the street.'

Because it was already dark when the three men returned from work they didn't see the yellow box, but Colin, in a bitter voice, and deliberately waiting until they were all together at the table, informed them of its existence.

'Not that I couldn't deal with any bloody burglar alarm!' he boasted. 'In fact I'd like to show the bastard just what I could do, teach him a lesson he wouldn't forget!'

'Don't even think of it!' Brian warned him. 'If you do what you have in mind you'll be back in gaol before you can turn round! And it won't be a short stretch! Not only that, it won't stop at that, you'll also put everyone in this house in the dirt. Where do you think would be the first place the police would look? Who do you think they'd go for?'

'True!' David agreed. 'We're a sitting target.'

'I was only saying,' Colin grumbled. 'I didn't say I'd do it. I'm allowed to think what I like, aren't I?'

'If that's the way your thinking goes,' Brian said, 'then you should think a bit further, like whether you actually belong here. It's not a place to plan further crimes. I know what Streeter's done is nasty. I'd say he's a nasty man, but he's only one. They're not all going to be like that.' No way would he tell them that two others were installing alarms. They'd either find out or they wouldn't, probably the former.

Mark spoke up, in a hard voice.

'It seems to me we didn't finish the punishment when we came out of prison. It seems to me it goes on.' The others nodded agreement.

'And I suppose we're expected to take it,' David said. 'For how long?'

'I don't know,' Brian admitted. 'And yes, the punishment does go on. I warned you about that. There's no sharp line where it ends, so you just have to learn to deal with it. There's no point in feeling sorry for yourselves, still less in planning to take revenge. That's the downward slope. In any case, you're more fortunate than most, none of you is fighting a lone battle and you've got time in which to sort yourselves out.'

'But we're not trusted, are we?' Mark persisted.

'By some you're not,' Brian agreed. 'But it's not everyone. Give it time. You'll have to earn trust – which you'll not do by being stupid! It's the wrong way.' He looked directly at Colin, but it was Fergus who spoke.

''Tis the natural way,' he said.

'I know,' Brian said. 'Don't think I don't sympathize.'

It was a subdued supper that evening, though in every case a hard day's work saw to it that their appetites weren't diminished. Brian did his best to keep them off the subject of burglar alarms.

'I thought,' he said, 'given a fine weekend we could do a bit in the garden. It would make a change from working indoors.'

'And what would we do in the garden in November?' Fergus asked. ''Tis all but dead.'

'No it's not!' Mark said. 'Sleeping if you like. Not dead.'

Colin gave him a derisive look. 'I suppose gardening's another of the things you know all about?' he said.

'Not exactly,' Mark said equably. He knew it annoyed Myers that he couldn't make him angry, or certainly not visibly, and he was determined to keep it that way even though at times he felt he'd like to wipe the floor with him. 'My mother's a keen gardener. Sometimes she roped me in. When she wasn't abroad with my father, that was. I'd do it for extra pocket money.'

'So you had a large garden, did you?' Fergus asked.

'Quite big,' Mark agreed.

Colin jumped up from the table and left the room. None of the others raised as much as an eyebrow at his going. They were used to his moods. Or rather to his mood, for it was a continuous one. Five minutes later they heard him working with his drill in the kitchen.

'So!' Brian said. 'How about you making a plan of how we should tackle the garden? I mean over a period.'

'If you like,' Mark agreed. 'I don't have to go into work until the evening on Saturday and I have to be there for Sunday lunches. But I could make a plan. We could discuss it.'

'Right,' Brian said, 'you've got the job! I suppose the first part will be clearing up – all the rubbish, dead leaves and so on. We should also dig up the borders, leave the soil in clods for the frost to break it up. We've time to do that. The frosts aren't likely to come early in this part of the country, are they? Too far south and west.'

'Shall we grow potatoes?' Fergus said. 'There's nothing beats taties! And if we were to grow cabbages as well we could have bubble and squeak.'

Brian shook his head.

'If all goes well we shan't be here to harvest vegetables. Nice idea, though, otherwise.'

Gardening had been a good thing to talk about, Brian thought as they left the supper table. Apart from Colin, who switched off the drill as they went into the kitchen, it seemed to have calmed things down.

'When we've finished this evening's jobs,' he said, 'we'll go along to the pub for a beer.'

The suggestion was deliberate. He intended to show Ralph Streeter and whoever else was having alarms fitted that the occupants of Number Fifteen were not intimidated by it, had nothing to be intimidated about. He also hoped to find out who the other two would-be owners of yellow boxes were.

'If that bugger next door is there, don't expect me to be polite to him!' Colin said.

'That's the last thing I'd expect of you,' Brian said. 'But if you'd any sense at all you'd know that your best revenge – and revenge is obviously what you're after – would be to show no reaction at all. Keep cool.'

He didn't want Colin's company in the pub but, on the other hand, he wanted all four men to be there. He wanted a united front of indifference to what Ralph Streeter had done.

Gary Anderson, emerging from Cornerways with Bruno on the lead, his intention being to go for their usual walk in Upper Mulberry Lane, looked across the road and saw, in the light of the street lamp, that misguided do-gooder with his band of ex-cons in tow coming out of Number Fifteen. They turned left. Obviously they were going to the pub. How they had the nerve to show their faces there he couldn't imagine, but they had.

Gary immediately changed his mind about his route. He would go a little way along Upper Mulberry, give Bruno his nightly treat of meeting with the Bichon Frisé, and after that he and Bruno would retrace their steps and walk along to the Green Man. The awesome combination of himself with Bruno, he told himself, would have more impact if they walked in when that mob were already seated. They would see what they were up against should any one of them have the temerity even to consider breaking into Cornerways. Mission accomplished in Upper Mulberry, though Frizzie had been very standoffish with Bruno, he turned back.

It was unfortunate, in the event, that Nigel Simpson was already in the Green Man with Titus when Gary arrived. Titus not only disliked Bruno, he was totally unafraid of him. Size meant nothing to Titus. Good stuff lies in little room was his motto and he had long ago discovered that large dogs tended to be wary of him. As, of course, were humans, especially the male sex who were paranoid about the possibility of being bitten on the back of the heel, or on their ankles, both of which areas, being within easy reach, were his speciality.

So when Bruno, dragging his master behind him, entered into what Titus for the time being considered to be his territory, Titus let fly. He did not actually attack Bruno, he wasn't stupid, but his confrontation, and the shrill sound of his barking, warning that attack could follow unless Bruno minded his p's and q's, reduced the big dog to a state of trembling apprehension. Nigel called Titus to heel, and Gary, with Bruno clinging to his side, skirted the company and found refuge in a far corner. Mark gave Bruno a friendly pat on his behind as he passed.

Brian and the men were sitting close to the bar and at the table next to them Ralph and Michelle Streeter were seated with Peter and Meg from Number Nine, whose last name Brian couldn't remember, only that they owned the errant cat, Samson. Brian didn't need to be told that it was on their house that this afternoon's burglar alarm had been fitted. Already on the lookout, he had seen it as they'd walked along the road, though he hadn't drawn the men's attention to it. He had, though, deliberately chosen a table close to Ralph Streeter's. It was his intention to attack head on.

'That's a very efficient burglar alarm you've had put in,' he called across pleasantly. 'Nearly blasted me out of the house this morning!'

Ralph Streeter responded with what for him passed for a smile – a slight upturning of one corner of his mouth.

'I won't apologize,' he said. 'It's intended to be good and loud. Michelle and I are going to feel much safer, knowing it's there and it works. One can't be too careful!'

'Oh, I do agree!' Brian said. 'In fact the lads and I were talking about it just before we came here. I think it wouldn't be a bad idea if we had one fitted at Number Fifteen. As you say, one never knows these days. Act first, don't trust anybody! And I know the lads agree with me.' He turned to them for confirmation, which they gave, looking grave, and nodding.

'Sure!' Mark said. 'We're all in favour of having one.'

Ralph Streeter's pale face flushed slightly.

'But . . .' he began, and had no idea what to say next.

He was saved from thinking of anything because at that moment an astoundingly loud ringing drowned every other sound in the pub. Ralph Streeter jumped to his feet and Michelle immediately pulled him down again. The landlord, recognizing a burglar alarm when he heard one and also having observed the installation that after-noon, was already ringing the police.

Esther heard the alarm. It intruded into a concert she was listening to on her stereo earphones and at first she thought it was, though strangely, part of the orchestral effects. When it became clear that the two sounds didn't match up she took off the earphones, switched off the CD and went to the window. There were possibly livelier things afoot. The night outside was dark, with a thin fog, but from the light of the street lamps she could see a certain amount. The interesting thing was that, though she had watched the morning's installation of the alarm next door and seen Brian's conver-sation with the man who had carried it out, this noise was definitely not coming from there. So where was it all happening?

Laura and Dermot heard it as they were eating a late supper. 'What in the world . . . ?' Dermot began. They had already noticed Ralph Streeter's alarm and deplored it – it was so obvious what he was saying – but this wasn't his. It was further along the road. What was everyone up to?

Jennifer heard it and ignored it. Let the whole street be burgled, she had more important things on her mind. She was speaking on the phone with Liam and things weren't going well. She held the receiver closer to her listening ear and stuffed a finger in the other one to shut out the noise.

'It's not ours,' Michelle said, 'it's too near! It must be Peter's.'

Peter was already on his feet, making for the door. Meg remained seated. 'Don't expect me to

287

come with you!' she called after him. 'I'm not going to face the burglars! You can do the hero bit! It was your damned silly idea to have the thing. I never agreed.'

She spoke in vain. Peter had already left. Ralph stood up again. 'Perhaps I'd better . . .' he began.

'Oh no you don't,' Michelle said. 'Don't get involved. They could be armed!'

'Oh no!' Meg was on her feet now.

'Stay where you are, Meg,' Ralph said. 'Jim has phoned the police. They'll be here any minute. Michelle is right, leave it to them.'

'But if they're armed . . .' Meg cried.

'Burglars don't usually carry guns,' Brian said. 'I'll go across and see what's happening.' He turned to the four men at his table. 'Don't any of you leave here until I'm back! That's an order!'

He had hardly left when the police car arrived. Several customers now went out, leaving their drinks on the table. If there was anything to be seen they wanted to see it.

Colin, who had been sitting silently ever since they'd come into the pub, spoke up in a loud voice.

'Well, at least we all know who the bloody burglars *can't* be!'

'Sure!' Fergus said. 'Don't we all have alibis?'

'And witnesses!' David added.

'So as everyone must agree we're as innocent as babes,' Mark said, 'who can it possibly be? And shall we have another half while we're waiting?'

They didn't have long to wait. Peter came back into the pub, followed by those customers who had gone outside to enjoy the spectacle. They returned smiling. Only Peter's face was as black as a thundercloud.

'Oh Peter, thank heaven you're safe!' Meg cried, flinging her arms wide. 'It was cowardly of me not to go with you, and I'm sorry! Tell me what happened?'

'That bloody cat!' Peter said. 'It tripped the alarm. I'll wring its sodding neck!'

Jennifer had spent most of the day thinking about things other than those she was actually doing. Walking head down from the lecture room to the library, she had literally bumped into the Vice-Chancellor, though that might have been averted had *he* been looking where he was going. He was known for being preoccupied but doubtless, Jennifer thought, when he had taken her gently by the shoulders and put her on the right track and they had both apologized profusely to each other, his thoughts were loftier than hers. He would be thinking about university finance, or the new physics building, or something highly mathematical, while she was considering whether she could give up the delights of Liam's body in order to dig up broken bits of pottery from the soil. She was not to know that the Vice-Chancellor's thoughts were on whether there was any chance that liver and onions would be on the Senior Common Room lunch menu.

In the library the pages of a learned critique of eighteenth-century essays swam before her eyes, resolving into visions of herself and Liam exploring the Parthenon, or as entwined figures in a sunburnt landscape with olive groves. In the end she had decided to give up and go home to Mulberry Lane. It was the only clear decision she did make. She was still uncertain about everything else in her life.

She was delighted, arriving back at the house, to find Grace there. Grace was just the person she needed. Grace would listen, she would understand, she would not make rash judgements, either of people or of situations.

'Oh Grace,' she said, 'I'm so glad you're here! I desperately want to talk to you.'

'Talk away,' Grace said in her calm voice. 'I'm listening.'

Jennifer began by showing Grace her aunt's letter. Grace read it through to the end then looked up and said, 'How absolutely marvellous!'

'It isn't really!' Jennifer said. 'Well, I mean it isn't and it is.'

Grace raised her eyebrows. 'What do you mean? What's the problem?'

'Liam of course!' Jennifer said. 'Surely you can see that? I wouldn't think for a moment I could take him with me, but how can I bear to leave him? I know he wouldn't wait for me. He'd find someone else.'

'I'm sure that's true,' Grace agreed. 'Are you seriously telling me you'd give up a chance like this for Liam?'

'I love him!' Jennifer pleaded. 'You don't understand . . .'

She broke off in mid-sentence as Stuart came into the room.

'Don't mind me, girls!' he said cheerily. 'I'm just going to make a cup of coffee and a sandwich. I haven't had any lunch. Unless either of you would like to do it for me, as a favour?'

'We wouldn't,' Grace assured him.

He sighed. 'Very well. I'll do it myself. Carry on with your girlie conversation. I'm not listening.'

Jennifer hesitated, and then, because he was

seldom interested in any conversation other than his own and she desperately needed to talk, she lowered her voice and continued.

'So there it is,' she said presently. 'You do see what I mean, Grace, don't you? About Liam?'

'Liam,' Grace said, firmly but pleasantly, 'is crap! Everyone except you knows that.'

Stuart, crossing the room, coffee cup in one hand and sandwich in the other, paused.

'Excuse me for butting in,' he said, 'but Grace is right! He is the utmost crap!'

'Do you mind?' Jennifer said. 'This is a private conversation!'

'It's for your own sake,' Stuart persisted. 'You could do a thousand times better than that. Nor would you have far to seek! I leave you with that thought.' He gave her a twinkling smile as he left the room.

There was a short silence as he closed the door behind him then Grace burst out laughing. Jennifer looked as though she'd been hit on the head.

'My God!' she said. 'Does he mean what I think he means?'

'I'm afraid so,' Grace gasped. 'Oh, you lucky, lucky girl! He'd probably let you type his manuscripts. What's more, your mother would approve of him.'

'I expect she would,' Jennifer agreed. 'It's bizarre. I'd no idea!'

'Oh, I had,' Grace said. 'I've seen it coming.'

'Isn't that alone enough to make one flee the country?' Jennifer said. 'Athens would hardly be far enough.'

'There's your answer then – except you'll have to wait until next summer.'

291

Jennifer dismissed Stuart with a sharp wave of her hand, as if she was brushing off a troublesome fly.

'Let's be serious,' she said. 'I have to give Liam a chance.'

'Why? Give me one good reason,' Grace demanded.

'Because . . . well, for one thing he might say I can go, give me his blessing, and be there for me when I get back. It's only a couple of months after all!' Not that she believed this. He'd be on with the new love with the speed of light. The trouble was – there was no getting away from it, no matter what anyone might say – she *was* in love with him. It was perhaps no more than physical, she couldn't judge, but it was real. It was as if he had a power over her which she wasn't sure she could break.

'Oh well,' she said. 'I'll phone him this evening. I'll put it to him and see how he takes it.'

'What you should do is to sit down right now and write to your aunt, accept the offer,' Grace said firmly. 'Tell him it's a fait accompli. I'll take the letter to the post for you.'

Jennifer shook her head.

'I can't. Not until I've talked to Liam.'

Which was why, when later the burglar alarm went off as she was doing so, she was the only person in the vicinity who didn't stop what she was doing.

'Are you fucking mad?' Liam demanded.

'I don't know,' Jennifer said. 'I do know I want to go. I might persuade Aunt Rachael to ask Professor Maitland if you could come along.'

'Not bloody likely!' Liam said. 'It's the last thing

I'd do. She's your mother's sister, isn't she? Enough said!'

'She's nothing like Mummy,' Jennifer protested. 'You might quite like her. It could all be fun.'

'Thank you,' Liam said. 'I don't intend to find out. Athens or me. It's a straight choice!'

Straight it was not, Jennifer thought. Why couldn't he see that? 'Think about it,' she said. 'I'll speak to you tomorrow.'

'Only if you've come to your senses,' Liam said, ringing off.

She looked at the receiver in her hand as if by so doing she could bring him back. Then she put it down, and wept.

Later, she wrote to her aunt. 'Dear Aunt Rachael, Thank you very much, and thank Professor Maitland for the offer . . .' She paused, then continued. 'I'm delighted to accept it. Can't write more now but will do so later.' Then she walked along the road and posted it.

17

To the outward eye it seemed, over the next week or two as November edged into December, that everything was back to what passed for normal in Mulberry Lane. Whatever was happening in the hearts and minds and houses of those who lived there, none of it was making waves. The third burglar alarm had been installed on the promised day at Number Two, the house of Winston and Bella Grange. That was surprising, Laura said to Dermot, since at the meeting neither of the Granges had raised any objections – indeed as far as she could remember, and Dermot concurred, they hadn't spoken at all – yet they must have ordered the alarm with great haste.

'I'm surprised at the Granges,' Laura said. 'You'd think, both of them being university lecturers, they'd be more tolerant, or at least have more open minds.'

'Where property's concerned,' Dermot observed, 'tolerance and open minds don't come into it.'

'They do with some of us!' Laura objected.

There hadn't, though, been so much as a bleep from any of the burglar alarms, though car alarms, especially that of a Renault whose owner was not known to anyone in the road other than by the name of the Phantom Parker, went off with monotonous regularity. Usually in the afternoon, waking Esther from her nap.

Esther had seen the Phantom Parker more than once. She had reported to Laura that he was middle-aged, of middle height, grey-haired, didn't wear a hat and was balding on top. He was also shifty-looking. When the alarm had been sounding for about fifteen minutes, driving her mad, he would appear, walking from the North Hill end of Mulberry Lane, get into his car and drive off.

'So what is he up to?' she'd demanded of Laura. 'I reckon he's visiting someone. Who could it be at that end of the road?'

'I'm sure if you don't know, no-one else will,' Laura had said. All the same, she did wonder.

Karen was back at work. She had resumed her treks forwards and backwards along the road, to and from the toffee factory, to and from both schools. Brian often happened to be working at the front of the house as she passed – putting the biggest possible distance between himself and Colin who was still getting on with the kitchen, now cladding the walls between the new units with primrose yellow tiles – and he and Karen, should he happen to look up, should she do so at the same time, would briefly wave to each other (observed by Esther).

One Thursday afternoon Brian was actually working in the front garden, digging a border, when Karen, with Fiona, passed on his side of the road. He stopped work and leaned on his spade.

'How are you?' he asked Karen.

'Fine!' she said.

'Not doing too much?'

'Just the usual. But I'm perfectly fit!' It was true. She was also less tired than she had been before her miscarriage, perhaps simply because she'd had an enforced rest. 'So how's everything with you?'

'Going quite well. The kitchen's almost finished. Why not come in and have a look at it? Colin's out – gone into the town to buy something or other he says he can't get at Potter's.' This was a not uncommon ploy on Colin's part and Brian, recognizing that the man needed to get away from the house – didn't they all, but the other men routinely could – went along with it. If Colin was absent longer than he need be then that was all right, as long as it didn't happen too often.

'I can't, not just now,' Karen said. 'I have to collect Neil from the nursery.'

'Then drop in on the way back,' Brian suggested. 'If you want to, that is.'

'Oh, I will,' Karen assured him. 'But I've got to hurry now.'

When she was out of sight Brian went back into the house and laid a table for tea. There were two currant teacakes, which he would toast, and orange juice for the children. Or perhaps they'd prefer milk and biscuits? In fact there was almost certainly ice-cream in the freezer which they could have. He wished he had a few sweets. Stop fussing, he told himself as he went around checking everything. He was acting like a silly young housewife giving her first tea party. He had only given the invitation in a bid to be neighbourly, nothing more than that.

Karen was back quite soon, Neil in his buggy and anxious to be out of it.

'Come in!' Brian said. 'The kettle's on. Would the

children like something to drink? Milk? Orange juice?'

'Thank you,' Karen said. 'Anything that's handy. I suppose there must be a reason why children are always thirsty?'

'I suppose so,' Brian agreed. 'I'm woefully ignorant about children.'

'You never had any?' Karen asked. 'Perhaps you didn't want them. Not everyone does.'

'Of course I did,' Brian answered. 'I like children. It just didn't happen.' Helen had hardly stayed with him long enough for anything to happen.

'Come into the kitchen while I make the tea,' he said. 'Let me show you what we've done so far.' Karen, with Neil holding on to her hand, followed him.

'Oh! It's great,' she cried. 'My goodness, what a difference! It's so light and bright. You must have worked hard.'

Brian shook his head. 'Not me! Colin's done most of it. When he puts his mind to it he does work hard. I'll give him that. The new oven and the hob should be delivered this week and then we're about finished in here.'

The kettle boiled, he made the tea, split the teacakes and put them in the toaster. He poured orange juice for Fiona and milk for Neil and opened the biscuit tin.

'Two each, no more,' Karen told the children. 'You'll have your tea when you get home.'

'Shall we take it through to the living room?' Brian suggested. 'It's a nice enough kitchen but there's not enough room for four people to sit down.'

In the living room Karen sat on the sofa with a

child on each side of her; Brian sat in an armchair and poured tea.

'I'm sorry I don't have anything to amuse the children,' he said.

'That's all right,' Karen said. 'But if you're really bothered, and you don't mind, you could put the TV on. There's always children's stuff at this time of day.'

'I want the TV!' Fiona said. 'I want to watch *Clever Creatures*.'

'You've fixed blinds since I was here last,' Karen remarked. 'They're nice!' They were cream, vertical blinds with wide slats, open now to let in what was left of the daylight.

'I've put them up in all the rooms at the front. It was a bit like living on a stage before. We'll probably fix them at the back later. They're nice enough, and they serve the purpose, but I think they look a bit austere in here, especially at night when they're closed.'

'I agree,' Karen said. 'Curtains would be softer, even if you only had them at the sides, for show. But if you had them to draw right across they'd be warmer. It's getting cold in the evenings, isn't it?'

'It's a case of getting them made,' Brian said. 'I haven't got around to having them done.'

'You don't have to,' Karen informed him. 'Oh! I don't mean I could do them, I'm not much good at that sort of thing. No, you can buy them ready-made.'

'I wouldn't want to pay a lot,' Brian said. 'We might not be here all that long and we have a budget.'

'They're not all that expensive, much cheaper than having them made to measure,' Karen said. 'I

298

think they'd have a good selection at Dean & Docker's in the town.'

A bright idea hit Brian. And a rather surprising one, he thought. Certainly it surprised him.

'I wonder . . .' he began. 'Well no, perhaps you wouldn't . . .'

'Wouldn't what?' Karen asked.

'It's a bit much to ask,' Brian said hesitantly, 'but I'm not good at things like that – choosing soft furnishings, I mean. I did just wonder if you might go into town with me and help me to do that? If you have time, that is.'

'Oh!' Karen couldn't quite keep the surprise out of *her* voice. 'Well, I would,' she said hesitantly. 'But you're right, it *is* finding the time. When the children are at school I'm mostly working. It really only leaves Saturday morning and that means taking the children. You wouldn't want that!'

It was Brian's turn to hesitate. It seemed . . . well . . . too domestic. He'd spoken before he'd thought, but how could he now draw back?

'I don't mind,' he said. 'If you're quite sure you have the time?'

'Well . . .' Karen said. They were treading as carefully as two cats on hot bricks, the pair of them. It was ridiculous. All it involved was a visit to Dean & Docker's, choose the curtains, come home. So why not? It would make a change, though she would probably have to bribe the children by taking them into the toy department.

'I could manage next Saturday morning.'

'Right!' Brian said. 'I'll call for you at half-past nine. That's not too early, is it?'

'Fine!' Karen said. 'There's no having a lie-in in our house, I can tell you.'

*　　*　　*

That evening, over supper, Brian said, 'I've decided to have curtains in this room. Any ideas about colour?'

'Curtains, is it?' Fergus said. 'That would be nice. I like something cheerful – you know, flowers and that.'

'Are we going to be here long enough to bother with fancy stuff like curtains?' Colin asked.

'Who knows?' Brian said.

'It's a nice idea,' Mark said. 'Who's going to make them?'

'You can buy them ready-made,' Brian informed them. 'I'm going into town with Karen on Saturday morning to choose something. Half-past nine. Anyone who likes to join in is welcome.'

He half hoped one of them would, but it was unlikely. On Saturday mornings, other things being equal and there being nothing of great urgency, the men were free to do what they wanted, which might well be to go into town, but was hardly likely to be to choose curtains. For some of them it was a chance for a lie-in.

'I was wondering . . .' David began, then hesitated.

'Yes?'

'On another subject. You know we asked if we could have visitors? Well, I'd like Sandra to come – and so would she. Would it be all right Saturday week?'

'I can't think of any reason why not,' Brian said. 'Just for the day, of course.'

'I know. But I wish she could stay overnight,' David said. 'It wouldn't be impossible, would it? I'm sure she wouldn't mind sleeping down here on the sofa.'

300

'Sorry!' Brian said. 'Not on. But perhaps you can arrange your jobs in the house so that you'll be free all day while she's here.'

'I'll give you a hand,' Fergus offered. 'Anything for true love!'

Jennifer, across the road, was not a happy bunny. Well, in a way she was, part of the time. She was thrilled and excited about the dig. She had posted the letter to her aunt, who had replied by return, promising to clinch matters with Professor Maitland and let Jennifer know the exact dates and all other relevant details. 'And you will need to come up to town, or possibly to Cambridge, and meet Norman and perhaps some of his students,' she'd written. No, it was not that side of things. Everything was fine there. It was Liam.

She had a guilty conscience about Liam although, on the other hand, he wasn't behaving exactly like a gentleman. Well, he wouldn't, would he? Being gentlemanly had never been part of his attraction. Quite the reverse. 'Gentlemanly' was what her mother liked, therefore it stood to reason that it was the last thing *she* wanted. All the same, he need not have slammed the phone down on her on the last two occasions she had tried to have a civilized conversation with him. She knew that if she had any sense she would simply leave it at that. Let him go, put him down to experience. But as far as Liam was concerned she hadn't yet come to her senses. She was still in love with him and she missed him desperately. But he couldn't be in love with her could he, she argued with herself, or he'd surely part with her for a few weeks to let her do something she so much wanted to do?

301

So life was not easy for Jennifer. She felt as if she was ever-lastingly on a seesaw – up, then down; up, then down. And naturally she confided all this to her friends. What were friends for?

'Really, Jen,' Imogen said, 'you are becoming impossible!'

They – Imogen, Grace and Caroline – had dragged her along to the Green Man to cheer her up, but at the moment she was on the down side of the seesaw and even the three of them together couldn't lift her up.

'What do you mean?' Jennifer asked indignantly. 'I thought you were my friends!'

'We are,' Grace said. 'But you are being a tiny bit boring.'

'It isn't as if we haven't all told you exactly what you should do!' Imogen's tone was quite forceful. 'It's either that you won't listen or you can't agree with any of us. So what more can *we* do?'

'And what more can *I* do?' Jennifer countered.

'You can do what you should have done ages ago. Just give him the heave-ho! Send him packing. Liam is a horrible, bloody bore,' Imogen said. 'Everyone except you can see that!'

'You don't know him like I do,' Jennifer began.

'If you mean I don't know him in bed, too right!' Imogen interrupted. 'Perish the thought. I wouldn't let him come within a mile of it and God knows why you do! He's foul. Why can't you see it? Sometimes I think you're doing it just to spite your mother!'

Grace raised both hands in the air.

'Hey! Let's chill this! Imogen, it's your round, and when you've got that we'll change the subject.'

'All the same,' she said in a gentler voice, when

Imogen and Caroline had gone to the bar, 'she *is* right, sweetie. You're not seeing straight. Going off to Athens could be the best thing you ever did. If Liam doesn't like it, dump him. Just dump him!'

Imogen and Caroline returned with the drinks.

'I've just had a brilliant idea!' Grace said. 'I think we all need a change of scenery. You know what it's like this time of the year, you get fed up. Why don't we . . .' She paused.

'Why don't we what?'

'Why don't we take off for the weekend? Why don't we up sticks, leave on Saturday morning and go off walking. Stay overnight somewhere, return Sunday evening. Just the four of us, no men invited.' At home, when she had problems, she would go for a long walk over the fells. It usually sorted things out, or at least put them into perspective. There were times when she missed the Yorkshire dales and fells desperately.

'In December?' Imogen queried.

'Why not? There's lovely walking weather in December. We'll find a hostel somewhere before it gets dark, or if not we'll check into a bed-and-breakfast. It won't break the bank.'

'OK,' Imogen said. 'I'm on!' She turned to Jennifer and Caroline. 'What about you two?'

'I agree,' Caroline said. But then she always did agree, Imogen thought. She was incredibly amenable, which could get a bit boring.

'Very well then,' Jennifer said. 'Where would we go?'

'Lots of places,' Grace said. 'The Cotswolds? We could get a coach or a bus to somewhere, then walk.'

'So it's agreed then,' Imogen said. 'Saturday morning, come rain or shine.'

Saturday morning dawned fine, indeed there was a wintry sun and the air was crisp. Grace had undertaken to wake the others by seven o'clock, and did so.

'We're all to have a substantial breakfast,' she said. 'No cup of black coffee and half a slice of toast. And we'll take a packed lunch, which will save expense.'

They had informed Philip the previous day that they'd be away for the weekend, and had asked him to tell Stuart, whom they might not see since he stayed out late these days. All the same, Grace decided, she would leave a note for him in case Philip forgot, or they didn't meet up. It could happen. The two men didn't live in each other's pockets. 'Almost certainly back Sunday,' she wrote, 'but don't send out search parties if we're not.'

'Not that he would,' she said to the others. 'He couldn't care less.'

By half-past eight they were out of the house. They had decided it would be more economical to travel to Cheltenham – or wherever – in Imogen's car, leave it in an overnight car park and collect it on Sunday afternoon.

'I'm really looking forward to this,' Grace said. 'And we are *not*, repeat *not*, taking our troubles with us!'

Though what troubles did the others have, Jennifer thought, in comparison to hers? However, she would do her very best to enter into the spirit of the weekend which, though no-one had said as much, she knew had been arranged mostly for her benefit and for which she was grateful.

*   *   *

Next to leave Mulberry Lane on Saturday were Brian, Karen and the children, and half an hour after that Dermot and Laura drove in the same direction. Everybody, thought Esther who had seen it all, is going out this morning. Where are they off to? She would quite like a trip in a car but no-one seemed to think of it, except for taking her to church. She got sick of staying in, seeing life through a window.

'Can I ask you a favour?' Karen asked Brian as they drove into the town. 'When we get to Dean & Docker's can we visit the toy department first? I've promised both children a present – something quite small – and if they get it first they'll have something to occupy them and nothing to nag about.'

'Sure!' Brian agreed. 'Except that I'd like to buy the toys. After all, this is my fault.'

'OK. Thank you,' Karen said. 'But it mustn't be anything at all expensive. They don't inevitably have a present every time we visit a shop – though that would be Fiona's idea of bliss – and seldom anything expensive. I wouldn't want them to get used to it.' Nor did she want to be beholden to Brian. That wasn't on the cards.

'Understood!' Brian said.

The choice was agonizing, and took for ever. In the end Neil chose a small model car, red, and Fiona a book of puzzles.

'Splendid!' Karen said. 'You'll have something to keep you occupied. Say thank you to Mr Carson.'

'Are we going home now?' Fiona asked.

'As soon as we've chosen the curtains,' Karen said.

There was a surprising choice in the curtain

department. In the end they settled on – it was a joint decision – a paisley-type design in tawny shades on a deep cream heavy cotton.

'Lovely!' Karen said. 'They'll show the dirt, of course, but they'll certainly brighten up the room. What about a curtain rail?'

'There's one there already,' Brian told her. 'A nice, old-fashioned wooden one with brass rings. I suppose it should have gone with the rest of the things, but I didn't notice and nor did the removal men. I'm not going to bother now. Shall we go somewhere for a coffee and something to eat? I expect the children are hungry.' It seemed the right thing to do and, unexpectedly, he was in no hurry to end the morning.

'That would be a treat,' Karen said.

Sitting at the table, looking for something to say, Brian remarked: 'David is having his girlfriend – well, his fiancée really, they're engaged – over for the day next Saturday.'

'That's a nice idea,' Karen said. 'I didn't think anything like that was on the cards.'

'I don't see why not. He's a bit disappointed she can't stay overnight, but that's not on.'

'That's a shame,' Karen said. 'Would it be any help if I said she could stay with me? The children could double up, she could have one of their rooms.'

'Good heavens! I imagine she'd be over the moon, and so would he, but I'm not sure from your point of view though. I don't know anything about her, only David's opinion and that's bound to be good, isn't it? On the other hand, she was the one who insisted that if David wanted her to stand by him he should come on this rehab course, so there must be something to her.'

'I suppose I could stand her for one night whatever she's like,' Karen said. 'Think about it. Only please warn her it won't be anything posh. Also that I've got two lively kids!'

At the moment when the children were eating the last of their doughnuts and Brian and Karen were finishing their coffee, Dermot and Laura were leaving the Shipfield library in the same street with a week's supply of books; and also at the very same moment Mrs Clarke was entering to change hers. The three of them met on the middle of the steps.

'Why, Mrs Clarke!' Dermot said. 'How are you?'

'I'm all right, thank you,' Mrs Clarke said.

'Darling, this is Mrs Clarke, Melanie's mother,' Dermot said to Laura.

'Hello!' Laura said, holding out her hand.

She had not expected to see anyone as attractive and young-looking as the woman who now shook hands somewhat diffidently. She was trim and slim and looked not a day over thirty, though of course she must be. Without actually saying anything, Dermot had given an impression of her as a drab, downtrodden sort of woman.

'Pleased to meet you!' Mrs Clarke said.

'We've just been changing our library books,' Dermot said.

And what else might we have been doing, coming down the library steps with an armful of them, Laura thought.

'I'm just taking mine in,' Mrs Clarke said. 'They're due today. I don't like paying fines.'

'Nor do we,' Dermot said.

That might have been it, they might have gone their separate ways had not Dermot said, in an

307

effort to be friendly: 'I didn't see you at the parents' evening last week, Mrs Clarke. I did remind Melanie.'

'I expect she forgot to tell me,' Mrs Clarke apologized. 'I would have come. How is Melanie getting on in school, Mr O'Brien? Has she been troublesome lately?'

How could he tell this woman that her daughter was as difficult as ever, that he tried not to speak to her except when he had to teach her, otherwise it seemed safest to ignore her, and that he looked forward to the end of the school year after which, thankfully, she would be out of his life. Which made him wonder if he himself was actually cut out to be a teacher.

'She should be going on to sixth form college next year,' he said. 'She's bright enough to do her "A" levels, even to get to university.'

Mrs Clarke shook her head. 'I can't see her doing any of that. I wish I could.'

Dermot couldn't see it either. She would abandon all her studies at the very first opportunity and take a dead-end job somewhere. But that was something else he couldn't say to her mother.

'Well, I'd better be going,' Mrs Clarke said.

Dermot and Laura went off for coffee. As they approached their usual coffee shop, Brian and Karen, with the children, were leaving it.

'Well!' Laura said, trying to sound not too surprised. 'Everybody seems to be in town this morning!'

'We've been buying curtains,' Brian said.

'Curtains?' Laura waited for an explanation but none came. 'Oh, really? We're just going in for a coffee.'

308

'We've just had one,' Karen said. 'They do very good coffee.'

'I know,' Laura said. 'We come here regularly.'

'And doughnuts!' Fiona added.

'See you around then,' Dermot said.

Seated at a table a few minutes later Laura began: 'That was interesting, wasn't it? Do you think . . . ?'

'Karen's a nice woman,' Dermot broke in, 'but I don't think you should read anything into it.'

'I'm not doing,' Laura protested. 'Anyway what about Melanie? You didn't say much to Mrs Clarke.'

'I couldn't,' Dermot said. 'How could I tell her mother that her daughter's invariably late for school and that when she does turn up she's half asleep. She doesn't work, she has no interest. In fact I feel sorry for the kid but I daren't show it.'

'I think you're wise not to,' Laura said.

'I feel sorry for the whole family,' Dermot said. 'Especially the mother.'

'Perhaps they need counselling?' Laura queried.

'Perhaps they do, but somehow Mrs Clarke's not the sort of woman you'd suggest it to.'

'I wonder why the husband left?' Laura mused.

'He'd been made redundant. He was depressed,' Dermot told her. 'Apparently there wasn't anyone else involved.'

On ten o'clock on Saturday night, somewhere in the Cotswolds, the four girls were already tucked up in a bed-and-breakfast (all rooms en suite) establishment where they had been obliged to check in because it had been impossible to find a hostel open. Even so, all the proprietor could offer them was one large room with a double bed and two singles – 'And lucky to get it,' he'd told them, implying that he was full to the ceiling.

'I don't believe he is at all!' Imogen said. 'I reckon he doesn't want to open up another room. He's packed them away for the winter. You must admit there isn't a sound from anywhere else in the house!'

'You're right,' Grace agreed. 'It doesn't matter though, does it? It's quite comfortable.'

'Except that four of us have to share one bathroom,' Imogen pointed out.

'Which we do in Mulberry Lane,' Grace reminded her.

Jennifer, who had had the luck to draw a single bed, pulled the bedclothes over her and gave herself up to her thoughts, which were alternately about Athens and about Liam, so that when she fell asleep she dreamt that Liam, armed with a gun, was pursuing her up a steep mountain in Athens and that the only way she could escape him was by plunging into the river which suddenly appeared from nowhere, where she would be safe because he couldn't swim. The water was icy cold, and so was she when she woke and found that most of the bedclothes were on the floor. And that it was already morning though she could have sworn that she had been asleep no more than ten minutes.

In Mulberry Lane, at around midnight, it seemed that most people had retired for the night. There were very few lights showing, though Laura and Dermot were still up, having been watching a video. Esther's house was in darkness; so were Numbers Thirteen and Fifteen and also the students'. No burglar alarms had sounded. As far as anyone knew, no house was being burgled and no-one was being murdered in his or her bed. At Cornerways Bruno was snoring in his sleep and at Number Eight Titus slumbered lightly, lying on his back with all four short legs straight up in the air, ready to spring to life immediately should anything at all threaten his domain.

Dermot heard a car draw up, heard a door slam, sounding particularly loud in the night air. The students, he thought, though Laura had told him that the girls were away and surely that was a girl's voice. And pretty loud. Nothing to do with him, of course. It was a free country.

He was about to leave the room and follow Laura upstairs when he distinctly heard what was no longer just raised voices, but a scream, and then another scream. He went to the window and drew back the corner of the curtain in time to see a man's figure – he thought it was Stuart but he wasn't sure, and in any case he was more concerned about the girl, who was leaning against the wall. She had stopped screaming and now she was leaning her head over the wall and being copiously sick. Then, when she had finished throwing up, she turned in his direction and the light from the street lamp lit up her face.

It was Melanie Clarke.

18

Dermot rushed into the hall and shouted up the stairs to Laura.

'It's Melanie! She's outside. She's in trouble!'

Laura appeared, already in her dressing gown, on the landing.

'Melanie? What's she doing outside our house?'

'That's what I'm on my way to find out!'

'Wait!' It was a firm command. 'I'm going with you! Let me put some shoes on.'

'Then hurry,' Dermot said. 'She doesn't look too good!' But Laura was already running down the stairs.

'What's it all about?'

Dermot didn't answer. He was already out of the front door, ahead of Laura.

Melanie was leaning against the wall, crying noisily. Tears ran down her face, smudging the heavy black mascara which ringed her eyes so that it ran down her cheeks. Her hair was wild, but perhaps that was its usual weekend style.

Dermot hurried towards her, Laura immediately behind him.

'Melanie!' he cried. 'What in the world . . . ?'

'Oh, Mr O'Brien!' she sobbed. 'What are you doing here?'

'I live here!' he said. 'More to the point is what are you doing? But never mind that now. Come in and let's sort you out.'

Laura stepped forward, took Melanie's arm and began to lead her to the house. 'I'm Mrs O'Brien,' she said. There was vomit on the girl's short skirt and she smelled strongly of drink. There had been no opportunity for Dermot to say what he had observed and Laura's first thought, insofar as she had time to think, was that the girl was seeking out Dermot. It was why she had been determined not to let him deal with her on his own. In spite of what had happened in the school she guessed he wouldn't have given a thought to any possible danger to himself in the situation. His concern would be for a pupil in distress and for that, while she deplored what she saw as his lack of common sense, she loved him.

They went into the house. Laura switched on the fire in the sitting room and seated Melanie in a chair close to it.

'Are you cold?' she asked. It was a chilly December night for which Melanie's clothing – the shortest of skirts, a low-necked cotton top revealing the curves of her high, rounded breasts, a flimsy jacket which wasn't fastened, shoes a few criss-crossing straps on five-inch heels – was totally unsuitable.

Melanie nodded. Apart from the one short sentence on first seeing Dermot, she hadn't spoken.

'Yes, I see you are,' Laura said. 'You're shivering.' She turned to Dermot. 'Bring a blanket from the cupboard, will you, and put the kettle on. A cup of tea will warm us all.'

Dermot fetched the blanket, which Laura draped

around Melanie's shoulders and tucked in as far over her legs as it would reach. Her feelings about Melanie were ambivalent – she smelled trouble – but for the moment she was a young person in distress, and that took precedence. She could have been one of her own daughters, though she liked to think that neither of them would ever have found themselves in such a situation.

'There,' she said. 'That's better. Now you can just sit quietly while I see how Mr O'Brien's getting on with the tea. When we've had that you can tell us what it's all about and we'll see what we can do to help.'

She left Melanie and joined Dermot in the kitchen.

'Have you the slightest idea what's going on? Why would she come to find you? For a start, how would she know where to look? The children don't know the teachers' addresses, do they? Not to mention why is she dressed as she is, why is she crying her eyes out and why has she vomit on her clothes?'

'Laura, she didn't come looking for me,' Dermot said sharply. 'It's nothing to do with me. The fact that I'm on the spot is nothing more than coincidence.' He told her what he had observed of the scene with Stuart.

'I never did like him,' Laura said. 'None of them do.'

'That's not the point now. As soon as Melanie's recovered enough,' Dermot said, 'I'll take her home.'

'Oh no you won't!' Laura declared. 'You'll do no such thing! Are you mad? She might look totally pathetic and harmless now, and don't think I don't feel sorry for her because I do, but have you forgotten what she's capable of? And you didn't ever tell me how very attractive, how sexy she was, even tearful, vomit-stained and stinking of booze!'

'Oh, Laura, she's just a kid!' Dermot protested. 'We can't possibly let her go home on her own. And I'm not letting you do it, then drive back on your own at this time on a Saturday night. So if you won't trust me on my own . . .'

'Not you. Her!' Laura said. 'And of course I wouldn't let her go home on her own.'

'Then we'll both have to go.'

Laura shook her head. 'Not so! We shall get her mother to come and pick her up. Do they have a car?'

'I've no idea,' Dermot said.

'Well, if they don't Mrs Clarke can get a taxi. But either way she'll have to collect Melanie. I wouldn't even let her go in a taxi on her own. What would the driver make of it?'

She poured three cups of tea, set them on a tray, added a plate of biscuits and went back to the sitting room, followed by Dermot.

'Here we are!' she said to Melanie. 'This will do you good. Are you any warmer now?'

Melanie nodded, still without speaking.

'Would you like to tell us what happened?' Laura said.

Melanie shook her head.

'It might help. You'd feel better afterwards,' Laura said.

'We might be able to do something,' Dermot said, though he didn't know what. In his view Melanie was born to trouble.

'How did you get here?' Laura prompted.

315

'With Stuart, in his car.' Melanie broke her silence reluctantly.

'Stuart next door?'

'I didn't know where he lived. I didn't know where you lived,' Melanie said.

'So where did you meet him?'

'In Jotters.'

'Jotters?' Laura asked.

'It's a club in the town,' Dermot said. 'Some of the older kids go there, whether they should or shouldn't. And the university students, of course.'

'I went with a friend,' Melanie said. Now that she had broken the ice she no longer seemed to mind talking. 'But she went off with someone, left me on my own. That was when Stuart came over. I've seen him there before, he's usually on his own. He bought me a drink, which I shouldn't have had because I'd already had three, but it was a fancy cocktail and I don't usually get those. They're expensive.'

'And how many did he buy you?' Dermot asked.

'Two more. Then I told him I'd have to leave because Mum had said if I wasn't in by midnight she wouldn't let me go out all next week. I quite liked him – well, I did then. He spoke nicely and he said some nice things. You know, compliments! He said he'd give me a lift home, so we went to the car park and we messed about a bit in the car – you know, nothing heavy. Then I said I'd really got to be home so we drove off . . .'

'Only he didn't take you home?' Laura said.

'No. I kept telling him he was going the wrong way but he took no notice. Then he stopped the car just outside here and said would I come in, just for a few minutes . . .' She stopped to sip her tea. 'I'd be all right, he said, but I didn't believe that. Then he said there'd be no-one in the house and I was real scared. I said I wanted to go home right away. That was when he got hold of my arms and dragged me out of the car. I started to scream and he tried to stop me. He was like an animal.'

She paused.

'And what happened next?' Laura asked.

A gleam came into Melanie's eyes.

'I kneed him. He doubled up. I hope I crippled him! He staggered off into the house. I think I was still screaming – or crying. He shouted back at me, told me to find my own fucking way home. I think it was all the screaming, and getting scared, and not knowing where I was, made me throw up.'

I reckon it was the six drinks inside you, Dermot thought, but it wasn't the time to say so.

'Well now,' Laura said, 'I think it's time we called your mother and told her where you are. She must be worried sick. Then she can come and pick you up, take you home and put you to bed. Does she have a car?'

'Of sorts,' Melanie said. It was an old banger she normally wouldn't be seen dead in, she hated it whenever her mother turned up at the school gates in it, but at this moment it would be wonderful to set eyes on it, with her mother in the driving seat, even though she knew she'd be in for trouble.

'Right! So give me her telephone number,' Laura said. 'I'll speak to her first – actually I met your mother only this morning – and then you can have a word with her.'

'I don't want to!' Melanie said. 'Not now. She'll be furious!'

317

'Most of all, she'll be pleased to know you're safe and sound,' Laura told her. 'Believe me!'

She keyed the number. Mrs Clarke answered immediately. No doubt she'd been sitting by the phone, Laura thought, I know I would have been. She explained briefly and quickly. 'But don't worry, she's all right,' she assured Mrs Clarke. 'I just thought you were the best person to take her home. Do you know where Mulberry Lane is? Good! It's Number Ten. I'll be looking out for you. Bring a warm coat for Melanie, will you?'

Within fifteen minutes Mrs Clarke was ringing the bell.

'She's OK,' Laura said, answering the door. 'A bit upset. It was the guy's fault, not hers. In fact she behaved very well in the circumstances. She stood her ground, stood up to him!' She didn't tell Mrs Clarke what Melanie had done to him. 'So don't be cross with her.'

'I won't,' Mrs Clarke said. 'But I don't know how to apologize to you and your husband. I really don't!'

'There's no need. I'm glad we were around.' Laura led Mrs Clarke into the sitting room. 'Here's your mum!' she said to Melanie. 'You'll be all right now.'

At the sight of her mother Melanie burst into tears again. Mrs Clarke stepped towards her and took her in her arms.

'I was so worried, love,' she said. 'But you're all right, and that's all that matters. We'll go straight home and you can go to bed. Explanations can wait until the morning.' She turned to Dermot and Laura, starting to apologize again, but they stopped her.

'Thank you both so much,' Mrs Clarke said. 'Melanie will be in school on Monday morning, I promise you.'

'This has nothing to do with school,' Dermot said. 'These things happen and school doesn't come into it.'

He saw them to the car, then came back into the house and locked the door.

'Actually,' he said to Laura, 'what I'd like to do is go next door and sort out bloody Stuart! And he would be bloody when I'd finished with him! It's time somebody did.'

'But not you,' Laura said. 'It's not your business. Besides, he's bigger than you, not to mention younger. Seriously though, if you were to interfere it could lead to all sorts of complications. It's up to the people involved to sort it out – if indeed they can. Anyway, I'm sure Melanie won't wish to be involved with Stuart ever again.'

'I daresay you're right,' Dermot acknowledged. 'It's just that I hate to see him get away with it.'

'Well, in a way he didn't,' Laura said, smiling for the first time. 'I guess he was well and truly thwarted! Shall we go to bed?'

Sunday dawned, though not that early since the year was approaching the shortest day. Three weeks from now it would be Christmas Eve. Before it was fully daylight Laura was wakened by the radio alarm. She stretched out and switched it off, then rolled over onto her other side and put an arm around Dermot, shaking him gently. 'Time to get up, darling!'

He mumbled in his sleep. He was always the same, as difficult to wake as any teenage boy.

'Come on,' she said. 'It's Sunday. We shall be late.'

'It's still dark,' Dermot complained.

'It is a bit,' Laura agreed. 'It would be lighter if you opened your eyes.' Though not much, she thought.

Reluctantly, Dermot did so, raising himself on one elbow. 'Do we have to go to Mass?' he grumbled. 'Can't we give it a miss for once?'

'Of course we can't,' Laura said. 'You know that.' Although Dermot was the cradle Catholic and Laura was the convert since just before their marriage, it was always he who looked for an excuse not to go to church. And Laura who didn't let him get away with it.

It didn't seem two minutes to him since they had come to bed. He supposed he had fallen asleep as his head hit the pillow, but now he remembered what had made them late. Poor Melanie! He hoped she was all right. He wondered, not very coherently because it was too early, what chance she had of ever being all right, the way things were. Then he gave up the thought. He would deal with it later.

'As a very special favour,' Laura said, getting out of bed with that typical sprightliness of hers, irritating so early in the day, and putting on her dressing gown and slippers, 'I'll go down and make the tea. I'll even bring you a cup.'

'You are wonderful,' Dermot said faintly. Then he turned, slid down under the bedclothes and was asleep again.

Before making for the kitchen, which was at the back of the house, Laura went into the sitting room and drew back the curtains. The street lights were still on and, apart from the paper boy just coming into view on his bicycle, Mulberry Lane was deserted. Even Esther's house – and she was the earliest of early birds – was still in darkness. I'll give her a ring when I've made the tea, Laura thought. It took Esther a long time to get ready for Mass. And always at the back of Laura's mind was the fact that Esther was really old, and quite frail of body, if not of spirit, and that she might, just might, one of these nights die peacefully in her sleep. It was always a relief when she called, as she did every morning, and Esther answered the phone. Not that she ever confessed this to anyone. Even to herself she hardly acknowledged how very fond she was of Esther, and to everyone else, Esther included, her businesslike though kind manner hid her feelings.

Stuart's car was where he had left it, very badly parked with the front wheel well on the pavement. He was no doubt dead to the world, sleeping off his excesses. Melanie had told them that he'd said there was no-one else in the house – in fact that was what had seemed to frighten her most in the end – so was Philip away? You wouldn't know, Laura thought. Philip was a person one didn't see, even when he was there. He could be in the same room and not be noticed. Anyway, she was glad Esther hadn't been disturbed by the screams, though Esther, if she found out, would probably be furious at having missed it all.

She wondered if the Andersons had heard. But Laura wasn't to know that Gary and Lisa's beautiful bedroom, with its top quality double glazing and thick velvet curtains, was at the back of the house, overlooking the garden. It could be said that they slept in *Upper* Mulberry Lane and would therefore be sheltered from the vulgar goings-on of Mulberry proper.

She made the tea and took a cup to Dermot. He was fast asleep and she had to shake him gently awake. She showered and dressed, choosing a long, wool skirt and a sweater. It was going to be a cold day. When she was ready, which as always was in good time, she telephoned Esther.

'Good morning, Esther!' she said cheerfully. 'How are you this morning?'

'I'm the same as usual,' Esther said. 'You don't need to phone me to see if I'm awake. I'm not one who sleeps much, more's the pity. I daresay I'm always awake before you are!' All the same she knew she'd be disappointed if Laura didn't ring. Laura, for her part, knew full well she'd be chided if she failed to do so. These were simply the usual preliminaries they went through with the morning call.

'Dress warmly,' Laura advised. 'I went out into the garden to feed the birds and it's quite nippy.'

'I shall dress as I always do,' Esther informed her. 'I don't have an extensive wardrobe, as you know.'

'I know no such thing,' Laura said. 'You are one of the best-dressed women I know – when you want to be. Anyway, usual time, Dermot will come across for you.'

Esther and the O'Briens would already have been in church by the time Jennifer and co. roused themselves from their beds in the Cotswolds. The plan had been to rise with the lark and be out on the hills almost before the early chill had gone from the day and it was the proprietor, quite used to these aspirations (more often than not unfulfilled) among his paying guests, who had said, 'Decide in

322

the morning. Don't hurry! I'll cook the breakfast at whatever time you come down for it.'

'Which goes to show,' Imogen said, 'that we *are* the only people staying here. In fact he could have given us a room each if he'd wanted to!'

'It doesn't bother me,' Grace said. 'With a family like mine you get used to queuing for the bathroom.' Until she'd left home for university she had never known the luxury of a room to herself. She still wasn't sure whether she liked it. She missed the late night chats with her sister before they both fell asleep.

It was, therefore, after ten o'clock when they went downstairs and almost eleven before they had eaten their way through cornflakes, bacon, eggs, tomatoes, mushrooms, fried bread, toast and marmalade.

'He might stint on the bedrooms,' Jennifer said. 'He certainly doesn't on the food!'

At about the same time that the girls were guzzling their breakfasts in the Cotswolds the men at Number Fifteen Mulberry Lane were eating theirs, with very much the same dishes on the menu and in this case cooked by Brian, who had taken on Sunday breakfasts as one of his chores. His style, deliberately chosen, was to make the men's stay as much like decent home conditions as possible, with the added safeguard of a few rules and disciplines designed to ease them back into the world and, though it was never stated, to guard them from some of the temptations which had probably landed them in prison in the first place. And if they were not resisted, would take them back there. It was his experience that most of the young

323

ex-prisoners he had dealt with were not so much wicked as weak, even those who saw themselves as strong and tough.

Sunday breakfast was therefore a moveable feast; you could come down when you liked, or skip it if you wanted to, except that eleven o'clock was the time for starting on the chores in the house.

They had decided, yesterday, that gardening would be the thing for Sunday, both morning and afternoon. There might not be many more fine weekends, Brian had pointed out, but they could work indoors however bad the weather was. So now it was half-past ten and three of the four men, with Brian, were seated at the table. Colin was still in bed. He preferred that to breakfast and would probably grab a slice of bread at the last minute before he went into the garden. Mark had already finished. He was on the Sunday lunch shift at the Shipfield Arms, which meant he had to work from eleven until three. He rose now, and piled his dishes together to take them into the kitchen.

'I'll have to go,' he said. 'There'll be trouble if I'm late.' It would take him twenty minutes to walk into the town.

Actually, he was enjoying his job in the hotel restaurant – well, most of it. He enjoyed the bustle, the comings and goings. He was happy in the surroundings of good furniture and furnishings; carpets, polished wood, quality china and cutlery, though one thing he would never learn to enjoy was that most boring of tasks, the polishing and buffing up of the cutlery and crockery when it came out of the dishwasher, which every lower-graded waiter, or dogsbody as he actually was, had to do. Standards at the Shipfield Arms were high and everything on the table had to be not only clean but gleaming.

'But next week,' he said now, 'I might get a very small promotion! One of the lads has to go into hospital, so we'll all have to do a bit more.'

'And will you be paid more?' Fergus asked. His job in the hospital and Mark's in the hotel paid much the same hourly rate.

Mark shook his head. 'I doubt that. I might get up to three seventy-five but I stand to get a better share of the tips, since there'll be fewer of us. The thing is, I'll get more interesting things to do. It won't all be clearing tables and helping to empty the dishwasher.'

So far he had been allowed very little contact with the customers. That wasn't his job, unless they actually asked him a question, but come next week he might be trusted to take an order and pass it to the kitchen, not to mention answer the telephone. 'Who knows?' he said. 'I might get to use some initiative!' He liked the atmosphere of the restaurant, especially when it was busy. Sometimes he thought that, given the chance, he might one day like to run his own restaurant, but for the moment that day seemed a long way off. A very long way off.

Colin, bleary-eyed, came into the room as Mark was leaving.

'Escaping?' he asked nastily. 'Of course you don't like gardening, do you? Dirties the hands!'

'I'm going to work,' Mark said tersely. 'I'll muck in with the rest of you when I get back.'

'Too bad it'll be over,' Colin said. 'It's dark by four o'clock.

'Oh, shut it, Colin!' David broke in angrily. 'You're boring!'

Colin went into the kitchen.

'He gets up my nose,' David said. 'Nothing's ever right with him.'

As Mark left the house he saw Gary Anderson emerging from Cornerways with Bruno on the lead. Bruno was a magnificent dog. Mark envied Gary his ownership of him. He had grown up with dogs, in his case German Shepherds, and having a dog was one of the things he had missed most in prison, and missed now, except that the boss of the Shipfield Arms had a black Labrador. He had some point of contact with him every day, even though the dog wasn't allowed in the kitchens or the restaurant. As soon as he had settled down in his own place one of the first things he would do would be to get a dog. Perhaps from a rescue place.

David, annoyed though he was with Colin, couldn't stay angry today. Things were right for him since yesterday afternoon when Brian had told him of Karen's offer to have Sandra to stay overnight. He had telephoned Sandra at once. If she got down from Croydon as early as possible on Saturday and left as late as the coaches would allow on Sunday, he had told her, they'd have practically two days together. He didn't have to work on Saturdays and Brian said he'd be excused everything in the house while Sandra was here. Unfortunately no night included . . . He hadn't worked out what, if anything, he could do about that.

It was one of the big drawbacks about living here. You were cut off from women. Well, not quite as bad for him perhaps. He had Sandra. Well, he had and he hadn't. He could phone her, write to her, plan the future with her – but it was not enough. There were times when he ached for her, when he had to try, deliberately, to put her out of his mind.

It was possibly worse for the others, or possibly not. It was a bit like living in a monastery except, since they hadn't taken vows of chastity, there wasn't anything to prevent them seeking the company of whoever they wanted. They had free time, they could go into the town and that, he suspected, was what Colin did – pick up a woman in Shipfield. About the other two he wasn't sure. Mark was gay, they all knew that, not that he said much about it, why should he? It was not likely that he had found a partner locally, though he might have had one when he'd been inside. As for Fergus – well, he talked a lot about sex but that seemed to be all. Unless by now he had a nice little nurse tucked away in the hospital? But would Fergus be able to keep it to himself? Words spilled out of him like water from a tap.

'I'll nip along to Karen this evening,' David said to Brian. 'Say thank you.'

Probably Mark and Fergus would go into the town, maybe to the cinema or to a pub, and if a pub, then preferably where no-one knew anything about them. There wasn't much going on on a Sunday. Usually David would go with them. Colin, also as usual, would go off on his own.

'If you're wanting to go out somewhere,' Brian said to David, 'I'll take the message for you. Karen won't mind.'

19

The next few days in Mulberry Lane were un-
eventful, everything taking its normal course.
Those who had to go out to earn a living dutifully
did so. Peter and Meg went off to Bristol (no-one
ever quite knew where Samson the cat went), Ralph
and Michelle Streeter set off together each day to
their salon, Michelle to cut, blow-dry and tint her
ladies' hair in various shades while Ralph dealt with
his ladies – they each had their own clients – did the
books and saw the reps. Laura went to the hospital,
Dermot to school. Nigel walked Titus twice a day,
every day. Gary Anderson, though weary in the
evenings from spending the day making money,
dutifully took Bruno for his walk. Fiona and Neil
were taken to and collected from school. Esther
kept up her Neighbourhood Watch and was a little
miffed that nothing happened.

The girls returned from the Cotswolds, declaring
themselves refreshed and invigorated even though
aching from unaccustomed hill walking, and
Caroline with a blistered heel. Jennifer, though
only a little less distressed about Liam, was still
determined to stick to her plan of going to Athens
with Professor Maitland's group. Little was seen of

Stuart by anyone (and still less of Philip). Unknown to the world, Stuart started off the week in a certain amount of pain and even more chagrin.

Melanie, though strictly not belonging to Mulberry Lane, merely having been drawn into it by circumstances, was perhaps the only one whose week deviated from its normal routine. On Monday morning she had not turned up for school and she was absent for the rest of the week.

'Her mother telephoned,' Dermot reported to Laura. 'Said Melanie had a nasty chest cold.'

'Which doesn't surprise me in the least,' Laura said (rather tartly for her). 'I wonder she doesn't go down with pneumonia, considering how little she wears. Especially in the chest area!'

Brian's week started off well. On the previous Sunday evening, at a time when the four girls were taking it in turn to have long, hot baths to soothe their weary limbs, Brian, as promised, and after the men had gone into town, walked along to Number Six to see Karen and to give her David's message of thanks. He took a bottle of wine with him, handing it to her when she invited him in.

'Oh, thank you,' she said, 'but you shouldn't!'

'It's a pleasure,' Brian said. 'Where are the children?'

'Tucked up in bed. Asleep, I hope.'

He told her why he had come – or, more accurately, gave her his excuse for coming. He couldn't quite admit, even to himself, that he was here because he wanted to see her. Women, he thought, he could take or leave. Karen wasn't like all other women, but he was not involved with her. Nor had he any intention of being so beyond a certain point, of his own choosing.

'David's really chuffed!' he said. 'I reckon he's counting the hours. It's very kind of you.'

'It's nothing,' Karen said. 'I just wish I could give the two of them some time here on their own but it's not easy taking both kids out for long.'

'I agree. Actually, I've thought about that and I have a possible solution,' Brian said. 'If you agree to it, that is. I thought if David and Sandra agreed to stay in and babysit while you and I go out, then they'd have the place to themselves. It seems to me the children go to bed reasonably early.'

'As early as I can possibly get them there!' Karen said with feeling. 'And as a matter of fact they go off to sleep quite quickly.'

'Well then! We'd be doing David and Sandra a good turn.'

Karen looked at him directly, and smiled. She wasn't the prettiest woman in the world, her nose was too long and her mouth too big for classic good looks, but her smile, which started in her eyes, lit up her face and gave her a beauty which went beyond perfect features.

'Put like that,' she said, 'how could I refuse?' Even so, at the back of her mind she still had this wariness. He was very nice, but that was it.

'Good!' Brian said. 'Where shall we go? A restaurant? The theatre? A movie? You choose.'

'A restaurant, then,' Karen said. 'It'll be nice to talk. A change from talking every evening only to small children. I sometimes think I'll forget how to talk with anyone except in words of one syllable!'

'I'll book somewhere,' Brian promised.

'Would you like a cup of coffee?' Karen asked.

'Why don't we open the bottle of wine?' Brian suggested. 'If you give me a corkscrew I'll do it.'

He followed her into the kitchen. She took a corkscrew from a drawer and two glasses from the cupboard.

'Let's take it back into the other room,' Karen said. 'It's more comfortable.' She went ahead of him, carrying the glasses, and sat on the sofa. Brian poured the wine and came and sat beside her.

'Here's to us!' he said, raising his glass.

Karen sipped at hers. 'Mmm! Very nice. I don't know a thing about wine but I like this.'

Helped by the wine, they chatted, though in the beginning awkwardness had them both searching for subjects of interest.

'Where are the men this evening?' Karen asked.

'Gone into town.'

'Oh! What's there to do in Shipfield on a Sunday evening?'

'Not much, I daresay,' Brian admitted. 'Pubs – but they don't have much money, and that's deliberate. Anyway, I don't enquire too closely into what they do in their spare time. If they tell me that's another matter. Perhaps I ought to?'

'I don't know,' Karen said.

'The point is, they're no longer prisoners, and they're not children. I suppose part of my job is to help them towards standing on their own feet, and that includes socially as well as economically. And I suppose another part is to try to keep them from temptation, particularly in these early days. It's a fine line between those two parts. I'm not sure I always tread it correctly.'

'I expect you do,' Karen said. 'So how long will it all take?'

Brian refilled their glasses.

'You mean what I'm doing here? I don't know

331

exactly. Three to six months perhaps. Or could be a year. Hopefully, I'll recognize it when the time comes. I'll recognize the time to push them out. With Colin Myers I doubt it's going to work anyway. I think I made a mistake there. I think for him it was board and lodgings for a bit while he sussed out what to do next.'

'And the others?'

'More hopeful. A lot depends on whether, when they leave here, they can get jobs. But one of the things about all this is that they'll have earned references from employers.'

Karen nodded. 'They'll need that. Will they go back to where they came from?'

'I don't know,' Brian said. 'I think it's on the cards that Fergus will go back to Ireland. The employment situation's better there than it was when he left, and he misses his family. And of course David will get married. I don't know about Mark. He's a bit of a puzzle. Well educated, intelligent, comes from a good family, though sometimes that makes surprisingly little difference. But I think perhaps he's got more ambition than the others. He'll set himself goals, hopefully legitimate ones.'

There was another silence.

'I suppose I'd better be off,' Brian said, breaking it.

'If you must,' Karen said – and was surprised to hear herself saying it. It must be the wine. She wasn't used to it.

'Well, actually, come to think of it I don't have to!' Brian said, smiling. 'There's nothing I have to be back for except that since there's an eleven o'clock curfew for the men I also keep to it.'

Karen looked at her watch. 'In that case you have

two and a half hours,' she said. 'It's only half-past eight. Shall we open another bottle of wine? I have one. I don't know what made me buy it because I don't buy wine. It's cheap plonk of course.' Nor did she quite know what had made her offer it.

'What a good idea!' Brian said.

In the kitchen Karen said: 'I could make an omelette in a bit, if you like.'

'Great!' Brian said. 'Not just yet, though. Let's drink your bottle of plonk.'

If I drink any more I shall get tight, Karen thought, but what the hell? She remembered, in a brief flash which she immediately banished from her mind, what had happened the last time she had drunk too much. It wouldn't happen again. Brian wasn't that sort of a man. There was respect between them. All the same, he was very attractive. She clamped down on her thoughts; they were on the way to leading her in the wrong direction.

'So what will *you* do when the men have left? Will you take in more? Or will the house be ready to sell? And if it is, where will you go next?'

'I don't know the answer to any of those questions,' Brian confessed. 'I wish I did. This was very much something I plunged into when I was at a turning point, didn't know which way to go. It's very much a question of doing something when the time is ripe, and hoping you do the right thing. I expect there'd always be someone ready to replace the men who left – there aren't all that many schemes like this – but it's also a question of what the Trust wants to do next.'

'I'd be sorry to see you go,' Karen said, 'though I expect you will, sooner or later.'

'I don't know,' Brian said. 'I don't suppose I'll do

333

it for ever. And what do you intend to do with your life?' he asked, refilling their glasses.

Karen shrugged, shook her head.

'I don't know. I certainly don't mean to work in the toffee factory for ever. I'd like to train for something better. I took the job largely because it was the only part-time one which fitted in with what I needed to do for the children. School and so on.'

'So what about your marriage?' he said. 'Or shouldn't I ask that?'

'My marriage is definitely over,' Karen said. 'Ray isn't going to come back and in fact I don't want him to. I've no feelings left for him. If he rang the doorbell right now I wouldn't let him in. When I get around to it I'll divorce him. I've made up my mind on that. The only thing is, I'm sorry for the children. I shall try to make it up to them as well as I can, but it's not the same as having a father around, is it?'

Her tongue, she was well aware, was running away with her. It was the wine, she thought, taking another sip. Did it matter? No, it didn't!

'You were married once, weren't you?' she asked.

'Yes, I was,' Brian said.

He told her about Helen, just about everything there was to tell, which surprised him because it was something he had never done with anyone before. It had eaten into him, coloured his view of life and of women and he had remained incapable of talking about it. 'She was several years younger than I was,' he said. 'I suppose I wasn't exciting enough for her. She wanted something more glamorous. Anyway, it's not something I think of trying again!'

'I'll make that omelette I promised you,' Karen

334

said. 'Do you like mushrooms? Do you want to eat here in the kitchen?'

'Yes to both,' Brian said.

When they had finished the meal, lingering over it far longer than it took to eat an omelette and a slice of garlic bread, Brian looked at his watch.

'Ten minutes to eleven,' he said. 'I'll have to be off! Another time I shall have to ask for a late pass! Anyway, I'll see you Saturday. I'll bring David and Sandra along as soon as she arrives and in the meantime I'll sort out something for you and me.'

'Supposing they don't want to stay in?' Karen asked.

Brian laughed. 'You don't think they're going to pass up the chance of being as good as alone in a house for two or three hours?'

Karen went with him into the hall. When she opened the door for him he gave her a friendly kiss on the cheek.

Did he, she asked herself when he had left, kiss me because he'd drunk too much wine? She hated the thought that he would have to get tight in order to kiss her. But it hadn't been that kind of kiss, not the sudden, fumbling, searching kiss of inebriation, not for either of them. It was simply a friendly peck, quite pleasant. She shouldn't read anything into it, though she was pleased at the thought that it might be the beginning of a friendship. But there was no rush, everything could take its time. Suddenly she felt happier than she had for a long time. Also, before they could go very far into a true friendship there were things she would have to tell him. And would they be enough to make her lose him?

*   *   *

Laura, drawing the bedroom curtains on that same Sunday not many minutes later, saw Brian crossing the road to Number Fifteen. She wondered where he had been. If he'd been to the pub, why weren't the others with him? They were obviously out, there were no lights showing in the house. Unfortunately for her, she drew the curtains across and left the window not more than five minutes before three of the men returned together, though she wouldn't have been wholly satisfied because Colin was not with them.

So went the week. Nothing exciting, no scandals, no accidents, no-one fell ill – or presumably not seriously since Dr Craven's car was not seen, even by Esther. Quite a lot of work was done in Number Fifteen. The kitchen was completed; a cupboard at the far end of the landing was converted into a small, claustrophobic shower cubicle; work started on dividing the large bedroom into two. At the Shipfield Arms Mark was permanently upgraded, his hourly rate rising to four pounds an hour plus tips. Brian decided that these extra earnings should be divided between the four men and added to their pocket money, which pleased everyone except Colin, who, while taking the extra money, complained again that he wasn't earning a wage outside.

Only on Friday did a real piece of news come into the road, and then only to Number Ten because it didn't affect anyone else. It was brought home from school by Dermot.

'The head had a letter from Mrs Clarke this morning,' he announced to Laura. 'Melanie isn't coming back to school! The two of them have been up to London to see the father and the upshot is that they're moving in with him.'

336

'Good heavens!' Laura said. 'Now that *is* surprising.'

'Not really,' Dermot said. 'There was never any real quarrel between Mrs Clarke and her husband. It was just that when he was made redundant after nearly twenty years in the same job – he'd gone into it straight from school – he simply couldn't face it. It was always on the cards that they might get back together again.'

'Well, that's good news all round,' Laura said. She liked, above all things, a happy ending. 'I'm sure you must be relieved.'

'I am and I'm not,' Dermot said. 'I didn't exactly dislike Melanie, you know, not even when she nearly drove me mad. She wasn't a *bad* girl. She was just going through a difficult time.'

Laura gave him a quick kiss.

'And you're a very nice man!' she said. 'You know, you *are* cut out to be a teacher, even though sometimes you think otherwise.'

'I hope she'll be all right,' Dermot said.

'I expect she will be,' Laura said.

That evening Mrs Clarke telephoned.

'I couldn't leave without speaking to you, Mr O'Brien,' she said. 'You've been good to Melanie and I won't forget it. You were good to me, too, just when I needed a bit of encouragement. We both have a lot to thank you for.'

'That's all right,' Dermot said. 'I'm glad I was around. When do you leave for London?'

'Next weekend. Melanie will have to go to a new school until she finishes the year out. I hope the headmaster won't give her too bad a report.'

'I'm sure he won't,' Dermot said. 'Give Melanie

my best wishes. You know I've always said she could do well if she worked hard.'

'I'll remind her of that,' Mrs Clarke said. 'I'm sure she's going to be a different girl, being with her dad.'

'I'm sure she will be,' Dermot agreed. 'Best wishes to you, too!'

He hung up. 'Sad,' he said to Laura, 'but hopefully a happy ending.'

The next day at eleven in the morning David, having met Sandra at the coach station, arrived with her at Number Fifteen. Brian opened the door to them and could not contain his surprise at the sight of Sandra, nor did he try too hard to do so since the surprise was so pleasant that for a moment he allowed himself to stare at her. He had seen photographs, of course, and in those she looked a pretty, though unremarkable, young woman – like a hundred others. The reality was quite different. She was, by any standards, stunning. She was tall – topping David by at least three inches. Her slender figure was wrapped almost to her ankles in a black coat which was crowned by a collar of creamy-coloured, long-haired fur which perfectly framed her beautiful face. Her hair fell like heavy, pale gold silk to her shoulders, mingling with the fur. Her rose-pink, full lips, which appeared to Brian to owe everything to nature and nothing to art (though any woman could have told him that this was not so), parted in a wide smile which revealed teeth worthy of Hollywood. She broke into his astonishment by holding out her hand, which he grasped without taking his eyes from her face.

'Very pleased to meet you!' she said.

Her voice, high-pitched and thin, brought him back to earth. It was pure, undiluted East End.

'And you too!' he said. 'David talks a lot about you.'

It was true, and true also that David had said she was a looker, but the rest of them had dismissed that as the language of a man in love. So how had David, who was shortish, had a homely face and short-cropped red hair, attracted this beauty? And to the extent that she wanted to marry him? There must be more to him than met the eye.

Sandra giggled. 'All good, I hope?'

'Of course!' Brian assured her.

He turned to David. 'I thought we'd go straight along to Karen's. She's expecting us. Sandra can get rid of her suitcase and settle in, and then you're free. First though,' he said to Sandra, 'I'd like you to meet the others. Unfortunately, Mark isn't here. He has a double shift today, both lunches and dinners, but Fergus and Colin are working on the bedroom. I'll give them a shout.'

There was no need to shout for Fergus. He had heard the arrival and was already running down the stairs, and being Fergus there was no way he could contain his feelings when he came face to face with Sandra.

'Wow!' he said. 'And where has David been hiding *you*?'

'Away from the likes of you!' David said. He turned to Sandra. 'Take no notice of this one. He's kissed the Blarney stone!'

'I can tell that!' Sandra said, smiling.

Brian called up the stairs, 'Colin, can you spare a minute?'

Without hurrying, Colin came downstairs, was

introduced and would not have shaken hands except that it was difficult to ignore the hand Sandra held out to him. Her 'Pleased to meet you' met with no reply.

'I'll get back to work,' Colin said to Brian. 'There's a lot to be done.'

'And take no notice of that one either,' David said to Sandra when Colin had left. 'He was born rude.'

Karen's reaction on seeing Sandra standing on the doorstep was the same as Brian's had been, but she recovered more quickly.

'Do come in,' she said. The children were in the hall. 'This is Fiona, and this is Neil.' The children looked up briefly; Fiona was colouring in a book, Neil was running a model car across the tiles while making sounds uncannily like a real car. 'Did you have a good journey?' Karen asked.

She showed Sandra to her room, David carrying the suitcase upstairs. 'I hope you'll be comfortable,' Karen said. 'If there's anything you need, please ask. The bathroom's right next door to you. The children sleep in the room at the end and I'm just next to them.'

'It all looks lovely,' Sandra said. 'It's very kind of you!'

'Not a bit!' Karen said. 'In fact, I'm going to ask you a favour, or has Brian mentioned it? I wondered if you'd look after the children while I go out for a meal with Brian? I don't often have a chance to leave them. They'll be asleep, probably before we go, but if not soon after.'

'We'd be pleased to,' Sandra said. 'Wouldn't we, David?'

'Of course,' David said eagerly.

Obviously, Karen thought, his mind was quick to see the possibilities.

'Would you like some coffee?' she asked as they went downstairs.

David hesitated.

'If you don't mind, we won't,' he said. 'Would you think it was very rude if we shot off? There's quite a bit I want to show Sandra.'

'Of course not!' Karen said. 'Feel free to come and go as you please. I'll give you a key.'

'What time do you want us to be here this evening?' Sandra asked.

Karen turned to Brian.

'I've booked a table for eight o'clock,' he said.

'So if you were to be back not later than half-past seven,' Karen said, 'then I could show you where everything is. I'll have some food for you. Is there anything you don't like?'

'Oh please, Karen, no need to do that,' David said. 'We'll bring something in. Or we'll ring for a takeaway.'

They were off within minutes.

'I can't stay either,' Brian said. 'I have someone coming to look at the wiring in the house. Colin's done it, but I want it to be inspected, just to make sure.'

'Then I'll see you this evening,' Karen said.

'I'm looking forward to it,' Brian said. 'I booked at Umberto's. I asked Dermot and that's the place he recommended. I hope you like Italian food?' The only other place he knew was the Shipfield Arms and he didn't want to go there, not with Mark waiting at the tables.

'Love it!' Karen assured him.

*   *   *

In the end Brian arrived at Karen's soon after seven o'clock. Sandra and David were already there – not surprisingly, really, since it was a dark, drizzling evening outside. Fiona was sitting on the hearth-rug, but there was no sign of Neil.

'Neil's already in bed,' Karen told him. 'I reckon he'll be asleep. They've both had a busy day – I've been trying to tire them out. Fiona's been promised one more story and then she'll be off too.'

'And I'm going to read it,' Sandra said.

'I've brought a bottle of champagne,' Brian said. 'The wine shop said it was already chilled but I reckon a few more minutes in the fridge wouldn't be a bad idea.'

'Ooh!' Sandra said. 'Champagne, wonderful!'

'It's a special occasion,' Brian said, smiling at her.

'I want champagne!' Fiona demanded.

'You shall have a teeny drink of it, the very last thing before you go to bed!' Karen promised. 'That is, if Brian says so?'

'A good idea,' Brian said. 'It'll make you sleep.'

It was Umberto himself who showed Brian and Karen to a table in a quiet corner, and gave them the menu.

'If it is what you like,' he said, 'the risotto is special – but there are many other things to choose from, all of them good. Would you like an aperitif while you are choosing?'

Brian looked to Karen.

'Not for me!' she said. She was still feeling the pleasant effect of the champagne.

'We'll have wine with the food,' Brian said to Umberto. 'Give us a minute or two.'

342

'All the time you want,' Umberto said. 'I'll leave you to it.'

'So what would you like?' Brian asked.

Karen studied the menu.

'Almost anything *except* risotto. Reminds me too much of rice pudding!'

'A good thing Umberto didn't hear you say that,' Brian told her. 'But I don't like it all that much either. So what shall we choose?'

'I would like,' Karen said eventually, '*penne primavera.*' She didn't much care what she ate. Being here was enough.

'A good choice,' Brian said. 'I think I'll have chicken and ricotta cannelloni.' He hesitated. 'No I won't! I'll have seafood lasagne.'

'Sounds delicious,' Karen said. 'Everything sounds delicious.'

'Dermot recommended this place highly,' Brian said as they gave the order, then drank wine and ate garlic bread as they waited for the food.

'Did you tell him you were bringing me?' Karen asked.

'I did.'

'It'll go the length and breadth of Mulberry Lane when he tells Laura,' Karen said.

'Does it matter?'

'Not a bit!' she said.

Karen felt as if she was enfolded in a warm, soft blanket. It was a long time since she had felt so cosseted, and for the first time she allowed herself a glimpse of a happy future before her, though she would have to allow herself also the courage to let it happen. That was the bit she wasn't sure about. She couldn't see what that future might be, she didn't entirely want to. A good friendship would be plenty to be going on with.

When they arrived back at Number Six, at about a quarter to eleven, David and Sandra were sitting side by side on the sofa, Sandra appearing slightly dishevelled, David looking like a man who had just won a prize. It was Brian's guess that they had made good use of the bed in Sandra's room.

'Were the children all right?' Karen asked.

'Wonderful!' Sandra said. 'Fiona went straight off to sleep – it must have been the champagne – and there wasn't a peep out of either of them. Did you have a nice time?'

'Great!' Brian and Karen said in unison.

Sunday went equally well. The Green Man was full at lunchtime. Brian and three of the men were there – Mark was working – plus Sandra. Nigel was naturally there with Titus and, unusually, and for no stated reason, so was Gary Anderson with Bruno, who skirted around Titus at a safe distance. Nothing untoward happened, between either the dogs or the people. The men from Number Fifteen were largely ignored, which suited them. Everything in the garden, it seemed, was lovely!

It was not to last. On Monday, either late in the afternoon or early evening, the time wasn't quite clear, the first of the burglaries occurred in Mulberry Lane.

20

The first houses to be burgled on Monday were Number Five and Number Seven. Which was the first to be broken into wasn't known, and it hardly mattered. Being next door to each other they were probably, the police said later, both done within a matter of minutes. One thing burglars didn't do was hang around, though in these two cases they'd stayed long enough to create a deliberate mess – books taken from the shelves and strewn on the floor, small items of furniture overturned, that sort of thing. Nothing really nasty.

It so happened that Eric and James at Number Five were the first home. Monday was always a quiet day in the shop. Eric had long argued that it was a waste of time opening on a Monday but James maintained that any halfway decent shop – and theirs was more than that – didn't stay closed on a weekday. They had, however, left on the dot of half-past five and were home before six.

Number Seven would normally have been occupied because Dawn worked at home. Monday was also a quiet day for her and today she had had only one appointment, at 10 a.m., so, since the twins were off school, recovering from nasty colds, she had taken them to visit her mother in Bath.

James rang the police at once, even before they'd checked what was missing. The sight of the house was enough to tell them that they'd been burgled. Eric started to tidy the room but James stopped him.

'Leave everything exactly as it is!' he ordered. 'The police won't want anything disturbed.' He was an avid reader of detective stories and knew the right moves. Then, while they waited for the police, they discovered what was missing, which included a comparatively new video recorder and several videos and, from a drawer in the bureau (early nineteenth century, mahogany, very pretty and in good condition) fifty pounds in ten-pound notes, which was housekeeping money, always kept handy. 'Too handy!' the policeman was to say.

He came quickly, but it was all a bit disappointing to James. He had rather expected a police car with blue lights flashing and sirens blaring, screeching to a halt in the street outside, but instead, when he answered the ring at the door, there was one uniformed policeman standing on the step. It was not at all as he'd seen such affairs on television.

'Good evening,' he said. 'I'm Police Constable Hendry.'

It was another small disappointment to James, which out of politeness he tried to hide. He had hoped for an inspector at least, possibly even a chief inspector, a sort of amalgam of Morse, Frost and Wexford, with possibly a sergeant as his side-kick.

PC Hendry seemed totally unfazed by the scene in the living room, no doubt because he had seen it all before.

'We've left everything exactly as it was,' James announced. 'We haven't touched anything – well, hardly anything. Fingerprints, you know.'

'Thank you,' the constable said. 'Then I'll just take down a few details. Now you say you arrived home just before six o'clock?'

'Ten to exactly,' Eric said. 'We left the shop dead on half-past five and it's a twenty-minute walk.'

'The shop?'

'Bygones. In the town. Just beyond the bridge. Antiques.'

'Oh yes,' the constable said. 'I know it.'

'We came in at the front door, as per usual,' Eric said, 'and I walked through to the kitchen to put the kettle on.'

'And I followed,' James added. 'We saw the broken window right away. It's actually in the top half of the door.'

'So having broken the window the thief only had to put his hand through and unlock the door. I suppose you'd left the key in the lock?' PC Hendry sighed.

'I'm afraid we did,' James confessed. 'And of course we shouldn't have, knowing what we're up against.'

'Up against? What do you mean, sir?'

'I mean that we have four ex-convicts living just a few doors along the road. You won't have far to look for the culprits on this occasion, constable.'

'Oh, really? What makes you say that?'

James looked at him in amazement.

'Well, it stands to reason, doesn't it? It's what we've all been expecting.'

'I see. And have you any other reason to think it might be one of these men?'

'Or two or three of them,' James said. 'Two to break in, one to keep watch. I wouldn't have thought you'd need any more evidence.'

'James,' Eric said, 'you're going too far! You can't assume all that.'

'Oh yes I can!' James disagreed. 'I reckon we don't need any more proof.'

'We'll see,' the constable said. 'Shall we go back to the room where the burglary took place? Is that the only room?'

'It seems to be,' James said. 'I had a quick look round. Everywhere else looks OK. I expect they were disturbed.'

'Possibly,' the constable agreed. 'Do you know what's missing?'

'The video recorder,' James said. 'It's quite new, state of the art – and several videos with it. And fifty pounds in notes from the bureau. He hadn't even bothered to close the drawer.'

'And that's all – I mean as far as you know?'

'We haven't discovered anything else,' Eric confirmed.

PC Hendry looked around the room.

'You have some very nice pieces here. That bronze bird, for instance. It's rather beautiful. And the pair of vases on the mantelpiece. Are they antiques? Valuable, are they?'

'They are antiques, and quite pricey,' Eric admitted. 'We bring pieces home from the shop and keep them here for a while so that we can enjoy them.'

'So they haven't taken anything like that? Do the men along the road know you're antique dealers?'

'I suppose so,' James said. 'Most people do.

Everybody knows what everybody else in this road does. I expect the thing is they don't know what's good when they see it. They're not the type to appreciate the finer things of life!'

'Is that so?' the constable said. 'You don't think they just looked for something they could sell quickly, get some money for?'

James shrugged. 'You could be right. I suppose it would be typical, wouldn't it – I mean of the ex-cons?'

'I can't say. I don't know the men in question. Now if you don't mind I'll sit down for a minute and take a few more details.'

He was prevented from doing so by the ringing of his mobile phone. 'Excuse me!' he said, taking it out of his pocket.

'Really?' he said. 'Number Seven? I'll be there in a minute!'

He switched off his phone and spoke to Eric and James.

'I'm afraid there's been a break-in right next door!' he said. 'Number Seven. I'll nip round there and see you both later.'

'I'm not surprised!' James said indignantly. 'I'm not in the least surprised.' He turned to Eric. 'Isn't it just what people said would happen? You should never have put me off when I wanted to get a burglar alarm fixed!'

'I didn't say you *couldn't*,' Eric said. 'I said it was a waste of money. I said professional burglars know how to deal with alarms.'

'Not all burglars are professionals,' PC Hendry said. 'Not by a long way.'

'I'm sure you'll find these are,' James said.

'I'll let myself out,' the constable said. 'I gather

it's a lady with children next door. She's bound to be nervous.'

It was true. Dawn was in a state. Like Eric and James, she had unlocked the front door and they had all gone straight through the hall to the kitchen, in this case because the children were desperate for a drink of water. Not only was there broken glass on the floor but the door was wide open, as if the intruders had left in a hurry. From the kitchen she had rushed to the living room, where the telephone was, and had found it in complete disarray, furniture and a standard lamp tipped over, a magazine rack emptied of its contents which were thrown around the floor. A small desk which stood in the corner had had the drawers taken out and the contents tipped onto the carpet.

'Sit down for a minute, madam,' PC Hendry said to Dawn. 'You've had a nasty shock!' She was chalk white, and trembling.

'Thank you,' she said. She sat on the sofa, a wide-eyed twin on either side of her.

'Can I make you a cup of tea?' he offered.

'No thank you. I'll be all right. It was so . . . well, it's not something you expect to find, is it?'

'I'm afraid it's not uncommon,' the constable said, 'though as likely as not it won't happen to you again. I take it you phoned straight away?'

'I did,' Dawn said. 'You were here very quickly.'

'I didn't have far to come,' he told her. 'I was just next door. Number Five.'

At first she didn't comprehend. She was too full of her own troubles to give even a passing thought to why a policeman might have been calling on the law-abiding Eric and James.

'The same thing,' the constable said. 'Their room's in the same state as yours. Have you had time to see what's missing?'

'My radio's gone!' one of the twins said. 'It wouldn't have if Mummy had let me take it to Grandma's, but she wouldn't!'

'I see,' Hendry said. 'Would you like to describe it to me, in a minute or two, and I'll write it down. What's your name?'

'Daren,' he said.

'And yours?' he asked the other twin.

'William.'

'It was a new radio,' Daren said. 'I had it for my birthday. I didn't want to leave it at home.'

'Daddy will buy you another one,' Dawn said. 'Don't nag!' She turned to the policeman. 'I don't see that there's anything else missing from here, though I haven't had time to look properly – except I left twenty-five pounds on the sideboard and that's gone. Well, it would, wouldn't it?'

'I'm afraid it would,' PC Hendry agreed. 'You mean you just left it there?'

'Yes,' Dawn admitted. 'It was stupid, wasn't it? But you don't think of being burgled when you just go off to see your mother for the afternoon. I'd had a client this morning – I'm a chiropodist – and it's what she paid me. I didn't put it in my purse, I never do. I keep my earnings separate.'

'May I ask where?'

'I have a small room upstairs where I see clients. I would have put the money away there but she didn't pay me until we got down into the hall, so I just popped it on the sideboard.'

'Have you been upstairs since you came home? I don't suppose you have?'

351

'No. As a matter of fact I was afraid to. I didn't know whether . . .'

'You were right not to,' the constable said. 'You did exactly the right thing, phoning the police. But shall we take a look now?'

She showed him the way, the twins following close behind. When she went into the main bedroom she gave a sharp cry. The dressing-table drawers were all open. She ran across the room and looked immediately into the top left-hand drawer.

'My jewellery!' she cried. 'It's all gone! Everything! The thieving bastards!' She sank onto the bed as if, suddenly, all her strength had left her. 'Michael said they weren't to be trusted but I wouldn't believe him.'

'Who is "they"?' Hendry asked, though he had a good idea what her reply would be.

'Those ex-cons at Number Fifteen!' she said fiercely. 'I was fool enough to think they were going straight. They seemed quite nice young men.'

'And is there any special reason why you think it would be them?' he enquired.

'I don't know,' she said. 'I'd rather it wasn't, but who else would it be?'

The constable shook his head. 'Could be anyone. Shall we go downstairs again and perhaps you'll give me a list of what's missing from your jewellery drawer?'

Downstairs she sat on the sofa, looking pale and distraught, trying to write a list.

'Do you two boys know how to make a cup of tea?' PC Hendry asked the twins.

''Course we do!' Daren said.

'Or coffee!' William offered.

'Well, why not make a nice pot of tea and we'll all

have a cup?' the constable suggested. They went off into the kitchen.

'Almost everything in my jewellery drawer was in boxes, and they've taken all those,' Dawn said. 'There were my pearls, a sapphire dress ring, and a very special ruby brooch which belonged to my grandmother . . .' Her face crumpled, tears came into her eyes. 'Oh dear! There were so many things – not many of them really valuable, of course, but bits and bobs I've had for years. Small treasures!'

'Well, for the time being just write down the valuables,' PC Hendry suggested. 'And perhaps anything which was an unusual design, something which could be recognized if it turned up. You never know, some of the items might surface.' He thought it was unlikely, but at the moment she needed a bit of encouragement.

'If only I hadn't gone to my mother's!' Dawn said. 'This wouldn't have happened.'

'You can't be sure of that,' the constable said. 'I reckon for a lady like you, with young children, it's better to be out than in when burglars call. What time did you leave?'

'Before lunch,' Dawn replied. 'And of course I did a stupid thing. I forgot to leave any lights on anywhere. Anyone could see the house was empty – and the curtains weren't closed. It gets dark so early at this time of the year.'

'What time do you expect your husband home?' PC Hendry asked.

'Not before half-past seven,' Dawn told him. 'It could be later. He had to go to Exeter today.'

'I see. Well, I'll give you a hand to put this room to rights, and then is there anyone you'd like me to

353

contact, someone who might stay with you until your husband gets home?'

'Thank you, but I don't think so,' Dawn said. 'I'll be all right with the boys. I don't suppose whoever did it will come back?'

'I think that's highly unlikely,' the constable agreed. He moved around the room, righting the furniture. The twins came in with mugs of tea. 'I'll drop by in the morning,' PC Hendry said. 'Do you think your husband could be in?'

'I'm sure he will. He'll want to be,' Dawn said.

The constable was rising to his feet, ready to leave, when the doorbell rang.

'Shall I answer that for you?' he asked.

Dawn nodded. 'Yes please.'

Eric and James stood on the doorstep.

'We thought we'd better just come and see if Dawn was all right,' Eric said. They walked past the policeman and into the living room.

'Oh, my dear!' Eric cried. 'Isn't this just too awful for words!'

Dawn nodded agreement. She really didn't want Eric and James, she wanted to be alone with the boys, waiting for Michael to come, but there was no way to stop them. She hoped they wouldn't stay. She had a nasty headache starting.

'I must say,' Eric said, 'your room is much tidier than ours. You should have seen the mess they made there.'

'It wasn't all that good here a few minutes ago,' Dawn told them. 'Constable Hendry kindly gave me a hand.'

'You know who we owe all this to, don't you?' James demanded. 'Those devils down the road!'

'Perhaps,' Dawn said. She wished he wouldn't go

on about it now. She wished he would go away. She didn't feel at all well. It was the shock catching up with her.

James turned to PC Hendry.

'I take it for granted that you'll be going along to Number Fifteen? That's where you'll find what you're looking for!'

'I shall be calling at several houses in the road,' Hendry said politely. 'Of course, if you have any more evidence . . . if you've thought of anything else . . .'

'Evidence?' James barked. 'What more do you need?'

'There isn't any so far,' the constable said. 'Unfortunately – or perhaps fortunately – police work depends upon evidence. But I shall certainly visit Number Fifteen, though so far there's nothing specific against them, or anyone else.'

'Someone's got to have done it!' James exploded. 'Furniture doesn't turn upside down, valuable property doesn't disappear of its own accord!'

'Oh, I agree, sir,' PC Hendry said. 'Naturally I shall be making further enquiries. Anyway, I'll leave you now but I'll see you in the morning. I take it you'll be available? Or should I come to your shop?'

James gave a cry of horror. 'Heaven forbid!' he said. 'We can't have the police coming into the shop. What would people think?'

'Well, sir,' PC Hendry said smoothly, 'they might think I was interested in buying an antique. It has been known.' He spoke to Dawn. 'If I were you, madam, I'd rest quietly until your husband comes home.'

'Yes,' Dawn agreed. 'That's exactly what I'd like to do. Thank you so much for coming, Eric and

James. It was kind of you, but I'll be all right now.'

Thus dismissed, the two men left with PC Hendry, turning left to their own home while he turned right and walked towards Number Fifteen.

It was a nasty night now, dark and drizzling, the wet pavements shining in the streetlights. He would see what the occupants of Number Fifteen had to say for themselves and then he'd report back to the station. It was time for his shift to end and he'd be glad to get back home, get a good meal inside him. He doubted whether the ex-cons would have done these jobs. They'd be fools if they had, but on the other hand you never knew. If it wasn't them it was possible he'd never find out who was responsible. It had all the appearance of ending up as one of those crimes that remained unsolved – to the intense annoyance of the public.

At Number Fifteen three of the ex-cons were in, as was the man in charge, Brian Carson, and PC Hendry had been in the house less than ten minutes – he was questioning Mark – when Colin Myers walked in.

'I've been in the house since mid-afternoon,' Mark said. 'Around half-past three, I think. I came straight home when I'd finished my lunchtime shift.'

'I see. Thank you.'

The constable turned to Fergus and David. 'And you two gentlemen?'

'I was at the hospital where I work,' Fergus said. 'Shipfield Private Hospital. I left just after five and came straight home.'

'I work at the toffee factory,' David said. 'I finished at half-past five.'

'And you came straight home?'

'Yes,' David said. 'I walked . . .'

He was interrupted by Colin Myers.

'What's all this about?' he demanded. 'Why all the questions?'

PC Hendry turned to him.

'There's been two burglaries along the road. Numbers Five and Seven.'

'And what's that got to do with us – as if we didn't know!'

'It's to do with everyone, sir,' the constable said smoothly. 'I shall be calling on other houses.'

'And I'll bet you came here first! Hot foot! No doubt you were given the lowdown!'

He was going to be the awkward one, Hendry thought. It had been obvious from the minute he'd walked into the room.

'And you are . . . ?' he asked.

'Colin Myers. Though I expect you already know! I don't doubt you were warned about us.'

Hendry ignored the remark.

'And would you tell me your movements today? Let's say from around eleven o'clock this morning?'

'I worked in the house until about three o'clock, and then I went into the town, shopping for the house. I didn't check the time and place every hour on the hour. I didn't know we were supposed to. I thought we were supposed to be free!'

'So you are, sir,' Hendry said politely. The more awkward people were with him, the more polite he became. It threw them – if anything could throw this one. But he'd got what he wanted out of all four. Any one of them was in the frame, especially as no-one knew quite when the break-ins had happened.

'And you, sir?' he asked Brian Carson. 'I'd be obliged if I could have your movements.'

'Certainly!' Brian said. 'As Colin said, we both worked in the house all morning but I had to leave just after one o'clock. I had a meeting of the Fraser Trust.'

'And where was that, sir?'

'In Bristol this time,' Brian said. 'I'd not been back long when you arrived.'

'Thank you, Mr Carson,' Hendry said. 'Well, I don't think I need trouble you any further at the moment. If you think of anything helpful, please get in touch.'

Not one of them is in the clear, PC Hendry thought as Brian saw him to the door, not that he suspected Carson for as much as ten seconds. And come to that, any of the men would be bloody fools to try it on with the risks entailed if they were caught.

'By the way,' he asked Brian, 'who lives at Number Thirteen?'

'Mr and Mrs Streeter,' Brian said. 'They have a hairdressing business in the town. They won't be home yet and you'll probably find they've been at work all day.' Much as he disliked Ralph Streeter there was no way he could imagine him breaking and entering. 'In any case,' he added, 'he has a burglar alarm as loud as a fire engine!'

'And Number Eleven?' PC Hendry enquired.

'You'll not find the burglar there,' Brian told him. 'Esther Dean's well into her eighties, and frail. She can't get out unless someone takes her.'

'She doesn't sound a likely suspect,' PC Hendry agreed, 'but it's my experience that people who are confined to the house see quite a bit of what goes on in the street.'

'You're right at that,' Brian said. 'She's known as the Neighbourhood Watch!'

'Which could be very useful,' Hendry said. 'I wonder if I should pop in and have a word with her now? I wouldn't want to upset her, still less to frighten her, and in the evening . . .'

'Perhaps if I went round with you and introduced you?' Brian suggested. 'Otherwise I think the sight of a policeman in uniform might startle her a bit. If she agrees to see you, then I'll leave you to it.'

'I think that would help,' PC Hendry said.

The two of them went round together. Esther was a long time in answering the door and when she did so she was undoubtedly taken aback at the sight of PC Hendry.

'Good heavens!' she cried. 'To what do I owe this? What's happened?' Something exciting, she hoped. It had been a dull day.

'Nothing to worry about,' Brian said.

He explained what had happened.

'So we thought you might be able to help us,' PC Hendry said. 'You might have seen something other people had missed.'

'I just might,' Esther said. 'Do come in!' She was sure she was going to enjoy this.

'I won't,' Brian said. 'I don't think you'll need me. But if you find you do, just let me know. Just pick up the phone. For the moment I'll leave you to it.'

'Now he's a very nice man!' she informed the constable when Brian had left. 'I like having him next door but one. In fact I like having all of them there. It's better than when it was Mrs Harper. She was very old, you know, and a bit funny in the top storey. And what can I do for you, young man?'

He gave her the facts. She was interested in every detail. 'Very exciting!' she said. 'In fact the most exciting thing that's happened in the road since Brian and the boys came.'

'I suppose that's one way of describing it,' PC Hendry conceded. 'Now the way you could help me – and it would be a great help – is if you could recall seeing anyone walk along the road since about half-past eleven this morning.'

'What would they look like, constable?' Esther asked.

PC Hendry drew a deep breath. 'I'm afraid I don't know that, madam,' he said patiently. 'You see, I haven't seen them. Just tell me about anyone you saw.'

Esther thought for a moment.

'Well then,' she began, 'there was the milkman. It's still dark when he comes but I know it's him because he rattles the bottles. I don't think it would be Ernest. He's a very nice man, and the milk's good, too.'

'No, I don't think it would be the milkman,' Hendry agreed. Not unless he came back at a later hour, he thought, which was unlikely. 'These break-ins couldn't have happened before eleven or so this morning because the lady was in the house up to then.'

'Oh, I see. Well, there was a young woman putting leaflets through the doors. Advertising pizzas and Chinese takeaways. I've never had one, have you?'

'I have,' Hendry said. Actually, he could do with one right now, preferably the Chinese. He was starving. Before she could ask him what it had consisted of, he jumped in. 'And was there anyone else?'

'No-one I knew,' Esther said. 'Oh, except Karen! She lives on the other side of the road and that's where she was, bringing the children home from school. She hasn't been too well lately, Karen.'

'I'm sorry to hear that,' PC Hendry said. 'And was there anyone else you knew?'

'Only Colin, from next door,' she replied. 'I saw him leave, early afternoon, I suppose it was. I didn't see him come back. It's quite dark, isn't it?'

'It is,' Hendry agreed. He was getting nowhere fast, and he didn't think he *would* get anywhere.

'Of course,' Esther said with faultless logic, 'if anyone was going to Numbers Five and Seven from the North Hill end, they wouldn't need to pass my house, would they?'

'You're absolutely right, and I won't trouble you any longer,' PC Hendry said. 'But if you do think of anything, don't hesitate to phone me.'

'Oh I won't!' Esther assured him. She really did hope she would think of something. It was most interesting to be interviewed by the police, and something she could tell Laura, who was used to bringing the news *to* her rather than hearing it *from* her.

'Good night, then!' PC Hendry said. 'Don't get up. I'll see myself out.'

'Good night, constable,' Esther said. 'And thank you very much.'

21

Long before PC Hendry had reported to Shipfield HQ, gone off his shift, and was at home eating a warming plate of Irish stew while watching *East-Enders*, Esther was on the telephone to Laura.

'You're not going to believe this . . .' she began.

'What in the world . . . ?' Laura broke in. Esther didn't sound at all like herself. Her voice was deep, and full of drama, and yet at the same time there was, surely, a faint note of pleasure. 'What is it?' she asked.

'If you would just listen and not interrupt,' Esther said sharply, 'I *will* tell you! That's what I'm trying to do!'

'Sorry,' Laura said. 'I'm all ears!'

Esther made a short but significant pause before replying.

'Mulberry Lane has been hit by a crime wave!'

'A crime wave? Did you say a crime wave, Esther?'

'That is exactly what I said,' Esther confirmed. 'And I chose my words carefully. A crime wave!'

'I do find it difficult to believe, Esther dear,' Laura said. She put her hand over the mouthpiece and spoke to Dermot. 'I think Esther's finally flipped!'

'It is absolutely true!' Esther was saying. 'The police have already consulted me.'

'*Consulted* you, dear?' Laura asked gently.

'*Consulted* me, yes!' Esther said haughtily. 'So I'd thank you not to be so condescending. The policeman said I could probably be very valuable to them.'

'Oh, I'm sure you could!' Laura said, raising her eyebrows at Dermot. 'So tell me, what's the crime wave all about? What exactly has happened?'

'*So far*,' Esther said ominously, 'two houses have been burgled. Eric and James – that's the gay couple at Number Five – though I've nothing against gays, as such – and Michael and Dawn at Number Seven. No-one was in either house at the time or who knows, we might now be dealing with murder! And I say *so far* because this could be just the beginning . . .'

'Or the beginning and the end,' Laura suggested.

Esther was not open to such a suggestion. 'Oh, I doubt that, I really do,' she said. 'You wait and see! We could all be at risk. Well, perhaps not me because I reckon the police will keep an eye on my house. Indeed, they said I was to ring them any time, any time at all, if I saw anything the least bit suspicious. So I shall keep a close watch!'

'I'm sure you will,' Laura said. 'Did they take much, the burglars?'

'This and that,' Esther said (PC Hendry not having given her that information).

'Well, it certainly is unexpected news,' Laura said. 'Are you all right? Would you like me to come across?'

'Not at the moment,' Esther said. 'I'm quite all right, and I'm going to be rather busy. I intend to telephone people in the road. I feel it's my duty to put them on their guard.'

'Why not let me do it for you?' Laura suggested. She would give a toned-down version to a small number of people. She didn't trust Esther not to raise panic throughout the length and breadth of Mulberry Lane.

'Thank you, but no,' Esther said firmly. 'I think it's up to me. I was, as I've said, almost the first person the police consulted – after the boys next door, of course, though I did tell the police they were on the wrong track there. They're such nice young men. Anyway, I can't spend time talking! Work to be done! In the meantime, lock your doors and hide your valuables.'

Laura was left with a silent telephone in her hand.

'Now who shall I inform next?' Esther asked herself out loud. She felt better when she spoke out loud, more purposeful. Who would Laura seek to tell? She would like to get in before her if she could. She wasn't quite sure that Laura would pass on the news with the importance it merited. She would blow it light. Especially my part in it, she thought.

Karen. Laura would almost certainly ring Karen first. The two of them were friendly, even more so since Karen's recent little misfortune. Esther took down her address book from the shelf – she had acquired, over a period of time, the telephone numbers of most people in Mulberry Lane, not because she needed them – she had scarcely used any of them – but because she liked to have them. And now they were about to come in useful.

364

She moved a chair across to the side of the small table where the telephone lived, and sat down. This could be a long job.

'Esther? So to what do I owe this pleasure?' Karen asked pleasantly.

'I'm afraid, my dear, you won't find it much of a pleasure when you hear what I have to say!' Esther said gravely. 'It's a duty I must carry out, especially since I promised the police I would give them every assistance I could.'

'The police?' What *was* Esther on about? Was she going a bit peculiar?

'So you haven't heard about the crime wave in Mulberry Lane?' Esther asked.

From then on the conversation between the two women went almost word for word as had Esther's earlier one with Laura, except that Karen didn't interrupt quite as much as Laura had and didn't try to take the job into her own hands.

'So look after those dear little children of yours,' Esther said finally. 'And mind you close all the windows before you go out of the house!'

Which won't make much difference, Karen thought, if they get in by smashing the glass. Should she ring Laura, ask her how much of all this she thought was true? On the other hand . . . if, as Esther said, Number Fifteen had already had a visit from the police then Brian would know as much, if not more, than anyone. And indeed he might be very worried. Surely it was a good enough reason for her to phone him? These days she often felt she would like to call him, just for a chat, nothing more – and indeed he had given her his number, 'In case you ever need it,' he'd said, but so far she hadn't had the courage to do so. Wasn't Esther's call a good enough reason, if only to check that he was all right? She picked up the phone.

Esther, having dealt with Karen, went back to her address book. Who next? She had met several people at the meeting in Laura's and Dermot's house, and she knew some of the neighbours from the days when she'd been able to get out and about. The Simpsons, for instance, with their yappy little dog; Jim and Betty Pullman at the Green Man. The Streeters, right next door, with their deafening burglar alarm, though thankfully it had not gone off since the day it was installed. All the same, she wouldn't tell them. Ralph Streeter was dead against the young men at Number Fifteen and she wasn't going to go out of her way to help anyone in that camp, quite the contrary.

There were the students, of course, straight across the road. She didn't know all of them but Laura had talked so much about them that she felt as though she did. The girls were nicely brought up, from good families and one of them, she knew for a fact, with titled parents. About the men students she wasn't sure. She hardly ever saw the red-haired one and she was afraid, from her memories of the meeting, that the good-looking one wasn't keen on the boys at Number Fifteen. On the other hand he *was* a well-set-up, incredibly handsome man and she had always had a soft spot for good-looking men. There was also, she thought, that horrible-looking loutish fellow who was Jennifer's boyfriend, though he hadn't been around as much in the last week or two. Still, it was possible he could have sneaked back and done the burglaries. That would be a splendid solution. She would mention him to Constable Hendry.

She didn't have the students' telephone number but she did have that of Mr Lambert, who owned the house and used to live there. Possibly it was still the same. She would give it a try and ask to speak to one of the girls.

'Yes, it's true!' Brian said to Karen. 'And yes, the police in the shape of one constable have been here. They were directed right here by the victims. Well, they would be, wouldn't they? Whatever goes wrong, my lot will be in the picture. Not that *I* suspect them!'

'Nor me,' Karen said.

But *did* he, Brian asked himself? How could he know? Not one of them had a real alibi – though again, if any one of them was the guilty party wouldn't he have had the brains to think up something watertight?

'Anyway,' he said to Karen, 'if Esther is on the job, and probably Laura O'Brien, it'll only be a matter of minutes before everyone in the road knows.'

'I'm ever so sorry,' Karen said. 'What are you going to do?'

'Certainly not hide away!' Brian said firmly. 'It's my belief that the pub will be bursting at the seams tonight – plenty to talk about – so I shall walk right into it, together with all four lads, whether they like it or not. Best to hear directly what people have to say about you.'

'I wish I could come just to show my own small support,' Karen said. 'I can't, of course. I can't leave the children.'

'Of course you can't,' Brian agreed. 'Though I wish you could be there. I'll tell you what, though. If I'm not needed by the lads I could call in after we leave the pub. Put you in the picture. Or would it be too late for you?'

'Certainly not,' Karen said. 'I'd like that.'

By eight o'clock that evening, at which time Brian announced that, come what may, they were all going along to the Green Man, it seemed that the news of the break-ins had travelled the length and breadth of Mulberry Lane. It was not entirely certain by what means every man, woman and child had been made aware but between Esther, Karen, Laura, the people they had each telephoned and the people *they* had spoken to, as well as the fact that James had been along to the corner shop and announced it there while buying a wholemeal loaf and a box of eggs, it was common knowledge. But what everyone in the road wanted to know was every last thing about it. They needed now to get together and talk.

For instance, was it true that someone thought they might actually have seen the burglars leaving Number Seven, arms suspiciously laden? Was one of them a woman? It could be. Women did everything these days, so why not burglary? But not, of course, if the ex-cons had done it, which they probably had. And then someone remembered having seen the one who worked at the toffee factory with a glamorous young woman on his arm only a couple of days ago. She could have been involved, couldn't she? And hadn't she stayed with Karen Jackson?

Few remembered from exactly which source they

had heard the different details – so many phone calls had been received and made – or whether some of them had been surmises which had grown, in the telling, into facts. That both houses had been left in a terrible state seemed to be well known. And hadn't the burglars urinated (or worse!) on the furniture? And what were the police doing? Most people had heard that the police had been to see Esther, but why would they do that? She was a batty old woman. Harmless, but batty! She *was* harmless, wasn't she? Could one be sure?

Which was why, though it was a cold, dark night, and raining, they had rushed like lemmings to the Green Man, which was now full to the doors and Jim Pullman was well into profiting from adversity.

The Number Fifteen contingent had not yet set off.

'Do we have to go?' David asked Brian. 'I don't fancy it at all.'

'I think we do,' Brian said. 'It's obvious that we're going to be suspected . . .'

'You mean *we* are,' David said. 'You'll be in the clear!'

'I suppose so,' Brian agreed. 'But not one of you – and not me for that matter – has an alibi which will hold water. On what's known so far any one of you could have done it. I'm giving you the benefit of the doubt and assuming you had nothing to do with it – you'd be fools if you did because you know what would be in store for you, straight back inside and a longer spell this time. And for what? A few pounds and some bits and bobs!'

'But we didn't!' Fergus objected. 'At any rate I know *I* didn't.'

It was the first indication that anyone had

supposed that one of them might be guilty. It was an indication which was not lost on any of them and it left an uneasy feeling in the room.

'If I find that any one of you had a hand in it, then I'll not show any mercy,' Brian promised. 'You'll have made things impossible for the rest of us. But if not one of us is guilty, then all the more reason why we should go and face it out, hear what everyone has to say,' he pointed out.

'And speak up if we want to!' David said.

'Certainly,' Brian agreed. 'But keep a tight hold on our tempers, which I know won't be easy.'

Colin Myers, who had so far sat silently smoking, broke in.

'I'm not bloody well going! You can all do what you like, but I'm not going. I'm not going to sit there and listen to a load of shit!'

'I can't make you go,' Brian said, 'but if you don't stand in with the rest of us you're a fool. You're making it worse for yourself.'

Colin shrugged, and lit another cigarette from the end of the one he was already smoking. Where does he get the money for all these smokes, Brian asked himself?

'We'll leave in ten minutes,' he said. 'So you can all make up your minds. I shall go whether anyone else does or not.'

In the end they all went, even Colin though he was still disgruntled and protesting.

'Don't let anyone say the wrong thing to me, that's all!' he threatened.

'Then let me tell you,' Brian said, 'that if you cause any kind of a disturbance I'll not only deal with you on the spot, I'll take steps in the morning I've been tempted to take for some time

370

now! There is no way I'm going to put up with your attitude.'

At twenty-two minutes past eight the volume of talk in the Green Man was hitting the ceiling and bouncing back again like waves on the seashore. At twenty-four minutes past the hour the pub door was pushed open and Brian Carson walked in, followed by the four men, Colin Myers a reluctant last. By twenty-five past the hubbub had died and there was complete silence in the place. All eyes followed the men as they walked across and took their places by the bar. Brian's keen eyes swept around the room, noting who was there. He saw Michael Blake, close to the bar. Ralph and Michelle Streeter, Gary Anderson with Bruno and Nigel Simpson with Titus. Probably all hostile, he thought, and then with some relief he noticed Laura and Dermot, who smiled as he passed them. By the time he had pushed his way through to the bar he had also spotted Eric and James, sitting with Peter and Meg. Also George Potter at the far side of the bar.

Jim Pullman took a deep breath. All right, it had been good for trade so far, but he didn't look forward to the next bit. Nevertheless, he was a fair-minded man.

'Good evening!' he said. 'What's it to be?'

'*Don't serve the buggers!*'

'Don't turn round!' Brian spoke quickly and quietly to the men. It was a voice he didn't immediately recognize, and was best ignored. Jim Pullman had other ideas.

'That will do, Michael!' he said. His voice was polite, but firm. 'No-one tells me who I can serve and who I can't in my own bar!'

'You weren't bloody burgled and I was!' Michael Blake said. 'And we can all guess who by!'

Jim Pullman raised his voice. 'Moderate your language,' he said, 'or I'll find I won't be able to serve *you*!'

He turned back to Brian. 'Three lagers and a half of bitter, is it?' Then he added quietly, 'You've done me no favour, mate, all of you coming in. You'd have been better to steer clear for a day or two.'

'I'm sorry, Jim,' Brian said in a particularly clear voice which, as he intended, carried across the room, 'I can't agree with you. And I was doing the favour to the lads. It's obvious what all this is about, and if these men are not guilty, which they maintain they're not, then I reckon they have a right to be here, to hear what's said. Everyone has a right to defend himself.'

'Point taken,' Jim said. 'But they'd better do it quietly.' He nodded his head in the direction of Colin Myers who was standing a yard or two away and looking murderous. 'And you'd better keep an eye on that one. It would give me a certain amount of pleasure to throw him out!'

There was a murmur, which grew in volume as everyone began to speak at once. Whether for or against what Brian had said it was difficult to tell, except for one voice, raised above the others.

'Sod off!' Michael Blake shouted. 'You're not wanted here!'

'That's enough!' Jim Pullman said. 'This is your final warning. You watch your language and you keep a civil tongue in your head, or you're out! I'm not having trial by mob in my pub. We leave the job to the police and the courts!' And the quicker the better, he thought. It also seemed to him that

Michael Blake would have been better occupied staying at home this evening, supporting his wife and family. Dawn must be in a bit of a state.

Jim Pullman's warning served, to a certain extent, to lighten the atmosphere, but there was still only one topic of conversation and that was the burglaries. He couldn't do anything to change that. People had a right to voice their opinions, to sit and talk with others about whatever they chose, as long as they didn't inconvenience anyone else. But he would nevertheless keep an eye and two ears open. There were still more than two hours to go to closing time and in his opinion grievances without solutions in sight grew bigger as the night went on.

The subject on everyone's mind and tongue didn't go away. It was too much to expect. There was still a rumble of talk and from time to time snatches of conversation came over to Jim Pullman, who remained uneasy, and to Brian and the four men standing by the bar.

'If the police had moved in quick enough and searched Number Fifteen they'd have found the stuff.'

'Oh no they wouldn't. That lot's too crafty. You can be certain it was taken down to the town and flogged in double quick time!'

'What good are the police?' James demanded. 'All they tell you is they can't search unless they're going to make a charge!'

'Rubbish!' Ralph Streeter said.

'Rubbish it might be, but it's true!' James said. 'We were definitely told that.'

Dermot and Laura remained sitting where they were, stifling the impulse to go and join Brian and the men at the bar for fear of adding fuel to the fire, but suddenly Dermot's voice came over clearly, though ostensibly he was looking at and speaking only to Laura.

'It would be interesting to know how many burglaries had taken place in Shipfield, say, in the last two years. I reckon quite a lot. I'm always reading about them in the *Courier*. So what's new?'

'I'll tell you what's new!' Peter Fenton said from the next table. 'What's new is it's happened in Mulberry Lane! We've never had that kind of thing before. Not in my time, and I've lived here a few years. We never thought we'd have to put up burglar alarms, did we?'

'Speaking of burglar alarms,' someone said, 'had any more trouble with the cat, Peter?'

'I've said it before and I'll say it again,' Nigel Simpson broke in, 'everyone should get a dog. If you have a dog there's no need for a burglar alarm.'

'I agree,' Gary Anderson said. 'I'd like to see anyone try it on in my house!'

It was amazing, Jim Pullman thought, that no-one reminded him that he had a dog *and* a burglar alarm.

'Anyway,' Gary Anderson continued, 'it shouldn't take the police too long to sort this one out! It's clear enough where to look. And the sooner it's sorted, and Mulberry Lane gets back to being the kind of place it was when I bought my house here, the better.'

Michael nodded in agreement. 'We've never had any trouble of this kind, not until recently. Never! It used to be a respectable community before . . . well, before certain people came here . . .'

'And will be again if the culprits – and I'm

naming no names,' Gary said with a glance at Jim Pullman, 'are despatched.'

It was too much for Colin Myers. He lunged forward in the direction of Gary Anderson and was immediately pulled back by Brian and David.

'Don't be a fool!' David said. 'He'll set that bloody great dog on you!'

'I most certainly will!' Gary said.

Jim Pullman thumped the counter.

'That's it!' he said. 'That's it!'

He turned to Colin Myers.

'Out you go! I don't allow fights in my pub. You're barred for a week!'

Then he turned to Gary Anderson.

'And it wouldn't be a bad idea if you were to leave. I reckon "incitement" is the word.'

'No problem!' Gary said. 'I don't know why I come in here anyway.'

Brian and the other men left at once.

'Sorry!' Jim Pullman said to Brian. 'I had no alternative.'

Brian nodded. 'I understand.'

Gary Anderson finished his drink and left shortly afterwards.

'Go home!' Brian said to the men when they were outside. 'Or do what the hell you like! I've had enough for one day.'

He made a sharp left turn and crossed the road to Karen's house. He felt a strong need to be in her presence.

22

Karen was at the door almost before Brian had finished ringing the bell. He followed her into the living room.

'Are you sure this isn't too late?' he asked.

'Of course not! I'm sorry I can't offer you a glass of wine. I don't have any at the moment. There's tea or coffee?'

'Neither, thank you.'

She motioned him to an armchair, and then dashed in front of him to remove a toy from it before he could sit down.

'Fiona!' she said. 'She leaves her things everywhere. Neil's a much tidier child even though he's so young. He always takes his favourites to bed with him. At the moment it's the red car you bought him.'

'Not very cuddly to take to bed,' Brian said.

'That doesn't seem to bother him. He's never been one for teddy bears.' She took the chair opposite him. There was an open book balanced face down on the arm. She saw him look at it.

'Yes,' she said, 'I've been reading. I shouldn't, because I've loads of jobs to do. I always read in bed, read myself to sleep, but I feel guilty if I pick up a book at any other time. I think I should be doing something more useful.'

'Like baking a cake?' he suggested.

Karen smiled. 'Something like that! Is that a hint that you'd like another?'

'Well, it was certainly very popular,' Brian said. 'It went like wildfire!'

'I'll think about it,' Karen promised. 'Are you going to tell me how it went in the Green Man?' He'd come into the house with a face like a thundercloud; eyes hard, his mouth a straight line. He wasn't quite like that now, but not his usual easy self. Pleasant enough, polite, but not relaxed.

'It didn't go well,' he admitted. 'In fact I think there might have been blows if Jim Pullman hadn't been his usual strong self.'

'I like Jim,' Karen said.

'So do I,' Brian agreed. 'He's a fair man – and he certainly knows how to run a pub. In the end he sent Myers off, told him to get out. I don't blame Jim but I can't say I totally blame Myers. He was provoked. The trouble is, Myers has a short fuse and he doesn't give a damn for anyone except himself. I confess I find Myers hard to handle. I reckon he's one of my failures. My biggest failure so far, I'm afraid.'

He sounded despondent. Karen thought she'd never seen him quite like this before. But come to that she hadn't seen all that much of him, not even if one put all their meetings together, end to end. How much did it amount to? And, nice as he was, she didn't want to get too sorry for him. Feeling sorry for an attractive man was not a good idea, not for her, not in her life.

'Oh, I wouldn't think so,' she said. 'I expect *he*'s the failure, not you!'

'Kind of you to say so,' Brian said in a flat voice, clearly not agreeing with her. 'Actually Michael Blake was also within an ace of being chucked out. Jim threatened him with it.'

'If you'd known Michael Blake as long as some of us have,' Karen said, 'you'd know he was just a big-headed bore! And you haven't told me what sparked all this off – I mean apart from your men being there.'

'That was all it took!' Brian said. 'Just for them to walk in at the door was enough. Even Jim would rather we hadn't come. He said so – though only to me.'

'So why did you?' Karen asked.

'Because I thought at the time it was the right thing to do. I still do, in a way. Better to know what you're up against – and who. Anyway, I don't want to bore you with all this.'

'It's what you came for,' Karen pointed out.

Had he? He supposed he had, but hadn't he also come because he wanted different company, because he wanted to talk to *her*?

'Let's change the subject,' he suggested. 'What sort of day have you had? Are you really well again? You look – well, I don't quite know what. Tired, I think.'

'You should never tell a woman she looks tired,' Karen said lightly. 'She usually reckons you think she looks plain, or old. Or both.'

'Whereas you never look either of those!' Brian said.

'Oh dear! I wasn't looking for compliments,' Karen said. She picked up her book, closed it, reached out and laid it on a table close by. 'I really wasn't.'

'I know that. But what I said was true, *is* true,' Brian told her.

All the same, there was something not exactly right about her. There was a sadness, and from time to time a slight withdrawal, as if she'd perhaps gone a little further than she'd intended, and then thought better of it. Let down the drawbridge and then suddenly hauled it up again so that he couldn't cross into her domain.

That was something he knew about. He was wary of women, having decided that life was easier without them. Then without thinking clearly about what he was doing he'd gone further with Karen than he had with any woman since Helen: taking her out to dinner, taking her shopping with the kids, and now sitting here with her in her home. He knew with one side of him – barely acknowledged, but true – that he did want to get closer to her, he wanted to enjoy her friendship, but with his other side he was holding back, not wanting to get too close. Closeness was not in his plans.

After Helen, when he had changed his job so dramatically, had rushed headlong into a totally different kind of life and had eventually got used to it and indeed come to like it, he had considered that he was managing his life quite well. If he was lonely, he brushed it aside, hardly acknowledging it. While never disliking women, he had no appetite for casual affairs, and anything more than that was not in his mind.

But now, if he was truthful to himself, did he still feel like that? He couldn't be sure.

Whatever had happened to him, he knew quite

well that it had happened at the O'Briens' house when Karen had stood up and spoken in defence of what he was doing. Even so it was probably true that he didn't trust her completely, not because she was Karen, but because she was a woman. How did one, having lost trust, get it back? And on her side, he was well aware, she was defensive. Pleasant, friendly, but with an invisible sign up which said 'This far, no further'.

'But surely not everyone was against you?' Karen queried.

'No, of course not. Dermot and Laura were there. They said the right things. But it's interesting what a few well-chosen, snide remarks by no more than two or three people can accomplish. Gary Anderson was a pest. I wondered how he knew about the break-ins. He doesn't mix with the rest of us. Perhaps it was coincidence that he was there, or perhaps someone told Lisa.'

'Lisa's not so bad,' Karen said, 'though I don't think she has any friends in the road.'

'It doesn't signify,' Brian said. 'Everyone hears bad news sooner or later!'

The truth of the matter was, it was all down to Esther's efficiency and persistence. She had assiduously rung everyone on the list of telephone numbers she possessed – though some people were inclined to disbelieve what she said. Unfortunately, the Andersons' number was not on her list. There had never been any reason for it to be there. Laura just might have it but she had no intention of asking her. Laura would simply offer to do the job for her, and that she didn't want.

There was, of course, the telephone directory.

Would the Andersons, she wondered, be ex-directory? Surprisingly, they were not. They might not like being telephoned but it was her duty. She was doing it for Mrs Anderson, who seemed quite nice, and those dear little children she sometimes saw walking along the road with their mother. She was not doing it for that pig of a man who had been so horrid at the meeting.

And that, though Brian would never have suspected it, was why Gary Anderson had been in the Green Man with his beautiful accessory, Bruno.

'Tell me,' Karen said, 'do you think any of the boys *had* anything to do with it?' Then she corrected herself quickly. 'No, don't tell me if you don't want to! It's not my business.'

'I'd like to tell you,' Brian said, 'except that I don't really know what I think. I wish I did! Cold reason tells me it's something they could have done because it's the kind of thing some of them have done in the past, but the whole point of what we're doing in the house is that the past is behind them and they're facing the future. So why would they be so stupid?'

'Why indeed?' Karen agreed. 'Is there any one of them . . .'

'Oh, there's always Myers,' Brian admitted. 'I always think of him first, simply because he's awkward and uncooperative – and, frankly, I don't like him.'

'You can't blame yourself for that,' Karen said. 'He's not likeable. Far from it.'

'Which is all the more reason why I should bend over backwards to give him the benefit of the doubt. Especially . . .' He hesitated.

'Especially what?'

'When I was in advertising,' Brian said, 'we had a number of leaks in the agency. Quite important ones. Advertising agencies are paranoid about keeping secrets about what they're working on and things were getting out far too often. Someone was guilty, and I was pretty sure I knew who it was; so sure that in the end I went to the chairman and told him of my suspicions. He took me seriously and a close watch was kept on the man from that minute. He was questioned. He was in danger of losing his job. But all that changed a couple of weeks later when the real culprit, a man I would never, ever have thought of, grew overconfident and careless, and was caught. What I was left with was the fact that I'd been only too ready to suspect the first man partly because I just didn't like him. I never saw that person again without feeling guilty, even though he didn't know what I'd done. I don't want to fall into that trap again and I just could with Myers.'

Karen nodded. 'And what about the others? What about Fergus and David and Mark?'

Brian shook his head in perplexity.

'I somehow can't see it – and at the same time I don't know whether it's because I don't want to see it. David has Sandra. He's set on marrying her as soon as he can. Why would he do anything to put that in jeopardy? Fergus has a new girlfriend at the hospital. He seems serious about her. She's Irish. He's already talking about them going back to Ireland. Why would he risk his future for whatever bits and pieces they've taken?'

'What about Mark?' Karen asked.

'I would say Mark was the most stable of the lot,' Brian said. 'He actively likes working at the

Shipfield Arms, hopes to stay on there and get promotion.'

'It could just as easily be none of them,' Karen said.

'I know that,' Brian said, 'but who else is going to believe that? What sort of chance are they going to get?'

He rose to his feet. 'Anyway, I must leave you in peace.' He didn't want to leave, but he must.

'Must you?' Karen said.

He nodded. 'I reckon I must keep the eleven o'clock curfew. Thanks for listening. A great help!'

'What are you going to do?'

'There's not much I can do,' Brian said. 'I'll see if the men can somehow come up with tighter alibis.'

'What will the police do?'

'I don't know that either. I expect they'll try to find out whether anyone has tried to flog any of the stolen stuff in the town – or perhaps in Bath. I don't know what was taken. PC Hendry was a bit cagey about that.'

He moved into the hall and Karen followed him.

'I'm sorry,' she said as she held open the door. 'I wish there was something more I could do.'

And then he spoke without thinking.

'There is,' he said. 'You could let me take you out to a meal again. If you can get a babysitter, that is.'

'I'm not sure . . .' Karen said. Her hesitation was not about the babysitter, though that might be a problem. It was because she was not sure that she wanted to go out in public with him again, so soon. Shipfield wasn't a village but it was amazing how quickly things got around. She wasn't ready for that. Also, what lay between them, on her side heavily, was that she hadn't told him about being pregnant, and about the miscarriage. She was surprised it hadn't got to him already, though equally certain that it hadn't. Of course it was nothing to do with him, but if they were ever to be real friends he would have to know. In any case, if she was to be seen with him in public then some kind soul would almost certainly tell him, warn him off.

She saw his look of disappointment at her hesitation. 'No matter!' he said, brushing the topic aside.

'On the other hand,' she said quickly – and afterwards wondered if she hadn't been too quick – 'you could come and have a meal with me.'

'I'd like that even better!' Brian said, at once more cheerful.

'I'm not the world's best cook,' she warned him.

'It doesn't matter a bit. In fact you needn't do it. I'll cook for you. What's more, I'll bring in all the ingredients.'

When he left, and in spite of the December cold, she stood in the doorway, holding the door open, and watched him until the darkness swallowed him up.

Before he crossed the road to Number Fifteen Brian turned around to see whether Karen was still standing in the doorway, but there was no sign of her, and the light was out. Although it was not yet eleven o'clock, there was hardly anyone around in Mulberry Lane which was not surprising on such a bitter night. The wind was cutting through him like a knife. He let himself into the house and went into the living room where David, Fergus and Mark were huddled around the gas fire. There was no sign of Colin. He hoped he hadn't gone into the town. If he had, then he'd be back late and that would mean more trouble. He'd had all the trouble he wanted for one day.

'Where's Colin?' he enquired.

'Gone to bed,' Mark answered. 'As soon as we came in. He was in a foul mood.'

'Not that the rest of us were feeling on top of the world,' Fergus said.

'I know,' Brian said, 'and I'm sorry. Do you want to talk about it now, or would you rather wait until morning?'

'What's there to talk about?' David demanded. 'They've decided who's done the jobs. They've decided it's us.'

'Not all of them,' Brian said. 'Only some.'

'Most, I reckon,' Mark said. 'Certainly the ones who make most noise! What is there *we* can do? Nothing, I reckon.'

'You could be right,' Brian admitted. 'But if you know you haven't done it—'

'Don't say *you* don't believe us,' David interrupted.

'I didn't say that,' Brian emphasized. 'If you tell me you'd nothing to do with it, then I'll take your word. If it turns out you're lying to me, any one of you, then I'll have no mercy. You'll be back where you belong.'

'Would I be so stupid?' David demanded. 'I've got my Sandra to think of!'

'Precisely!' Brian said.

'And I've got Moira,' Fergus said. 'She's a lovely girl. There's no way I'd let her down. I'm going straight!'

'We've not yet met Moira,' Brian said. 'You must bring her along.'

'Not while this is going on,' Fergus said firmly.

'On the contrary, it would be a good thing to do. It would cheer you up,' Brian pointed out. 'In fact it might cheer us all up. And, in the meantime, I reckon you should all think very hard about your alibis. Try to pin down exactly where you were at given times. Did you meet anyone while you were out? Did you call in at a shop? Exactly what time did you leave work, and get home? That sort of thing. The more precise we can all be, the better – especially when the police get closer to finding when the break-ins took place.'

'I doubt Policeman Plod will do that,' Fergus said.

'Don't underestimate him,' Brian said. 'In any case, it's my opinion he'll be here again. He'll have more questions to ask, so beat him to it. Ask yourselves. Did you pass the houses on your way home? You wouldn't, David, because the toffee factory's in the other direction—'

'Oh, but I did!' David interrupted. 'I'd written a letter to Sandra and I went to North Hill post office for some stamps.'

'There you are!' Brian said. 'So what time? And was there anyone in the post office who knew you, or would the postmaster remember you?'

'He might,' David said. 'He was waiting to close. I was the last customer.'

Mark stood up. 'If it's all the same to everyone else,' he said, 'I'm going to bed. I'm knackered. I'm not sure I can think straight about any of this.'

'Fair enough,' Brian agreed. 'We'll talk tomorrow.'

'If there's anything left to say!' David put in.

'Think about what I said,' Brian advised. 'As many times and details as you can. But on the other hand, by this time tomorrow the police might have caught someone.'

'Pigs might fly!' Fergus said.

Mark turned around as he was leaving the room.

'Oh, I don't know!' he said. 'They caught us, didn't they?'

On the next day, Tuesday, Jennifer arrived home at half-past four. She had had a busy day, lectures both morning and afternoon and two or three hours' making notes in the library, and it had been her turn to do some food shopping for the house. Thank goodness there was a shop on campus which sold most things. She didn't feel like going further afield. She had a cold coming on, possibly even flu. Her head felt as though it had been boiled and her throat was red raw.

There were no lights on in the house. She was clearly the first home. She parked her car, fished out her door key, gathered up the shopping bags and the canvas bag she carried her books in and walked up the path. As she put her key in the lock she heard the phone ring. She rushed into the house, switched on the hall light, dumped the bags and flew to pick up the receiver. It wasn't that she was expecting a call, just that she could never hear a phone ringing without dropping everything to attend to it.

It was Liam.

She sat down on the hall floor, prepared to listen though not sure that she wanted to. It was three weeks since they had spoken, on which occasion she had spent her time repeating that she had no intention of changing her mind about going to Greece. It was all fixed up, or as good as. Her name was on the list and she had a date to meet Professor Maitland some time during the Christmas vacation. Did she, in fact, want to speak to Liam now, or should she simply hang up on him? A lifetime's training in what constituted good manners meant that she couldn't bring herself to put down the phone.

'Have you come to your senses yet?' Liam asked without preliminaries.

Jennifer took a deep breath.

'Well?' Liam demanded, breaking the silence. 'Have you? Let me tell you, this is your last chance!'

'A chance I've no intention of taking. I came to my senses weeks ago,' Jennifer said. 'I came to my senses when I told you I was going to Greece. As you will recall, I asked if you wanted to go along. You said no.'

'I'm not going on any fucking archaeological trip,' Liam said. 'Digging bits of stone out of the ground? Not bloody likely! We could go to France! We could go to Italy!'

Jennifer spoke slowly and deliberately.

'I . . . am . . . going . . . to . . . *Greece*! You can go to hell! And don't ever ring me again!'

Then she put down the phone, sank her head on to her knees and burst into tears. But not for long. Eventually she stood up, picked up her bags, went into the kitchen and put on the kettle. She made tea in a mug, swallowed two aspirins, and decided to go to bed. It was nothing to do with Liam, she told herself firmly, it was everything to do with her foul cold, which felt more like flu by the minute. She filled a hot-water bottle and crawled into bed, and it was there that Grace found her when she came home an hour later.

'I think I've got flu – or worse,' Jennifer said. 'And I've done the most stupid thing! I've left my laptop in the car. I brought the shopping in and then the phone rang and I forgot to go back for it. But it's OK. I did lock the car. Will you be an angel and get it for me? It's on the back seat. The keys are by the telephone.'

'Sure,' Grace said. 'Right away!'

She was back within five minutes.

'Oh Jen, the car's been broken into. There's no sign of the laptop.'

Jennifer sat upright.

'Oh God, no!' she cried. 'I don't believe it! I've only been home an hour!'

'I'm afraid it's true,' Grace said. 'I looked in the boot to make sure. There were bits and pieces in there, but no laptop. Was it insured?'

'Yes,' Jennifer said. 'Daddy insures everything. But it's got hours of work on it I haven't backed up or printed out.'

'You'll have to let the police know,' Grace said. 'The insurance won't pay out if you don't. Shall I ring?'

'I'd be grateful,' Jennifer said. 'Oh, what an idiot I am! If it hadn't been for Liam . . .'

'What's that creep got to do with it?' Grace asked.

'He phoned me just as I came in.'

'Then I hope you sent him off with a flea in his ear!'

'Oh, I did!' Jennifer assured her. 'At least I got that right!'

Police Constable Hendry, walking down North Hill, answered a call on his mobile from Shipfield Police Station.

'Two car break-ins in Mulberry Lane. Number Two, name of Grange, and Number Twelve, owner of car a Miss Jennifer Winton. Number Twelve is a students' place. Both calls in the last few minutes.'

'Right,' Hendry said. 'I'll go to Number Two first since it's nearest. Mulberry Lane's keeping me a sight too busy at the moment! I take it the cars haven't been stolen? No hot-wiring?'

'No. Just broken into and valuables nicked. Probably a coat-hanger job!'

'OK,' Hendry said. He wished these petty thieves wouldn't do their stuff shortly before he was due to finish.

Dr Winston Grange and his wife, Hendry discovered, had driven home from the university, where they both worked, at around four fifteen that afternoon.

'We left early because we had a joint early evening appointment. The first session of a conference in Reading,' Dr Grange said. 'Normally we're home much later. I parked the car in the road, right in front of the house, and I definitely locked it.'

'Right, sir,' Constable Hendry said. 'Do I take it the car wasn't alarmed?'

Dr Grange looked uncomfortable. 'Unfortunately the car went in for servicing this morning so it was turned off for that. I forgot to turn it back on again. We were in a hurry. We had to snatch a quick bite to eat before we left, so we were both in the kitchen. We couldn't have seen anything.'

'We couldn't have, anyway,' Bella Grange said. 'It was dark. I'd closed the front-room curtains.'

'We didn't discover anything wrong until we went

out to drive off,' Dr Grange said, much preferring the story to be in his own hands. 'The car wasn't locked and I knew I had locked it. I realized at once it was a coat-hanger job.'

Constable Hendry sighed. 'I sometimes think the whole world knows how to break into a car with a wire coat hanger!' he said. 'So what was missing, sir?'

'A CD player – new, expensive – and all the CDs, quite a collection.'

'Anything else, sir?'

'No, that was all,' Dr Grange said. 'But quite enough!'

'Thank you for reporting it promptly,' Hendry said, putting away his notebook. 'We'll do what we can. I don't know how much it'll be. Theft from cars is very common – in fact there's been another one just along the road, at what might well be around the same time. I'm on my way there now.'

'I hope you do catch them,' Dr Grange said. 'It's come to something when you can't leave a locked car outside your own door without this happening.'

'It has,' Hendry agreed. 'But it could be worse, sir. They could have hot-wired the ignition, driven the car away and torched it. That's also very common.'

At Number Twelve he heard Jennifer's story, which was depressingly similar.

'And I suppose you forgot to set the alarm?' he asked.

'No,' Jennifer said. 'I don't have one. My car's years older than Dr Grange's. I'm a student, he's a senior lecturer and his wife's a librarian. I know them.'

'You're a fortunate young lady to have a laptop,' Constable Hendry said.

'I know,' Jennifer admitted. 'My father gave it to me for my birthday. And luckily he insured it.'

'So you won't lose out?'

'Oh but I will!' Jennifer told him. 'I had hours of work on it! Quite difficult stuff, some of it, and including a whole essay. Yes, I know, I should have backed it up, but I didn't.'

'That's a shame, miss,' Constable Hendry said. 'We'll do what we can. We just might be lucky. In the meantime, as I said to Dr Grange, you can be thankful your car wasn't driven away and torched. Though actually he was luckier than you since they seem to prefer torching the newer cars to old bangers! I sometimes think it's revenge.'

'Revenge? What's Dr Grange done that they'd want revenge for?'

'Simple. He possesses a nice car that they'd like to have. They tell themselves they have a right to steal it.'

It would make sense, Constable Hendry thought as he left, to cross the road to call in at Number Fifteen, see who was home and who wasn't. Strike while the iron was hot. He knew, because he'd consulted the records, that theft from cars was among the various crimes of which they'd been found guilty. In any case he was sure they'd all know how to do it. There was no-one else in the frame so far, and if his experience was anything to go by there might never be.

He rang the bell and the door was answered by Brian.

'I'd like a few words with you, and any of the men

who are here,' Hendry said. 'There've been one or two developments.'

'Good!' Brian said. 'Come in.'

Hendry followed him into the living room. The only other occupant was Mark Leyton, sitting in an armchair, watching television.

'Not so good, actually,' Hendry said. 'Two thefts from cars in Mulberry Lane this afternoon.'

'So naturally,' Mark said in a steely voice, 'you want to know where we've all been? Now I can really help you there. I was home at three fifteen, since when I've watched racing, *Fifteen to One* and *Countdown*. I did quite well with *Countdown* today. Like to look?' He handed the constable the small pad on which he had worked out the words and the numbers.

'Thank you, sir! Very impressive!' Hendry said. 'You should try to get on it. You might win a special goody bag with a teapot. Do you know how to break into a car?'

'Who doesn't?' Mark said.

Hendry sighed. It was true. They probably showed you how on TV.

'It doesn't take long, does it?' he said. 'I mean, someone skilled could nip across the road, do the job and be back again before the *Countdown* interval was over, couldn't they?'

'They could,' Mark agreed, 'but I didn't.'

'Which I can vouch for,' Brian said. 'We've both been in this room the entire afternoon. I've been doing accounts while Mark, as he says, has been watching wall-to-wall television.'

'I'm glad to hear it,' Hendry said. He wasn't sure whether he was or not, but he believed it. In his mind Leyton was too smart to risk prison for a laptop, or the cash he'd get for selling it. 'So where are the other gentlemen?' he enquired. 'Wouldn't they be home by now?'

'Colin Myers has gone to the dentist. Fergus doesn't finish until half-past five. He should be here in ten to fifteen minutes. David said he'd be doing some overtime. They're busy, close to Christmas.'

Which leaves him wide open, Hendry thought.

'Wait a minute,' Brian said, reading the policeman's thoughts. He picked up the telephone. 'I'm ringing the toffee factory.' He waited a minute, then said, 'Would it be possible for me to speak to David Jessop? He's in Packing. I wouldn't trouble you but it is rather important. Thank you very much.' He handed the phone to Hendry. 'They're fetching him. Speak to him yourself,' he suggested.

They waited, then David's loud voice could be heard in the room. 'David Jessop. Who's speaking?'

'Police Constable Hendry.' The constable sounded awkward. 'Just a question or two! What time will you be home this evening?'

'Not before seven. I told Brian. I'm on overtime. What's it all about?'

'Just routine questions,' Hendry said soothingly. 'I'll call at the house another time.' He handed the phone back to Brian. 'That seems satisfactory for the moment,' he said.

'Good!' Brian answered. 'If you'd been a bit earlier we could have rung the hospital, spoken to Fergus. In fact . . .' He picked up the phone again – 'I'll give it a try. He might just be around.'

The phone was answered quickly.

'I wonder if I could speak to Fergus O'Connor?' Brian asked. 'He's on the portering staff.'

'I know,' the operator said. 'I would think he's left, but I'll check.' After a short interval she spoke again. 'I'm afraid he left only five minutes ago. I'm sorry!'

I'm not, Brian thought, putting down the phone and looking at his watch. 'Twenty to six,' he said to Constable Hendry.

'Fair enough,' Hendry said. 'Which leaves only Myers.'

'I told you, he's gone to the dentist. His appointment was at four o'clock but they keep you waiting, don't they? He had a few fillings to be done.'

'Then I'll leave you to it,' Hendry said. 'I'll call in and see Myers some time tomorrow.' He didn't have much hope of anything. It seemed to him that Number Fifteen was a dead duck.

I'm getting a bit too familiar with Mulberry Lane, he thought as he walked back to the station. It had been part of his beat for a long time but until now it had caused almost no trouble at all. A nice quiet road, respectable people. Of course it was his duty to check on the ex-cons but he still had nothing more than prejudice to go on. Police work wasn't about prejudice, it was about evidence.

What might or might not be evidence turned up the next day. Brian Carson telephoned the police station – reluctantly, but he had to do it – to report that Colin Myers had returned from the dentist but had, in fact, left the house later that evening, unobserved by the others who'd thought he was in his room. He had taken with him all the tools which belonged to the house – worth around three hundred pounds – thirty-five pounds from the joint housekeeping purse, and the petty cash box which had contained eighty-two pounds and seventy pence.

23

Colin Myers, it seemed, had vanished into thin air. Brian was able, on the phone, to give the station sergeant the last address known to him, which was in East Croydon. 'Though that was his address before he went to prison,' he pointed out. 'I don't know that he ever went back there. Certainly in the short time I've known him he hasn't been out of Shipfield, though of course that doesn't mean he hasn't been in touch with anyone, does it?'

'That's right,' the sergeant agreed. 'Did he talk about his home life?'

'Hardly ever,' Brian said.

'Very well, sir. We'll be in touch with East Croydon right away. They'll send someone round to check on him. PC Hendry is due here any minute, so he'll be with you shortly. He'll go through all the details with you.'

PC Hendry arrived at Number Fifteen half an hour later.

'I reckon I should take up residence in Mulberry Lane,' he said affably as Brian showed him in. 'It would be simpler!' He nodded to Mark who, since he wasn't on duty until eleven, was reading the newspaper.

'I take it the other gentlemen are at work?' the constable said.

'That's right,' Brian said. 'They'd already left before I discovered Myers was missing.'

'So fill me in,' Hendry said. 'When and how did you find out?'

'He usually comes down around eight o'clock. Fergus and David leave about ten past, quarter past. When Colin hadn't appeared at half past I took it he'd overslept so I went up to his room to wake him. There was no sign of him, not in his room or in the bathroom or anywhere else, though his bed had been slept in. If it had been anybody else I might have thought they'd gone out for an early walk, but not Colin. A walk for a walk's sake wasn't his style. It was more likely, I reckoned, that he'd slung his hook. Not for good, of course, but for the day.'

'Was that something he was likely to do?' Hendry asked.

Brian nodded. 'He's done it before, when he was in one of his frequent bad moods, though only for an hour or two. He's been particularly fed up in the last few days. We all have, and not without cause. My men feel they've been in the front line – which might be why Myers took off.'

'Or possibly he *was* the cause?' Hendry suggested.

He *could* be the cause, Brian thought. He hoped he wasn't but he couldn't close his eyes to the possibility.

'And the tools?'

'I didn't realize he'd taken the tools until just before I rang the station,' Brian admitted. 'It was the reason I rang. You see, there were clothes around the room so it didn't occur to me at first that he wasn't coming back. He seems to have left in what he stood up in. I noticed later his fleece jacket wasn't on its hook in the hall, but it's a cold day, isn't it?'

'And what about the tools?' Hendry prompted.

'I didn't miss them until I wanted a particular spanner, which would usually have been kept in the bag. He was methodical with tools. He put them back where they belonged – but of course the bag itself was missing.'

'What were they worth? I think you said about three hundred pounds.'

'That's right,' Brian said. 'Most of them new. I have the bills and the receipts. They'd have been a heavy weight to carry far, but he's a strong man.'

'He'll probably sell them, first opportunity,' the constable said. 'What about the cash?'

'We have a communal purse, for the house-keeping. We all had access to it and anyone who was doing the shopping took money from it. There'd have been about thirty-five pounds in it. The petty cash box had just over eighty-two pounds in it.'

'And he had access to that?'

'Sure! It was the float we had for buying materials for the house. Myers and I both had access because we were the ones who did that sort of shopping. I know how much was in it because I balanced it the day before yesterday.'

Mark spoke up. 'Why didn't he take all his clothes if he was leaving? Not that he had many, but his suitcase is still in the bedroom.'

'Your guess is as good as mine,' Brian said. 'He was never one for rational thinking.'

'Well, I'll take a description, what he looks like,

how he was dressed. I suppose it's too much to hope you might have a photograph?'

'I'm afraid so!' Brian said.

Helped by Mark, Brian described Colin Myers as best he could, though he was not a man who would stand out even in a short bus queue. Five feet ten, thin, light brown close-cropped hair, blue eyes, no distinguishing marks. Dressed in blue jeans and a grey fleece jacket. Totally nondescript. It would describe fifty thousand men, Constable Hendry thought.

'Well,' he said, 'we'll do what we can.' He seemed to go through life saying that. 'I'd like to find the man. It will also be very interesting to see if the trouble in Mulberry Lane dies down from now on.'

Brian was not sure whether he wanted that or not. He didn't want it to be any of his men, not even Myers. He had tried to keep an open mind – as, he believed, and it was to the constable's credit, had PC Hendry – but if it *had* been Colin Myers and things did quieten down, then at least it would let the others off the hook. But presumably they'd have to find him to prove it.

The constable was about to leave when his mobile rang. He put it to his ear, and listened.

'I see! OK. Pity, though.' He turned to Brian. 'The Croydon police have already visited the address you gave. It's apparently just around the corner from the police station. No joy! The flat is occupied by someone else, has been for more than a year. He knew nothing of Myers. A neighbour remembered him but hadn't seen him around for a year or two. He said he didn't know him well, didn't think many people did. Would you say Myers was a loner?' he asked Brian.

'Definitely,' Brian agreed. 'He didn't mix, even with the men here. He seldom talked about other people. I doubt he had many friends.'

'Which will possibly make it easier for him to disappear into the blue,' Hendry said.

As he reached the gate and turned left into the road he heard a sharp, staccato tapping. He looked up and saw Esther standing at her window, rapping impatiently on the glass and signalling him to come in. Might as well, he thought. She might just have seen something. Old ladies often did. On the other hand, Myers would seem to have made off in darkness.

He walked up her path and waited patiently while she struggled to the door.

'Good morning, constable!' she said brightly. 'I'm pleased to see you. Do come in and tell me how you're getting on. I hope you're making progress in these crimes which are sweeping through Mulberry Lane. Terrible about the cars, isn't it?'

He followed her into her sitting room while she was talking. So she already knew about the thefts from cars? Well, she would, wouldn't she? Someone would have told her, or she would have dragged it out of them.

'We're looking into it,' he said.

'And what were you doing at Number Fifteen?' she asked outright. 'I don't think you'll find who you're looking for there. They're very nice young men, very polite and helpful.'

There was no point in not telling her. It wasn't a secret and without a doubt the whole road would know, though goodness knew how, before the end of the day.

'One of those very nice young men has skipped off without a word to the cat!' he said.

'Oh dear!' Esther said. 'You do surprise me. How do you know he's actually left? Did he leave a note?'

'Not a word,' he said. 'We just know! Everything points to it.'

'Which one?' she enquired.

'Colin Myers. Did you know him?'

'Not as well as the others,' Esther admitted. In fact she knew him only by sight. He had never come in to do one of the little jobs for her that the others were so willing to carry out. And when from time to time she had tapped on the window, simply by way of a friendly greeting, he'd ignored her. She didn't like being ignored. 'He wasn't very friendly,' she added.

'I don't suppose by any chance you saw him leaving the house?' the constable asked.

'I'm sorry, I didn't,' she admitted. 'It's dark so much at this time of the year, isn't it?' She wished she had. It would have been such a coup, such a help to the police. She would probably have got her name in the paper, even been interviewed for radio or television.

'Yes,' Constable Hendry replied. 'He probably did make off in the dark. Well, as I say, if you do see anything the least bit interesting give us a ring!'

'Oh I will, I will,' Esther assured him. 'I shall keep my eyes peeled. And please do call again, any time you're in the neighbourhood. So nice to have an interesting visitor!'

As PC Hendry, and indeed anyone else who had a practical view of human behaviour, had expected, and due to everyone's avid cooperation in spreading the news, such details as were known about Colin Myers's flight were around Mulberry Lane by supper time at the very latest.

'They'll all be in the Green Man,' Brian said as between them they cleared the dishes after a satisfying meal of sausages and mash. 'Do we want to go?'

'No!' Mark said. 'At least I don't. Let them sort it out for themselves.'

'I think I'd like to be going there,' Fergus said. ''Twould be nice to hear what conclusions they've come to.'

'What about you, David?' Brian asked.

'Not me!' David said. 'I'm going to phone Sandra and then have an early night. I've got a cold coming on.'

'OK, Fergus,' Brian said. 'I'll go along with you. I'm not staying long, though.' He might, he thought, call in on Karen on the way back.

As he had expected, the pub was fairly full and the main subject of conversation was Colin Myers. What did surprise him, however – or did it? – was how Colin's going off with the tools and the cash was somehow taken as proof of his guilt for everything else which had happened in Mulberry Lane in the last week. They didn't much care where he had gone, or even whether he would be caught; they doubted he would be. The important thing was, he had left Mulberry Lane. That was what counted. Brian and Fergus were treated with a certain amount of coolness, especially Brian, who had first brought the ex-cons to Mulberry Lane.

'Well, let's hope the law catches up with him,' Nigel Simpson said. 'Criminals should get their just deserts!'

'Oh, they won't catch him,' Ralph Streeter said.

'They seldom do. Everybody knows the country's full of unsolved crimes, with the perpetrators free as air to commit more. The police are too busy chasing after motorists.'

'Personally,' said Gary Anderson (who had been greeted by Lisa with the news the moment he arrived home, and had come along to the pub to get the whole story), 'as it turns out I don't care! I hope he burns in hell of course, and if he came anywhere near my wife or children I'd see that he did, but just as long as he keeps away from Mulberry Lane . . .'

Dawn, who was there with Michael, rounded on him like a tiger. 'You wouldn't, would you? Nothing happened to you and yours and that's all that matters! You didn't have your house broken into, your jewellery stolen. He took my ruby brooch! It was real rubies! What's more, it was left to me by my grandmother, and it meant the world to me! You suffered nothing!' Her face was flushed, her eyes filled with tears which rolled down her face. Michael handed her a handkerchief.

Gary did not deign to reply.

'You can be certain of one thing,' Ralph Streeter said. 'You'll never see it again.'

'Thank you!' Dawn retorted. 'Thank you very much! That's all I needed!'

Nigel Simpson spoke up, turning to Brian.

'I have to say, I never took to him. He was different from the others. You're better off without him!'

I suppose that's true, Brian thought. Myers had never fitted in and would probably not have stayed the pace. All the same, he was interested in the way they – certainly everyone here – seemed to have assumed that Myers alone had been responsible for everything, including the thefts from the cars. It was a surprising volte-face. But perhaps he was responsible. It was possible. But this evening's atmosphere wouldn't last. By this time tomorrow they would be back to remembering that there were still three of them left. And they were still ex-cons. They would never be flavour of the month.

He ordered another drink each for himself and Fergus.

'I'm going after this,' he said. 'I want to pop in on Karen.'

As Karen opened the door to him she put her finger to her lips, signalling him to be quiet. He followed her into the living room and she closed the door behind them.

'They've only just gone off to sleep,' she said. 'It's all Fiona's fault, the little monkey. She deliberately keeps Neil awake. She's been awkward all day. Really, though, I suppose it's my fault. I don't do enough interesting things with them. Fiona likes to be entertained. She likes to go places, and I've neither the time nor the energy.'

'Well, I did venture to say you looked tired,' Brian said. 'Perhaps we can do something about that, I mean for the children.'

'That would be nice.' Her tone was non-committal, deliberately.

She had been thinking about Brian. If they were to be friends – and there was surely nothing against being good friends, they were already neighbours – then it could only be if they could trust each other, at least that far. If I had a woman friend, she had thought, one who had been around, though not necessarily knowing about the event, would I have kept the knowledge of what had happened to me from her? Especially if we saw each other reasonably often? She had decided that no way would she do so. So why shouldn't that apply to Brian? She didn't *have* to tell him, but to keep it from him deliberately when other people in the road knew about it seemed unfair. So she would tell him, as soon as the right occasion presented itself. If it made any difference to their friendship – well, that would be a pity but it would only confirm her opinion of men. She didn't think it would, she hoped it wouldn't, but she would risk it.

He handed her a bottle of wine which he had bought in the Green Man.

'Oh! How nice,' Karen said. 'Shall we open it?'

'Why not?'

She went into the kitchen and he followed her. He drew the cork while she got out the glasses, then they took the wine back to the living room.

'I suppose you've heard about Colin Myers?'

'Oh yes,' Karen said. 'Most things get around in Mulberry Lane. Laura phoned me. She'd heard from Esther, so whether I've heard the truth or a blown-up version I don't know.'

Brian gave her the details.

'That's as much as I know,' he said, 'but if you'd been in the Green Man this evening you'd have realized that everyone has it all worked out. Colin did the two break-ins plus the two car jobs, then stole the stuff from the house and hopped it. They were so pleased to hear he'd gone. They assume he's taken all their troubles with him.'

'And what do you think?' Karen asked.

'I don't know,' Brian said. 'I really don't. It's quite possible that he did the lot. It's certainly not beyond him. And in a way it would be easier if I knew he'd done it because it would let the others off the hook. In another way it's worse for them. It's exactly what the people in Mulberry Lane expected to happen, and the other three will be tarred with the same brush.'

'Do you think they'll find him?' Karen asked.

'I doubt it – at least not easily,' Brian said. 'He's a slippery customer. And they won't know where to look. I had an address in East Croydon but they drew a blank there. After that the world's wide open. I doubt he has any contacts anywhere. Mind you, I'd never be surprised to hear that he'd landed himself back in prison. He's probably not quite as clever as he thinks he is. Anyway, let's talk about something else. Sometimes I wonder why I let myself in for this job!'

'You do know why,' Karen said. 'And a good thing you did, too! But I would like to talk to you.' She took a long drink of wine.

She looked serious. He had no idea what it could be about.

'Go ahead,' he said.

Now that she'd made up her mind to do it, she didn't know how to begin. She paused for a few seconds.

'Well?' Brian said. 'Don't look so worried. It can't be that serious.'

'Oh, but it is,' she said. 'It certainly is! But I want you to know. Even if I didn't think someone else would eventually tell you, I'd want you to know. We are friends, aren't we?'

'I hope so,' Brian said.

She told him everything. She kept nothing back, nor did she try to mitigate her part in what had happened. She gave him the whole truth. She didn't look at his face as she was speaking. She didn't know what she might see there. When she had said everything, nothing added, nothing held back, she was silent. So was he. Then he reached across to her, put two fingers under her chin and raised her head so that she had to look at him, had to meet his eyes. What she saw in them was not coldness, or blame – but first of all anger, which changed quickly to sadness, compassion.

'Oh, my dear Karen!' he said. 'Oh, my poor, dear Karen!'

'I had to tell you,' she said. 'If we were to be friends I couldn't have this hidden between us.'

'I'm glad you told me,' Brian said. 'And there's one thing I'd like you to promise me. Will you promise that, even if you can't put it behind you, you won't go through life thinking you were guilty? It's all too easy to feel guilty, I know about that, but you weren't. You weren't. You must never think you were.'

'Thank you!' Karen said. 'I'll try not to.'

Brian refilled her glass.

'There's no need ever to talk about it again,' he said, 'but I'd like to think that if ever you do want to, you'll talk to me.'

'I don't think I shall – I mean want to.' She felt herself in the last few minutes to be a new person.

'Right!' Brian said briskly. 'Now we'll go back to what we might do to interest the children! How about us going to Bristol at the weekend, to the zoo? I've never been there myself, and most children like to see animals.'

'They'd love it!' Karen said. 'For that matter, so would I. Oh, it *is* kind of you, Brian! Are you sure you have the time?'

'I'm more than due for a day off,' Brian said. 'So we'll do that on Saturday, but on one condition . . .'

'What's that?'

'That I come back afterwards and cook that meal we mentioned.'

24

Saturday was clear and bright, a sunny December day with no wind but a decided nip in the air. Fiona and Neil, wearing woolly hats, scarves and gloves, were ready and waiting, impatiently watching from the window, when Brian arrived at half-past nine to pick them up.

'They've been on the lookout for the last twenty minutes,' Karen said. 'Very different from a school day, I can tell you! I have to drag them out of bed then.'

'I'm not late, am I?' Brian asked.

'Of course not!' Karen said. 'Dead on time, in fact. I thought I'd take the buggy, if that's all right. Neil might get tired if he has to walk too far, and he's too heavy to carry.'

'I won't get tired!' Neil said. 'I don't want to go in the buggy!'

'Then I'll go in it!' Fiona said.

'No!' Neil objected. 'I won't let you! It's my buggy!'

'And if you two argue like this when we're out I shall bring you straight back home!' Karen threatened.

'Not until we've seen the animals!' Fiona said.

'If you're naughty you'll not get to see the animals!'

'But you're not going to be naughty,' Brian said. 'I'm quite sure you're not! We're going to have a wonderful day. Isn't that so?'

'Yes,' Fiona said agreeably.

And they would, Karen thought, smiling.

Brian had a good effect on these two. She wished she had his secret. Perhaps it was that, never having had children and not knowing much about them, he didn't particularly treat children as children. He didn't use childish words, or assume that they couldn't understand; he dealt with them as people who just happened to be not quite as tall, but were otherwise equal. He had the gift of treating them with understanding, but then, she thought, from her observation he had that with people of any age.

It was a wonderful day. The drive to Bristol went quickly. With the children secured in the back of the car while Karen sat next to Brian, they all sang along to the music on the tapes. When they reached the zoo Brian parked the car, then Karen took the buggy out of the boot and lifted Neil into it. Of course, he protested loudly.

'Oh, Neil! I never know where I am with you,' Karen told him. 'One day you don't want to go in the buggy, another day don't want to walk.'

'I want to walk,' Neil said. 'I'm a big boy!'

'I know you are, darling,' Karen agreed. 'And later on you *shall* walk. But for now you must go in the buggy and I'll push you. We'll find the café and have a nice drink of orange juice and a biscuit. You'd like that, wouldn't you? I expect you're thirsty.'

'Can we have chocolate biscuits?' Fiona asked.

'Probably,' Karen said, 'if you're good.'

'I want Brian to push me!' Neil said.

Karen turned to Brian, raised her eyebrows.

'Of course I will, young fellow!' Brian said. 'As long as you drive. I'll be right behind you. I'll hold on to the handles in case you drive too fast! Don't forget to sound the horn if anyone gets in the way. We don't want to run over anyone, do we?'

'He can't drive!' Fiona said. 'And there isn't a horn! There isn't a steering wheel!'

'Oh yes there is!' Neil retorted. 'There's a wheel, and there's a horn, and I *can* drive!' He grasped an imaginary steering wheel, twirling it around in his small hands; then he pressed an imaginary horn and made a high-pitched, piercing noise which startled two women walking along in front of him.

'See!' he said. 'They got out of the way!'

'You're potty!' Fiona said.

'I'm not potty!' Neil protested. 'You're potty!'

'If I were you, old man,' Brian said, 'I'd watch the road, watch for the traffic. That's what good drivers do.' He glanced at Fiona. 'And passengers shouldn't talk to the driver!' Then he cried out suddenly. 'Look out, driver! We have to turn left here. Put your hand out. Give a signal. Keep the other hand on the wheel! That's right!'

'Stupid!' Fiona grumbled. She was envious.

When they reached the café a reluctant Neil was persuaded out of his buggy so that it could be folded up and taken inside. The place was crowded but they found a table and Brian went off to join the queue for drinks; juice and biscuits for the children, coffee for himself and Karen.

'I've finished!' Fiona announced in no time at all.

412

'I want to see the animals. When are we going to see the animals?'

'Any minute now,' Karen assured her, wiping chocolate from Neil's face. Brian unfolded the buggy and since it was no longer a buggy but a high-powered car Neil was into it at once. Karen made as if to push him.

'No! No!' he cried. 'You don't know how! Only Brian!'

Smiling at Karen, Brian took over.

And then, within minutes, there were the animals and everything was suddenly magical. The children had never seen wild animals close to, only on television or in books.

'Can I stroke the lions?' Neil asked.

'I don't think that would be a good idea,' Brian told him.

'I like the monkeys best,' Fiona said. 'They make me laugh! Can we see them again?'

'I expect so,' Karen said.

By the time they had seen every single animal, and the monkeys twice (and the snakes, which made Karen shudder so that she had to turn away), it was almost lunchtime and they were hungry, but, most fortunately, there was a restaurant almost in front of them.

At the table Karen read out to the children from an extensive menu, lavishly illustrated.

'As it's a special day,' she said, 'you can both choose whatever you like best.' Without hesitation they chose fish fingers and chips. 'Which they have about twice a week at home,' she told Brian.

'I believe you,' Brian said. 'And I'm going to have shepherd's pie, which I eat frequently. It's the comfort of the familiar in a strange place.'

'It's the lack of a sense of adventure,' Karen said.

The idea was – it had been hatched between Karen and Brian, though not told to the children – that in the afternoon they should visit one of the city's large stores where there was known to be a Christmas Grotto, with Santa Claus in attendance. The children had not been told in advance because Karen feared that they might be too tired for it, but fish fingers, chips and ice-cream had clearly revived them.

'But how can Father Christmas be here?' Fiona demanded as they entered the store, which already looked like fairyland.

'He gets everywhere!' Brian told her.

And there he was, attended by a Christmas fairy and several green-clad elves. They joined the queue, and when it came to their turn he gave them presents from a large sack – a toy car for Neil to add to his collection and a glittering hair ornament for Fiona, which she insisted on wearing immediately.

'You must have a present,' Brian told Karen when they had been guided rather quickly out of the grotto to allow other paying customers to come in.

'The whole day's a present for me,' Karen said. 'I don't need anything else.'

Nevertheless, Brian insisted, and in the jewellery department he bought her a pair of earrings: small, oval amethysts set in silver. Very beautiful, but not so expensive that she couldn't accept them.

Going home in the car, it was already dark; they sang again, but not for long. Well before they reached Mulberry Lane the children were asleep. When they got to the house Brian lifted Neil into his arms, carried him up to his bedroom, laid him in his cot – Neil scarcely moving – and carefully undressed him.

What a pity he never had children of his own, Karen thought as she took care of a half-asleep Fiona. He's a natural.

They covered the children and went downstairs.

'Would you like a cup of coffee? Or there's a glass of wine. I vacuumed what was left over the other night. It'll be quite drinkable. Or do you have to go? It's been a wonderful day but I don't want to keep you!'

She was nervous. She'd looked forward to this day, and it had gone well – wonderfully well for the children – but she didn't want to make too much of it. She didn't want to be unwelcoming but she wasn't sure that she wanted another tête-à-tête with Brian just yet. The last one was still in her mind. In any case, she was bone tired, ready for bed and sleep.

'I don't have to go,' Brian said, 'though I don't want to be too late. Call me fussy, but actually I like to have an idea what the lads are up to on a Saturday night. So why don't we just finish the wine? You stay put. I'll get it.'

She waited, leaning back in the chair, her eyes closed.

'There's half a bottle,' he said. 'Just under. Not too little, not too much.' He poured a glass and handed it to her, and then he poured one for himself. Karen raised her glass in his direction.

'Here's thanking you for a lovely day!' she said.

Brian raised his glass. 'I enjoyed every minute of it,' he said. 'They're nice kids. We'll do it again some time.'

She didn't sleep well. She had no idea how long she lay awake – certainly several hours – but it seemed to her when she wakened next day that she'd been asleep no more than ten minutes and now already the children were wide awake and Neil was calling for her.

It was certainly later than she'd intended. When she drew back the curtains she saw the O'Briens' Volvo outside Number Eleven. They would be going to Mass, taking Esther, as they did every Sunday morning. She envied them. They were so contented with each other, so steadfast in their faith. She felt they would always know what to do, always help each other to make the right and proper decision. She wished she had not lost her faith, but it was a vain wish, she thought. She'd done so, and that was that. You couldn't lean on something you didn't believe in. That was cheating.

Laura, Dermot and Esther were probably the only people in Mulberry Lane bound for church. It was not a churchgoing community. Of the rest, some were indulging in a leisurely breakfast of the kind only enjoyed on Sundays and bank holidays: bacon, eggs, tomatoes, mushrooms, fried potatoes. Full of cholesterol, as Bella Grange pointed out to her husband, and totally delicious, as Winston retorted, so what the hell! The students were brewing the usual Sunday coffee, thanks to Lady Winton and Fortnum & Mason's delivery service. The Streeters, both on diets, were pretending to enjoy crispbreads and low-fat spread.

Some people, of course, were still in bed: Eric and James, Peter and Meg. (Samson had not yet returned home from wherever he'd spent the night.) Jim and Betty Pullman had been up and about early, getting the Green Man ready for opening at noon after an exceptionally busy Saturday night. Nigel Simpson was grooming a protesting Titus prior to taking him round to the pub. Gary Anderson was at the gym – though not for many more Sundays since he was having one built in his own house. The basement would lend itself very well to that.

At Number Fifteen the men were reading the papers – the *Mail on Sunday*, the *Sunday Express* and the *News of the World*.

Brian had been thinking about Christmas. It might be a good idea to spend some time with Karen and the children. She was in need of cheering up. What about having them here for Christmas dinner? He would see what the men thought.

'What shall we do about Christmas?' he asked at breakfast.

'Do you think I could invite Sandra over?' David asked quickly. 'And do you think Karen would have her to stay? It's almost impossible to travel on Christmas Day.'

'You'd have to ask Karen,' Brian said. 'There's no reason why Sandra shouldn't come here to her meals. As a matter of fact I had been wondering whether we might ask Karen and the kids for Christmas dinner. I doubt they'll be going anywhere. What do you think?'

''Twould be nice to have children around on Christmas Day,' Fergus said. 'More like home. And if Sandra's invited could I not ask Moira? She'll not be able to get home to Ireland. She doesn't have enough time off.'

Brian looked across at Mark.

'What do you think?'

'OK by me,' Mark said. 'I'll be working flat out at Christmas and the New Year. I'll not be likely to see anyone.'

He didn't mind that. He was learning something every day, and being given more responsibility. Also, Brian had said that as compensation for having to work over the holiday he could keep all his tips for himself instead of having to put them in the kitty. He supposed he might have liked to see his parents at Christmas, but they would be abroad.

'Right! Then I'll give Karen a ring, and you two can invite Sandra and Moira. Though I'd better check with Karen about Sandra staying,' he added to David.

He telephoned her later that morning.

'I'd love to come for Christmas dinner!' she said. 'So would the children. If you're quite sure, that is?'

'I'm sure,' Brian said.

'And of course Sandra can stay,' Karen added. 'Tell David she can stay all over the holiday if she wants to.'

On Monday, late morning, Police Constable Hendry visited Number Fifteen again.

'Come in, constable, I'm afraid there's only me here,' Brian said. 'The lads are all at work. Would you like a cup of coffee, or a beer?'

'A cup of coffee would go down nicely,' Hendry said. 'It's a cold morning. Seasonal, I suppose.' He followed Brian into the kitchen.

'Soon be Christmas,' Brian said, switching on the kettle. He found himself looking forward to it.

'It was you I wanted to see,' Hendry said. 'And

really only to report progress, or rather no progress.'

'Nothing on Myers, then?' Brian asked.

'Afraid not! Nothing at all! He seems to have disappeared into the blue. We'll keep on trying, of course, but I can't promise what'll come of it. We haven't many leads on where he might be. Possibly London, and that's a good place to hide.'

Brian made the coffee and they both sat at the table. The constable stirred two spoonfuls of sugar into his mug.

'We've not traced any of the stolen goods either, neither your tools nor the stuff from the other jobs in the road.'

'Though we don't know he was involved in those,' Brian reminded him.

'True, sir!' Hendry agreed. 'And we're not totally assuming he was, but it points that way, doesn't it? Anyway, nothing traced. And most petty thieves sell the stuff quickly. More often than not they're on drugs and they're desperate for the money.'

'I can assure you Myers wasn't on drugs!' Brian said. 'I'm positive about that. I'd have known. I'd have recognized the signs. If he had been he wouldn't have lasted ten minutes here. This isn't a suitable set-up for drug rehabilitation. It was never seen as that.'

Hendry nodded. 'Well, the other lads' alibis for the car thefts seem watertight so far. We can't be sure on the house jobs. We're no nearer pinning down the times those took place. A funny job, mine. Believe nothing, prove everything. Doesn't allow for much faith in human nature, does it?'

'Different from mine,' Brian said. 'If I didn't have faith in human nature I couldn't do it at all.'

'You look for the best, me for the worst,' Hendry said. 'But to be fair, I'm usually pleased when I can really let someone off the hook.'

'And start looking for someone else!' Brian said.

'That's right. I don't like closing a case that hasn't been solved.' He paused, took another drink of his coffee. 'So what will you do for Christmas?' he said conversationally. 'I suppose you don't get it with your family, not in this job?' He wondered about Brian Carson, knowing this wasn't the first time he'd done a stint like this. Did he not have any family?

'I don't have any family,' Brian said, answering the unspoken question. 'My parents are both dead and I haven't any brothers or sisters. I'll be spending it here with the three men. And perhaps a friend or two.'

'I must say,' Hendry said, looking around, 'you've made a nice job of this place between you.'

'Mostly Colin Myers,' Brian admitted. 'He's a good workman when he puts his mind to it. Fortunately he's finished most of the skilled work. We can manage the rest of it between us.'

PC Hendry drained his mug and stood up. 'I'll let you get on with it,' he said. 'And thank you for the coffee. It was nice and warming. I'll let you know if anything comes up, and I can take it you'll inform the station if anything more occurs to you?'

'I will,' Brian promised.

Esther saw Constable Hendry leave Number Fifteen and walk in her direction along Mulberry Lane. She tapped on the window and he waved to her but, to her great disappointment, didn't stop. She would dearly have liked to know what was afoot: Monday was always a boring day, often the prelude to a dreary week.

It turned out to be another of those weeks in which little of note occurred in Mulberry Lane which, though dull from Esther's point of view, came as a benefit to many of the inhabitants who felt that rather too much had been happening recently and it was a relief to return to their usual unexciting and respectable existence. There were no more burglaries, no accidents, no sudden illnesses, no-one ran off with someone else's wife. Those who had been unlawfully deprived of their belongings had put in their insurance claims and Jennifer's father, while chiding her for her carelessness, promised her another laptop for her Christmas present. Nothing, of course, would compensate Dawn for the loss of the ruby brooch.

On another level, Jennifer's cold had turned out to be a mild case of influenza (though at no point did it feel mild to her) and a few other people were laid low by a similar bug, but that was no more than could be expected at this time of year, especially as after a cold, dry Monday the weather turned unseasonably wet and muggy. Dermot was one of those who was smitten, but since it was almost the end of term and the pressure of work was less – also because he did not want half his class to be flu-bound over the Christmas holidays – he had no compunction in taking two days off and sweating it out under the duvet, with Laura looking after him – filling hot-water bottles, making hot drinks – when she wasn't at work or out Christmas shopping.

It was not entirely true that *nothing* was happening, since several people were gearing up for

Christmas. The Streeters worked late on Wednesday evening, decorating the salon in the best of taste, blue and silver, nothing over the top, and laid in a bottle or two of cream sherry so as to be able to give a glass to all their clients on Christmas Eve. As far as business went, they were assured of a bumper season since almost every hour in the week beforehand was filled with appointments.

Fiona brought home gold and red foil stars she had made in school which Karen promised to hang on the Christmas tree as soon as she had time to get it down from the loft and put it up. Neil was being coached to be one of the three wise men in the Christmas tableau, for which he would be draped in a striped beach towel, wear a paper crown and carry a present wrapped in gold paper for Baby Jesus. The Blake twins had been chosen as the Babes in the Wood in the school play and in between sorting out her clients' feet for the rigours of Christmas shopping Dawn was making their costumes (the twins', not the clients').

Although it was a bit early, the Green Man was already abundantly decorated. Paper chains almost obscured the ceiling and the walls, there were additional fairy lights wherever a space could be found for them, and a huge Christmas tree was ablaze with lights in all available colours and in the shape of bells and bows. Betty Pullman was possibly the only lady in Mulberry Lane who would not have a minute to have her hair done.

'It won't matter, love!' Jim said. 'You'll be wearing a paper hat from morning 'til night! Anyway, you always look lovely!'

On the Thursday Gary Anderson took a couple of hours out of his busy day to go into Bath to buy presents for his wife and children. Shipfield could offer nothing fine enough, nothing worthy of them. Had time allowed he would have liked to have gone up to Harrods. And since Lisa's mother and father were coming down from Yorkshire to stay with them until the New Year he must also choose something for them.

In the Green Man, though neither Brian nor any of the men had been in there for several days, desultory grumbles still lingered about the thefts, mostly about the inadequacy of the police and the statistics on the number of unsolved crimes across the country. Feeling remained high against Colin Myers and from time to time there were threats about what might happen to him should any one of them meet up with him, but aside from that he seemed to be thought of as perhaps the one rotten apple in the barrel. Filled with the spirit of Christmas, most of them at least seemed not inclined to blame the other men.

On Thursday evening the students packed, ready to leave Mulberry Lane the next day, then sat around briefly drinking coffee. Briefly, because most of them planned on an early start on Friday morning, Grace particularly so since she had to make the long journey by rail to North Yorkshire. 'I'm dying to see everyone again!' she admitted. 'It seems so long, though I know it was only September.'

'What will you do at Christmas, I mean apart from seeing your family?' Caroline asked. In her eyes Grace was the most fortunate person in the world. Her own parents were divorced and she had no siblings. She would spend an uneasy Christmas in two different flats, divided between her parents and their new partners. She didn't look forward to it.

'All the usual things,' Grace said. 'Very simple, really. Carol singing around the village on Christmas Eve, church on Christmas morning and a huge family lunch – brothers, sisters, grandparents, aunts and uncles. Presents after lunch – there isn't time before. And of course the work on the farm goes on – animals to feed and so on.' She didn't mind that, in fact she loved it, in the same way that she loved the countryside there: the high fells, the dales with their swift streams, the brownish water racing over rocks, the fields dotted with ancient stone barns. It was her spiritual home. She hoped once university was over never to have to live away from it for long.

They all knew that Imogen, after spending Christmas at home, would be taking off two days later with a group of like-minded friends for a skiing holiday in Switzerland. 'We always ski in January,' she said matter-of-factly. 'I'd hate not to! I can't think what else I'd do.'

Stuart wondered briefly if Imogen might not be a better matrimonial target than Jennifer. Obviously there was money there, and a wife who would support him until such time as his first novel was in print, and in the charts, was essential. Imogen was also attractive, intelligent, presentable. She would never let him down when he began to move in the more exalted circles of literature and the arts. Not that Jennifer would let him down in those areas, but she had this archaeological bug. He didn't want a wife who would always be off to foreign parts, not unless she was accompanying him on an author tour.

The problem with Imogen was that – and it

genuinely surprised him – she didn't seem to fancy him.

Jennifer was going home to Reigate, though whether she would be able to stand it for the whole of the Christmas vacation was, she thought, another matter. Still, duty called, at least for a few days, and for two or three of them Aunt Rachael would be there and they could talk about Athens. After that she would take off to Brighton and stay with Ruth and the baby. She had, after all, been invited to be the godmother. Daddy was being very generous about the new laptop. It would be better than the one which had been stolen, everything up-to-the-minute. Her mother was surprisingly happy about the Greek expedition and would probably take her up to town to kit her out in the very best gear for it. Part of Lady Winton's pleasure, as she confided to her husband, was because it was the end of that awful Liam. 'Jennifer will probably meet some very nice people,' she said to him. 'Especially on an expedition led by Professor Maitland!' She had looked him up in Debrett's *People of Today* and had been quite impressed.

Some of the students at Number Twelve were mildly disappointed that they would miss the carol singing in the Green Man on Christmas Eve, also the party planned there for Boxing Day evening (at which it was rumoured the Salvation Army band would play) – but not too seriously disappointed. They were, after all, birds of passage. A year from now some of them would have left Mulberry Lane for ever. Two years on and they would all have fled.

25

Christmas Eve arrived, and with it came Sandra in the early afternoon. Moira, who had worked a day shift in the hospital and had then gone home to change, did not arrive until evening. Sandra looked as tall and ravishing as ever; Moira was petite, with a neat short crop of blue-black hair falling in a fringe over her forehead, and sea-green, thickly lashed eyes. She was as attractive as Sandra in a totally different way, plus she had a soft voice and a West of Ireland accent. Fergus, Brian thought, had done well for himself.

The four of them were going out to a meal in the town, and afterwards to a club or a pub – perhaps the Green Man to finish with, perhaps not. It being Christmas Eve, there was no eleven o'clock curfew. Mark had already left the house and would be working late.

Karen had said that she definitely didn't wish to go out on Christmas Eve. She had called in at Number Fifteen, with the children, on her way home from the shops. It was then that David and Sandra offered willingly (more than willingly) to forgo their dinner in the town should Karen wish to go out.

Karen shook her head. 'No way!' she said. 'Christmas Eve is for the children. I'm all theirs this evening! And you'd have no peace. Even if they go to bed early, which for once they won't mind doing, they'll not go to sleep. They'll struggle to keep awake.'

'We're going to stay awake to see Father Christmas,' Fiona confided. 'But you have to be in bed or he won't leave anything. And you mustn't let him know you've seen him. You have to pretend to keep your eyes shut.'

'I also have to make two dozen mince pies,' Karen said. 'And wash my hair. So I'll be very well occupied.'

All of which Brian took to mean that she didn't want him there. And that was all right. He had things to do, not least to make some preparations for tomorrow's dinner. Eight people! And he'd never cooked a Christmas dinner before. He knew most of the work would fall on him, though no doubt they'd all offer to help. He didn't want that. The kitchen was small; he'd rather have it to himself, make his mistakes in private. All the same, he didn't want to spend all morning in the kitchen, so anything he could do in advance, this evening, he would do.

'We might make a start on the decorations before we go out,' David said.

He smiled at Sandra, remembering what they had discussed together, that next year, if they were lucky and all went well, they might be putting up Christmas decorations in their own place. Even if it was only two rooms, and no matter where.

'I must go,' Karen said. 'We'll see you all tomorrow. Around noon?'

'I look forward to it,' Brian said.

'Will Father Christmas be coming to you?' Fiona asked him.

'I hope so!' he replied. 'I've been very good!'

He saw them to the door. For a moment he was tempted to suggest that he should join Karen later this evening, but he resisted it. She'd made it plain, though without any animosity, that it was not what she wanted.

Walking to the gate with them, he saw that Esther's window was lit, the curtains not yet drawn, and the old lady herself was standing there, looking out. He waved to her, as did Karen, and then the children.

'I wonder what she's doing tomorrow?' Brian said.

'She's OK,' Karen said. 'She's having Christmas dinner with Laura and Dermot. They're taking her back with them after church. Laura told me.'

'Good!' he said. 'See you tomorrow then.'

Karen and Sandra, with the children, arrived at Number Fifteen soon after midday. What time Sandra had let herself in on Christmas Eve – or Christmas morning – Karen had no idea. She had been asleep and heard nothing. But this morning, admittedly after a long sojourn in the bathroom, she had emerged as fresh as a daisy, as beautiful as a butterfly.

'Merry Christmas, everyone!' she cried.

'Father Christmas came!' Fiona said. 'I stayed awake *ages*, but I didn't see him, and Neil was asleep.'

'Well, I can see he's been!' Sandra said.

The room was littered with bright wrapping

paper. Fiona herself was dressed in a nurse's outfit – cap, apron, plastic thermometer, bandages and toy watch – and was attending to a new doll which had presumably already contracted some nasty illness. Neil was wheeling a tipper lorry, loaded with small wooden bricks, across the floor. The doll and the lorry had been bought with money Karen's mother had sent. 'You choose for them,' she'd said in the note to Karen. 'I don't know what they like.' (You would, Karen thought, if you took the trouble to come and see them more often.) From the children's father there had been nothing, not even a Christmas card.

The nurse's outfit had been bought by Karen, not that she credited her daughter with the caring qualities of a nurse-in-the-making, but Fiona liked to be in charge. She was bossy. For Neil she had chosen a toy xylophone. Neil had rhythm, and with a little encouragement, Karen fondly hoped, some latent musical talent might emerge. Guiltily, she thought he would probably have preferred a drum.

'It's time we were getting ready to go to Brian's,' she said.

Neil looked up from tipping another load of bricks on the area of the carpet chosen by him as his delivery point, from which he would eventually reload them and return them to the starting point. His face puckered, his lower lip stuck out in defiance.

'Don't want to!' he protested.

'Of course you want to!' Karen said cheerfully. 'You like going to Brian's.'

Fiona broke off from taking her patient's temperature for the fifth time.

'Oh, Mummy! He means he wants to stay with his tipper lorry,' she said painstakingly.

'Oh! But he can take it with him,' Karen said. 'I didn't expect him to leave it behind, or his xylophone.' Not that he had shown any more than a fleeting interest in the latter, she thought. 'I'm sure Brian won't mind. You can both take your presents.'

'Brian likes tippers!' Neil stated.

'I shall wear my uniform,' Fiona said. She would also, she planned, take everyone's temperature and feel their pulse. She knew how to do that, she had seen it on television.

'We must tidy up here first,' Karen said. 'Smooth out the Christmas paper and save it for next year!' She did that every year – sometimes she actually ironed it – but seldom reused it, either because she forgot where she'd stored it or, if she did find it, it was all in the wrong sizes.

The four of them left Number Six soon after noon, Neil in his buggy, clutching his tipper lorry, Fiona carrying her new doll. Karen and Sandra were weighed down by parcels and as they left the house Karen wondered out loud if she had been wise to refuse Brian's offer to break off his cooking and collect everyone in his car.

'We'll manage,' Sandra said. 'It's not far.'

Esther, already back from church, was comfortably ensconced in the O'Briens' front window, supping a glass of dry sherry and, for once, viewing life from the other side of the street.

'You didn't tell me Karen and the children were going to Number Fifteen today!'

'Didn't I?' Laura said. 'That was remiss of me.'

'So are they going to Christmas dinner or just for drinks?' Esther enquired.

'For dinner,' Laura said. 'I don't know what's on the menu but I daresay I can find out afterwards and let you know.'

'Doesn't matter,' Esther said. 'Everybody eats the same at Christmas these days. Now when I was a girl we used to have a goose. Much tastier than turkey. Turkey is a dry meat. I hope you have basted yours well.'

'I have,' Laura assured her. 'Would you like Dermot to pour you some more sherry?'

'Why not?' Esther said, draining her glass.

The children's faces lit up with surprise when they entered Number Fifteen, as, in fact, did Karen's and Sandra's. Fergus and David had made a wonderful job of the decorations, concentrating on silver, gold, red and white. Paper chains, tinsel, ribbons, bows, holly, mistletoe and lots of sparkle everywhere.

'Oh,' Fiona cried, 'it's just like fairyland!'

'It certainly is!' Karen agreed. 'When did you do all this?'

'This morning,' David said. 'Far too early!' He pointed at Fergus. 'That one dragged me out of bed, hangover and all!'

Brian, aproned, came out of the kitchen to greet them all. He was followed by Moira, whom he had not been able to keep out of his territory. She had been useful peeling vegetables but he had refused to let her lay the table. That he wanted to do himself, and by now he had already done it, in a manner so festive that the everyday crockery, which was all they had, was vanquished.

Neil tugged at Brian's apron.

'I bringed my tipper lorry,' he said, man to man.

'Oh, good!' Brian replied. 'We'll have a good game with it this afternoon.'

Fiona had taken her coat off and now stood before Brian in the glory of her uniform, waiting to be noticed.

'My goodness!' he obliged. 'What have we here? A nurse! In fact, two nurses!' He pulled Moira forward. 'Moira is a nurse! Nurse Moira, let me introduce Nurse Fiona!'

There was a slight unhappiness in Fiona's face which Moira spotted at once.

'But I'm not in uniform,' she said quickly. 'So you will have to be the head nurse. You'll have to tell me what to do.'

Fiona brightened up at once.

'Well,' she said. 'Rosie – she's my new doll – isn't at all well. I think she has a temperature, and she has a rash. And I think she might have a broken arm because she fell off the chair. Or a leg!'

'Goodness gracious!' Moira said. 'She does sound in a bad way! Shall the both of us take a look at the poor child?'

'You can be the doctor, if you like,' Fiona said graciously.

'There's more presents for everyone,' Fergus said.

'Shall we open them all after dinner?' Karen suggested.

'I think that would be best,' Brian agreed.

Christmas dinner was a great success. Brian, justifiably pleased with himself, accepted compliments on the meal from everyone. When they had finished eating, he said, 'Now we'll clear the table and it's present time.'

There was something from everyone *to* everyone, some of the gifts small and inexpensive, others less so. Brian gave Karen a fine silver necklace with a small amethyst pendant; she gave him a leather notecase embossed with his initials. Afterwards David, Sandra, Fergus and Moira offered to wash up.

'Can I help?' Karen asked.

'No,' Brian said. 'Four is quite enough.'

'I don't know about that,' Moira said. 'I've seen the state of the kitchen! 'Twould take an army to put it straight! But really, Karen, there isn't room for you.'

Karen wasn't sorry. She was pleasantly full of food she hadn't had to cook, relaxed and rather tired. She would happily lie back in a comfortable chair and watch whatever television offered.

'Mummy can help me to look after Rosie,' Fiona announced. 'She's a bit better but she shouldn't be left.' Rosie had been diagnosed as having chicken pox, a broken arm and a sprained ankle. She had been sponged down, her ankle bandaged, her arm put in a sling made from one of Fergus's new Christmas present handkerchiefs and she had spent dinnertime lying on a cushion on the sofa with her eyes closed.

Brian, reminded by Neil that he had promised to help with the tipper lorry, went down on his hands and knees. Loud conversation and peals of laughter came from the kitchen. Karen's last conscious thought before she fell asleep was to wonder why Irish laughter sounded different from English.

When she wakened it was to the sound of Neil

banging on his xylophone. Fiona, unusually for her, had fallen asleep sitting by Rosie.

'We decided the tipper lorry was tired,' Brian explained. 'Also it ran out of petrol and there was nowhere open so we thought we'd have a bit of music. I'm sorry if it woke you. The others have gone out for a walk.'

'I'm sorry I dozed off,' Karen apologized.

'Don't be,' Brian said. 'It's good to see you so relaxed.'

'Listen, Mummy!' Neil commanded.

He gave a loud and totally discordant offering on the xylophone.

'Lovely, darling!' Karen said. She turned to Brian. 'I think we might be in for wall-to-wall music! I hope you can stand it?'

'Sure!' Brian said.

'It's been a lovely Christmas Day,' Karen said.

Brian nodded agreement. 'Yes, it has.' And how strange it was, he thought, that in spite of spending it with a bunch of ex-convicts, no family around him, the shadow of the burglaries still hanging like question marks over the men's heads, it had been one of the happiest Christmas Days he remembered for a long time.

When the four came back from their walk they made tea, after which Karen said, 'I think we really must go. The children are tired, they were up early.'

'If you must,' Brian said. 'I'll walk back with you, help with the parcels.'

It was Fiona who reminded them. The four of them were standing in the hall, wearing their coats and woolly caps – it was freezing cold outside, David said – and the other four were waiting to see them off, when she cried out, 'We haven't done it!'

'Done what, darling?' Karen asked.

'We haven't done the kissing under the mistletoe! Everybody kisses underneath the mistletoe at Christmas! Miss Perkins said so.'

'Miss Perkins is Fiona's teacher and there is nothing she doesn't know,' Karen said solemnly.

'Well then, let's not waste any more time!' Fergus said. 'Come right here, Nurse Fiona!'

The mistletoe, a meagre branch – there had been a shortage this year – had gone unnoticed among all the other decorations, being under the light fitting. Fergus swept Fiona off her feet, held her high in the air, under the mistletoe, and gave her a smacking kiss.

Everyone kissed everyone else, there was a feast of kissing. When it was Brian's turn to kiss Karen, for a second or two, which seemed to each of them a long time, they looked at each other without speaking, without moving, not even smiling. Then Brian put his arms around Karen and drew her close. She twined her arms around his neck, and they kissed: a long kiss. He could smell the sweet, spicy scents of her perfume. Without realizing she was doing so, Karen stroked her fingers along the back of his neck. It was as if, for one moment, the chattering crowd around them was not there at all. They heard none of it. Then Karen lowered her arms and Brian loosened his hold on her and let her go. Their bodies no longer touched. After that they exchanged a quick under-the-mistletoe kiss, and it was time to go.

They walked along the road towards Number Six, Brian toting two carrier bags filled with presents,

Karen pushing the buggy in which Neil clutched the precious tipper lorry, Fiona carrying Rosie who was wrapped in Karen's scarf in case whatever ailed her should be made worse by exposure. Brian had opted not to take them in the car, not only because the distance was so short but more because everyone at Number Fifteen, himself included, had had a few Christmas drinks, mostly alcoholic.

They walked in near silence, Karen and Brian not talking at all, Neil almost asleep. Only Fiona made a few remarks to the poorly doll. 'You'll soon be home, and in bed,' she assured Rosie. 'And as you're tired you needn't have a bath tonight!'

Karen's thoughts were back under the mistletoe. She wondered what Brian was thinking about now. Had it been, could it have been, alcohol that had induced what had happened between them at that particular moment? For herself she was certain it hadn't been, but how did she know about Brian? At the time she had been sure – without any need to stop and think – that the feeling between them had been strong and deep, and mutual. Now, in the cold darkness of the December evening, she was less sure. If Brian were to take her by the hand, or put his arms through hers . . . but how could he, burdened by carrier bags, she reasoned with herself. How silly she was being!

Reaching the house, she unlocked the door and they went in.

'I won't stay,' Brian said. 'I can see the children are tired. Unless you want me to help you, of course?'

'I'll be all right,' Karen said. Of course she wanted him to stay, but he had already made the decision not to.

'*I*'m not tired,' Fiona said, 'but Rosie is. Can she have a hot-water bottle, Mummy?'

'I expect so,' Karen said.

'Then I'll see you tomorrow evening,' Brian said. 'It's been a wonderful day!'

'For me too,' Karen said. 'Thank you for having us.'

'It was a pleasure!'

He didn't want to leave. He would have liked to help her to put the children to bed and then stay for the rest of the evening, but she looked tired. He was not sure that she would want him. Her voice, in the very little she'd said since they'd left Number Fifteen, sounded uncertain. Perhaps she had not felt what he'd felt, though he'd thought she had. Perhaps for her it had been no more than the result of the relaxing atmosphere of Christmas Day.

'I'll see you tomorrow, then,' he said. 'Around seven.'

He was to take her out to supper in the town, and after supper to drop in on the festivities at the Green Man, which had an extension until midnight. It was an arrangement for the purpose of giving David and Sandra time together on their own. Perhaps, Brian thought as he left, he and Karen would have more to say to each other tomorrow evening.

This last thought was Karen's exactly as she watched Brian walk down the path and away along the road before she closed the door.

'Now,' she said to the children, 'bedtime! It's really quite late and you've had a long day.'

They were in bed in no time at all, and fell asleep quickly. Not long afterwards she herself went to bed. Sandra had a key so there was no need to wait up for her, and to tell the truth she would be glad to be in bed, not only because she was tired, but because she wanted to lie there in the darkness, thinking her own thoughts, letting them take her wherever they would.

Karen was wakened by a loud ring at the front door. She felt sure she had been asleep no more than twenty minutes, but when she switched on the light the bedside clock showed a quarter past one. The bell rang without ceasing as she reached for her dressing gown. Stop it, Sandra, she thought. Stop it, you'll waken the children! It had to be Sandra. She had no doubt mislaid her key. Karen ran swiftly down the stairs and along the hall to the door, intent above all on stopping the noise.

'Really, Sandra! Must you—?' she cried as she opened the door.

It was not Sandra. There, on the doorstep, where she had expected to see David and Sandra, stood Ray.

For a long moment Karen could not believe what she was seeing, nor would her mind take it in, and his appearance did not help. He wore a shabby grey anorak, his black hair was untidy, his eyes red-rimmed. He looked seedy. His breath made small alcoholic clouds in the frosty air. This was not the Ray she had known. Whatever his faults he'd always been meticulous about his appearance.

She stared at him, speechless.

'Well?' he said. 'Aren't you going to ask me in?' He swayed towards her.

'What are you doing here?' Her words came out harshly. He was the last person in the world she wanted to see. She felt she'd been wakened from her sleep only to be plunged into a nightmare.

'Come on, Karen!' he said. 'I can't stand out here! I'm frozen!'

'Why are you here?' Karen demanded.

'I've come back to you!' he said. 'My true love! I've come back to you and my children!'

'You're drunk!' Karen said. 'And even if you weren't I don't want you back, now or ever. It's over.'

'I can explain!' Ray said. He raised his voice. 'Please let me come in.'

What else could she do? Any minute now he would waken the neighbours. Also, standing here barefoot, in her thin dressing gown, she was shivering. Reluctantly, she let him in.

'But you can't stay!' She was adamant. 'No way can you stay! I'll give you ten minutes to explain – and please do it quietly.'

'You don't understand,' he said. 'Of course I'll explain. In the meantime can I have a drink? Whisky. To warm me up. I'm frozen!'

'I don't have whisky,' Karen said. 'I never did, as you well know. In any case it's obvious you've had more than enough. You'd better come into the sitting room where I can shut the door on you. If you waken the children I'll kill you!'

He followed her in. She closed the door. He sank onto the sofa. Almost immediately the telephone rang, a sinister sound in the early hours of the morning.

'If it's that whore Freda,' Ray said, 'I don't want to speak to her!'

It was David.

'Oh, Karen, I'm sorry to ring you so late,' he said, 'but I thought if I didn't you might be worried when

439

Sandra didn't turn up. The thing is, she's had one little drink too many – Christmas Day and all that – and she's passed out on the sofa. Brian says she can stay where she is until morning. So we'll see you then. I'm really sorry! Were you asleep?'

'No, I wasn't,' Karen said. 'It's all right.'

She was pleased Sandra wasn't in the house. She wanted no witness to the scene she was going through.

'Who was that?' Ray asked. '*Was* it Freda?'

'No, it wasn't,' Karen said. 'I'm going into the kitchen and I'm going to make some strong black coffee. Don't you dare to move from here! And when you've drunk the coffee you're leaving. And please don't ever come back.'

'I don't want to leave,' he whined. 'I want to stay. I want to see the children. They're my children as well as yours!'

'That's a new thought, I must say!' She was bitter. 'I doubt you've given a thought to the children since you left. No birthday cards, no presents. Nothing at all for Christmas. Never a word out of you! I don't suppose Neil would even recognize you.'

'I want to see them,' he persisted.

'Well, you can't. They're in bed, they're fast asleep.'

'Then let me stay until the morning. I'll see them then, and after that I'll go, I promise you.' He had put on a wheedling tone which was more obnoxious, Karen thought, than his bullying.

'I can't go back tonight,' he said. 'I can't drive all the way to London. You can't turn me out. I've had too much to drink. It wouldn't be safe, Karen. You know it wouldn't.'

'I'd be more concerned that you'd kill someone else,' she retorted.

But he was right, damn him! How could she let him drive a car in the state he was in, and the roads almost certainly frosty? With all her heart she hated the thought of spending the night under the same roof as this man, but what else was there? For a moment she longed for Brian, longed to pick up the phone, hear his voice, to ask, 'What am I to do? Tell me what to do.' She couldn't of course. It was out of the question.

'I'm going to make the coffee,' she said. 'Stay right where you are. I mean what I say!'

In the kitchen she went through the motions of making coffee, her mind in a whirl. She stared at the hot, dark liquid filtering into the glass jug. Automatically, when it had gone through she filled the mugs, adding milk to hers, leaving Ray's black but stirring in two spoonfuls of sugar. Why should she remember that he took two sugars? She didn't want to remember it. She didn't want to remember anything about him.

She knew that she had to let him stay; he was in no state to drive a car and since she was stone cold sober, though deeply, deeply angry, she knew she had to prevent him doing so. And wouldn't that lead on to him seeing the children in the morning? How would she prevent it? She hated the thought of it happening. It might well upset them, especially Fiona, who had taken it badly when her father had left, at which time he'd made no bones about not wanting to keep in touch with the children. Freda didn't like children, and that was that.

She picked up the mugs and went back to the sitting room.

He was lying full length on the sofa. He had taken off his tie, loosened his collar. He was fast asleep, dead to the world, breathing noisily. The air around him already stank of drink.

She stood there, a mug of coffee in each hand, looking down at him. How had he come to this? For a brief moment she was stirred by pity, but she quickly pushed it away. He had invaded her life again at a moment when she least wanted him, at the very point when she had glimpsed a better future. Why did this have to happen? It wasn't fair!

There was no point at all in waking him. What good would that do? By the look of him he would sleep for hours. She would trust to luck, she would leave him where he was, get up very early in the morning and send him packing before the children wakened. It was all she *could* do.

She returned to the kitchen and poured the coffee down the sink, both his and hers. She didn't want it. It was not kindness, she told herself, which made her then go to a cupboard and find a blanket. She was doing it because otherwise he might grow cold in the night, and therefore wake and make a noise.

She draped it over him. He didn't stir. Then she went quietly upstairs and with the key from her bedroom, which stupidly fitted the children's rooms as well, locked them in. She hated doing that, but she must. She couldn't take any chances, not that she thought he would hurt them but she couldn't bear to think of him frightening them.

Then she went into her own room and locked herself in.

26

Brian awoke on the morning of Boxing Day with an unusually light heart, then immediately thought of Karen and knew that she was the reason for it. He had not felt like this for a very long time, not since those first heady weeks when he had fallen in love with Helen, when she had graced his workplace with her beauty, and then later his home with her quick wit and charm. Long after she'd left him he'd continued to love her, had thought it impossible that he would ever again think about any other woman in the same way. And when, gradually, the hurt had grown less raw, he'd ceased to look at women as individuals but saw them all as members of a group who would not be allowed beyond the outer edges of his life. He had avoided their company and had come to believe that the celibate way of life would be his for ever. In time the bitterness had left him, but not the mistrust. He had lost confidence in himself when it came to women.

And now, suddenly, all that had changed. Yet it was not sudden, he thought as he lay awake, luxuriating in his thoughts before getting out of bed. That first evening at the O'Briens' had been the start, and since then the feeling had been growing, though he had not recognized it for what it was until that silly, simple thing – no more than a game, really – the kiss under the mistletoe. You sound like an infatuated swain, he chided himself. But it was not infatuation. He was in love. It was like – he searched for words to describe it, but couldn't find any.

Today, he decided, he would tell Karen. They would tell each other, for he was sure that his feelings were also hers. He would see her this evening. But no! he couldn't wait until then. He wanted to see her now.

He jumped out of bed, showered, dressed. There was no-one else stirring in the house. He ran downstairs to the kitchen, tip-toeing through the sitting room where Sandra lay dead to the world on the sofa. Filling the kettle for a cup of tea – he didn't want anything to eat – he checked the time. Eight thirty. Was it too early? Today, after all, was a holiday. But wouldn't she already be up and doing because of the children? Young children, or so he was told, woke at the crack of dawn. It was only as they graduated to teenagers that they became happy to stay in bed until noon.

What excuse would he give her for calling on her at this hour? He had to see her, it wasn't enough to telephone. Did he need an excuse? And then, quite by accident, he lighted on the perfect solution. There on the kitchen stool was the toy thermometer, part of Fiona's nursing set. Possibly even now she was searching for it and raising Cain because it was lost. He slipped it into his pocket. Ten minutes later, with a spring in his step, he was walking along an almost deserted Mulberry Lane towards Number Six. It was chilly. The roofs and windows of the cars, parked almost nose to tail along the road, were white with frost. Whatever brave plants were left standing in the front gardens appeared withered by it. But frost had no part in Brian's being this morning: all was blue sky and sunshine. When he reached Number Six he bounded up the path and pressed his finger on the doorbell.

Karen had lain awake for a long time, then slept fitfully and wakened early, and the moment she woke she jumped out of bed, put on her dressing gown and went quietly downstairs. Thank God there was no sound from the children!

Ray was still asleep, though no longer snoring. The flush had left his face and he was horribly pale. She knew she would have to wake him, she had to get him out of the house as quickly as possible. She shook his shoulder. He stirred, muttering in his sleep, so she shook him again and he opened his eyes. Then he sat up, suddenly wide awake.

'What the devil—?' he began.

'Be quiet!' Karen ordered. 'I'm going back upstairs to shower while you pull yourself together, then I'll make you some breakfast and you can leave. The alternative is that I'll have you thrown out!' It was an idle boast. She had no idea how she would accomplish it. She could only pray that he wouldn't put her to the test.

'I'll be down again in less than fifteen minutes,' she said. 'Please keep quiet. The children are asleep.'

He didn't answer, just watched her as she left the room.

It was the sound of the shower raining down on

her at full strength which caused Karen not to hear the doorbell. Ray went to answer it.

Brian, standing on the top step as the door opened, saw not Karen but Ray, not that he knew the man was Ray. All he knew was that a man stood there, putty-faced, dishevelled, no tie, his shirt open, his hair falling damply over his eyes.

For a split second Brian wondered had he pressed the wrong bell? Had he come to the wrong house? But that was stupid. No way could he have done that. So who was this man? Karen had made no mention of a visitor over Christmas. Could it be her brother? Did she have a brother? He had not been mentioned, but then there were lots of things between them still to be mentioned, things he wanted to know, small details of her life. Thoughts chased one another through his mind with the speed of light.

'Yes?' the man said.

'I wanted to see Karen,' Brian said.

'I'm sorry! She's in the shower.'

What was happening? Brian wanted to push past this man, force his way into the house. Find Karen. But the man blocked the doorway. In any case, he couldn't do that, could he? Brian took a grip on himself, forced himself to speak calmly.

'And you are . . . ?' he asked.

'I'm her husband.'

'Husband?'

'That's right. Husband. You can't see Karen. I told you, she's in the shower. But if you'd like to leave a message I'll pass it on.'

'Thank you,' Brian said.

Why was he thanking this man who said he was Karen's husband? And why should the man say it if it wasn't true? Though, automatically, he had thanked him politely, he didn't feel polite. He felt savage. He would like to hit the man in the face. But Karen hadn't hit him in the face, had she? By the look of him he had spent the night here.

'Well?' Ray prompted.

Brian found his voice.

'No message,' he said.

'Right then! Who shall I say called?'

'Tell her Brian called.'

The door was closed immediately. Brian turned and walked back down the path. Halfway down he thrust his hands into his pocket. His fingers touched the thermometer. He took it in his hand, swerved round and threw it hard against the closed door so that it smashed to pieces on the top step. But why did I do that, he asked himself immediately. What has Fiona done to me?

He let himself into Number Fifteen and opened the door into the sitting room. Sandra stirred, opened her eyes and saw him. There was neither sight nor sound of anyone else.

'Oh! You've been out,' Sandra said. 'Is it very late?'

'No,' Brian answered. 'And I'm going out again. Tell the others to expect me when they see me. I don't know when I'll be back.'

'Where shall I say you've gone?' she asked.

'You needn't!' He didn't know the answer.

He got into his car, which by now had defrosted enough for him to see through the windscreen. He turned on the engine, which fired at the first touch, and drove off. When he came to the main road he would let the car decide whether to turn left or right – Bath or Bristol. He didn't care. All he knew was that he had to get away.

At the corner of Mulberry Lane he turned left down North Hill. Shipfield was quiet, almost deserted. Most of the shops in North Hill were closed, though not so in the centre of the town, where the post-Christmas sales were already under way. At the junction with the main road without thinking about it he turned left, perhaps simply because he was on the left side of the road, and was on his way to Bath.

When Karen had showered and dressed she listened again at the children's door. There was no sound. She unlocked the door but decided against entering. That might be all that was needed to wake them, which was the last thing she wanted. She had matters to sort out with Ray first.

She went quietly downstairs. When she went into the room Ray was looking out of the window. He turned around to face her. He had buttoned up his shirt and put on his tie, so that he looked fractionally better – though by no means good. He was unhealthily pale, in need of a shave and clearly hung-over. How could she ever have been in love with this man? But she had been, she couldn't deny that, though it was all gone.

'We have to talk!' she said.

'No!' Ray said. 'I want to talk to you first!' His voice was surprisingly firm. She waited, without answering.

'First of all,' he said, 'I'm sorry. I'm sorry I came. I shouldn't have. We had this great bust-up – nothing that can't be mended, I see that now but I didn't at the time. I'm happy with Freda—'

'How very nice!' Karen interrupted.

'Please hear me out,' he said. 'I don't know why I came here, I wasn't thinking straight, I shouldn't have.'

'But you did,' Karen said.

'I know. And I'm sorrier than I can say, and now I'm going. I'm not going to ask to see the children. It would be wrong. I haven't set eyes on them for nearly two years and it's best if they forget me. I expect they already have – which is no more than I deserve, but then I was never any good with children, as you know.'

Nor could Karen believe what she was hearing, though it was true what he said, he had never wanted children. He and Freda were well matched in that respect.

'So I'm off!' he said. 'I'm sorry, I'm sorry, I'm sorry! I won't ever trouble you again.'

Karen couldn't believe what she heard herself saying next. She wanted to burst into tears of relief and all that came out of her was a small, polite voice saying, 'At least let me make you some breakfast!' Had that really been her reply to all that he'd said? It must have been, for he answered her.

'No, thanks all the same. I'll stop somewhere on the way.'

They were at the door, she was seeing him off in a surreally civilized fashion when he suddenly remembered.

'Oh! I answered the door when you were in the shower. A man, name of Brian. He didn't leave a message.'

Karen stared at him in horror.

'You answered the door?'

'Of course I answered the door,' Ray said. 'You weren't there, were you?'

'What did he say, what did you tell him?' Karen demanded.

'I've told you! I asked him if he'd like to leave a message. He said "Tell her Brian called." '

'What else did he say? What else did you say?'

'Nothing! He asked who I was, which I must say I thought had nothing to do with him, but I was quite civil. I told him I was your husband. That's all.'

'Go!' she said. 'Please *go*!'

'I'm going,' Ray said. 'No hard feelings, eh?'

'Just *go*!'

He left. She closed the door on him, went through to the kitchen. What now, she asked herself. What now?

It was plain enough. She had to talk to Brian. At all costs she had to talk to him, and the sooner the better.

She picked up the phone. After some delay – why wasn't he answering? – it was answered by Sandra.

'Is Brian there?' Karen asked.

'Brian? No, he's gone out.'

'Do you know where?'

'I don't,' Sandra said. 'He got into his car and drove off. He seemed in a bit of a hurry.'

'Did he say when he'd be back?' Karen asked.

'No. He said, "Expect me when you see me." Are you all right, Karen?'

'Of course!' Karen said. 'When he comes in will you ask him to give me a ring?'

'Sure!' Sandra promised. 'Anyway, I'll be along with you in about an hour.'

'No hurry,' Karen said quickly. 'You stay right

where you are, with David. In any case, I have things to do.'

'Are you sure?' Sandra asked. David was still in bed, but if he came down soon they might at least have a few minutes together. She longed to spend every bit of time with him.

'Absolutely,' Karen assured her. 'Why not wait until this afternoon? And you will give Brian my message when you see him?'

''Course I will,' Sandra said.

As Karen put the phone down she heard Neil's cry. He almost invariably awakened with a cry, which worried her. She always wondered what he had been going through which led to the cry.

'I'm coming, darling!' she called out.

She went to the children. Fiona was also awake. She saw them into their dressing gowns and slippers and went down with them to the kitchen. She made and served the children's breakfast hardly knowing what she was doing. They were chattering like magpies and it went over her head.

'You're not listening, Mummy!' Fiona said.

'I'm sorry,' Karen said. 'What was it?'

'I said can we go to the shops?'

'I'm not sure,' Karen said. 'It's Boxing Day, they might not be open.'

'Then can we go to the park?'

'I don't know, Fiona. I might be too busy. I'll have to see.'

She had, she just *had* to see Brian. Where was he? And what was he thinking? Was he remembering that she was a woman whose husband had left her – it was he who had done the leaving, not she – who had been pregnant from a casual encounter, and whose husband was now presumably back with her?

She *had* to speak to him, she had to tell her side – but where was he?

And then she remembered – why hadn't she remembered earlier? – that he had a mobile phone. She immediately telephoned the house. Fergus answered.

'I'm sorry, he's not here,' he said. 'We don't know when he'll be back.'

'Oh!' Karen said. 'I do want to get in touch with him. It's important. Do you have his mobile number?'

'It'll be somewhere here,' Fergus said. 'Can you hang on a minute?'

Where could he be, she asked herself as she waited. There was no need to ask why he had taken off; it was all too clear.

'I've found it,' Fergus said. 'And Sandra wants a word with you.'

She wrote down the mobile number, only half listening to Sandra. 'So will that be all right?' Sandra asked. 'I mean if we came along in about half an hour. David and me.'

'Sure!' Karen said. 'Whenever!' She couldn't think about that now. All she wanted now was to call Brian on his mobile. Thank God for mobile phones, she thought. She would explain everything. Surely he would understand? Or at least listen.

She dialled the number. The line was dead. She tried again with the same result. He had switched off his phone. But why had he done that? Where was he? What was he doing? She was desperate. She had to talk to someone, but who? There was only one person, and that was Laura O'Brien. She picked up the phone.

At Number Twelve the telephone rang. As Dermot stretched out his hand to answer it his heart made a small leap. This must surely be Frances. To his surprise and Laura's she hadn't called them on Christmas Day. 'After all she *is* in Spain,' Laura had pointed out. 'They do have telephones in Spain,' he had snapped back. Snappy because he was disappointed. It was the first Christmas of her life that he hadn't seen his younger daughter.

'Or perhaps she called when we were on the line to Therese?' Laura had suggested. Therese called them early on Christmas Day. She was the conscientious one.

So now he was certain it would be Frances, and when the voice said, 'It's me, Karen. Can I speak to Laura?' he experienced a sharp pang of disappointment.

'I'll get her,' Dermot said. 'She's in the kitchen.'

Laura dried her hands and came to the telephone.

'Oh, Laura!' Karen cried, without preliminaries, 'I don't know what to do! He's not answering his mobile! No-one seems to know where he's gone!'

'Whoa!' Laura said. 'Who's he? Who are we talking about?'

'Brian, of course! I really do need to talk to him! Heaven knows what he must be thinking.'

'Karen, dear,' Laura said quietly, 'you're not making sense. If you start at the beginning I might just understand.'

'It's so difficult on the phone,' Karen said. 'Oh Laura, can I come round? I'm sorry to disturb you, but *please*! I wouldn't ask if it wasn't important.'

'Of course you can,' Laura said.

453

'Sandra and David will be here any minute. I can leave the children with them,' Karen said.

'Come as soon as you're ready,' Laura told her – and put the phone down. 'Karen,' she said to Dermot. 'Some sort of trouble, I'm not sure what. She's coming round.'

'Oh, no!' Dermot protested. 'It's Boxing Day. We're supposed to be relaxing! Do you always have to be at everyone's beck and call? Can't it wait?'

'According to Karen, it can't,' Laura told him. 'And it's not like Karen to panic. She sounded very upset. But we won't disturb you. I'll take her into the kitchen. Women talk best in the kitchen anyway.'

Laura was looking out of the window when she saw Karen approaching. Before Karen could walk up the path and ring the bell Laura was standing there with the door open.

'Come into the kitchen,' she said. 'I've just put the kettle on.'

They seated themselves on either side of the kitchen table. Laura's was such a nice kitchen, Karen had always thought, homely and smart at the same time, with its pinewood furniture and jazzy cushions, but now she hardly saw it.

'Oh Laura!' she said. 'This is awful!'

'Tell me,' Laura invited.

Karen told her everything, sometimes racing along, sometimes stopping altogether, overcome by the dreadfulness of it all. The relating of it, especially of the parts with Ray, seemed now almost less bearable than they had at the time. Then she had kept her cool, appeared strong and in charge, partly because of the children and partly because she hadn't wanted Ray to know that she was afraid, but now there was nothing in the way, and telling it she relived it, only with greater intensity.

Laura reached out and covered Karen's hand, which was shaking, with her own.

'It must have been dreadful,' she said. 'You should have sent for me!'

'I didn't have time to think,' Karen said. 'And yes, it was terrible, but nothing was as awful as when I heard that Brian had called and Ray had answered the door.'

'You can explain all that to him,' Laura said. 'I'm sure when he hears the truth he'll understand.'

'But how can I when he's not here?' Fresh tears filled Karen's eyes, and overflowed. Laura passed her a tea towel to wipe her face.

'Oh Laura, where is he?' Karen cried. 'I know he hadn't planned to go anywhere. We were going to spend most of the day together with the children, and then go to the pub this evening while David and Sandra stayed in.'

'He'll be back,' Laura comforted her. 'I'm quite sure. And when you've talked to each other, everything will be all right. You'll see!'

'Everything was going so well between us,' Karen said. 'I just know we'd reached—' She broke off. She wasn't prepared to tell anyone, not even Laura, just how she had felt last night, and how sure she was that Brian had felt the same. All that had still to be said between herself and him.

'Well,' Laura said, 'I'll make that cup of tea, and then I think you should go home in case Brian rings you. You wouldn't want to be out, would you?'

'Do you think he will?' Karen asked bleakly.

'I'm sure of it!' She would keep a watch for him returning, and make sure he did.

455

*   *   *

Brian drove slowly around the centre of Bath, searching the streets for a place to park, but in vain. Although it was Boxing Day, and not yet mid-morning, the place was busy: cars, buses, bicycles and, above all, pedestrians. Visitors, he guessed by the way they walked leisurely around, crossing and recrossing the road, standing to gaze into shop windows even though many of the shops were closed. No-one seemed to be walking with any purpose, as if they might have a job to go to, as if they had to be somewhere at a given time.

And I'm getting nowhere, he thought, and turned left at the next road junction. There was a large car park close to the station. He would have to use that, though he hated large car parks, especially if they were multi-storey ones.

He found a place, parked the car, locked it and walked out into the street. Standing on the edge of the pavement, wondering whether to go right or left, he thought, what does it matter? What am I doing here anyway? He had less purpose than those people who had irritated him not many minutes ago by their meanderings. At least they were on pleasure bent.

He turned right and walked in the direction of the abbey. It seemed the natural thing to do. It was dominant; high above everything else, so strong, so permanent, so 'I will always be here'. So at the centre. Not that he felt any affinity with the abbey. Usually when in Bath he walked past it without a thought. He had been in of course, though never to a service, only to look around. Nor, though at this point he turned into the abbey churchyard, did he intend a visit now. The abbey churchyard was not so much a churchyard as a busy though traffic-free thoroughfare, but what it did have was cafés. The only thing he could think of now was to sit with a cup of coffee and try to get his head straight.

'Anything to eat, sir?' the waitress asked.

He was about to say no – though he hadn't eaten since teatime yesterday because this morning he had been too eager to rush out of the house to see Karen – when it occurred to him that something to eat would allow him to sit here longer, to kill more time.

'I'll have a bacon sandwich,' he said.

When it came it smelled good, though he ate it without tasting it and then ordered another cup of coffee.

'What does it mean?' he asked himself for the thousandth time. He knew what he had seen with his own eyes. The man had answered the door as one who had a right to do so. He had stood there not at all fazed. It was early in the day, he *must* have stayed the night. He had said he was Karen's husband, and what reason would he have for saying that if it wasn't true? Of course they were separated, but obviously this man still had the entrée to her house, she let him stay. She had made no mention of him at all yesterday. She might have said that, since it was Christmas, he was coming to visit the children. But she hadn't. Nothing had been said. Whatever the arrangement, she hadn't intended him to know. His thoughts went round and round, always arriving back at the point they had left.

He paid his bill, tipped the waitress well, partly out of gratitude because she had not seemed to mind that he had stayed so long, had not attempted to clear away around him, then walked through the abbey churchyard towards Milsom Street. A juggler in the churchyard, standing in front of the Pump Room, had attracted a small crowd, but Brian walked past as if on his way to somewhere.

But where, he asked himself, eventually standing in Milsom Street, looking in a bookshop window. There's no sense in this. He knew, it stared him in the face, that he had to go back to Shipfield. He had to confront her. He had to *know*.

He turned round and walked – almost hurried – down Milsom Street in the direction of the car park.

27

Esther did not see Brian's return to Number Fifteen. She had observed him leave in the morning and had wondered where he could be going so early on Boxing Day and though she had looked out several times during the day, his car had not been there. At the point when he did return she had been having a nice little lie-down, to prepare her for the evening, when Laura and Dermot were to take her along to the Green Man for whatever festivities were afoot. In fact, as Brian got out of his car and walked up the path Esther was in the Land of Nod, lying on her back on the sofa, snoring gently.

Not so Laura. As far as she could, with the other things she had to do in the house, she had kept a sharp lookout for Brian – Dermot had complained that she was as fidgety as a hen with chickens – and now as she saw him draw up her patience was rewarded.

For a minute she was uncertain whether to ring Brian, ask him to come across then tell him what she knew or whether to let Karen know he was back and leave her to it.

'*Of course* you must leave it to Karen!' Dermot

said forcefully. 'It has nothing to do with you. It's between the two of them.'

'She did tell me,' Laura pointed out. 'And I only want to do what's best. But I suppose you're right, I should leave it to them.'

'I'm sure I am!' Dermot said.

Laura phoned Karen.

'He's just arrived back. I leave it to you,' she said. 'If you want me for anything, let me know.' She rang off.

Karen sat with the receiver in her hand. She knew she had to do something. She didn't know what to say, how to begin. She took a deep breath and tapped out Brian's number.

He answered the phone quickly. If there'd been anyone else around he thought he might not have answered it at all, but everyone was out.

'Yes?' he said.

'It's me,' Karen said. 'I have to see you. I have to talk to you.'

At first he didn't answer. The silence between them seemed to last for ever.

'*Please*, Brian!' Karen said. 'I have some explaining to do. Nothing is quite what you think. Please let me tell you – but not on the phone. Please come here.'

He was still slow to answer, even though he had driven fast from Bath for the purpose of seeing her. When it came to it what was he going to say?

'Is he still there?' he asked quietly.

'Of course not!' Karen said. 'He was away by half-past nine. I'm not expecting to see him again. And David and Sandra have taken the children to the park. Please come!'

He hesitated again, then said, 'OK. I'll be along in a minute.'

She opened the door to him and he stepped into the hall. He felt awkward, almost like a stranger, and yet as they stood there looking at each other, neither of them for the moment speaking, he wanted to take her into his arms, to enfold her, to hold her close and never let her go. He wanted everything that had happened between them in the last few hours – and though it seemed like a large chunk of his life it *was* no more than a few hours, not even adding up to half a day – to be pushed aside, buried, hidden, ignored. But he knew at the same time that that wouldn't do. What those few hours had shown was how fragile his trust in her had been. And perhaps hers in him? He didn't yet know that. If there was to be anything worthwhile between them, then that trust had to be there, and be stronger.

He couldn't know, they hadn't spoken, how akin Karen's thoughts were to his. She was hurt that he had jumped to false conclusions. She was also aware that up until now, pleasant though their relationship had been, she had kept him on the edges of her life. She had not opened up what she truly was; it had not been possible to know her. She had held back what she might have given, not because of her mistrust in him but because of his gender. She constantly protected herself from being hurt.

He followed her into the sitting room. Karen sat on the sofa but instead of joining her he took an armchair. She was the first to speak.

'It wasn't how it looked,' she said. 'He arrived after one in the morning, fairly drunk, having driven himself from London. He'd quarrelled with the woman he lives with. One of those Christmas Day quarrels when everyone says too much. He wanted to see the children then and there and I wouldn't wake them. But I couldn't have let him drive back anyway. He'd had far too much to drink. He might have killed himself – or someone else.'

'Why didn't you phone me?' Brian demanded. 'Why didn't you ask for help?'

'I didn't want to involve you,' Karen said. 'I wanted to keep it from you.'

'I would have come!' he said.

'I know. And I should have done that. I thought I could handle it all myself. Nothing happened, you know, nothing that you might have thought of. I went into the kitchen to make some strong coffee. I'd made up my mind to tell him that if he set so much as one foot on the stairs I would ring for the police . . .'

'The police?' Brian said. 'Why not me?'

'I've told you,' Karen said. 'I didn't want to involve you. Anyway, when I came back with the coffee he was fast asleep. I left him there and went to bed, but I locked my bedroom door, and the children's. Next morning he decided of his own accord to leave – but if he hadn't I'd have sent him off, and he knew it. When you came to the house I was in the shower, I didn't hear the bell. It was only when he was leaving that he told me you'd been. I would have told you, although I didn't want you to have any part in the sordid bits of my life. I wanted everything to be new. You do understand that, don't you?'

'I do,' Brian said. 'But you can't start anew without knowing something about the past, what brought you to this point, what brought me to it.

We bring our baggage with us and we have to take on each other's baggage. I was wrong because I didn't allow for anything that had made you what you are. I didn't know. You said so little. But I was wrong not to have trusted you.'

'How could you? I never allowed you to get close . . . and yet . . .' She hesitated.

'What?'

'I knew that on Christmas Day we had come close. I saw, or I thought I saw, a new beginning.'

'And you were right,' Brian said. 'It was. It *is*!'

He moved from his chair, joined her on the sofa and took her in his arms. A minute later the children burst in, followed by Sandra and David.

'We went on the swings!' Neil said.

'*I* went on the slide,' Fiona boasted. 'I came down head first and on my tummy!'

The Boxing Day party in the Green Man was nicely under way. Well, not so much a party; the first drinks for all comers were on the house, courtesy of Jim Pullman, and there were paper hats for everyone who could be persuaded to wear them, and savoury nibbles, which Betty had made, on every table. The Salvation Army band was not in evidence – there had been a rumour that it would be but no-one was quite sure who had started the story – so Jim had put on tapes of seasonal music. Unfortunately, by the evening of Boxing Day everyone had had a surfeit of 'Hark The Herald Angels' and 'Silent Night' and there were growing calls for someone – anyone – to play the piano: 'Something lively!' they demanded.

A total stranger took up the challenge, a short, middle-aged man with wild grey hair. The only person to whom he was not a total stranger was, presumably, the plump, tight-suited, forty-ish blonde with whom he had been drinking and who now followed him as he pushed his way towards the piano, sat down at it and ran his hands up and down the keyboard in a series of flashy arpeggios.

'A bit of classy stuff here!' Jim Pullman muttered to Betty. 'I hope he knows a few songs as well.'

'Oh, you needn't worry,' the blonde said. 'Norman can play anything. You name it, he'll play it – and never a sheet of music needed.'

'Come along then, ladies and gentlemen,' Norman called out. 'Name your tune!'

The ladyfriend's boast was true. He *could* play anything. The requests came thick and fast and there was nothing he didn't know, from 'Lily Of Laguna' to 'My Way' and back again. In no time at all, half-pints of best bitter (his chosen beverage, said his ladyfriend, who turned out to be called Violet) were lined up across the top of the piano, courtesy of appreciative members of the company.

The place was packed, and people were still coming in.

'This is a bit of all right!' Jim said to Betty as she passed him, flushed and perspiring, in search of a fresh supply of nibbles. 'This is just what we wanted!'

Almost everyone from Mulberry Lane was there: the Streeters, Michael and Dawn (courtesy of Dawn's mother who had come over from Bath for Christmas and was looking after the twins), Eric and James, the Simpsons with Titus, George Potter. No students, though. They were scattered to far places. I miss the students, Jim thought. Especially the girls. Laura and Dermot were there with Esther

who, surrounded by drinks, was queening it at a
table in the centre of the room. The two empty
chairs at the table were being saved for Brian and
Karen, who had not yet arrived.

'If they don't come soon,' Laura remarked,
'they'll lose the seats. We can't keep them for ever!'

She had seen Brian walking in the direction of
Karen's house quite soon after she'd telephoned,
but more than that she didn't know. Did the fact
that so far they hadn't shown up mean they weren't
coming, that things had continued to go wrong?

The Andersons were at the next table. An
evening in the Green Man was not quite what Gary
would have chosen for Boxing Day evening. It was
Lisa who had begged to come.

'I never get to the pub,' she'd said. 'I never get to
know any of the neighbours.'

'Why would you want to meet the neighbours?'
Gary had asked. 'They're not our style.'

They might be, she had told him, if she had a
chance to know them. If she were in Leeds she'd be
down at the pub, or in a club, and it would all be
nice and friendly. Besides, she didn't want to stay in
the house, watching wall-to-wall television. They
did that most nights. And since her parents were
down from Leeds and were only too happy to
stay in with the children, Gary had had no further
excuses. Naturally, Bruno was with them, sprawled
by the side of Gary's chair, in a perfect position to
be tripped over by anyone carrying a couple of
glasses of beer.

Bruno's owner, though, had not submitted him
to the indignity of wearing a paper hat, as had
Titus's owner a yard or two away. It sat perkily on
the dog's small dark head and somehow went well

with his long, auburn moustaches. He also sported a red bow on his tartan collar.

'Oh! Isn't he a sweetie?' Lisa cooed.

Titus squared his small shoulders and sat up straighter. Gary gave Lisa a look.

At that moment the door opened and Brian and Karen entered. With one glance at them Laura knew that everything was all right. She had never seen them look happier. Unfortunately, this wasn't the time to ask questions.

'Hi, Karen! Hi, Brian! We've saved you seats,' she called out.

Dermot stood up. 'What will you have to drink?' he asked them.

'Oh no!' Jim Pullman said as he was passing. 'First drinks on the house! I'll be with you in a minute.' He went back behind the bar. 'Have you seen that Karen?' he said to Betty. 'She looks as if she's won the lottery.'

Betty looked up sharply, glanced across to where Karen was talking to Laura.

'You're right, Jim!' she agreed. 'That's just what she does look like. Now I wonder why?'

Jim shrugged his shoulders. He wasn't going to tell her that Brian and Karen had come into the pub hand in hand, though they had almost immediately separated. Let them get on with it, whatever it was, in peace. Privacy didn't last long in Mulberry Lane – not that people were unkind, just nosy!

'You're not saying anything,' Betty said, 'but I can see you're putting two and two together and making five. You're an old romantic, that's what you are!' All the same, she thought, good luck to them, if there's anything in it. She'd like something nice to happen to Karen for once.

Lisa now persuaded Gary to move their chairs so that they could join the others at the O'Briens' table. He hadn't wanted to, but she'd dug her heels in. 'The O'Briens *are* our near neighbours,' she said. 'What have they ever done wrong to us?'

If Brian Carson had brought the men with him, Gary decided, there was no way he would have given in to Lisa. But he hadn't, there was no sign of them. And if they were to come in and sit at the table, he'd leave at once. As it was, he ordered drinks all round and sat down.

Lisa was waving her arms about, making wide gestures. Why, Laura thought. And then she saw the pearl and garnet bracelet Lisa was wearing on her right wrist, the deep red stones flashing in the lights. She didn't think Lisa was doing it intentionally, at least not in a swanky sort of way; she wasn't like that. Perhaps she just needed someone to notice it.

'I *love* your bracelet, Lisa!' Laura said.

'I noticed it too,' Karen added. 'It's beautiful. Is it new?'

Lisa smiled happily. 'Gary gave it to me for Christmas. It is nice, isn't it? And of course he has such good taste, my Gary! Actually, he spoils me rotten.' She smiled fondly at him, laid her hand on his arm, the bracelet glinting and sparkling for all to see. His spirits suddenly lifted.

'Nonsense, darling,' he said, in deeply gratified tones. 'Nothing is too good for my wife! Or for my children! My dearest possessions!'

All was instantly sweetness and light, the Spirit of Christmas at its very best. Forgotten, it seemed, were the trials and tribulations of the last few weeks, buried were their differences. It was for all the world, and for the moment, just like Charles Dickens. (Except for Dawn, who was sadly still missing her grandmother's ruby brooch.)

'Good wishes to one and all!' Lisa cried squeakily, raising her glass. 'Peace and good will to all men!' She was possibly just the teeniest, teeniest bit tipsy.

Brian and Karen raised their glasses to each other, saying nothing – and then to the rest.

'But will it last? I mean with all of them. Not those two,' Jim Pullman whispered to Betty as she passed on her way to the kitchen, where there were mince pies in the oven.

28

It is now 8 January. Christmas and New Year cele-
brations are well over and the decorations have
been taken down and packed away for next time.
People in Mulberry Lane, if you were to ask them,
would say, slightly surprised, yes, they had had a
very nice Christmas, but it's been and gone now,
hasn't it? These things come and go in a flash,
don't they? For Karen and Brian, however, it will
never be gone and forgotten. It was a very special
time for them and now they can look forward to a
New Year in which all manner of good things can
and will happen.

Esther has also enjoyed her Christmas. She likes
to look back on things. There's more to be gained
than by looking forward and it helps to pass the
time. So she goes through it once again. Mass on
Christmas Day, Christmas dinner at the O'Briens'.
She was sure she had helped to cheer up Laura and
Dermot who were missing their daughters. It had
been Therese's turn to spend it with her in-laws and
Frances had gone to Spain with a group of friends.
That's what happens when your children grow up
and fly the nest.

Then there had been the pub on Boxing Day

evening. She really enjoyed that. It is possible, she thinks, that she drank just a little too much on that occasion – people were so generous, and she couldn't be rude to them, could she? She couldn't not accept the drinks. She doesn't remember too much about getting home but she does remember that she slept like a log – all night, without even getting up to go to the lavatory. But now she is well back in routine – watching out of the window. Not that there's much to see at this time of the year, with the weather cold and damp, the days short and the nights long. Even so, and only three weeks after the shortest day, darkness seems to come just a little later each day, which is a bonus for her.

The children are back at school and any time now the students will return. In fact she saw Jennifer's car earlier today, but it's not there now. She has probably gone shopping. Esther had a Christmas card from Grace, also one from Jennifer. It will be the last year for them and Imogen. She will miss them – but then there'll be new ones. One must try to look forward!

What Esther does not yet know is that when Jennifer returned there was a letter for her from Stuart.

Dear Jen and all

Just to let you know that I shan't be returning to the fold! I started on my novel on Boxing Day and it's going great guns. A sure-fire winner! So what is the point, I ask myself, of slaving for a degree? And the answer comes 'none at all!'

Look out for me in the bookshops!

Aye yours,

Stuart

Good riddance, Jennifer thinks!

Nothing more has been heard of Colin Myers. Constable Hendry popped in for five minutes to wish Esther a happy new year, though it wasn't in his line of duty. What a nice man he is, she thinks. She has assured him she will still be at her post, keeping a sharp lookout for whatever might happen in the road, and if she sees anything the least bit suspicious she will immediately phone the police station. He seemed pleased by this. It was he who told her that they'd had nothing more on Colin Myers. 'Would you say the police were baffled?' she'd asked him, and he'd said, 'Yes, it does look a bit like that. But you never know,' he'd added, 'something could turn up out of the blue.'

Lisa's parents returned to Leeds at new year. They had enjoyed themselves, it had been lovely to see the kiddies, and Lisa had a lovely home, you couldn't say otherwise. Everything top quality. But they were glad to go back. Leeds was their home. Always would be. Lisa felt a little sad and lonely when they left – not that she'd like to have them living with her all the time, but the children had thoroughly enjoyed having grandparents, especially the spoiling which went with them.

Brian is working in the house. There isn't a great deal left to do – a certain amount of decorating, and some small finishing touches in some rooms. Nothing he can't take care of. The garden needs much more attention but now isn't a good time. Brian is quite happy to work largely on his own. It's much easier than working with Colin Myers. Of course, as always, the men will help him when they're not at work. For instance, Mark is at home right now because this week he's on the evening shift.

Brian and Karen have had many discussions about what they will do when the men finally leave, which might not be too long now. They have not come to any firm conclusions, except that whatever it is they will be in it together.

It has now moved on to mid-afternoon, not yet dark of course but not exactly brilliant daylight either. Esther has had an early lunch – every meal is early for Esther, which comes of living alone and not having enough to do. Meals are the punctuation which breaks up the day; a cup of tea is a comma, tea with a biscuit or a bun a semi-colon, lunch or supper a full stop and a rare, special meal, especially if provided by someone else, an exclamation mark. After lunch today she had her usual little zizz, sitting in the armchair with Classic FM on the radio. They do lunchtime requests and they're nearly always easy listening, the kind of music one can fall asleep to without feeling guilty. But her naps don't last long and now she is fully awake and alert again.

Very little is happening in the road. A black car passes, going towards North Hill, and then a large white delivery van in the opposite direction. It slows down, the driver presumably looking at the house numbers, but unfortunately doesn't stop and deliver anywhere within Esther's view, and then – having been watching the delivery van she didn't see where they came from – she observes two youths walking up the drive of Cornerways and disappearing from view around the back of the house. Since she is into suspecting everything in her new role as amateur detective and honorary assistant to the Shipfield police force, she decides that the youths (or young men – difficult to decide in so brief a glance) are definitely shifty-looking.

It is time for action. She must alert someone but not, at this moment, the police. She doesn't want to make a fool of herself. Her first choice would be Laura or Dermot but they are both at work, as are most other people in Mulberry Lane. But not Brian!

'They're probably workmen,' Brian says when she phones him. 'There to do a job.'

'I don't think so,' Esther says firmly. 'They weren't carrying anything – tools or whatever – though I think one of them had a rucksack on his back. In any case, Lisa Anderson is out. I saw her set off with the dog in the car more than an hour ago. I expect she's gone shopping. She does a lot of shopping. Anyway, I reckon they were up to no good! They haven't reappeared. So what are you going to do? Shall I ring the police?'

'Not yet,' Brian says, sighing. He doesn't quite believe her. 'Mark is here. We'll go across and have a look-see. Anyway there's one good thing: if these guys are up to no good it lets out my men, doesn't it? They're all accounted for!'

Brian and Mark cross the road to Cornerways and go round to the back of the house. There, to Brian's surprise, they find a window broken and the back door unlocked. Clearly one of the men has gone in through the window and unlocked the door for the other. The door is left ajar, presumably so that they can make a quiet getaway.

Brian and Mark enter quietly, being careful to lock the back door behind them and pocket the key. They can hear that the men are upstairs because, believing the house to be empty, they don't bother to move quietly. Brian and Mark wait silently in the hall, hidden behind the staircase, for the men to come down.

Lisa, back from shopping and fetching the children, pulls into the drive in her Landcruiser and draws up precisely in front of the steps which lead to the front door. She is a skilful driver and could quite easily park this large vehicle on a doormat. The children are belted into the seat behind hers and Bruno is in his separate area in the back. Bruno likes to go out in the Landcruiser. It is large and roomy, very suitable for a dog of his eminence.

Lisa leaves her keys in the ignition, gathers up her shopping bags, then speaks to the children.

'Wait there for two minutes! I'll let Bruno out, take my shopping up the steps and unlock the door. Then I'll be straight back for you.' If Lisa had remembered to set the burglar alarm it would have gone off as she opened the door – indeed it would have gone off at the back of the house also – but she frequently forgets about it. It is a bone of contention between herself and Gary, who would *never* forget to set it.

Esther, watching, sees Lisa's arrival and since there has been no sign of either the youths or of Brian and Mark common sense tells her that they must be in the house. Where else? She is filled with excited horror at the thought. This is definitely her cue to phone the police! She does so without delay, and if her account is a little picturesque – woman and children in danger, four men involved – at

474

least it convinces the police that a crime may well be in progress and for this reason they rush into two squad cars and, with blue lights flashing and sirens wailing, speed towards the scene.

The burglars find exactly what they had hoped for – Lisa is not only careless about burglar alarms, she is the same about her jewellery. Even though Gary has had a safe cunningly fitted behind a picture on the bedroom wall she usually takes her jewellery off and leaves it on the dressing table or in the top drawer, which is where the burglars now find it. Easy-peasy! As one of them chucks it into the rucksack still on his companion's back, they both hear the Landcruiser draw up and Bruno's deep bark as he is let out (Bruno's bark is the most frightening thing about him). A look passes between them. 'Shit!' one of them says quietly. Then they leave the bedroom, run down the stairs and make for the back door.

Brian and Mark are waiting for them. They have also heard the Landcruiser but their priority is to catch the felons. They spring upon them but the agile youths break free and, unable to get to the back, rush towards the front door, which Lisa at that very moment is opening.

Since the burglars stop for nothing in their flight, Lisa is knocked down the steps to the ground, the contents of her shopping bag spilling everywhere. One youth, however, is stopped by Bruno, who pins him against the steps. No-one has ever really thought that Bruno was capable of this! It surprises even him! The other youth makes a straight line for the Landcruiser and, since Lisa has left the driver's door open, he jumps in, turns the key and starts the

475

engine. The children, still strapped in the back seat, scream at the tops of their lungs.

Mark is in hot pursuit and before the youth in the driving seat can move off (the other one is still pinned down by Bruno, who is now actually licking his face) Mark sets about him and pulls him, with a mighty heave, out of the vehicle. The youth, slippery as an eel, eludes Mark again and begins to run away down the drive.

Onto the scene arrive the police cars, one at either entrance to the drive. The car at the left entrance narrowly avoids knocking the youth to the ground, but neatly blocks his escape.

Meanwhile Brian is busy assisting Lisa to her feet. She is not badly hurt but she is shaken and surprisingly angry. By this time tomorrow she will have some ripe bruises to display.

The police waste no time. They arrest the burglars (but not until Lisa has called off Bruno) and one car takes them away while the occupants of the other remain behind. The children are freed – they have stopped screaming now but Amber is noisily sobbing. They are not sure what is happening. Everyone goes into the house.

To Esther's intense disappointment there is nothing more to be seen until, not long afterwards, Gary races along the road in his red BMW, having been telephoned by the police. He dashes inside and closes the door behind him so that Esther is now left with nothing. Her only hope is that PC Hendry will call later and give her all the details, not to mention commending her for her prompt action. Possibly there is some sort of award? Not financial, of course. She doesn't have anything like that in mind. Just an acknowledgement, perhaps

something she can wear, like a brooch or a lapel
pin.

Inside Cornerways, Gary is absolutely overcome at
the thought of what might have happened to his
darling wife and children. He sits on the sofa with
one arm around Lisa, the other around Nathan, and
Amber on his knee. He is trying to express his thanks.

'Well, sir,' the senior policeman says, 'I must
say you owe a lot to your neighbours across the
road. Especially this one.' He indicates Mark. 'If he
hadn't been so quick off the mark the kid – they're
not much more than kids – would have driven off
with your children. And since he probably doesn't
know how to drive . . . well, who can say?'

'Mark pulled that horrible man out of the car!'
Nathan says. 'He just *pulled* him out!'

'Bad man!' Amber cries. 'I was frightened.'

'You're all right now, darling.' Gary frees the
arm which was around his wife, to hold his small
daughter closer. 'And Mark was a very brave man.'

He looks across at Mark.

'I can't thank you enough. I shall never be able
to thank you enough. I don't even know where to
begin.' At this moment he would gladly give Mark
half his kingdom.

'And you also owe a lot to the fact that these two
men came to your house the minute they suspected
something,' the senior policeman says. 'Most people
don't bother. If we had prompt action like that more
often, there'd be fewer crimes committed!'

'I know that, too,' Gary says.

'But one of the people we have to thank most,'
Brian reminds everyone, 'is Esther Dean! She's
a very old lady, but if she hadn't been watching, if
she hadn't acted when she did, if she hadn't been

persistent, it would all have turned out very differently.' And part of the reason for Esther's action, Brian thinks, was because she had never considered his men to be responsible for the previous burglaries. He won't bring that up now. He rather thinks, judging by his reactions, that Gary Anderson has got the message – although it is still to be proved that today's break-in has anything whatsoever to do with the previous ones.

'Would that be the old lady who seems to be a friend of Constable Hendry's?' the junior policeman asks.

'That's the one!' Brian confirms.

Then a thought comes to him almost out of the blue. It might not be the time to bring it up . . . nevertheless . . .

'Do you mind if I ask you one question?' he says to Gary. 'I apologize in advance if I've got it wrong, but I'd like to know.'

'Anything!' Gary says. 'Anything at all. Whatever I can do.'

'Soon after we came here,' Brian says, 'there was a letter pushed through the door. A rather nasty letter. Was it from you?'

Over the months he has come to the conclusion that it was either Gary Anderson or Ralph Streeter, but he has not been able to decide which. Now he has his answer in the dark red flush which rises from under Gary's collar to the roots of his hair.

'I'm sorry!'

'I did wonder,' Brian says calmly.

'What's this about a letter?' the senior policeman says sharply.

Gary, who is in the mood for confession, tells him all.

'Threats!' the policeman says. 'I reckon you could be in trouble with the law about that. If Mr Carson had reported it to the police . . .' He looks questioningly at Brian.

'Forget it!' Brian says. 'It's in the past. I'm just pleased to be saved from going through life suspecting the wrong person.'

In fact it is easily proved, when it comes to questioning them, and later in court, that the two youths who broke into Cornerways were indeed the very same ones who had committed the other crimes in Mulberry Lane – and elsewhere in Shipfield. And as PC Hendry had prophesied earlier, they *were* on drugs and they had immediately sold the proceeds of the thefts to feed the habit, though they had sold them in Bristol, not in Shipfield, and Bristol is a large city. Dawn will never see her brooch again.

It is falling dark when everyone except the Andersons themselves leaves Cornerways, so that all Esther can see is figures silhouetted in the light from the doorway as they make their farewells. It seems like the end of the action for the time being, she thinks, but it has been an interesting day. She will ring Brian in a few minutes, after which she will phone Laura, if she's home, and tell her all about it. She wonders whether she might also ring Karen but then decides that she can leave that to Brian. They are very close, those two. Very close. It stands out a mile.

THE END

A SELECTED LIST OF FINE NOVELS
AVAILABLE FROM CORGI BOOKS

14060 0	**MERSEY BLUES**	*Lyn Andrews*	£5.99
14685 4	**THE SILENT LADY**	*Catherine Cookson*	£5.99
14451 7	**KINGDOM'S DREAM**	*Iris Gower*	£5.99
14895 4	**NOT ALL TARTS ARE APPLE**	*Pip Granger*	£5.99
14538 6	**A TIME TO DANCE**	*Kathryn Haig*	£5.99
14771 0	**SATURDAY'S CHILD**	*Ruth Hamilton*	£5.99
14820 2	**THE TAVERNERS' PLACE**	*Caroline Harvey*	£5.99
14868 7	**SEASON OF MISTS**	*Joan Hessayon*	£5.99
14603 X	**THE SHADOW CHILD**	*Judith Lennox*	£5.99
14772 9	**THE COLOUR OF HOPE**	*Susan Madison*	£5.99
14823 7	**THE PATHFINDER**	*Margaret Mayhew*	£5.99
14753 2	**A PLACE IN THE HILLS**	*Michell Paver*	£5.99
14947 0	**THREE IN A BED**	*Carmen Reid*	£5.99
12367 6	**OPAL**	*Elvi Rhodes*	£5.99
12607 1	**DOCTOR ROSE**	*Elvi Rhodes*	£5.99
13185 7	**THE GOLDEN GIRLS**	*Elvi Rhodes*	£5.99
13481 3	**THE HOUSE OF BONNEAU**	*Elvi Rhodes*	£5.99
13309 4	**MADELEINE**	*Elvi Rhodes*	£5.99
12803 1	**RUTH APPLEBY**	*Elvi Rhodes*	£5.99
13636 0	**CARA'S LAND**	*Elvi Rhodes*	£5.99
13870 3	**THE RAINBOW THROUGH THE RAIN**	*Elvi Rhodes*	£5.99
14057 0	**THE BRIGHT ONE**	*Elvi Rhodes*	£5.99
14400 2	**THE MOUNTAIN**	*Elvi Rhodes*	£5.99
14577 7	**PORTRAIT OF CHLOE**	*Elvi Rhodes*	£5.99
14655 2	**SPRING MUSIC**	*Elvi Rhodes*	£5.99
14715 X	**MIDSUMMER MEETING**	*Elvi Rhodes*	£5.99
14792 3	**THE BIRTHDAY PARTY**	*Elvi Rhodes*	£5.99
14867 9	**SEA OF DREAMS**	*Susan Sallis*	£5.99
14907 1	**SONS AND DAUGHTERS**	*Mary Jane Staples*	£5.99
14846 6	**ROSA'S ISLAND**	*Valerie Wood*	£5.99